NOVEMBER
22

BOOKS BY BRYAN WOOLLEY

November 22
Time and Place
We Be Here When the Morning Comes
Some Sweet Day

NOVEMBER 22

Bryan Woolley

SEAVIEW BOOKS

NEW YORK

Copyright © 1981 by Bryan Woolley

All rights reserved. No part of this book may be reproduced, stored in a retrieval system, or transmitted in any form by an electronic, mechanical, photocopying, recording means or otherwise, without prior written permission of the author.

Manufactured in the United States of America.

FIRST EDITION.

Seaview Books/A Division of PEI Books, Inc.

Library of Congress Cataloging in Publication Data

Woolley, Bryan.
    November 22.
      1. Kennedy, John F. (John Fitzgerald), 1917–1963—
Fiction. I. Title.
PS3573.067N6   813'.54   80–54524
ISBN 0–87223–690–0   AACR2

Designed by Tere LoPrete

For Isabel

Author's Note

ALTHOUGH THE TRAGEDY at the core of *November 22* actually occurred, this story is fiction, and most of its characters are figments of the author's imagination. Any resemblance between them and any real persons, living or dead, is coincidental. However, a few of the secondary characters *are* persons who lived in Dallas on that fateful day. They are Stanley Marcus, Barefoot Sanders, Jesse Curry, Will Fritz, and M. N. McDonald. I owe it to them and to the reader to emphasize that although they are real, the scenes in which they appear and the words they speak in *November 22* are fictitious.

On the other hand, the events taking place within the presidential party—related here in the italicized passages between the chapters—are history, and I have tried to be accurate in my description of them.

The author of a story of this nature necessarily owes debts to those who have written before him, and I wish to acknowledge my larger ones. They are to the reporters of the *Dallas Times Herald*, whose coverage of the assassination of John Kennedy and its aftermath is preserved in the newspaper's files; the report of the Warren Commission on the Assassination of President Kennedy; Warren Leslie's *Dallas Public and Private;* and William Manchester's definitive history, *The Death of a President*, which is the source of most of the italicized passages here. The editorial attributed to Byron

Hayes in "The Twenty-first Hour" actually was written by A. C. Greene, and appeared in the *Dallas Times Herald* on November 23, 1963.

I also wish to thank several friends who helped me in various ways with my task. They are Charles J. Sopkin, Gloria Safier, A. C. Greene, the late Preston Jones, Elaine Walden, and my wife, Isabel Nathaniel.

The Trents lived in a house on Pleasant Avenue that was the finest street in Dallas that was the biggest and fastest growing town in Texas that was the biggest state in the Union and had the blackest soil and the whitest people and America was the greatest country in the world and Daughter was Dad's onlyest sweetest little girl.

John Dos Passos, *U.S.A.*

NOVEMBER
22

When Air Force One *dropped below the clouds, its landing gear was whining and clunking into place. It wasn't until then that the lights of the two cities became visible. Off the tip of the starboard wing, the skyline of Dallas protruded from the dark prairie. Thirty miles to the west, at the other end of a line of smaller towns, the fewer towers of Fort Worth shone through the rain. It was toward these that the big plane banked and descended onto Carswell Air Force Base, an outpost of the Strategic Air Command on the outskirts of the city.*

The First Hour

JAKE

BYRON HAYES UNFOLDED THE PAPER and handed it across the table. Jake had seen the pictures in *Time*, but not arranged as they were now in the full-face and profile of a post office poster, nor with WANTED FOR TREASON in heavy black across the top. He refolded the leaflet and handed it back.

"You didn't read it," Hayes said.

"Does it say something new?"

"No. A guy in front of the Baker Hotel handed it to me at lunchtime. Real class, huh? On the day before he's coming?"

"Probably one of Colonel Byrd's men." Jake reached for the brown bag containing their bottle and poured bourbon over what remained of his ice. There was too little left to cool the liquor, but he was beyond the need of ice anyway.

"Maybe," Hayes said. "Or one of Bruce Alger's men, or Barry Goldwater's men, or a Bircher. Maybe he belonged to them all. What does it matter?" He set his glass as precisely as he could on the wet ring it had made on the table and waved the bottle toward him. Jake poured him another. Donnie, the bartender, saw it.

"Hey! It's closing time!" he said. "You want the cops on me?"

"Fuck you," Jake said. He corked the bottle and twisted the brown bag around its neck. "Sick," he said. "Fucking sick town. Why do we stay here, Byron? Why don't we go someplace healthy? Some part of the United States?"

Hayes lifted his horn-rimmed specs to his forehead, a sign he was drunk. His pale eyes were sentimental. "I've always been here," he said. "I was raised in Oak Cliff, went to SMU, went to work for the paper and never left. I'd be scared, going out there at my age. What's different, anyway?"

Jake shrugged. "Better papers. Less sickness. Something to make you write better . . ."

"Yeah, tell me about it, Jake. Tell me how you went to Little Rock and became Scott Fitzgerald, and how Tulsa made you Ernest Hemingway, and how you went to Korea and turned into Ernie Pyle, and then came to Dallas and became Jake fucking Callison."

Hayes had raised his voice, and in the corner of his eye Jake saw a stool swivel away from the bar and Tim Higgins gather his beer bottle and glass and cigarettes and matches. "Oh, shit," Jake said. "A broadcast prick."

Higgins loomed over the table. "Mind if I join you? I wouldn't ask, but there's nobody else."

"We're about to leave," Jake said.

"Just till you finish your drink." Higgins laid his belongings on the table and eased his heavy body into a chair. He grinned. "Big assignment tomorrow, Jake?"

"The courthouse, as usual."

Higgins frowned. "Not covering the visit? Who is?"

"Everybody else, I guess. The Washington bureau people will be here. The Austin people. General assignments. Fuck, I don't know."

"I made the press pool," Higgins said.

Hayes snorted. "*Made* the press pool! That ain't exactly winning the Pulitzer."

Higgins raised his glass in a mock toast. "To ink-stained wretches everywhere," he said. "Hey, that was a pretty good editorial, Byron. 'We hope the president will learn that what he may have heard isn't true. Dallas is not a city of hate.' Did you write that?"

"I'm not supposed to say," Hayes said. "It's the newspaper's opinion, not mine. That's why they don't put by-lines on editorials."

"Well, give me *your* opinion, then. *Will* he learn that? *Is* Dallas a city of hate?"

"Oh, shut up," Hayes said.

"Actually, I hope there's a little action," Higgins said. "Something like that Stevenson thing, you know? Jesus, I could make the net with that."

"Shut up, goddamn it," Jake said. "Christ, you're as sick as they are. Jesus! Wishing for it!"

Higgins nudged Jake with his elbow. "Losing the old journalistic instincts, Callison?"

"What do *you* know about journalism?" Hayes asked. "You wouldn't make a pimple on a newspaperman's ass."

This was an old recital, and Jake wasn't in the mood. "Donnie's getting pissed," he said. "Let's drink up."

They drank and banged their glasses on the table with an air of finality. Jake rose and had to touch the table to keep his balance. The neon beer signs over the bar weren't double yet, but they were fuzzy. He couldn't make out the features of the bathing beauty on the bright front of the pinball machine.

They stood in the doorway, assessing the rain. Not bad. Just a drizzle. The bar's sign cast eerie pink reflections on the sidewalk and the small puddles in the street. The damp, cool air felt good, meeting the whiskey in Jake's skin. He wished he could walk home.

"Need a ride?" Higgins asked.

"No, thanks, we've got machines," Hayes said. "Machines" was a favorite word of his when he was drunk and feeling old. Jake had read it . . . where? Fitzgerald? Dashiell Hammett? He loved its quaintness. He wished he had lived when automobiles were "machines." He loved Hayes when he said it.

Higgins dashed across the narrow street and disappeared into the dark parking lot that served the newspaper and the radio and television stations that the paper owned. "You need a ride, Jake?" Hayes asked.

"No, I've got my machine."

Hayes smiled wearily and laid his hand on Jake's shoulder. "Why don't you come by for a nightcap?"

"No, it's late."

"Jean wouldn't mind. We could talk."

"I'll take a rain check."

Hayes's hand dropped. They stepped onto the sidewalk and strolled up the street toward the newspaper end of the parking lot. The rain was heavier, wetter than it looked, but still felt good after the smoky, dead air of the bar. They crossed the street and stopped at the edge of the lot. Only a few cars remained, shining wetly in the shadows. "If this keeps up, maybe they'll cancel the motorcade," Hayes said.

"Not likely."

"I wish he weren't coming. What's he got to gain here, Jake?"

"I don't know. Maybe he wants to prove he's not afraid."

"Come with me," Hayes said. "Let's talk."

"No, thanks, Byron. I'd be lousy company."

"Well . . ." Hayes extended the bag with the bottle in it. "Go find somebody better, then, you bastard."

WARNER

He preferred the blonde one, he decided, and felt a little guilty for it. His wife was brunette, and he guessed that was the reason—not for liking the blonde, but for feeling the guilt. And he was drunk. He wondered if he could get up and find his way to the hotel. The bald man with the cigar—the bartender, he remembered—was standing at the door, saying goodnight to his customers. He called some by name, but the names meant nothing to Warner. He was glad they didn't. He didn't like people who hung around joints like this. Babe's. He had never been in Babe's before, but had been in places like it, full of men reeking of beer and cigarettes and sweat. The sweat was bad tonight, maybe because of the rain. And what was that other odor? Piss. Piss and those chemicals that people like Babe use to try to keep you from smelling the piss. The odor had been in Warner's nostrils all night. His table was close to the john. Or maybe the whole place smelled like piss and chemicals. The bald man was moving his way. Warner was the only customer left in the place. The bald man stopped beside the table and took the cigar out of his mouth. "Time to go, buddy," he said.

"What time is it?"

"A little after midnight. Closing time."

"Closing time isn't till two."

"Where you from?"

"San Antonio."

"Ah. Well, this is Dallas. In Dallas, closing time is twelve."

"How about one more setup?" Warner said. "One for the road."

"Can't do it."

"Let me see Babe, then. Babe will give me a setup."

"I'm Babe," the bald man said.

"Pleased to meet you." Warner extended his hand, and Babe shook it listlessly. "I'm Warner Barnhill."

"Ah. Two last names," Babe said. "You rich? Most people with two last names are rich."

"My daddy's rich. He gave me two last names because he's rich, I guess. He gave me my mother's maiden name. You're right. Rich people do that. They put your whole damn family tree in your name. How about a setup, Babe?" Warner waved his empty glass.

Babe moved the cigar from side to side with his tongue, appraising him. "Ask me to join you and we can call it social," he said. "In case the vice cops come."

"Sure."

"Let me lock up," Babe said. "Then it'll be all right."

Warner gazed at the dark stage while he waited. He heard a key turn in the lock. Babe rattled the knob, testing it, then moved behind the bar. Ice cubes clinked in glasses. "What's your pleasure?" Babe asked.

"Water."

"I'm a soda man."

Babe set the glasses on the table, and Warner uncorked the bottle in the paper bag and poured for both of them. Babe raised his glass in salute and sipped. "Nice stuff," he said.

"Cutty Sark," Warner said. "What's your last name?"

"Slater. Jerome Slater. Nobody calls me Jerome since my mother died, though. So call me Babe. I ain't rich."

Warner raised his glass. "You ought to be, charging seventy-five cents for a glass of water."

"In New Orleans, you can sell real drinks and stay open all night if you want to," Babe said. "Here it's beer and wine and setups and close at midnight. Crazy fucking place. Ain't a bartender got as much right to sell whiskey as the guy in a liquor store? Ain't that what bartenders are for?"

"It's the Baptists," Warner said. "They're afraid somebody might get drunk. It's them and the brown paper bag companies." He giggled.

"It's the fucking legislature," Babe said. "They'd change it if they wasn't hypocrites. *They* get drunk enough."

"I can't allow you to impugn the reputation of that august body," Warner said. "I'm a member of it."

"Yeah?" Babe's dark eyes lit briefly. "Then why don't you change it?"

"The Baptists wouldn't like it."

"Well, between the state law and the city's midnight cur-
few, I've got it tough, even at seventy-five cents for water. By
the time I pay the rent and the band and the girls, I ain't got
nothing." He grunted. "And that's a fact. Where you from?"

"San Antonio."

"Oh, yeah. You said. The old Alamo City."

"Right."

"You really in the legislature?"

"Yeah. The House."

Babe rolled his cigar between thumb and forefinger, in-
specting its gnawed, soggy end. Warner tilted his head for
the last of his drink. "How about another?" Babe asked.

"Might as well."

Babe picked up their glasses and walked behind the bar.
"You here for the visit?" he asked.

"Yeah. I missed him in San Antonio."

Babe laughed. "You must not be important."

"I'm not."

"Where is he tonight?"

"Fort Worth."

"You like him?"

"Yeah."

"You're a pinko liberal. No wonder you ain't important."
Babe returned to the table and watched Warner pour the
whiskey. "How'd you like my girls?"

"The brunette had a bruise on her thigh."

"Shit. You noticed."

"Couldn't help noticing."

"I told her to cover it up. With makeup, you know. Her
boy friend did it. Fucking boy friends. I keep warning them,
but they don't listen."

"The blonde is nice."

"Ain't she? That's Sheila."

"Yeah, Sheila's nice. Nice tits."

They stared at the ashtray in the center of the table, drinking quietly. The haze in Warner's head made the butts in the tray seem to move. He groped his pack from his pocket and lit another.

"You here alone?" Babe asked.

"Yeah."

"Maybe you'd like to meet Sheila. She likes politicians." Warner raised his eyes to Babe's. "She lives at the Plaza," Babe said. "Couple of blocks from here. If you wanted to drop by, I could call. She wouldn't mind."

"I don't want to go to the Plaza."

"Maybe she'd come down here. It's up to you."

Warner shrugged. "Why not?"

Babe got up and picked his way among the tables and chairs toward the telephone near the door. He walked with a limp. Warner heard the nickel drop into the phone and the whirr of the dial.

"Hi, honey. You busy?" Babe spoke softly, intimately, like a father to a daughter. "I got somebody I want you to meet. . . . Yeah, I know . . . I know. But this is special. A favor for Babe, huh? . . . Well, he don't want to come there. He's important, a state rep . . . yeah . . . yeah . . . Listen, honey, just get your ass in gear and come down here, okay? . . . Well, you got an umbrella, ain't you? . . . Okay. Good. Step on it, okay? Good. Fine. Thanks, sweetheart."

Babe sat down and relit his cigar. "Sheila's anxious to meet you," he said.

"She coming right away?"

"She'll be along. She's got to get herself together, you know. How about a drink?" Not waiting for Warner's reply, Babe picked up the glasses, got the ice, and refilled them. "How long you in town?"

"Just till tomorrow."

"Just for the visit, huh? Big deal for a politician, I guess. You going to meet him? Personally, I mean."

"That's why I'm here. I'll have to get lucky, though."

"Well, maybe you will. Mind if I clean up a bit?"

"Go ahead."

Babe moved among the tables with a tray and a towel, picking up glasses and ashtrays, wiping the tables, arranging chairs. Warner rested his chin on his chest, saw a speck of ash on his necktie and considered flicking it off, but didn't. He wished Babe hadn't called the girl. He wished he weren't sitting alone, that he was in his room where he belonged, sleeping, resting for tomorrow. When Babe limped past him and said, "That's Sheila," he raised his head, but he had heard nothing. Babe went through a door next to the stage and closed it, and Warner heard him talking but didn't understand his words. Then the door opened and Babe was shaking a collapsed umbrella. The girl was unbuttoning her blue plastic raincoat. She smiled. "Hi," she said.

"Hello," Warner said.

"This is Sheila," Babe said. "Sheila, this is Representative Barnhill."

Warner stood. Sheila offered her hand, so he shook it. "Pleased to meet you."

"Likewise," Sheila said.

Babe laid the umbrella on a table and helped the girl out of her coat and folded it over a chair. The girl stood like a statue, avoiding Warner's eyes. Her blonde hair and red satin sheath and gold earrings reminded Warner of Marilyn Monroe. Men probably were supposed to think of Marilyn Monroe when they looked at Sheila. She was about twenty. Maybe twenty-one. "Have a seat," he said. He pulled out a chair.

"Thank you." Her voice was small. She perched on the edge of the chair. Maybe the sheath was too tight to let her really sit down.

He nodded at the brown bag. "Drink?"

"I don't like the hard stuff. Mind if I have something else?"

"Whatever you like."

Sheila smiled at Babe. "I'll have the usual, Babe."

"I'd like a beer," Warner said.

"Sure. What kind?"

"Whatever's handy."

Sheila placed her elbows on the table and folded her hands and propped her chin on them. A gold charm bracelet clicked down her arm. Her nails were long and red. Her eyes dropped. Babe set a brown Lone Star bottle and a fresh glass before Warner and a long-stemmed glass of something bubbly in front of Sheila.

"Champagne," Warner said. "You're an expensive lady."

"It's Champale," Babe said. Sheila gave him a small frown. "He's a friend," Babe said. "Besides, it's on me. Look, you kids have your drink. I got work to do." He moved away, and Sheila smiled at Warner. Her eyes were blue.

"Babe says you're a state rep," she said.

"That's right."

"I expected someone old and greasy."

"Babe says you like politicians."

Sheila laughed.

"You're a—good dancer," Warner said.

She sipped the Champale. "Thank you."

"Do you like it? Dancing?"

"Sure. Why wouldn't I?"

"I don't know. I just wondered."

"Do people ask you if you like being a state rep?"

"No. Maybe they should. They might be surprised at the answer."

"Okay, then, do you?"

"Yes and no." Warner laughed, and she did, too. The beer was clearing his head. He offered her a cigarette.

"No, thank you. They stain the teeth."

"You have lovely teeth."

"Thank you. You sure are complimentary. You don't have to do that."

"You don't have to say 'thank you' all the time, either."

"What do you do when you're not making laws?"

"Guess."

She looked him up and down. "You're a lawyer."

"That's right. How did you know?"

"You look like a lawyer. If you saw me on the street, what would you think I was?"

Warner hesitated.

"An exotic dancer, right?"

"Right."

"And that's what I am. People look like what they are."

"What about Babe?"

She laughed. "Babe looks like Babe. He says you're rich. Are you?"

"Well, I wouldn't say 'rich.' I'm a state representative and a somewhat successful attorney."

"As you said, I'm an expensive woman. You can afford me, can't you?"

"I think so."

Her smile took on the sultry quality she had used on the stage. Her apparent shyness was gone. She picked up Warner's hand and held it between her own. "It's raining. Where's your car?"

"I don't have one. I flew in."

"Hey, Babe!" she called over her shoulder. "Call us a cab, will you?"

Babe limped to the phone and dropped a nickel. "Five minutes," he said when he hung up. "I told him to honk."

"Babe told me you don't like my place," Sheila said.

"Mine's better."

"Where is it?"

"The Adolphus."

"That's fine."

LUCIUS

Lucius Jackson never objected to working the night shift, although both the fares and the tips were lighter then, except on the airport runs. He enjoyed the dark, empty streets and the black ghosts of buildings with the lights burning in them. He wondered who the lights were for. Watchmen? Janitors? Burglars? He wondered if they liked being alone in the buildings as much as he liked being in the empty streets. There were almost no cars, and the few there were seemed to move so much more quietly and slowly than in the daylight. In the daylight, they roared. In the night, they whispered. On rainy nights like this, they were even quieter. The police cars, especially, moved almost silently. Lucius hated it when in the night he would look into the mirror and see a police car creeping behind him. He had never been in trouble, never even gotten a traffic ticket, but he didn't like cops. They made him nervous, more nervous hidden in their creeping cars than in person, for he always thought they were watching him, waiting for him to make a mistake, looking for an excuse to arrest him. He wondered if white people felt that way, too. He never broke the speed limit, even when his passengers asked him to, even when they were in a hurry to catch a plane and promised big tips. He never ran a red light, even late at night when he could see for blocks in every direction and no headlights were shining anywhere. That was the sort of thing the cops were waiting for him to do. If he ever did it, blinking lights would come out of nowhere, from behind him where the cops were stalking, and he would be in trouble.

It had been a slow night, and he hoped this would be an airport fare, but his hope was slim. People didn't go to Love Field from Babe's. He hoped it wasn't a drunk. That was the bad thing about working nights, the drunks. Especially those who staggered out of the strip joints. There were only two kinds of them, those who wore name tags and moved in groups and laughed and cursed and called him "boy" and demanded to know where they could get laid, and the lonely ones who babbled about home or got sick or passed out in his cab. He didn't blame Babe Slater and the others for calling a cab instead of the cops, but it was the one bad thing about working nights.

It was late for drunks, though. The clubs had closed almost an hour ago. Maybe Babe himself was going somewhere.

When Lucius rounded the corner, Babe's sign and the signs of the other clubs were dark, but he found the place and pulled to the curb and honked. A figure stepped out of the doorway, and Lucius leaned across the seat and rolled down the window. "You call a cab, mister?" he said.

The figure stepped toward him. "Huh? Me? Not me. I thought you was the cops."

It was a man, but Lucius couldn't see his face. The voice was weak and shaky, as if frightened. "You need the cops?" Lucius asked.

"Huh? No. I was just kind of expecting them."

Babe's door opened, and a man and a woman were silhouetted for a moment against the dim light inside. The woman started to open an umbrella, then didn't. The man carried something tucked under his arm. The frightened man opened the back door of the cab, and Lucius thought he was about to climb in, but he just held the door for the woman.

"Henry!" she said. "What are you doing here so late?"

"Just trying to get by, Miss Sheila," the man said.

Lucius recognized the whine of a wino. "Hey, mister!" he said.

The man ignored him. "I wonder if your friend has any use for that bottle," he said to the woman.

The other man laughed. "I guess not," he said thickly. "She won't drink it, and I've had enough." He gave the wino the bundle under his arm.

"Bless you," the wino said. "Have a nice evening, Miss Sheila."

The couple got into the cab, and the wino slammed the door. Lucius looked back to ask where they wanted to go, but they were already in a clinch, kissing. Lucius turned his eyes to the mirror and tried to watch, but it was too dark. The woman was breathing hard. Her plastic raincoat rustled. "Where to?" Lucius asked without turning.

"Adolphus," the man managed to say.

Lucius started the meter and cursed silently. The hotel was only four blocks away.

The Second Hour

BETTY LOU

DURING COCKTAILS and most of dinner, Rodney and Elsie Dart had been almost charming. Of course, Rodney had bragged about his glory days as the SMU Mustangs' star tackle and his courtship of Elsie, the school's prettiest and most popular cheerleader. The Yankee guests, Mr. and Mrs. Leary, must have found it hard to believe, since both Darts had run to fat and Rodney to baldness, and maybe Rodney felt their skepticism. "Ain't that right, Alex?" he would ask after his description of some gridiron feat, and Alex, who had been in law school in those days, would nod. "Ain't that right, Betty Lou?" Rodney would ask, and Betty Lou, who had been an undergraduate in those days, would say, "That's right, Rod."

Betty Lou Carpenter hadn't liked Rodney and Elsie at SMU, and she didn't like them now. If Alex had told her where they were going, she would have refused the date. Maybe Alex knew that. "One of my biggest clients has asked me to dinner," he had said, "and it's not the kind of thing I can turn down. I don't like to go alone. The fifth wheel, you know, the odd man out." Betty Lou didn't often get asked for a date, and she forgot to ask who the client was.

Rodney rambled through his whole football career, and

from there into an immodest account of his brilliance and success in the home-construction business and how Dallas was definitely the place to make a million these days. Mr. Leary, a freckled Irishman, showed considerable interest in that part of Rodney's discourse. He was in insurance, after all, and new homes meant new policies. Elsie rolled her eyes at Mrs. Leary across the table, and Mrs. Leary smiled and spoke occasionally in crisp New England monosyllables. Betty Lou said little, and Alex said nothing, but the first half of the evening hadn't been bad.

It was the third bottle of wine that launched Rodney's tirade against Roosevelt's "queer deal" and Truman, "that little haberdasher," and even Eisenhower, who "gave Germany to the Russians." Kennedy, of course, had given away Cuba and was trying to give away the rest of Latin America and Vietnam and Cambodia and Laos and was turning the United States itself over to the niggers. Rodney's brow seemed to get narrower as he talked. His eyes, fueled by alcohol and spleen, burned black as onyx. "Kennedy ain't just soft on them," he said. "He's *in* with them. He's part of the conspiracy. Ain't that right, Alex?"

Alex mumbled something noncommittal, and Rodney took it for agreement. "The Russians would be in the White House tonight if the pope didn't want it, too," he said.

Both Learys flushed, and Betty Lou decided to intervene. "Oh, Rod! You don't really mean that!" She knew he meant it, but the Learys' discomfort embarrassed her. This was their first dinner party in Dallas, they had said, their first experience of Texas's famous hospitality.

Rodney shook a beefy, freckled finger. "Look who's defending the pinkos! Look who's speaking up for St. John of Boston! This wouldn't have anything to do with that account of yours, would it?" He smiled at Mr. Leary. "Betty Lou's firm has been hired to drum up a rousing welcome for St. John, you see. Every commie in Dallas will be in the streets tomorrow, won't they, Betty Lou? At least you hope they will."

"I don't understand," Mrs. Leary said. Her husband looked at her as if he wished she hadn't spoken, but her eyes were on Rodney.

"Betty Lou's been brainwashing the press," Rodney said. "She's been paid to show St. John that Dallas loves him. Ain't that right, Betty Lou?"

"But why—" Mrs. Leary said.

Betty Lou interrupted. "Rod, you know the image of this city—"

"To hell with the image!" Rodney boomed. "It's a *disgrace* for Dallas to kowtow to the likes of him! What's he ever done for us?"

"Rod, darling," Elsie said sweetly, "why don't we continue the discussion in more comfortable chairs, over a brandy?"

So they had moved to the living room, where Elsie, waving her arms like a traffic cop, assigned each a seat. Alex and Mrs. Leary were given the ridiculous purple French provincial love seat, Betty Lou was assigned the hard-seated antique rocker, and Elsie trapped Mr. Leary beside her on the pink sofa. Elsie waved Rodney to the black, imitation-leather recliner, but he ignored her and lined six snifters along the marble mantel, poured from the crystal decanter, and passed the snifters around.

Betty Lou seized the moment of shuffle as a chance to change the subject and asked, "What business are you in, Mr. Leary?" He had answered that hours ago, but he smiled gratefully.

"Insurance," he said. "Regional office manager. We were moved here just last month."

"I guess you're hardly settled, then," Betty Lou said.

"Heavens, no!" Mrs. Leary said. "We'd barely gotten Jason settled in school in Hartford. Then we moved here and had to start all over."

"They like the Kennedys up there, don't they?" Rodney said. He was standing at the mantel, his legs spread wide, holding the decanter in one hand and his snifter in the other.

"Well, yes. . . ." Mrs. Leary seemed flustered. She was a small, dark woman, birdlike in a quiet, nervous way. She reminded Betty Lou of New England schoolteachers she had seen in movies. Betty Lou guessed she had intelligence but was too shy or modest to show it often.

"Are you active in politics, Stacy?" Elsie asked.

Betty Lou cringed inwardly. It was the first time Elsie had used Mrs. Leary's first name. She was digging now. She wanted information.

"Well, yes, I—"

Mr. Leary caught his wife's eye this time and shook his head slightly.

"I vote, if that's what you mean," Mrs. Leary said.

"Ha! If you stick around Elsie, you'll be doing a lot more than that!" Rodney said. "I'm a politics widower! There's hardly a night Elsie's not off at some meeting. White Citizens Council, National Indignation Committee, John Birch Society, Friends of General Walker, Texans for America . . . Always on the go, ain't you, honey?"

Both Learys looked startled. They had just realized where they were. Poor Learys!

"I think she loves Bruce Alger more than she loves me," Rodney said. "Ain't that right, honey? She's even promoting a Goldwater-Alger ticket for 'sixty-four. What do you think of that?"

"Well, what's wrong with it?" Elsie said.

"Balance!" Rodney roared. "Geographical balance! Texas and Arizona are just one state apart, honey!"

"Uh, who's Alger?" Mrs. Leary asked.

"He's your congressman, Mrs. Leary," Betty Lou said. "Like it or not."

"Why wouldn't she like it?" Elsie said. "Do you know of a better one?"

Rodney brandished the decanter. "Betty Lou's on the other side, honey. Until tomorrow. Ain't that right, Betty Lou? But Bruce won't make it, even if he wants it. They'll have to get some Yankee to run with Barry." He laughed. "I kind of like old J. L. Fisher's idea. Billy Graham and Barry Goldwater. By God, who could vote against that?"

"That old fool," Betty Lou said.

"Fool? J.L.'s one of the richest men in the world, young lady. He's brought in more oil wells than a dog has fleas. I wouldn't call that a fool. Would you, Alex? And he's a damn good Baptist, too. Ain't that right, Alex?"

Alex grunted.

"We go to Highland Park Baptist," Elsie told Mrs. Leary. "I've tried to get him to try my church, the Episcopalian, but he won't."

"Dyed-in-the-wool Baptist I am!" Rodney said. "Every inch of my hide baptized—and once saved, always saved. What church do you folks go to, Mark?" He and Elsie looked at Mr. Leary, who looked uncomfortable.

"Catholic," Mrs. Leary said quietly. "We're Irish Catholics. And we both voted for John Kennedy. Mark, have you forgotten the baby-sitter?"

The room was quiet. Rodney set the decanter and his snifter on the mantel. Alex looked at his watch. "Yeah, we'd better go, too," he said. He and Mr. Leary rose and headed toward the coat closet in the hallway. Rodney and Elsie said nothing.

When they were ready for the street, the Learys thanked the Darts and departed into the mist. Alex and Betty Lou said their goodbyes quickly, too. Elsie kissed Alex on the cheek. "I'm sorry, Alex," she said. "I thought they were *nice* people. I hope they get on that plane with their pinko Catholic Yankee and go back where they belong."

Alex's headlights caught the Learys walking slowly along the wet sidewalk. He slowed, and Betty Lou rolled down her window. "Need a ride?" she called.

"No, thanks," Mr. Leary said. "We live just around the corner."

"Well, welcome to Dallas," Betty Lou said.

JAKE

Jake had never had trouble sleeping, until lately. It had to do with the separation. Or maybe not. Maybe it was this lousy apartment and its grimy carpets that felt greasy to his bare feet and the cockroaches that scurried about the cracked linoleum in the kitchen when he turned on the light. Maybe it was the two open suitcases at the foot of his bed. For two months he had held in the back of his mind the thought of unpacking and getting settled. He ought to hang some pictures and clean the refrigerator, do something to give himself a stake in the place, something to make it his own. But he hadn't, and maybe that wasn't the trouble at all.

He flung the covers back and sat on the edge of the bed and lit a cigarette in the dark. Sometimes that helped. Sometimes all he needed was one last cigarette after he went to bed. He liked to smoke in the dark. The orange glow of the cigarette was a comfort, almost like a person. He resented needing another person or even wanting one. He had always thought of himself as a loner. Liz had called him that. "You're a real loner," she used to say. "You don't need anyone, do you?" And Jake had believed that. He always felt betrayed somehow when he realized it wasn't true. Oh, he needed James. He didn't mind admitting that, even to Byron and Jean. It was a way of hanging onto a shred of his fatherness, admitting that he needed James. "Fatherness." Was that a real word? It ought to be. It wasn't the same thing as "fatherhood." "Fatherhood" had to do with copulation, conception, birth. Biology. "Fatherness" was something else. Reading to James, bathing him, arranging the covers over him, kissing him goodnight. He wondered how James was doing in school. Whenever Jake asked him, he said, "Fine," and when he asked Liz, she said, "Fine." Fine. It wasn't much to know about a son's experience in first grade. There was no fatherness in "fine." Thinking of James made Jake's gut ache. He couldn't go to sleep thinking of James.

He should have gone home with Byron. If he had gotten too drunk to drive, he could have slept on the couch, and Jean would have awakened him and given him a good breakfast and gotten him off to work. God, he envied Byron, married to the same woman all his life and still in love with her. Why couldn't everyone be like that? Why couldn't Jake Callison be like that? Byron's whole life was measured in ones. One city, one newspaper, one wife, one son dead in Korea. One house, even. Maybe that was the secret. Never count beyond one. Never let other possibilities into your mind. Never dream. Never want. What did wanting get you? Greasy carpets. Cockroaches. Walls without pictures. God, he hated the place. He should have looked around some more, found a place he really liked. It was dumb, taking the first place he looked at. But he could afford it, and hadn't felt like looking. Maybe he hadn't thought he would be here long. Hell, couldn't he still look if he wanted to? This place might be all right if he fixed it up. But what for? He couldn't bring James to a neighborhood with dopers and hookers on the sidewalks. He wouldn't even bring Sherry here. Like most bankers, she despised untidiness. She would think less of him if she saw the cockroaches and the suitcases. She would want to fix it up, take him shopping for bedspreads. Shower curtains. Pictures. A picture of James was in one of the suitcases.

Maybe more bourbon would do it. The bottle that Byron had given him was on the kitchen counter, still in its brown bag. No. He couldn't take any more bourbon. He wished he had some brandy, or even a beer. God, he felt lousy. Jesus H. Christ. Maybe he should see a doctor. "What seems to be the trouble?" the doctor would ask. "I'm coming apart, doc. I drink too much, smoke too much, can't sleep, hate my job, don't have any money, and my kid keeps asking me why I'm mad at mommy and don't live with them anymore."

Maybe he should call Byron. Byron would have some brandy. Jean wouldn't mind. Byron was a lucky son of a bitch. The couch unfolded into a bed. Clean sheets.

He picked up the telephone receiver and held it in his lap while he lit another cigarette, then dropped the match in the ashtray and dialed. Sherry answered on the first ring.

"Hello?" Her voice was groggy, irritated.

"Hi, hon. What you doing?"

"Jake? Is this Jake?"

"Sure it is, hon. Did I wake you up?"

"Jake, do you know what time it is? It's—almost two."

"I'm sorry. I—lost track. I said I would call you."

"Well, I was expecting it a wee bit earlier. I stayed in all evening—"

"I know, honey. I'm sorry. Byron and I . . ."

"Yeah, I figured. Well, now that I'm wide awake, what do you want?"

Jake hesitated. He didn't trust her mood. "I'd like to come over."

"Jake, it's two! I have to work tomorrow, and so do you. How about tomorrow night? I'll fix you dinner."

"I accept. But I'd still like to come tonight. I won't give you any trouble. Go back to sleep if you want to. Just unlock the door and I'll lock it when I get there."

"I'm afraid to. I ought to give you a key." She was more awake, more pleasant now. She sighed. "Okay. But hurry. I don't want to be a wreck tomorrow."

"Right. I'm on my way."

Jake hung up and switched on the lamp beside the bed. He rummaged in the suitcases for clean clothes, found socks and underwear. Nothing else was clean. He laid them on the bed beside the damp suit, shirt, and tie he had just taken off. What the hell, it was raining, anyway. He walked naked over the greasy carpet to the bathroom and spread dirty towels on the dirty white tile floor and turned on the curtainless shower. After his shower, he shaved and splashed aftershave on his face and brushed his teeth. He kicked the wet towels into a pile beside the toilet and returned to the bedroom to dress. Sometime during all this, he started to whistle.

JONATHAN

Jonathan Waters poured the milk into the pan and set it on the stove and got the jar of Ovaltine down from the shelf. He got down the silver beer stein with J.L.F. engraved on it in Old English and spooned the Ovaltine into it. When the milk was warm, he poured it over the Ovaltine and stirred it until the crystals dissolved, then set the stein on a small silver tray and carried it into the front hall. He always used the front stairs when it was late and nobody was around. They weren't as steep as the servants' stairs.

Late at night, when it was so quiet, the Fisher house reminded him of a funeral home, although it was more elegant than any he had visited. The lights turned low, the reflections of electric candles in the huge, gilt-framed mirrors, the heavy velvet draperies and their heavy gold fringes and tassels seemed the perfect setting for corpses in mahogany caskets.

Jonathan's slippers whispered up the curve in the wide stairs and down the wide hallway to the front corner bedroom. He knocked and waited for Mr. J.L.'s brusque "Come in! Come in!" He opened the door quietly and closed it quietly. He couldn't see Mr. J.L., but knew he was sitting in the velvet wing chair in front of the fireplace, hidden by the chair's high back. Jonathan waited in front of the door for the rest of the ritual.

"Is the place secure?" the voice asked from behind the chair.

"Yessir. Calvin locked up about three hours ago, sir."

"Are the yard lights on?"

"Yessir. Calvin turned them on, too. Everything's just fine, sir."

"Good. Good."

That was Jonathan's signal to advance and place the Ovaltine on the small table beside the chair. Mr. J.L. was staring into the flames in the fireplace, his bare, bony feet resting on the velvet ottoman in front of the chair, his hands clasped over the maroon silk robe covering his round belly. In the big chair, he looked as small as a child.

"Anything else, sir?" Jonathan asked. "Except turning down your bed, I mean?"

"Throw another log on the fire, Jonathan, and sit down."

Jonathan folded the fire screen aside and selected the smallest log from the stack on the hearth and laid it across the andirons. Sparks flew up the chimney. He jabbed at the fresh log with the poker until it nestled comfortably among the remains of the others, then replaced the screen and sat down on the small wooden stool by the rack of fire tools.

"Miss Anna has retired, has she?" Mr. J.L. asked.

"Yessir. Almost four hours ago."

"Good. Good. Resting comfortably, is she?"

"Far as I know, sir."

Mr. J.L. hadn't looked at Jonathan. The fire brightened his watery blue eyes and bald, knobby head. "Are you a Christian, Jonathan?" he asked.

Jonathan had dreaded the question. It meant that Mr. J.L. was in a talking mood. "Oh, yessir," he replied. "You know that."

Mr. J.L. glanced at him sharply. "What church?"

"Why, African Methodist Episcopal, sir. All my life."

"Ah, yes. Methodist. Good folks, Methodists."

"Yessir. You better drink your Ovaltine, sir, before it cools off."

Mr. J.L. lifted the stein and sucked at it. "Nice and warm, Jonathan, as always."

"Thank you, sir."

Mr. J.L. stared into the fire. "Calvin says some coloreds are Catholics, Jonathan. Is that true?"

"Why, yessir, I believe that's right. I don't know any, but I believe that's right."

"Why's that, you reckon?"

"I don't know, sir. Maybe they always been, like I always been Methodist."

"Mmm! They're in on the conspiracy, I guess, like the rest of them. That Martin Luther King's one of them, isn't he?"

"Nosir. Dr. King's a Baptist, I believe. Yessir, he's a Baptist, I'm almost sure."

"I mean, he's in on the conspiracy, Jonathan. What do you think all that rioting is about over in Alabama? Coloreds eating with whites at Woolworth's? In a pig's eye! What's he doctor of, anyway, Jonathan?"

"I don't know, sir. Preaching, I guess."

"Preaching! Rabble-rousing, you mean! Rioting! Agitating!"

Jonathan always hated this part of the conversation. He had once sent a check for five dollars to the National Association for the Advancement of Colored People. He still worried that Mr. J.L. might find that out, although he had burned his canceled check as soon as his bank statement arrived.

"What is it those people want, Jonathan? What do they *really* want?"

"Why, I don't know, sir. I sure don't."

"At least George Wallace is standing up to them. That's

more than the nervous Nellies who run this town are doing. I never thought I'd see the day when coloreds would walk right into Neiman-Marcus and sit down at a table in the Zodiac and eat. Did you, Jonathan?"

"Nosir. I never did."

"Jew store. They're in the conspiracy, Jonathan. Just sit down and eat. Where was the Citizens Charter Association then?" Mr. J.L. laughed. "The big dudes. The old movers and shakers, eh, Jonathan? Pissants! Can you see Buck Pool putting up with the likes of that?"

"Nosir. I sure can't."

"Have I told you about Buck Pool, Jonathan?"

"Oh, yessir."

"Well, Buck and I were doing some oil prospecting down in Mexico back in—back in 'sixteen, I think it was—and these bandits came upon us. *Villistas. Muy malos hombres*, Jonathan. Six of them. They wanted our horses. . . . You sure I haven't told you about Buck, Jonathan?"

"Oh, yessir. You told me about Mr. Pool, all right."

"Well, anyway, Buck just cut down on them with his Winchester and killed two of them. Just like that"—Mr. J.L. snapped his fingers twice. "The others turned tail and ran, and Buck and I wound up with two extra horses." Mr. J.L. laughed. "It was hotter than hell down in Mexico in those days, Jonathan."

"Yessir. I've heard about that."

"Old Buck just cut down on them and killed two. A Winchester is a mighty good rifle, Jonathan. People pay attention to a Winchester."

"Yessir. I reckon they do."

Mr. J.L. swallowed the last of the Ovaltine and set the stein on the tray.

"You ready for me to turn down your bed now, sir?" Jonathan asked.

"In a minute, Jonathan. Calvin Coolidge was the best president we ever had. If he had served another term, there wouldn't have been a Depression or a Roosevelt. Do you know what he did one time, Jonathan? He went to church by himself one Sunday, see, and when he got back, Mrs. Coolidge asked him, 'What did the preacher preach about today, Calvin?' And he said, 'Sin.' And she said, 'What did he say about sin, Calvin?' And he said, 'He's agin it.' " Mr. J.L. slapped his knee. "Got right to the heart of the matter, didn't he? God, for a president like that! You know who would make a fine president, Jonathan? Billy Graham. Billy Graham, and Senator Goldwater for vice president. Who could vote against a ticket like that? Would coloreds vote for a ticket like that, Jonathan?"

"Why, yessir. I reckon they would."

"Except for the Catholic coloreds. How many do you reckon they are, Jonathan?"

"I don't know, sir. I don't know none of them."

"And the Catholic whites. And the Red whites. Get that, Jonathan? Red whites? Ha! And the Jews. But they're all in it. They're all against us. All against America. All trying to get our horses, aren't they, Jonathan?"

"Yessir. I reckon so."

"Well, God will not be mocked, will He?"

"Oh, nosir."

"Nosir. Martin Luther King ought to put *that* in his pipe and smoke it. God will not be mocked. Buck Pool's dead, you know. Fell off a derrick out in the Permian Basin in—I don't remember—long years ago."

"Yessir."

"Broke every bone in his body. Limp as a dishrag when we picked him up."

"Yessir. You told me about that, sir."

"I thought he was never going to hit the ground, Jonathan. He just hung up there, like a hawk, you know? His shirt sleeves just a-flapping."

"May I turn down the bed now, sir?"

"Yes, Jonathan. I'm ready."

Jonathan's slippers whispered across the thick carpet to the old four-poster. He turned back the crocheted counterpane and the heavy white wool blanket and the white sheet. He fluffed the big feather pillow. "It's ready for you, sir," he said.

Mr. J.L. rose and shuffled quickly across to the bed, untied the fringed sash of his robe, and Jonathan lifted it from his shoulders and laid it on a chair. He lifted the bedcovers, and Mr. J.L. sank into the deep feather mattress with a sigh. Jonathan arranged the sheet and blanket over him and folded the counterpane back to the foot of the bed.

"The Ovaltine was nice and warm, Jonathan," Mr. J.L. said. "As always."

"Thank you, sir."

"They'll be here tomorrow."

"Who, sir?"

"But we'll wind up with the extra horses, won't we, Jonathan?"

"Oh, yessir."

"Miss Anna's resting comfortably, is she?"

"Yessir. She's fine."

"Well, goodnight, Jonathan."

"Goodnight, sir."

The suite was cramped and musty and painted green. Its windows overlooked a parking lot and the neon of the Greyhound and Trailways stations, a movie theater, a garage, and two loan companies. Five floors above, in the more spacious Will Rogers Suite, Lyndon Johnson hooted and hollered with local party chieftains and old political cronies. In the Texas Hotel Coffee Shop, John Connally held forth for the press and anyone else who would listen, delivering clarion calls for party unity.

She was exhausted from San Antonio, Houston, the motorcades, the plane flights. She laid out her clothes for the next day and joined her husband.

"You were great today," he said.

The Third Hour

STACY

WHEN MARK LEARY LEFT to drive the baby-sitter home, Stacy went to the small bedroom in the back of the house to look in on Jason. The baby-sitter had said he was sleeping soundly, so there was no reason to go in and chance waking him, but Stacy never felt comfortable about an evening out until she got home and saw that Jason was all right.

She tiptoed into the room without switching on the light and sat down on the edge of the bed. Jason had kicked the covers off and his pajamas had worked their way up his legs. His face and legs and feet were pale in the dim light that came through the doorway from the hall. His face was serene as an angel's, and his legs were long in the slender, coltish way of ten-year-olds who are going to be tall. Stacy pulled the covers up to the boy's chin. He stirred and turned onto his back. His mouth opened and made a little snoring noise, then he turned back onto his side and the noise stopped. Stacy kissed him lightly on the forehead and stood up. Where had her baby gone? Whatever happened to the precious little bundle she had carried so proudly from the hospital on that humid August day? She was still proud, of course. No mother would want her baby to remain a baby forever, and Jason was growing up so fine. But she was a little sad, too, whenever she noticed how quickly he was doing it.

She tiptoed into the hall and pulled the door almost closed, but left it ajar. Why? Did she still expect him to cry out in the night with hunger or an earache? He hadn't in years, but silliness was no reason to break a habit she found comforting.

She felt tired and heavy from the wine and brandy. Undoing her clothes and stepping out of them exhausted her. She slipped on her gown and slid into bed without removing her makeup or even brushing her teeth, and thought she would be asleep before Mark returned. But the scrape of his key in the lock and the back door closing roused her from her doze. She lay open-eyed in the darkness when he crept into the bedroom and began undressing, so careful not to make noise. She listened to the care with which he laid his shoes on the floor and kept his hand on his belt buckle to keep it from rattling, and then she said, "Never again."

"I thought you were asleep."

"Never again," she said.

"Never again what?" Mark's voice was thick and defensive, as it was when he had drunk too much. She didn't like to talk with him when his voice was like that, because some of their worst fights began that way. Sometimes it would take several days or even a week to be close again, and the equilibrium of the household would be cockeyed, and everyone would be edgy until it was over. Sometimes at the end of one of those times Mark would promise to stop drinking, but Stacy knew that wouldn't work and didn't really want him to stop anyway, because he wasn't a drunk and enjoyed his liquor. She wished he wouldn't drink too much, that's all, and that she wouldn't get into conversations with him when he had. But he couldn't help drinking a lot with Rodney Dart standing at his elbow with the bottle all the time, and now she couldn't help getting into this conversation with him. "I'm never going to that house again," she said.

"Why not?" Mark had his pajamas on now and asked the question on the way to the bathroom. He closed the door, and Stacy heard him pissing and then flushing and then brushing his teeth, so it was some time before she got to answer.

"Because they're nuts," she said as he slipped between the sheets.

"Who's nuts?" He sounded insulted.

"The Darts. They're crazy. I never heard so much baloney in my life. And you just sat there and took it."

"They're not crazy. They're just different," Mark said. "There are a lot of people like them around here. This isn't Connecticut, you know. Yale isn't just down the road. People think differently here."

"*Think!* You call that *thinking?* There wasn't a thought in that house, unless that Betty Lou Carpenter had one and kept it to herself. Who in the world are the Texans for America? Who else would Texans be for?"

"Go to sleep, baby. We'll talk about it in the morning."

Stacy knew what that meant. Mark saw that they were moving toward a fight and was trying to avoid it. He was right. She ought to shut up and go to sleep. "I don't want to talk about it," she said. "I'm just telling you I'm not going there anymore, or anyplace like it. Why were we there, anyway? Why were we sitting there like dummies, listening to that garbage?"

"Because I'm in the insurance business," Mark said. "Because Rod Dart is one of the biggest home builders in Dallas County and has just bought a big policy from our company." His voice was patient, condescending, as if she were a child asking why she couldn't play in the street. "Because Rod Dart can recommend our company to a lot of people who buy his houses. Because if I don't sell insurance, you and Jason and I go without shoes."

"Don't be sarcastic."

"Besides, they're neighbors of ours and were trying to

show a little hospitality to the newcomers, even though the newcomers are Yankees. But one of the Yankees turned around and bit the hand that fed her."

"*Bit!* Who did I bite? That Elsie?" Stacy sat up and propped her pillow against the headboard. "All I did was tell the truth! And believe me, she was trying hard enough to drag it out of me!"

"Well, you didn't have to give her that Irish and Catholic and Kennedy business. That's private stuff and they don't need to know it."

"You sound ashamed of it!"

"I'm not ashamed. Our religion and politics are nobody's business, that's all."

"Well, they were telling us plenty about theirs! I never heard such boring *bullshit* in my life!" The anger rose in her hot and glowing with alcohol.

Mark laid his hand on her shoulder. "Stacy, let's—"

"Don't touch me."

The hand remained on her shoulder for a moment, then dropped away. Mark rolled onto his side, his back to her. "Goodnight, then."

She waited until she knew he wouldn't speak again, then moved her pillow down and stretched out and pulled the sheet around her. She was sorry. She wished she had been asleep when he got home, so everything would be all right in the morning. She knew one thing, though. Stacy and Jason Leary would be among those "Communists" who would wave and cheer when the president rode by. She didn't care what Mark thought.

DENNIS

Dennis Pointer pushed his chair away from the chrome-and-plastic breakfast table that served him and Judy both for eating and for work and went to the tiny kitchenette to empty the ashtray into the trash. He lifted the electric percolator to weigh how much coffee remained and got his mug and refilled it, then settled himself at the table again, in front of the typewriter. He struck a match and lit a cigarette and balanced it on the edge of the ashtray, then took off his thick glasses and wiped them with his handkerchief. He picked up the Revised Standard Version Bible that Judy had given him last Christmas. He loved the feel of the soft morocco leather and the golden glow of his name embossed on the cover and the thin India paper and the golden edges of the pages. It was a fine, expensive Bible. He turned the pages with care, scanning them.

He envied some of his fundamentalist classmates, who believed in inspiration. They never labored over sermons, they said; they depended on the Holy Spirit to tell them what to say, and never knew what their message was going to be until they stood in the pulpit. Dennis had heard their sermons in his homiletics class at Southern Methodist. They were full of fire and maudlin sentimentality. They convinced him more strongly than ever that he was doing right, writing the sermons in full, like essays, and delivering them in his conversational way. What he lacked in fervor he made up in reason, in common sense, in intelligence.

But the page in the Underwood portable remained blank, and he was getting nervous. He wished he believed in the power of prayer, in divine guidance. He picked up the cigarette and took a puff, then a swallow of coffee. Maybe he should just start typing, just type whatever came into his mind. Maybe that would bring an idea. He snuffed the cigarette and placed his fingers on the keys.

Sometimes I wish the old phophets of Israel and Judah were still alive. Their messages were so current, so timely, and yet they contained that small, hard kernel of immortality that makes them relevant, even urgently important, for all men in all ages. Sometimes I wish I could sit down with Jeremiah or Amos or majestic Isaiah and get his advice and encouragement.

Advice and encouragement about what? What relevant, urgently important message did the prophets have this week for his tiny flock at the Broadway Junction Methodist Church in a grove of blackjack trees beside a narrow road on a prairie full of farmers a hundred miles northeast of Dallas?

These inspired men knew how to read the signs of the times and place them under the judgment of God. They placed their fingers on the pulse of a sick nation, pinpointed the causes of the disease, and predicted the inevitable outcome of the illness if the patient refused to admit it was sick and call on God to heal. . . .

Call on God to heal? Was that too Pentecostal? Being the weekend pastor of the Broadway Junction Church made him aware of the Pentecostals and the sermons they wished he would preach. There had once been a Pentecostal church at the Junction, and a Baptist church, but now only his remained. So the Baptists and the Pentecostals came to hear him, too, in that grove with the outdoor privy behind the little white church and the black soil into which he sank to his ankles when it rained, a century removed from Dallas and Southern Methodist University and the debates and discussions of the Perkins School of Theology.

"Who caused the boll weevils, preacher?" a farmer had asked him once. "The Lord or Satan?"

He remembered the question more clearly than any he had asked or been asked at Perkins, but couldn't remember what his reply had been. He wished he could. There might have been a clue to himself, to what he was about, in that answer. He didn't believe in a personal Satan or demons or any of that, but the farmer hadn't seemed disturbed by his answer. Did he even believe in a personal God? Had he blamed the boll weevils on Him? He wished he could remember. He wondered if the farmer did.

    Micah of Moresheth is one of my favorite prophets. He lived in a society which was very similar to our own. The nation Judah was prosperous. The people were still enjoying the remnants of King Solomon's glory. On the surface everything looked strong and permanent. But beneath the surface the nation was sick, and Micah knew it. The people were given to drunkenness and immorality. The rich were exploiting the poor, seizing their lands, cheating them out of their money, making them live in hovels on the outskirts of the city, in filth and poverty. Then the rich were telling each other that it was because the poor were naturally inferior, or lazy, or less blessed in the eyes of God, that things were as they were.

Why didn't he just come out and say the sermon was about the Negroes?

He didn't know Judy was up until she put her arms around his neck. She smelled of sleep, and he felt her warmth through her quilted nylon robe. He craned his neck and smiled at her. "How you feeling?" he asked.

"I don't know. Groggy. I just woke up."

He turned in his chair and felt her forehead. "You've still got a fever, I think."

"Maybe it's because I just woke up," she said. "God, I don't want to spend another day in bed." She glanced at the page in the typewriter. "What are you doing?"

"Trying to get a sermon started."

"How's it going?"

"I don't know what I want to say."

"Well, it's only Thursday."

Dennis looked at his watch. "Friday."

"You've got plenty of time," Judy said.

"Yeah, but I wanted to get a good start on it. Tomorrow's going to be busy. It would be easier to finish if I got a good start now. If I knew what I wanted to say."

Judy removed her arms from his shoulders and moved to the couch. She sat down as if the walk had been an effort, then stretched out and laid her head on one of the blue flowered pillows. Her blonde hair was matted. Her blue eyes were unnaturally bright.

"What are you doing?" Dennis asked. "Go back to bed."

"I'm tired of bed. It feels good to be up."

"If you still have a fever in the morning, I'm going to take you to the doctor," Dennis said.

"It's just the flu. He would tell me to take aspirin, drink liquids, and go to bed. I'm already doing that. Anyway, you would miss Kennedy."

"I could take you after that."

"What time are you going to Love Field?"

"His plane arrives about eleven-thirty, I think. I'd like to be there by eleven."

"Is that early enough? Won't there be a big crowd?"

Dennis grunted. "I wish. I may be the only one there."

"Is it really like that?"

"No, but almost."

"Why don't you ask somebody to go with you?"

"I asked Ben and Weldon, but they said they didn't want to cut class. I think they were afraid."

Judy sat up. "What do you want?" Dennis asked.

"A Coke. I can get it."

"No, I'll get it." Dennis took his mug into the kitchenette and poured the last of the coffee and unplugged the percolator. He got a Coke from the refrigerator and rummaged in a drawer for the bottle opener and pried the cap off. He handed the cold bottle to Judy. She moved her legs enough for him to sit down beside her.

"What are you cutting?" she asked.

"Greek. And ethics, if I don't get back in time. I'm okay in both of them."

"Dennis . . ."

"What?"

"Don't you ever miss Boston?"

"Sure. I miss it right now. It may be snowing there by now."

"Why don't we go home for Christmas?"

"You know why. We can't afford it."

"Well . . ." Judy moved her finger over the sweating Coke bottle as if drawing a design. "I talked to papa today, and he offered to pay the fare."

"I still can't," Dennis said. "A minister can't leave his church at Christmas."

"Oh, darling! I don't think they would mind. They'd probably *like* not having to go to church on Christmas. They'd certainly understand your wanting to be with your family."

Dennis shook his head. "I can't, Judy. Why don't you go?"

"Without you? What fun would that be? And who would play the piano for you?"

"We could sing *a cappella*. You don't need a piano for Christmas carols."

"Thanks. You make me feel real important."

"Well, we don't, do we?"

"Dennis, I have an idea. Why don't you work out some kind of laymen's service they could do without you if they wanted? Leave it up to them. If they want a Christmas service, they can have one without you. If not, everybody can stay at home and have fun."

"Judy—"

"We could go skiing. . . ."

"Get thee behind me, Satan," Dennis said. "I'll think about it. We've got time."

"If we're going, we have to make plane reservations."

"I'll think about it. Go to bed."

"Nuzzle me."

Dennis leaned to kiss her, but she said, "Not on the mouth, idiot." He kissed her neck just below her ear. Her skin was too warm.

"You're not going to try to teach tomorrow, I hope," Dennis said.

"No. I still feel lousy." She groaned. "I'd better set the alarm to call Wilkes. He gets upset if he has to find a substitute after seven-thirty."

"Won't they use the same one they had today?"

"Well, he'll have to call her before she gets assigned to somebody else."

"Get to bed, then." Dennis stood up and grasped Judy's hands and helped her from the couch. He held her close for a moment, then released her and backed away. "Take some aspirin."

Judy pulled her robe closely about her and shivered and turned toward the bedroom. "Don't work too long," she said.

Dennis returned to the typewriter and stared at the page while Judy brushed her teeth and set the alarm. His head ached. He had smoked too much. The coffee was making him nervous. He searched for his train of thought, wondering if he even had one. He longed for something to click in his mind, for some door to open and let light in. But he couldn't wait for it. He touched the tabulator key for a new paragraph.

Micah thought it was time somebody said something. So he did.

BULL

"There it is." Bull Waggoner pointed past the sweeping windshield wipers at the crumpled mass of metal against the bridge abutment, now glistening in the periphery of the patrol car's headlights.

"Jesus," the rookie said.

Bull eased the car into the emergency lane behind the wreck. Miraculously, the taillights of the ruined car still burned. The car was tilted against the abutment, as if trying to climb to the bridge above. The revolving red lights of the patrol car moved across the crumpled hood, then off, then on again, then off. The drizzle pelting Bull's windshield and the sweep of the wipers gave the wreck the aspect of a grotesque Christmas tree.

"You seen many dead bodies, Larry?" Bull asked the kid.

"Just my grandmother."

"Well, this ain't going to be like your grandmother."

Bull grabbed his flashlight and stepped out of the patrol car, and the kid followed. Bull went to the driver's side of the wrecked car, and the kid went to the other. Bull tried the door, but it wouldn't open. He shined the light through the shattered side window. The driver had been a young man. Now he was pressed between the steering wheel and the back of his seat like a flower between the pages of a book. He must not have had a whole bone left in his chest. "This one's gone," Bull said. He shined the flashlight across the seat and the dashboard. The woman had been young, too, he guessed, although he really couldn't tell. Her blood on the dashboard reflected his light, and he saw bits of brain.

"Jesus," Larry said. Bull heard him retching on the other side of the wreck. He had retched himself once, when he was a rookie, but it had been over a suicide, a guy who had stuck a shotgun in his mouth.

"Call for the meat wagon," he told Larry. "Call for a

wrecker. Tell the dispatcher there ain't no way we can get them out. Tell them how bad it is."

The kid wiped his mouth with a handkerchief and opened the patrol car door and leaned across the seat for the mike. He wouldn't sleep tonight. He would lie awake a long time, wondering why he had become a cop, wishing he hadn't. He would consider other career possibilities, maybe go for a couple of job interviews. Then the memory of the bodies in the wrecked car would fade, and the next time he saw one he wouldn't think much about it. He would remember these two, though, just as Bull remembered the guy who stuck the shotgun in his mouth. Bull didn't remember many of the corpses he had seen since then, but he still remembered that one.

Traffic was light on the North Central Expressway, but the drivers were slowing down, first because they saw the revolving lights of the patrol car, then to rubberneck at the wreck. One seemed to be stopping and Bull waved him by with the flashlight, throwing his whole huge body into the wave, ordering him away.

Bull went to the patrol car and got some flares. Larry was hanging up the mike, and Bull said, "Stay with the radio." He set out the flares, listening to the frying sound of the tiny raindrops hitting their bright pinkish light. The drizzle was wetter than it seemed from inside the car, and he was getting chilled. He should put on his slicker, but there wasn't time. He stood in the light of the flares, waving his flashlight. One of the drivers stopped anyway. Bull yanked off his hat and charged at the car, his crew cut bristling. The driver rolled down his window and spoke quickly, frightened. "I'm the one that called the police," he said. "They told me to come back to the scene."

"You a witness?" Bull asked.

"Yeah. I seen it happen."

"Okay. Pull in over there behind the patrol car. I'll be with you in a minute. Don't get out of the car."

The driver rolled up the window and eased his car within the perimeter of the flares. There were sirens in the distance now. First the fire engine, then the ambulance, then another police car. The firemen arrived first, and the rookie got out of the car to meet them. They began their work on the doors of the wreck. Then the ambulance arrived, then the police car, and finally the wrecker.

"You got a torch?" one of the firemen asked.

"Sure do," the wrecker driver called.

"Well, get it."

McDonald, the cop from the backup car, carried a yellow slicker to Bull, grinning. "Put this on, old man," he said. "You trying to get some sick leave?"

"I could use some," Bull said. He took the slicker, but didn't put it on. "Put Larry on traffic," he said. "I got a witness over there."

"Right. It's a bitch, ain't it?"

"Go look for yourself."

"Captain wants you to come in and write your report and then go home," McDonald said. "Rest up for the big day."

"Right. Soon as I talk to my witness."

The wrecker man was wearing goggles now, working at the door with his torch. Sparks were flying amid the revolving lights and the dark figures of the men. Bull folded the slicker and walked to the beat-up Chevy and climbed into the front seat beside the driver.

"They dead?" the driver asked.

"Don't know," Bull said. "May I see your driver's license?"

The man took off his cowboy hat and tossed it into the back seat, then fumbled in his hip pocket. He brought out a wallet and opened it and offered it to Bull.

"Just the license, please," Bull said.

The man took out the license and handed it to him, and Bull shined his light on it. He was talking to Jimmy Otis Phillips of Texarkana, it said.

"This your correct address, Mr. Phillips?"

"Yessir."

"What line of work are you in?"

"I work for a trucking outfit up there. Out of Texarkana."

"What brings you to Dallas, Mr. Phillips?" Bull was writing on his clipboard. Mr. Phillips was watching him carefully.

"I got a couple of days off and just thought I'd come down and look around."

"You been drinking, Mr. Phillips?" Bull smelled beer on him.

"Just a couple of beers on the way down. I ain't even hit town yet."

Bull shined his light into Mr. Phillips's eyes and decided he was telling the truth. "Okay," he said. "Tell me what you saw."

"Well, I was just coming down this road here—"

"U.S. Seventy-five."

"Yessir. And this guy passed me. Real fast. Then he pulled back into the lane in front of me. And then, when he was—oh, I guess about a hundred yards in front of me, well, he just sailed into that bridge."

"Did he hit his brakes first?"

"Yessir. I seen his brake lights. Then he hit the bridge."

"Did he skid much?"

"Well, he skidded, but I couldn't say how much. All I could see was his lights. But he fishtailed, all right, and then he hit the bridge."

"And what did you do then?"

"Well, I stopped and went over and tried to open the door, but it wouldn't come open. I tried to peek in the window, but I couldn't see nothing. And I said, 'Anybody hurt?' and I didn't hear no answer. So I got back in my car and drove to that Texaco station up yonder and called the cops. The police. And they told me to come back down here and talk to the officer at the scene. I ain't going to get no ticket or nothing, am I?"

"No, you've been very cooperative, Mr. Phillips. How

long do you plan to be in Dallas? Is there a phone where we could reach you, in case we need more information?"

"Yessir. I'm staying with Bob Timmons." Bull wrote down Bob Timmons's number. "I got to be back in Texarkana by Sunday night. I ain't got no phone there, but the company will know where I am." Bull wrote down the company's number. "I bet them suckers is dead. How many was there?"

"We're not sure yet," Bull said. "Thank you, Mr. Phillips, and drive carefully. These wet roads can fool you."

"Don't I know it. I'm a professional driver."

Bull stepped out of the car and held his folded slicker over his clipboard. "Much obliged," he said as he closed the door.

The old Chevy roared into life and moved slowly away, and Bull walked toward the wreck, where the ambulance people were laying a body on a stretcher in the brightness of the fire truck's spotlights. McDonald stepped out of the light to meet him. "How's it coming?" Bull asked.

"Okay," McDonald said. "You and your rookie go on in."

"You need somebody on traffic?"

"We can handle it. Go ahead."

Bull walked over to the flares and touched Larry on the arm. "Let's go," he said.

When they were back into the traffic, Bull turned off the revolving lights and settled himself into the seat. "Nasty night," he said.

HENRY

"Fuckin' scotch," Muffin said.

"You're particular for a nigger," Henry said.

"Mother-fuckin' scotch," Muffin said.

"If you don't like it, don't drink it," Henry said. He took

the bottle away from Muffin and held it up, trying to see how much was left, but it was too dark under the viaduct for him to see. He shook the bottle. There was some left. He drank it. "Listen to them sirens," he said.

"Fuckin' sirens," Muffin said.

"I bet there's a big wreck somewhere."

"Fuckin' wreck," Muffin said. "Give me that scotch."

"Ain't none left," Henry said.

"Fuckin' scotch," Muffin said.

"You're sure uppity for a nigger," Henry said. "You know who give me that scotch? The most beautiful lady in Dallas. Sheila Towers. Right outside of Babe's place. You know Babe's place. Well, that's where she give it to me. Right out in front. Just give it to me. Just like that."

"Fuckin' Sheila," Muffin said.

"You know Sheila? Naw, you don't know Sheila. Sheila wouldn't know no nigger. Sheila wouldn't give no nigger no scotch."

"Fuckin' Sheila," Muffin said.

"Ain't no use thinking about that," Henry said. "Ain't no nigger fuckin' Sheila. Sheila's got her man for the night, Muffin. He's the one that give me that scotch out in front of Babe's place. He just held it out to me and said, 'Here, Henry, you take this here scotch. I don't need it no more. Have yourself a good time, Henry.'"

"Fuckin' scotch. Give it to me," Muffin said.

"Ain't none left," Henry said. "You just roll over and pull this viaduct up under your chin and go to sleep, boy. Ain't no use worryin' about no scotch. Ain't no scotch left."

Muffin started crying. "Fuckin' rain," he said.

The Fourth Hour

THOMAS J.

"Ain't gonna be no dogs in heaven. Ain't gonna be no George Wallace in heaven. Ain't gonna be no billy clubs in heaven. Ain't gonna be no bullwhips in heaven. Ain't gonna be no cotton fields in heaven. Ain't gonna be no scrubbin' in heaven. Ain't gonna be no Kluxers in heaven. Ain't gonna be no hate in heaven. Ain't that right, reverend?"

"That's right, sister. You said it right," the Reverend Thomas J. Durant said. "You said it exactly right."

Many of the old ones claimed more years than they had. Sister Emma claimed she was born in slavery. Thomas J. doubted it, but it was possible. The old ones often claimed that, and believed it. They ought to organize the Sons and Daughters of Slavery, Thomas J. thought, like the white women organized the Daughters of the Confederacy. They were proud of it. They liked to say they were born in slave cabins. Maybe this one was. She claimed to be a month past her hundredth birthday. It was possible. She looked like an Egyptian mummy there on the yellowing white sheet in the yellow light from the old lamp beside the bed. Her flannel nightgown, the nap worn off it in spots, was yellow, too, or seemed to be. She could be a hundred. She could be a daughter of slaves. Definitely a daughter of slaves. Maybe a slave herself. Her dark scalp shone through her thin white hair. She couldn't weigh more than seventy-five pounds.

"You know what heaven's gonna be like, reverend?"

"Sure, Sister Emma. Like the Zodiac." Thomas J. smiled. She had gone with them the day they desegregated the restaurant on the sixth floor of Neiman-Marcus. She had said it looked like heaven.

The old woman laughed weakly. "Naw, reverend, not the Zodiac. Ain't no fried chicken in the Zodiac. Ain't no watermelon in the Zodiac. Heaven's gonna be like Juneteenth every day. Lord, Lord, how them white women looked at us in that Zodiac. Naw, heaven ain't gonna be that. Heaven's Juneteenth, reverend."

It was a tradition in Mount Zion Baptist Tabernacle that on the Sunday before Juneteenth, Sister Emma Rawlins would stand in the pulpit and tell about the Union general coming ashore at Galveston on June 19, 1865, and proclaiming that the slaves in Texas were free. In the fourteen years that Thomas J. had been her pastor, her narrative had never varied. He was sure the proclamation hadn't been as dramatic as Sister Emma imagined it, with hundreds of flags flying and trumpets sounding, and Sister Emma didn't claim to remember the flags, since, she said, she wasn't yet two years old at the time. But her mama and daddy told her about the flags, she said, and she did remember the sun shining so bright on the trumpets. She had celebrated every Juneteenth there had ever been, she said, and she remembered the sun on the trumpets.

"Come take me, Jesus. Lord, Lord, I'm ready. Ain't gonna be no rent in heaven. Ain't gonna be no light bills in heaven. Ain't gonna be no cockroaches in heaven. . . ." She paused, frowning. "Will there be white folks in heaven, reverend?"

"There'll be some, Sister Emma. They aren't all bad."

"No, not all. President Lincoln will be there, won't he?"

"Yes, he'll be there."

"Him and me was alive at the same time. Did you know that, reverend?"

"Yes, sister, I did."

"Come take me, Jesus. Set me down by Abraham Lincoln. You know what heaven's gonna be like, reverend?"

"Juneteenth every day."

"That's right. And State Fair. Them lights and that music. And cotton candy and walking by the lagoon and watching the fireworks. State Fair and Juneteenth at the same time. Lord, won't it be fine?"

Sister Emma's house was two blocks from Fair Park, where the fair was celebrated every October. She would move her rocker to the porch in the evenings when the air was cool and listen to the music of the nightly parades and the midway and the noise of the crowds at the Cotton Bowl that sounded like waves crashing on the beach at Galveston. On the last night of the fair, Thomas J. and Lucius Jackson would take her to the midway and find her a bench where she would sit and watch the swirling lights of the rides and smile at the screams of the youngsters riding them and admire the young couples strutting by with their corn on the cob and the panda bears they had won. A month before this night that Thomas J. was sitting beside her bed, he and Lucius had taken her there in Lucius's taxicab, and she'd called it the happiest night of her life because she had received a birthday card from President Kennedy that day.

"You'll be there, reverend. And all the members of the Dallas County United Poll Tax Committee."

"I hope so, sister."

"Oh, you'll come, all right. I'll greet you at the pearly gates and make a little curtsy, just like at church. That won't be for a long time, but time don't mean nothing in heaven, does it?"

"No. You said it right, sister."

A small gas heater burned brightly in the corner of the room and Thomas J. was sweating. He wanted to take off his coat, but it wouldn't be dignified, so he pulled his handkerchief out of the breast pocket and mopped his brow. "Are you still cold, sister?" he asked.

"Yes. Would you pull the blanket over me?"

Thomas J. bent over the bed and pulled the old wool army blanket up to Sister Emma's chin and tucked it around her. "Would you like some water?" he asked.

"Yes. That's mighty kind of you, reverend."

The floorboards creaked under his feet as he walked to the kitchen. He pulled the chain on the light socket hanging from the wire in the middle of the ceiling. The bare bulb, moving like a pendulum from the force of his pull, made shadows ebb and flow across the faded, water-stained wallpaper above the sink on one side of the room and the ancient gas range on the other. The porcelain back of the sink had two holes like eyes where faucets were intended to be, but Sister Emma carried her water from the faucet in the yard. The galvanized water bucket sat on a low bench beside the sink, and the dipper hung on a hook on the wall above it, but the bucket was empty. Thomas J. picked it up and walked back through the front room to the door. "I'm going to get you some water, sister," he said.

He paused on the porch while his eyes adjusted to the darkness, then stepped onto the flat stone that served for a step, then to the ground. The rain was a fine mist, almost like fog, and made a halo around the streetlight down the block. He breathed deeply, craving the damp air after so long in the hot, dry room with the airless smell of sickness in it. The faucet was by the gate, and he stepped carefully toward it, still not sure of himself in the dark. He found the faucet and set the bucket under it and turned it on.

"Is that you, reverend?"

The voice startled him and he stood quickly erect. "Oh, hello, Lucius," he said. "What are you doing, sneaking around here at this hour?" Lucius Jackson was a deacon in his church, and they had been friends a long time.

"Just checking on Sister Emma. I saw her light on. I brought her a TV."

Thomas J. bent and turned off the faucet. "Where did you get it?"

Lucius hesitated. "Bought it from a guy. Just a while ago. I promised Sister Emma I'd take her downtown tomorrow to see the president, but I guess she can't go."

"No."

"So I brought her a TV to watch him on. She doing okay?"

"No," Thomas J. said. "She may not get to watch him on TV, either."

"Well, I'll bring it in."

"You need help?"

"No. It's a little one," Lucius said.

"I was getting her a drink of water." Thomas J. picked up the bucket.

"Uh-huh," Lucius said. He disappeared, and Thomas J. heard him open a car door. He waited until Lucius reappeared at the gate, carrying the TV. "It's a little one," he said, "but I'll set it close to her bed. It would have to be close, anyway, so she can reach it."

They walked together into the house. "Lucius is here," Thomas J. said. "He brought you a present." He went to the kitchen and set the bucket on the bench and dipped water from it into a jelly glass sitting by the sink and took it to the front room. Lucius had set the TV on the chair in which Thomas J. had sat and was on his hands and knees, reaching under the bedside table to plug it in. "I think sister's asleep," he said.

Thomas J. sat down on the side of the bed, holding the glass. "Sister Emma? I brought your water." The army blanket covered most of her face, and Thomas J. grasped its edge and turned it back. "Sister Emma?"

Lucius stood up and rubbed his palms on his pants legs.

"Happy Juneteenth, Lucius," Thomas J. said.

"Huh?"

"She's gone, Lucius. Call the funeral home." He set the jelly glass on the little table and went to the corner and turned off the gas heater.

Lucius pulled off his cap and squeezed it in his big hands and stared at the still, small figure on the yellow sheet under the army blanket. Two huge tears welled into the corners of his eyes and coursed slowly down the valleys between his cheeks and nose.

Thomas J. laid his hand on his friend's shoulder and said, "Time don't mean a thing in heaven, Lucius. Nothing at all."

SHEILA

She tried to pretend she was still asleep, but the hand on her breast became insistent. "What?" she asked.

"I want it," the man said.

Sheila tried to remember who the man was and where she was. It didn't matter, but she hated to lose track. The man's hands were waking her body, not sexually, but rousing it out of sleep. "You've had it," she said.

"I'm just trying to get my money's worth," the man said.

"You got it," she said. "Why don't we get some sleep now?" Barnhill. That was his name. And this was the Adolphus. "What time is it?"

"I don't know. Who cares?" His words were slightly slurred, although he hadn't had a drink since they left Babe's. He grasped her wrist and moved her hand up his thigh to his erection. She curled her fingers around it but didn't move them. She just held it.

"Let's wait till morning," she said. "It must be very late now."

"There's no time in the morning. I've got too much to do

tomorrow." He leaned and kissed her nipple, but she didn't respond, didn't move her fingers. "There's an extra fifty in it for you," he said.

Babe wouldn't have to know. She could keep it all. "All right," she said. Barnhill moved to her, but she said, "Let's see the fifty."

"Jesus Christ." He rolled away from her and got out of bed. He rummaged in his trousers in the darkness, then got back in bed and handed her a folded bill. She switched on the lamp to make sure it was a fifty. "You're a trusting little soul, aren't you?" he said.

"It pays to be careful." She opened her handbag and put the bill in and laid the bag back on the table.

"You ought to be in politics," he said, and she remembered that he was a senator or something. She moved her hand toward the lamp switch, but he said, "Let's leave it on this time."

"The customer's always right," Sheila said. She settled herself back into the bed, and Barnhill moved against her and tried to kiss her on the mouth. Pretending to misunderstand his intention, Sheila turned her head aside so that the kiss landed on her neck. She spread her legs, and Barnhill positioned himself between them, and she grasped his erection again and guided it into her and closed her eyes. In the darkness, Sheila always kept her eyes open, gazing at the dark ceiling, but when they wanted the light on, she closed them. She didn't like to see the faces looming over her. She disengaged her mind from what she was doing and began moving her hips as if she were doing her dance lying down and made little moaning sounds.

"Is it good?" he asked.

"Oh, yes, it's good. It's so good." Sheila had had better, but worse, too. Much worse. Kinky worse. Barnhill stuck to basics, and it wasn't bad. She wouldn't be worse for wear when morning came, and she appreciated that. He might be pretty good with the right woman. She wondered if he was married. He didn't wear a ring, but he probably was. He was pretty good-looking, a brown-eyed blond, pretty prosperous, pretty nice. Well liked, probably, since somebody had elected him to something. Barnhill wasn't with her because he particularly needed to be, and that made him a pleasant enough trick. He was on the verge of coming, so she quickened the rhythm of her hips and moaned more loudly. He came then, and collapsed on her, breathing hard. Sheila breathed hard, too, and made a gasp.

"Did you come?" he asked.

"I—I think so."

She hadn't, of course, but he probably believed her. Most men knew that orgasm wasn't part of the bargain, but every man thought he was different, the exception, the one who could make a woman forget she was involved in a business transaction. Most men didn't ask if Sheila came, but if they asked, she always said she thought so. Barnhill probably believed it, but he apparently wasn't going to crow about it as some did, telling long stories about other women they had made come and how they did it. Barnhill just lay quietly on her, so quietly that she thought he was asleep. She nudged him. "I have to pee."

He disengaged himself and moved to the other side of the bed, and Sheila went to the bathroom and peed and washed herself. She wished she had a toothbrush. She usually carried one in her handbag, but had left it in a suite at the Baker the night before. She would try to remember to buy another in the morning. She went back to the bedroom and opened her purse and got the Prince Albert tobacco tin and the packet of papers. "Would you like a joint?" she asked.

"A what?"

"A joint. Marijuana."

"No. I don't do that. It's a felony, you know."

"Mind if I do?"

"Go ahead."

"It helps me sleep sometimes." Sheila licked her thumb and

peeled two papers out of the packet and stuck them together. She rolled the joint quickly, expertly, and lit it with a match from the hotel matchbook on the table. She inhaled the smoke deeply and held it in her lungs as long as she could, then exhaled and watched it swirl toward the heat of the lamp. She propped the thin pillow against the headboard and sat upright against it.

"You told me you didn't smoke." Barnhill was lying on his side, watching her, smiling. Sheila knew she made a pretty sight, sitting with her knees bent so he could see the firmness of her thighs and calves.

"This doesn't stain your teeth," she said. "Anyway, you don't smoke it all day like cigarettes."

Barnhill leaned on his elbow. "You're a good-looking woman," he said.

"Thanks. I know that."

"Sitting there smoking like that, you remind me of Marlene Dietrich in *The Blue Angel*. Did you ever see that?"

"No. I've seen pictures of her, though."

"It's about a nightclub singer in Berlin before the war. I sort of feel like I'm in that movie tonight. You're Marlene Dietrich, and Dallas is Berlin. It's not hard to imagine."

"How's Dallas like Berlin?"

"It's full of Nazis."

"And what are you? A Communist?"

Barnhill laughed. "See? You're doing it. If you're not a Nazi in Dallas, you must be a Communist. I'm a Ralph Yarborough Democrat. That's close to being a Communist here, I guess. He believes in labor unions."

The marijuana was taking hold of Sheila. Her head was lighter. She was relaxing. "Politics is boring," she said.

Barnhill watched her breathe in the sweet-smelling smoke.

"You didn't have to come here, did you?" she said.

"Jesus, you sound like you're from Highland Park." Barnhill shook a cigarette out of his pack and lit it. He moved the ashtray to the mattress between them. "You're not from Highland Park, are you?" He was mocking her, but she didn't care.

"I'm from Greenville," she said.

"And Sheila Towers isn't your real name."

"How do you know that?"

"Nobody's named Sheila Towers."

"Babe named me that. I wanted to call myself Greenville Green, but he wouldn't let me."

"Babe was right. What's your real name?"

"Thelma Ruth. Thelma Ruth Green."

Barnhill snickered.

"What's so funny about that?"

"Nothing. I just can't imagine a stripper named Thelma Ruth Green."

"I'm an exotic dancer."

"Whatever." He rolled over and picked up the telephone. "Give me a wake-up at six-thirty, will you?" he told the operator.

"You're an early riser," Sheila said when he hung up.

"I'm not. Barefoot Sanders is."

"Who's that? Sounds like a comedian."

"Barefoot has his funny moments. Makes his living as U.S. attorney, though. And I've got to get to him before anybody else tomorrow. He's my best chance of getting a ticket to that damn luncheon."

"Why don't you have a ticket? Aren't you important?"

"Berlin ain't my town, baby."

"So you're going to beg a Nazi for a ticket." She was getting nasty, but didn't care. He had started it.

"Barefoot may be the only liberal in Berlin. Except maybe Judge Sarah Hughes. Kennedy appointed them both. To undermine Dallas from within, you know."

"Politics is boring," Sheila said again. She snuffed out the joint in the ashtray. Barnhill put out his cigarette, too, and moved the ashtray to the table. He shifted himself closer to her and laid his hand on her thigh. She removed it. "No more tonight, cowboy. You've had your ride."

"What happened to the sweet little exotic dancer from Babe's?"

"She's tired. Her bumps don't want to grind anymore."

"Suit yourself." He fluffed his pillow and rolled onto his side, his back to her.

"Well, maybe for another fifty . . ." she said.

"Forget it. Turn out the light."

Sheila switched off the lamp and went to the bathroom and showered. Barnhill was asleep when she returned, so she dressed quickly and picked up the blue raincoat and the umbrella and her handbag and tiptoed into the hall, pulling the door softly closed behind her.

She didn't like to wake up with them.

LUIS

The man on the mattress beside Luis was lying on his back and snoring. Luis wanted to wake him up, but he was afraid. The man had arrived only that day, and Luis didn't know his name, and Luis was too young to wake up an older man he didn't know. Luis was seventeen, and he remembered how tired he had been when he arrived in this place six months before. The man beside him was probably tireder than he had been. He looked old. Maybe forty-five. He had a wife and many children at home, no doubt. If he had come from the interior, he had missed them a long time already. Even if he had come from a border state, as Luis had, he already had missed them a long time. The journey was hard and tiring, and the farther north you came, the more you missed your family and home and village, as poor as all of them were. He missed his own village in Tamaulipas, even now that he had been in Dallas for six months and had a job and friends.

It was the fear that made it bad. It was worse than the work, the fear of the Border Patrol in its khaki uniforms swooping into the workplaces and taking the people away. Many of the people who had come to the house where Luis lay on the mattress had already been taken away, some of them just a week or two after they finished the hard journey. It would have been better for them if they had never started. But it was a chance you took. And if you could avoid the Border Patrol long enough, it was worth the work and the fear and the risk to go to the Western Union office every week and send the money home. It made you something in your village.

And something besides the money was going to make Luis something. In the morning, when he rose from the mattress where he lay, he would see the president of the United States. At least he hoped he would see him. He would be working in the kitchen while the president was having his lunch. And Jackie. *Jack y Jackie.* Even the people in his village knew of them, in a village where nobody important, not even a Mexican of importance, had ever come. Maybe Jack would speak of the Alliance for Progress. *La Alianza para el Progreso.* The great partnership between the *Gringos* and Mexico that would take the poverty away from his village and let him go home and work in his village just as he was working here, without the *Gringo* bosses and the fear of the Border Patrol. That would be a great thing.

He would write a letter home. He would write the first letter home that he had written since he crossed the Rio Grande, and the priest would read it to his mother and father and his sisters. He would tell of *Jack y Jackie* coming to the Dallas Trade Mart to have lunch, and he would say that he shook hands with them, even if he hadn't, and that they said nice things to him, even if they hadn't, and that he had served their table, although he knew he wouldn't. And he would say that the president spoke of *La Alianza para el Progreso*, even if he didn't, and that life was going to be better in Tamaulipas. That's what he would do. And even the priest would be impressed. Luis would be something. And that is what he had learned since he had come to Texas—that everyone could be something, if they worked hard and learned English and were lucky and the Border Patrol didn't take them away.

The Fifth Hour

LUTHER

THE CLOCK STRUCK ITS SINGLE NOTE for the half-hour. Colonel Luther Byrd didn't have to guess which hour it was half-past. For as long as he could remember, he had awakened every morning at 4:30, and for eighteen of those years he had awakened to the same single note of the same clock. He retired every night at 11:00 sharp and went immediately to sleep, hearing none of the clock's chimes except the single note for 4:30. It was strange and amusing that he had never heard the chimes for 2:00 or 2:30 or 3:00 or 3:30, but always heard 4:30.

The clock was from a house on the Rhine, and it was in that house, in 1945, that he first heard it strike 4:30 and knew that he had to have it. The woman who owned it, and in whose house and bed he was, didn't want to sell it to him. It had been in her family for a long time, she said, and wasn't a valuable clock. She was sure the American captain could find a more beautiful, more valuable clock elsewhere for less than he was offering for hers. But when he told her he was taking the clock whether she took the money or not, she accepted the twenty-dollar bill that he offered her. Now the clock sat on the antique walnut table in Colonel Byrd's living room, below the Nazi flag in its huge glassed frame on the wall. And Colonel

Byrd never heard it strike 4:30 without remembering the first time he had heard it and the woman and the house on the Rhine and the war.

It was good that the United States had won the war, of course. If a country is going to fight a war, it ought to fight to win. But Colonel Byrd believed in 1945, and still believed, that he and his comrades-in-arms had been engaged against the wrong enemy. Maybe Hitler and the Nazis had been a little extreme in their methods, but they had done a damn good job of containing the Communist threat, which couldn't be said of anyone since. Roosevelt. Truman. Eisenhower, the bastard who let the Russians take Berlin. And Kennedy. Kennedy, who had forced Colonel Luther A. Byrd to give up his command and retire at fifty-five simply because he had called his men to attention at each dawn to instruct them on the evils of communism. Whose side was Kennedy on? Luther Byrd knew. It was there in the leaflet.

Colonel Byrd slipped his feet into the fleece-lined slippers beside his bed and wrapped himself in his brown silk robe. He went into the living room in the dark and switched on the reading lamp beside his chair and picked up a leaflet from the small stack on the table where the clock was. He sat down in the chair and propped his feet on the leather ottoman and studied the paper. The quality of the printing wasn't good. The pictures, the full-face and profile of the traitor, would have reproduced better if he could have provided glossy prints to the printer. And the expressions on Kennedy's face weren't as evil as he would have liked. But it was a rush job, and, anyway, its message was clear. WANTED FOR TREASON. There was no mistaking the meaning of that. Even Caroline and John-John could figure out what that meant. Maybe even Jackie.

How many of the leaflets had his people distributed that day? Not all of them, he hoped. There should be some left to distribute along the route of the motorcade. The reporters should get some. The White House press corps would pounce on that. It would make the wire services, and maybe the networks. The world would know that not everyone in Dallas was in love with Jack and Jackie. Maybe the Citizens Council and the newspapers and the half-assed public-relations people were willing to let principle fly out the window for a day, but the friends of Luther Byrd weren't. There were still enough patriots left to expose the so-called president for the commie-loving papist turncoat that he was.

Kennedy would see the newspaper ad, whether he saw the leaflet or not. The White House crowd couldn't resist the newspapers. They would want to read about themselves, and they would see the ad. The ad would let them know they weren't fooling everybody. The ad would cram the message up their asses.

Colonel Byrd crossed the living room and slid open the glass door to the balcony, as he did every morning when the clock struck 4:30. The view from his balcony, on the fifteenth floor of the only high-rise apartment building in Dallas, was the best in the city. Below him, the empty pavement of Turtle Creek Boulevard glistened under the streetlights, and on the horizon the skyscrapers were ablaze with lights.

Two years ago, only a few months after his disgrace, Colonel Byrd had decided to make Dallas his home. The people who welcomed and entertained him bragged that there was no reason for a city to be where Dallas was; there was no seacoast, no large lake, no navigable river, no pass through mountains, no scenic vista, no natural resource except the flat, fertile prairie itself. The city was where it was, his hosts told him, because a man named John Neely Bryan had decided to build a town here and had been glib enough to persuade others to buy land from him and join him. Others had followed and built more, until the prairie was important only as a place on which to build. Money itself, and the smart movement and placement of it, had become the fount of still more money, and the buildings to house the money and the paper work concerning it continually grew larger, until they dwarfed the other structures of the city. The banks and insurance com-

panies ruled the blazing skyline, and two more towers, even
taller than the rest, were under construction. Colonel Byrd
could see their few lights along their bare girders shining with
the rest, hinting of the grandeur to come.

The people of Dallas were proud of themselves because
they owed nothing to Nature, nothing to God, and, most
emphatically, nothing to the federal government. That pride
was the reason Colonel Byrd had chosen the city as his home
after years of wandering and persecution in the service of his
country. Like the original Creator, the Dallas people had built
their city out of nothing. They had created their world in
their own image and had gone to great lengths to keep it free
of blemishes and the influence of coloreds and commies and
labor unions. Only important people made important deci-
sions here, which was as the founding fathers had intended the
whole country to be.

Colonel Byrd wasn't one of the decision makers of Dallas
yet, but he would be someday. There were many here who
shared his values, who recognized the danger that the country
was in, who were alarmed by the steady destruction by the
termites at work inside the timbers of the Republic, and Dallas
didn't lack the will to fight. There were right-thinking people
here, and he had found a remarkable number of them in such
a short time. His organization of them into an effective political unit was progressing nicely. Many of them, especially the
women, worshiped him. And why not? Wasn't he a hero?
Hadn't he served his country well, even ignoring the will of
his so-called superiors when they tried to turn him from his
duty as he saw it? The time would come when Dallas would
invite him to the inner sanctum of the decision makers, and
he would be ready. Dallas, the city built on guts and daring
and nothing else, would become his headquarters for a great
crusade. Dallas would be to Luther Byrd what Geneva had
been to John Calvin. The center from which the true gospel
of Americanism would spread.

Colonel Byrd realized that he was standing at attention.

And why not? His thoughts were honorable, and it was an honorable cause on which he was embarked, more honorable than fighting the Germans had been, more honorable than defeating a country that had meant no harm to right-thinking people, more honorable, certainly, than getting fired for having beliefs and acting on them.

Fired. That's what the Jew-dominated eastern newspapers had said. How the pinkos had crowed over that. How smug they were in their belief that Luther Byrd had been muzzled at last, that the Paul Revere of the modern age had been shut up. He felt more honorable, cleaner, purer, standing at attention in his silk robe in the damp night air of Dallas than he ever had genuflecting to the will of the Pentagon and the White House. He regretted only that Hannah wasn't with him on his balcony, that he couldn't speak his thoughts aloud to her and hear her quiet agreement. They had killed her. Their persecution of him had weakened her heart. She couldn't bear to see what they were doing to him, and seventeen days after his humiliation, she died. Poor Hannah. Poor, poor Hannah. He had tried to tell her he wasn't through, that he would go on fighting and would finally win, but she never really believed. Not really. If she had believed, she would be standing beside him now, listening to his thoughts and admiring the beautiful Dallas skyline.

The traffic light down on Turtle Creek, going idiotically through its sequence of signals—green, yellow, red, green, yellow, red—sending its orders to no one, controlling nothing, was what his life in the army had become. A sequence of futile signals, useless warnings to no one. He was glad to be out of it. Maybe he could use the traffic-light image in one of his pamphlets or speeches. The red could signify the Reds, and the yellow—what? The cowards? The yellowbellies who merely cautioned, but commanded nothing, controlled nothing? Well. It would take some thought. It could be effective, though, thought through and printed in color.

Maybe he should get out his uniform and wear it tomorrow.

The map in the evening paper indicated that the motorcade would move down this very street, through this very intersection. He would have his flag flying from the balcony, upside down as usual, sending its message of distress to those who knew enough to know what an upside-down flag meant. The men in the motorcade would know. Kennedy would know. Johnson would know. The Secret Service would know. They would look. They couldn't help looking. What if he were standing beside the flag in full dress, at attention? Would they know who he was? Would they recognize Colonel Luther A. Byrd, whom they had tried to disgrace? A dignified protest. The press boys would see it and use it, especially if they saw it was Luther Byrd sending the message. Would they know? The Secret Service would know. They would know where Luther Byrd was when Kennedy came to Dallas. But would they tell the press?

The clock struck five. Colonel Byrd always heard it strike five, the time for the security check. He stepped inside and slid the heavy glass door closed and locked it. He reached between the wall and the back of the sofa and got the length of pipe that he always slid into the groove in which the door slid, to keep it from opening if the enemy somehow got to the balcony and picked the lock. He drew the drapes over the glass and moved to the heavy, solid wooden door he had installed to the hallway and checked the three deadbolt locks. All secure. He opened the drawer of the little antique chest beside the door and lifted out the heavy army Colt .45 automatic. Yes, the clip was full, and a round was in the chamber. The Luger in the bathroom was loaded, too. He tucked it back under the towel on top of the toilet tank, then pissed and washed his hands and brushed his teeth again. He picked up the pair of military hairbrushes beside the sink and ran them through his silver hair and snapped to attention in front of the mirror, admiring the contrast of the gray eyes and the leathery skin, kept brown in secret by a sunlamp, approving the crow's feet at the corners of his eyes, the lack of flab, the stern set of the thin mouth. He turned off the light and returned to the bedroom and opened the drawer of the night-stand. The .45 there was ready, too, as he knew it would be. He laid his robe carefully across the end of the bed and set the slippers on the floor.

If he decided to wear the uniform, he must be careful that Kennedy couldn't interpret it as a sign of respect. Maybe a black armband . . .

Two hours before dawn, the first ones arrived. They leaned against the storefronts, smoking, trying to stay out of the rain. They were union men, Ralph Yarborough men, stopping by to see the president before they went to work. As the parking lot slowly filled, they joked with each other, joked with the cop in the yellow slicker on the bay horse, whistled at the young secretaries holding umbrellas.

"You think he'll show up in this rain?" one of them said.

"Hell, yes," his friend replied.

In the Will Rogers Suite, Lady Bird Johnson was dressing for the day. She was dreading Dallas, and her hands were trembling.

The Sixth Hour

RAYMOND

"YOU'VE BEEN IN THE BOONIES too long, Ray," the White House man had said the first time they drove the route together. "The object of the motorcade is to let the people see him."

"Our job is to protect the president," Raymond had replied.

"Well, yeah. But you've got to be reasonable."

Raymond Medley reached to the nightstand and plugged in the percolator, then lay back in bed. Every morning for two months, the thought of the motorcade had been the first to pop into his mind. He closed his eyes and visualized its route again, and was glad that this was the last morning he would have to think of it.

He had driven every block of it ten times or more with the man from the White House detail, and another dozen times alone. He knew every street, every intersection, every building, every billboard. Mockingbird Lane. Then right onto Lemmon Avenue. Then right onto Turtle Creek Boulevard, which suddenly and without explanation became Cedar Springs Road. Then a jog to the right onto Harwood Street. Then a sharp right onto Main Street, the canyon between the downtown skyscrapers and the leg of the journey that he dreaded most. Then the little jog to the right onto Houston Street to reach Elm Street. Then left on Elm, through Dealey Plaza. Then under the Triple Underpass and onto Stemmons Expressway to the Trade Mart.

If you had to have a motorcade, an expressway was the place. The limousines could move swiftly along behind their motorcycle escort, and there were no buildings close to the roadway and no sidewalks for crowds. When Raymond was informed that the president was to visit Dallas, he had suggested that the entourage go directly to the Trade Mart, a short, swift drive from Love Field. When the White House insisted on a motorcade, he recommended North Central Expressway as the fastest, safest route downtown. The White House vetoed that, too. The politicians wanted Dallas to see Kennedy.

Raymond went into the bathroom and pulled the white bath mat from the rim of the tub and spread it in front of the toilet to protect his feet from the cold white tiles. He pulled the drawstring on his pajamas and sat down and stared at the words "Stoneleigh Terrace" on the mat. He had seen the same words from the same perspective almost every morning for the ten years he had served in Dallas, and only a couple of times had he wished for more than he had. A wife, maybe. Kids, no. A transfer to the White House, only in his ambitious moments when he was younger. The Stoneleigh, threadbare as it was becoming, still provided a fair restaurant, a good bar, maid service, free parking, and had never raised his rent. The manager had told him the other permanent tenants, old ladies and gentlemen, most of them, felt secure with a Secret Service man on the premises. He had everything he really wanted, and the only thing he had that he didn't want was the president coming to Dallas.

Adlai Stevenson had warned the White House against it a month ago, and then chickened out and told the president to go ahead if he thought it was important. The picture on the front page of the evening paper had been a lulu, all right. The congressman from Dallas, the darling of the right-wingers, snarling into the camera and, presumably, into Stevenson's face, just before Adlai got bopped with the picket sign. And Johnson. He couldn't want to come here. A mob of screaming women had spit on him and Lady Bird in Dallas during the campaign, and since then the Johnsons' visits had been quiet and brief. Raymond had watched Lady Bird's face turn tense and her hands clench whenever she had to leave a hotel suite or a friend's home and be exposed, even for a moment, to the anonymous Dallas public.

Yarborough had warned the White House about Dallas, too, and so had Henry Gonzalez. They were liberals, though, and had nothing to gain here. Gonzalez had been anxious enough to show off the president in his own congressional district in San Antonio. And Yarborough had never carried Dallas, not for governor, when he lost, and not for senator, when he won. He couldn't carry Dallas for dogcatcher. He was paranoid as hell, too, as most Texas liberals were, especially when in Dallas. And Kennedy. Could he carry Dallas? Not in a month of Sundays.

So why were they coming? Just because Dallas was the state's second-largest city and would be insulted if Kennedy visited Houston and San Antonio and Fort Worth and Austin and didn't come here? Why should Kennedy care?

Raymond thought of the city as a Republican castle surrounded by a Democratic forest, a castle where money was king and needed no excuse, no explanation, for running things. He didn't mind that. Almost half of his twenty years in government service had been spent here, and he had grown to love the city and the smooth, quiet way it did things. It didn't deserve all the bad press it had gotten, nor the reputation that Luther Byrd and the Birchers and Edwin Walker and the rest of the lunatic fringe were giving it. He wished Kennedy weren't coming to stir it all up again.

The visit was probably John Connally's idea. He was the nearest thing to a Republican that Texas was likely ever to

elect as governor. He loved Dallas, and Dallas loved him.
They saw and did things the same way. He understood the
city. What was it he had said? "I've been poor, and I've been
rich, and rich is better." That was the Dallas point of view,
all right. But why did Connally want to come here with
Kennedy? Maybe he didn't. Maybe Kennedy wanted to
come here with Connally. Maybe he was so confident of his
charm that he thought he could win over even the Connally
people in Dallas. Or maybe he just wanted to prove that the
president of the United States wasn't afraid of Dallas. Or
maybe it was Jackie's idea. Since the election, she hadn't ac-
companied her husband on a single political trip. So why
Texas? Did she want to see what Neiman-Marcus women
looked like?

The aroma of coffee drifted into the bathroom, and Raymond got up and flushed the toilet. *Theirs not to reason why,
theirs but to do or die*, he thought. He went to the tiny foyer
between the bedroom and the sitting room that he seldom
used and opened the hall door. The newspaper hadn't arrived
yet. He closed the door and fastened the chain latch again.
He returned to the bedroom and poured his coffee and pulled
the cord to open the drapes. In the dimly lighted parking lot
the cars were still shiny wet, but the rain was only a drizzle.

"Damn," he said aloud. But a drizzle might be enough to
keep the crowds small. Maybe the bubble top would have to
be put on the limousine to protect Jackie's hair. He hoped
the rain wasn't ending.

JONATHAN

When the bell sounded in their top-floor bedroom in the
Fisher mansion, Lanell rolled over and pressed herself against

Jonathan's back. "Be an angel," she said. "Go down and keep her company. I can't pull my old body up yet."

"All right," Jonathan said. "You owe me one."

Lanell kissed him on the neck, and he got up and put on his robe and slippers. The narrow wooden back stairs creaked under his feet, and when he entered the kitchen, Miss Anna turned from her flowerpots and looked at him.

"Oh. Good morning, Jonathan," she said. "I was expecting Lanell."

"She's catching a few more winks. I'll fetch her if you want her."

"No. That's all right." Miss Anna turned back to the African violets on the oak sideboard in the breakfast alcove. Jonathan poured water into the kettle and set it on a burner and turned on the flame under it. "I don't think these things are ever going to bloom," Miss Anna said.

"You're up bright and early this morning, Miss Anna," Jonathan said.

"Early, but not bright at all. It looks like it's going to be a wretched day."

Jonathan glanced toward the huge bay window that formed the alcove, but it was still dark outside and he could see nothing. "Yes, ma'am," he said. He got the silver tea ball from the drawer and filled it from the canister. He got the carton of milk from the refrigerator and filled the plain white china cream pitcher.

"Do you know anything about African violets, Jonathan?" Miss Anna asked.

"No, ma'am. Calvin might, though."

"I've already asked him. I guess I'll have to buy a book. You'd think they would have bloomed by now."

Jonathan opened the cabinet to get a cup and saucer. "Get one for yourself, Jonathan," Miss Anna said.

"Thank you, ma'am," he said. "I'm having trouble coming awake."

"Did Mr. J.L. keep you up late?"

"Yes, ma'am. Pretty late."

Miss Anna turned from the violets again, a look of concern on her face. "Is he well?"

"Oh, yes, ma'am. That man of yours is just a night owl, Miss Anna." Jonathan lifted the kettle and poured the boiling water into the white china pot. "He just likes to talk sometimes, you know."

"Politics, I suppose."

"Yes, ma'am, politics. And religion. And the old days in Mexico. And Mr. Pool."

Miss Anna laughed. Her laugh sounded so much younger than she was, and made Jonathan feel younger, too. "Buck Pool again? How many times have you heard those tales, Jonathan?"

"Lord, no telling. You want something to eat? I could toast you an English muffin."

"No, thanks. Just the tea. Did he tell you about his Billy-Graham-for-president scheme?"

"Oh, yes, ma'am."

Miss Anna ran her hands down the front of her flowered housedress as if smoothing wrinkles. The diamonds on her fingers flashed in the light of the small chandelier over the breakfast table. "It's terrible to get old," she said.

Jonathan set the tea things on a wicker tray and carried them to the table. He poured a cup for her and one for himself.

"Sit down, Jonathan," she said. She often invited him to the table, and Lanell, too, but he was uncomfortable sitting with her, even in the kitchen early in the morning before anyone else was up. He never refused, though.

Miss Anna had grown old more gracefully than any white woman Jonathan knew. Even so early in the morning, her white hair was immaculately brushed and pinned. The pale skin of her face had scarcely a wrinkle and was carefully made up. Her brown eyes still sparkled with life and wit and intelligence. Only her thin hands, blotched with liver spots and trembling as she lifted her cup, seemed old. "Getting old is better than the alternative, Miss Anna," Jonathan said.

"What's that?"

"Dying young."

She laughed. "I'm not so sure, Jonathan. I'm not sure that's true. Sometimes I think Mr. J.L. envies Buck Pool."

"Oh, Miss Anna! He died a young man. Look at all Mr. J.L. has done since then."

Miss Anna leaned across the table. "Did he talk about the *conspiracy*, Jonathan?" she whispered.

"Yes, ma'am. He nearly always talks about the conspiracy."

"Well, do you think that's good? That's *all* he talks about anymore."

"Oh, I don't think it's good or bad. It's just what he thinks about, you know?"

"Do you think there *is* a conspiracy?"

"Now, Miss Anna. You know I don't know anything about politics. Even if there isn't a conspiracy, there's no harm in thinking it."

Miss Anna held out her cup for more tea. It rattled on the saucer. "If Mr. J.L. were an ordinary man, I would agree with you. But he's very—influential. I just pray every night that he won't take it into his head to do something about it."

"Like what, Miss Anna?"

"I don't know. Just keep him from going to town today, will you?"

"I'll try. But Calvin would be the one to drive him."

"Well, tell Calvin to tell Mr. Fisher that there's something wrong with the car. If he asks."

"What are you worried about, Miss Anna?" Jonathan asked.

"I don't know," she said.

MARY ELLEN

The last hour or two before dawn was the only time in the day when the house was quiet and Mary Ellen Waggoner could work without interruption and think her own thoughts. Sometimes she would speak her thoughts aloud to Buster, whose toenails clicked on the linoleum tile floors as he followed her from room to room. He was a moose of a dog, a cross between a German shepherd and some other large breed. Bullard thought the other half was collie, because of Buster's nervous energy. He was probably right, but Mary Ellen thought of the dog as the world's biggest cocker spaniel because of his liquid brown eyes and his insistence on sitting in her lap whenever she was on the couch. He probably *thought* he was sitting in her lap. Actually, he was lying across it, for her lap couldn't contain his long legs and his eighty pounds. Bullard, in his stern cop's voice, often said she had spoiled the dog, letting him lie on the couch and her lap, but she didn't care. Buster was a comfort to her during the long nights when her husband was on duty, after the children were in bed. She talked to the dog for hours sometimes, and he would prick his ears and look at her, his eyes full of understanding, and tilt his head from side to side as if weighing the truth of what she said. Buster was the best listener in the family.

Mary Ellen knew the dog was standing behind her, but she jumped when his cold, wet nose touched her bare calf. "In a minute, Buster!" she half whispered. "Let me get a load in first." She had dumped the contents of the laundry hampers onto the kitchen floor and was bent over the pile, her hands working quickly, separating the whites from the colors and the cottons from the wash-and-wears. There would be at least four loads, for there was little clean in the house. "I can't let the kids go to school in dirty clothes," she said. "You don't want that, do you?"

Buster moved to the other side of the pile, facing her, his eyes beseeching, his long tongue lolling from the side of his toothy mouth, panting. "You'll have to wait, Buster," she said. "Just one load, and then it's your turn." The first load would have to be a uniform shirt for Bullard, the red cotton skirt and red-and-white-striped blouse for Kim, the blue jeans and Dallas Cowboys sweatshirt for Joey, the green corduroy overalls and gold knit shirt for Albert. She dropped the garments one by one into the machine and held the green overalls up to the light. Joey had worn them before Albert, and the corduroy nap was worn off the knees. The bib was splotched with—what? Carrots? Squash? Something orange and baby-foodish. Her baby. Her last baby. She dropped the overalls into the machine and poured in the soap powder without measuring. She closed the lid and turned the dial and listened with satisfaction as the water spewed into the machine. Her day had begun.

"Now you." She reached into the cabinet under the sink for the bag of Purina Dog Chow, and Buster followed her, tail wagging, to his large bowl beside the refrigerator. She poured the bowl full of nuggets and stood back, but Buster still looked up at her, wagging his tail. "What? Outside?" At the sound of the word, Buster bounded twice, his nails clicking, and stood, his nose pointing at the back door. Mary Ellen turned the knob and he bounded out as quickly as the door opened wide enough for him to pass. Mary Ellen's nostrils caught the odor of wet grass, like hay, and she opened the door wider and stepped through onto the small concrete patio. It was drizzling. She would have to catch Buster when he came inside and wipe his feet, else she would have every floor to mop today.

Buster sniffed along the chain-link fence, lifting a hind leg at each metal post to mark the boundaries of his territory. He sniffed his way into the carport and anointed a tire of Mary Ellen's station wagon, and another on the pickup that Bullard drove to work. Mary Ellen lifted a hand to her chin and regarded the carport appraisingly, as she had a hundred times before. It was the only possibility. They would have to borrow the money to make it into a room. Kim had two more years in high school, and Joey was already complaining about sharing his room with Albert. Mary Ellen didn't blame him. A twelve-year-old should have a room of his own, and it was either convert the carport or move.

Bullard talked of moving to Mesquite and buying a bigger house, but she wouldn't hear of it. She had lived her whole life in Oak Cliff. Her mother was only two blocks away. She and Bullard had bought this house on a VA loan only a month after their wedding, and she didn't intend to leave it. She had planted the lawn herself and had watched the pecan tree and the mimosa grow from almost nothing, and there was nothing wrong with the house that replacing a few broken squares of siding and a little painting and caulking and weather stripping wouldn't fix. And, of course, the additional room and bath. Kim would want the new room, but maybe she and Bullard would take it as their own. The carport was larger than the master bedroom, and it would be nice to have a private bath and leave the kids to fight over the old one in the mornings. It would beat the cost of moving and the higher mortgage payments, even for a brick house in Mesquite. And Bullard could do nearly all the work himself. The repairs, anyway, and maybe most of the carpentry on the new room. He was awfully handy when he was in the mood, and she could help with the paneling and the floor tiles.

She sighed. Poor Bullard. She didn't blame him for putting off the chores, and she hated herself when she nagged him. The room could wait until spring, but the weather stripping, at least, ought to be done before winter. Poor Bullard. How haggard he had looked last night. She knew as soon as she saw him that he had handled something awful, but he wouldn't tell her much. A wreck, he said. Two fatalities. She thought he hated car wrecks worse than anything, they were so pointless. Poor Bullard. She loved him so. He was such a good man, such a fine officer. She wished she didn't nag him.

Buster bounded to her and jumped. She felt his nails sharp against her breasts, and his huge feet left streaks of mud down the front of her nightgown as they slid down. "Oh, damn you!" she cried. "Bad dog! Get down!"

Buster slunk from her, tail between legs, and lay down on the wet concrete beside Albert's tricycle. His fawn-colored hide had turned dark in the drizzle, and Mary Ellen realized that she was wet, too.

"Come on," she said. "Come on, bad doggy. Time to go in."

Buster bounded to her again, but she grabbed his heavy collar and held him away. She tugged him to the door and opened it and pulled him through. She held him while she grabbed a dish towel from the drainboard and rubbed his muddy feet and damp hair. When she released the collar, Buster made two aimless turns about the kitchen, then noticed his bowl and began eating, picking up the chunks of food and crunching them between his long, white teeth, looking at Mary Ellen with what seemed to be a grin.

The washing machine had stopped, and she opened the lid and shook the twists out of the heavy, wet garments and tossed them into the dryer and switched it on. She bent to pick up a bundle of white cottons and tossed them into the washer. She shivered in the damp of her nightgown and held the front of it out before her to examine the muddy streaks, then lifted it over her head and worked herself out of it and tossed it into the washer.

She felt deliciously wicked, working naked in her kitchen with only Buster to see her. She bent, looking for the new can of coffee in the cabinet where she stored the canned goods.

"My God! What have you and this dog been *doing?*"

Mary Ellen almost screamed. She whirled, her hand to her

breast. Bullard stood in the center of the room, robe loosely tied, hands on hips, grinning. "Hey, nice tits," he said. He stepped to her and hugged her. He lifted her left breast and looked at the welts that Buster's nails had made. "You guys play kind of rough, don't you?"

"You bet. I love it."

"Do you carry on like this every morning?"

"Oh, yes," Mary Ellen said. "Every morning. Buster's terrific."

"Better than me?"

She nestled closer into his arms. She was almost as tall as Bullard, but felt tiny when he held her. "Mmm. Well . . . He gets up earlier."

"I'm up."

"You shouldn't be. I haven't made the coffee yet."

"I'm not staying up, and I don't want coffee. I came looking for a woman. My bed's getting cold."

Mary Ellen laid her head against his neck and inhaled the smell of sleep and moved her pelvis slowly deeper against his crotch. "Oh, dear," she said. "A woman's work is never done."

The Seventh Hour

JAKE

SHERRY MURRELL'S HAND COVERED the mouthpiece. Her eyes were wide, angry. "Your *wife!*"

When Jake reached for the phone, Sherry threw the covers back and got out of bed. She stalked to the breakfast bar on the other side of the room and banged a pot on the stovetop.

"What is it?" Jake asked. "Is James okay?"

"Yes, James is fine." Liz was angry, too.

"Well, what is it? What time is it, anyway?"

"It's six-thirty."

"Jesus Christ, Liz—"

"Your friends are well trained, buddy boy. The guys on the city desk acted like they'd barely heard of you and had no idea where you might be. Jean Hayes didn't—"

"You called Jean? When?"

"Last night. She didn't even know where Byron was. And I called your place four or five times—"

"Well, I was there. Part of the time. What do you want, Liz? Why are you calling me here at six-fucking-thirty in the morning?"

Sherry banged the coffeepot onto the stove so hard that water sloshed from the spout and sizzled on the burner, then she flounced past the bed to the bathroom. She gave Jake the finger as she passed.

"Money!" Liz cried. "It's about money, Jake! Do you think I *enjoy* interrupting you with your—your—whore?"

"Now just a goddamn minute, Liz! We're getting a divorce, remember? You've got no right to—"

"Okay. Okay. You're right." Jake felt her trying to control her voice. "You have a perfect right to—sleep anywhere you want. But the money situation is really bad, Jake. I've still got the mortgage payments and the car payments and the bills, and it's just not enough."

"Well, Liz, you've got all there is to have. From me, anyway. I'm trying to make it on seventy-five dollars a week. Seventy-five fucking dollars, Liz! I made more than that when I was a cub reporter!"

Liz was breathing heavily into the phone. Jake thought she might be crying. "Oh, I know, Jake," she said. She was crying. "Oh, it's just awful."

"You've got a job now," Jake said. "That's a help, isn't it?" He spoke calmly. When Liz didn't shout, he didn't shout. It was a rule of his.

"Well, yeah, it helps. But I don't make that much, Jake."

"You make more than seventy-five a week, don't you?"

"No, I don't, actually. Not after deductions."

"Close to it, though. Right?"

"Well, yeah. But things were tight enough when you were here, and now . . ."

"What can I do?"

Sherry turned on the shower. Jake heard the curtain slide open on its rod, then close.

"Meet me," Liz said. "Take me to lunch or something, and let's talk about it. Maybe we could get a loan and consolidate some of the bills. Do you owe the credit union anything?"

"No, thank God. How could I pay off a loan on seventy-five bucks a week?"

"Well, let's talk about it, okay?"

"When?"

"How about noon? Lunch? Hell, I'll even buy."

"All right. But let's make it eleven. I don't want to get stuck in that motorcade crowd."

"Okay, eleven. Where?"

"How about the Blue Front?"

"Fine. . . ." Liz hesitated, as if she had something else to say, but said nothing.

"Is James up?" Jake asked.

"No."

"Well, tell him I love him and I'll pick him up at ten tomorrow morning."

"What are you going to do with him?"

"I don't know yet."

"You aren't going to take him to that—woman's place, are you?"

"Of course not."

"I don't want him to know about her."

"He doesn't."

"Well, I don't want him to. Are you serious about her?"

"I can't talk about that now."

"Okay. Eleven at the Blue Front, then. I'm sorry, Jake."

"Leave a message at the office next time, okay? I'll return the call."

"All right. I'm sorry."

Jake hung up the phone and noticed that the shower had stopped. "How are things on the home front?" Sherry called.

"She wants more money."

Sherry sashayed into the bedroom, her breasts and hips wrapped in a green beach towel. Her face and shoulders were scrubbed and rosy, her short blonde curls wet. "Are you going to give it to her?" Her voice still held its sharp edge.

"I can't. I don't have it. Shall I check the coffee?"

"I'll get it."

Jake smiled, watching her sashay to the stove. He knew she was tending the coffee not to be kind but to make him notice her in the towel.

"I hope you aren't angry with me," he said.

"Of course I'm angry. What right has she to—"

"That's what I told her."

"Well, tell her not to call here. She makes me feel like a home breaker." Sherry carried two steaming mugs to the bed and leaned to give one to Jake. He hooked a finger into the towel where it was tucked closed between her breasts and let it drop.

"Fresh!" Sherry said.

"Just don't be angry."

Sherry handed her mug to Jake, too, and crawled over him to her side of the bed, then took it from him. "Cigarette me," she said.

Jake lit two and passed her one. "Jesus," he said, "I've got a headache you wouldn't believe."

Sherry tousled his hair. "Poor Jakie-poo! Women after him night and day!"

"Why are we waking up so early, anyway?"

"The phone rang."

"Why aren't we going back to sleep? The sun's not even up."

She laid her wet head on his shoulder. "Do you love me?"

"You know I do."

"Well, drink your coffee and prove it."

LUIS

The stranger lying beside him was no longer snoring, but something had awakened him. What? Luis's arms were crossed on his chest. He was cold. He sat up on the mattress and stretched his thin legs before him on the bare floor. His legs could feel the cool air coming from under the house, between the planks. In the gray light that came through the window, he saw the stranger huddled under the frayed quilt that Luis had bought from the woman next door. It angered Luis that the man had taken his quilt, even in his sleep, but the man was old and had just arrived. Maybe he would find a job and buy his own quilt soon. And his own mattress. Although the house had only two rooms, there was room for another mattress. Or maybe the Border Patrol would take one of the others away, and the new man could take over his mattress.

If the Border Patrol took someone away, Luis hoped it would be Ignacio. Ignacio, from the mountains of Chihuahua, had a knife scar across his nose and down one cheek that made him look ugly and mean. He carried a switchblade tucked into his pants under his shirt. When he got drunk, he liked to take out the knife and brandish it and try to start fights. Although he had never hurt anybody, everyone was afraid of him because he was the biggest man in the house. Luis, who was the smallest man and the youngest, was afraid of him, too, but Ignacio sometimes gave him beer and had never tried to start a fight with him. Ignacio worked as a carpenter, building houses, and so did Juan and Rogelio. Antonio was good with plants and worked for a nursery. Antonio was Luis's favorite because he was gentle and told stories about working on ranches in west Texas and hiding from the Border Patrol plane when it flew over. Luis was glad he slept in the room with Antonio, and that Ignacio and Juan and Rogelio slept in the other room. Maybe the new man would get a job building houses with them and go to sleep in their room.

The light told Luis it was time to get up. The other men would get up soon, wanting their breakfast. Luis was their cook, because he worked in a kitchen. He had never cooked before, but he was learning and didn't mind, since the other men paid for the food. He stood up and put on his white T-shirt and blue jeans and slid his feet into the sandals that he had worn up from Tamaulipas.

He switched on the kitchen light. A rat, larger than a kitten, was in the sink, drinking the water that dripped from the faucet. He stopped drinking and looked at Luis, who stood very still, wanting to scream out to the other men but not daring, for they would think him womanly. The rat's eyes were bright and black, and he looked at Luis, then drank again from the shallow puddle in the sink. Then he jumped out of the sink onto the cabinet, and down from the cabinet to the floor, and ran to a spot beside the refrigerator, where a hole had rotted in the floor. He paused at the edge of the hole and looked at Luis again, then dropped into the hole.

Luis stood still for several seconds, afraid the rat would return.

WARNER

Warner awoke on the side of the bed, not in the middle, where he slept when alone. That meant somebody was in bed with him. He rolled his head to the right. No one was there, but the pillow was rumpled and the sheet was wrinkled. Ah, yes. The bitch. He had paid her for all night, and she had skipped. How much had he paid? Thelma Ruth Green. Had she been worth what he paid? He reached for the phone. "I asked for a wake-up call," he said. "I didn't get it."

"You asked for six-thirty," the operator said. "It's six-twenty-five." Her voice was the gray-haired tough-mother type.

"Okay, give me Room Service, then," Warner said.

"You sound awful," the operator said.

The Room Service voice was Mexican and bored.

"What have you got that's greasy?" Warner asked.

"Pardon?"

"What do you have with lots of grease?"

"Nothing, sir. Nothing is greasy here."

"But I *want* grease. *Sabe?* I want three greasy fried eggs and two orders of greasy bacon. And toast. With lots of butter. And coffee. *Sabe?*"

"Yessir."

"Bring me a couple of beers, and there will be a big tip."

"Yessir. I will try."

"And hurry. I want *warm* grease."

"Right away, sir. What room are you?"

"Eleven-oh-nine. Barnhill. B-a-r-n-h-i-l-l."

Warner laid the phone in its cradle and eased himself up. He staggered to his suit coat, which was draped on the back of the desk chair, and took his address book from the inside pocket and looked up Barefoot Sanders's home number. Sanders answered with a crisp cheerfulness that Warner tried to copy. "Ready for the big day, Barefoot?" he asked.

"Who is this?" There was a touch of caution in Sanders's voice.

"Warner Barnhill."

"Warner! How the hell are you?"

"I'm fine. How about you?"

"Busier than a one-armed paperhanger, but getting by."

"Barefoot, I need a favor." Warner became aware of his nervousness. He wished he knew Sanders better.

"Don't we all? What can I do for you?"

"I need a ticket to the luncheon. I thought you might know where to find one."

"You're in Dallas?"

"Yeah. At the Adolphus."

"Didn't you catch him in San Antonio?"

"No. I was in Austin."

"You should have stuck around. He's going to be there tonight."

"Connally didn't invite me to the damn reception."

"He didn't invite Yarborough, either."

"You're kidding!"

"No. The Yarborough people say Connally and Ralph have been playing gingham dog and calico cat the whole trip. Connally has glued himself to Kennedy, and Yarborough's been relegated to Johnson's car. He's royally pissed. Yarborough, I mean. He and Lyndon get along like matches and gasoline."

Warner saw his opening. "Well, Barefoot, shouldn't a few Kennedy supporters be at that luncheon?"

Sanders laughed. "How many do you need?"

"Just one."

"You're lucky. That's about how many I've got left. You didn't come all the way to Dallas just for this, did you?"

"Yeah, Barefoot. Hero worship."

"Okay. But no foot stomping or whistling, hear? Pretend you're a banker or something."

Warner smiled. "You'll be proud of me."

"How come Gonzalez didn't fix you up?"

"Dallas is *your* town, Barefoot."

"Don't I wish! Come by the office. I'll leave the ticket with my secretary."

"Thanks, Barefoot. I owe you one."

"You damn sure do."

"I won't forget."

"I won't let you."

Warner was elated. If he could get close enough to Yarborough, or even Connally, he might get an introduction. Maybe even a picture, shaking hands. Kennedy ought to know who his friends were in Texas. Maybe he did. It could be a great day.

He went into the bathroom and found the Bufferin in his shaving kit, then saw a little pile of gold beside the kit and picked it up. It was the stripper's charm bracelet.

The valet walked past the Secret Service sentries and entered Suite 850. He knocked gently on the door of the master bedroom. "Mr. President," he said. "It's raining out."

The president, coming out of sleep, replied, "That's too bad."

The Eighth Hour

STACY

STACY AND MARK and Jason all were quick wakers, glad to see the morning, and breakfast was usually a cheerful time in the Leary household. But the evening at the Darts' had soured Stacy further on the city to which she had moved against her will, and Mark's refusal to agree that their hosts' behavior had been crude—insane, even—made her feel betrayed. In the month they had lived in Dallas, had her husband already abandoned his integrity, his heritage, his principles for the sake of selling insurance to a mob of fanatics? Had his promotion warped him so that only business mattered now? She nursed her hurt, glaring hard-eyed at Mark, whose head was bowed over his plate of burned toast and rubbery scrambled eggs, refusing to acknowledge her look. She hoped he was feeling shame. His apology for their bedtime quarrel would come later, maybe days from now. During such times she regretted loving him so much.

"Mom, can I have some cereal?" The whine in Jason's voice told her that he felt the tension. She moved her gaze to him. His head was down, too, staring without focus at the blue plastic plate. His fork moved listlessly among the eggs without picking them up.

"All right," she said.

Jason jumped up and busied himself with cornflakes, sugar, milk. "Can I put a banana on it?"

"Yes, but hurry." The taut silence bothered her, too. She rose and switched on the portable TV on the kitchen counter and watched the tube warm up and fill with a bland face speaking in an atrocious drawl. "We will take immediate action to block any improper conduct," it said.

The police reserve and the fire department and the Texas Department of Public Safety had been mobilized. The Texas Rangers were in town. Sheriffs and deputies from neighboring counties were coming to help. Citizens observing unseemly behavior were authorized to make citizen's arrests. Dallas was being warned.

"Citizen's arrests!" Stacy cried. "Who *is* this clown?"

"Police chief," Mark mumbled.

"Oh, God! Are they *all* crazy? Citizen's arrests!"

"He's trying to keep the crowd small," Mark said.

"For the president of the United States? Where are we, Mark?"

"Will you turn that thing off? It's driving me nuts."

Stacy twisted the knob so hard that it came off in her hand. She hurled it against the countertop. It shattered into pieces that bounced onto the floor.

"Beautiful!" Mark looked at her, his mouth twisted into as much of a sneer as his genial face would permit.

"Well, I'll tell you *one* thing!" She shook her finger. "They aren't keeping me away, or Jason, either! And if you had any—any—*fortitude*, you'd be on the sidewalk with us!"

"Mom—"

"Waving a flag, too!"

"Mom—"

"What *is* it, Jason!"

"I can't go, mom."

Stacy glared at the small, upturned face.

"I forgot to tell you," he said.

"Who says you can't? The superintendent said children

whose parents come to school and get them will be excused from class."

"Mrs. Claymore says she won't excuse anybody, even if their parents come." Jason's eyes were round with worry. He wiped away his milk moustache with his shirt sleeve.

"Why?" Mark asked.

"She says Kennedy's bad and we can't go look at him."

Mark's hand moved his cup slowly from his lips to his saucer. His face was fiery red. "Maybe he shouldn't go, sweetheart," he said.

"Shouldn't *go?*"

Mark turned to Jason. "Brush your teeth and get your books, son," he said. "I'll drive you to school."

When Jason left the kitchen, Stacy started to speak, but Mark raised his hand. "It's not what you think," he said. "Maybe it really *isn't* going to be safe."

Stacy shuddered and hugged her robe about her. "I hate this place," she said. "I can't believe these things."

"It can't be as bad as it seems," Mark said. "They're still nervous about that Stevenson thing. They don't want it to happen again. They're sensitive, and I can't blame them."

"But that *teacher*, Mark."

"I'll speak to her when I take Jason to school."

"No, *I'll* speak to her when I pick him up."

"Baby—"

"I can't let this happen. I can't let our son . . ."

Mark sighed and pushed his chair away from the table. "Okay. Bring him to the office. I have a good view of the street."

"No, I want Jason to really *see* him. Don't you know what it means to a child to see the president of the United States in person? It wouldn't be the same, seeing him through a window."

Mark turned without reply and went into the bedroom. He returned wearing his raincoat, carrying his briefcase. "Jason!" he called. "Let's go!"

Jason came out of his room, fumbling with books and windbreaker, and Stacy bent and kissed him. "I'll pick you up at ten o'clock," she said.

"You want me to tell Mrs. Claymore?"

"No, I'll just come."

Mark opened the back door, and Jason ran past him to the car in the driveway. Mark hesitated, his hand on the doorknob, and looked at Stacy, standing in the kitchen door, hugging herself. He set his briefcase on the floor and crossed to her and embraced her. She stiffened. "Come on," he said. "We Irish Catholic Communists have to stick together." She relaxed and kissed him, and he smiled. "Bring him to the office," he said. "I'll go down to the sidewalk with you."

SOLOMON

Rabbi Goldstein read the full-page, black-bordered ad again.

Welcome, Mr. Kennedy,
to Dallas ...

. . . A city so disgraced by a recent liberal smear attempt that its citizens have just elected two more conservative Americans to public office.

. . . A city that is an economic "Boom Town," not because of Federal handouts, but through conservative economic and business practices.

. . . A city that will continue to grow and prosper despite efforts by you and your administration to penalize it for its non-conformity to "new frontierism."

. . . A city that rejected your philosophy and policies

in 1960 and will do so again in 1964—even more emphatically than before.

Mr. Kennedy, despite contentions on the part of your administration, the State Department, the Mayor of Dallas, the Dallas City Council and members of your party, we free-thinking and American-thinking citizens of Dallas still have, through a constitution largely ignored by you, the right to address our grievances, to question you, to disagree with you, and to criticize you.

In asserting this constitutional right, we wish to ask you publicly the following questions—indeed, questions of paramount importance and interest to all free peoples everywhere—which we trust you will answer . . . in public, without sophistry.

These questions are:

Why is Latin America turning either anti-American or Communistic or both, despite increased U.S. foreign aid, State Department policy, and your own ivory tower pronouncements?

Why do you say we have built a "wall of freedom" around Cuba when there is no freedom in Cuba today? Because of your policy, thousands of Cubans have been imprisoned, are starving and being persecuted—with thousands already murdered and thousands more awaiting execution and, in addition, the entire population of almost 7,000,000 Cubans are living in slavery.

Why have you approved the sale of wheat and corn to our enemies when you know the communist soldiers "travel on their stomachs" just as ours do? Communist soldiers are daily wounding and/or killing American soldiers in South Viet Nam.

Why did you host, salute and entertain Tito—Moscow's Trojan horse—just a short time after our sworn enemy, Khrushchev, embraced the Yugoslav dictator as a great hero and leader of communism?

Why have you urged greater aid, comfort, recognition, and understanding of Yugoslavia, Poland, Hungary, and other communist countries while turning your back on the pleas of Hungarian, East German, Cuban and other anti-communist freedom fighters?

Why did Cambodia kick the U.S. out of its country after we poured nearly 400 million dollars of aid into its ultra-leftist government?

Why has Gus Hall, head of the U.S. Communist Party, praised almost every one of your policies and announced that the party will endorse and support your re-election in 1964?

Why have you banned the showing at U.S. military bases of the film "Operation Abolition"—the movie by the House Committee on Un-American Activities exposing communism in America?

Why have you ordered or permitted your brother Bobby, the Attorney General, to go soft on communists, fellow-travelers, and ultra-leftists in America, while permitting him to persecute loyal Americans who criticize you, your administration, and your leadership?

Why are you in favor of the U.S. continuing to give economic aid to Argentina, in spite of the fact that Argentina has just seized almost 400 million dollars of American private property?

Why has the foreign policy of the United States degenerated to the point that the C.I.A. is arranging coups and having staunch anti-communist allies of the U.S. bloodily exterminated?

Why have you scrapped the Monroe Doctrine in favor of the Spirit of Moscow?

Mr. Kennedy, as citizens of these United States of America, we demand answers to these questions, and we want them now.

The American Fact Finding Committee

An unaffiliated and non-partisan group of citizens who
wish truth

Bernard Weissman,
Chairman

Rabbi Goldstein stared at the name. He had thought he
knew every Jew in Dallas, but he didn't remember Bernard
Weissman. There was no face in his congregation that he
could connect with those words. His wasn't the only congregation in the city, but he had been in Dallas a long time
anyway. Everyone Jewish, at least. But there were other
congregations, and the city was growing so fast.

His eyes, behind gold-rimmed glasses, moved from "Bernard Weissman" to "The American Fact Finding Committee." He scanned his memory for such an organization.
The White Citizens Council, the John Birch Society, the
National Indignation Committee, the Minutemen, the Friends
of General Walker, the Texans for America. He kept track
of them all, for committees and societies with righteous names
often wound up painting swastikas on synagogues. He found
no American Fact Finding Committee.

"Clara," he said. "Do you know Bernard Weissman?"

Mrs. Goldstein was squeezing lemon into her tea. Her brow
knitted in thought. "Weissman? What business is he in, Sol?"

"Troublemaking, I think." Rabbi Goldstein lifted the page
and he thought he knew everyone. Everyone important,
with the ad from the newspaper and handed it across the
table. "Have you heard of the American Fact Finding Committee?"

"I don't think so, but the names of those committees all
sound alike to me." Mrs. Goldstein pushed her glasses farther
up her nose and began reading the ad, half-forming the words
aloud to herself. "Oh, dear!" she said, looking up.

"You've never heard of Bernard Weissman?" Rabbi Goldstein asked.

"Oh, you know me, Sol. I'm never sure. Do you know him?"

"No." He sipped his tea, watching his wife until she laid the newspaper on the table and picked up her cup.

"I can't read it all," she said. "It's too awful."

Rabbi Goldstein picked up the paper and stood up. "I'll take my tea into the study. I have a lot of work to do."

"Have you finished your sermon?" Mrs. Goldstein asked.

"No. That's the work I have to do."

"Well, make it a good one. Are you going to say something about Mr. Kennedy?"

"Yes, but I don't know what. Today I wish I were a Christian, so I would have the extra time."

The rabbi walked around the table and kissed his wife on the cheek, as he always did when he retired to his study. When he closed the study door, he went immediately to his desk and picked up the telephone directory and leafed through the W's. There was no Bernard Weissman. Then he flipped to the A's. There was no American Fact Finding Committee. Then he dialed.

"Is Mr. Marcus in?" he asked the servant who answered.

"May I ask who's calling, please?"

"Rabbi Goldstein. It's rather important."

"Mr. Marcus has already left for the store, sir."

"How long ago? Should he be there by now?"

"Yessir. I believe so."

Rabbi Goldstein thanked the servant and dialed Marcus's private number at the store. The voice that answered was a deep grumble.

"Stanley! Is it such a bad day already?" Rabbi Goldstein asked.

"Sol! Good morning. Yes, it *is* a bad day. Who the hell is Bernard Weissman?"

"That's what I was going to ask *you*. You don't know him?"

"Never heard of him."

"What about the American Fact Finding Committee? Ring any bells?"

"No. Maybe it's a new one that General Walker dreamed up. Or Colonel Byrd. Or J. L. Fisher. Or maybe it's a fake. Maybe this Weissman *is* the American Fact Finding Committee. Or maybe there's no Bernard Weissman. Maybe it's just some right-wing bastard who wanted to add a little anti-Semitic touch to his masterpiece."

"Well, it gives another black eye to the city," Rabbi Goldstein said.

"Yes, his timing was perfect. It'll probably bring them all out again. I wish they hadn't insisted on that damn motorcade."

"I wish the paper hadn't taken the ad," Rabbi Goldstein said.

There was a long silence, then Marcus said, "Sol, do you know Betty Lou Carpenter? Her agency's in charge of the visit, trying to encourage a cordial reception and freeze the crazies out. You might give her a call."

"Do you have her number?"

"Hold on." There was another silence, then Marcus read him two telephone numbers. "The first one is her office," he said. "She's probably still at home. If she knows anything, call me back."

Rabbi Goldstein smiled. "Are you sure Weissman doesn't work for you, Stanley?"

"If he did, I would know what to do with him."

Rabbi Goldstein hung up and dialed the Carpenter woman.

"Yes?" The voice had an early-morning languor in it, but didn't sound sleepy.

"Miss Carpenter? Rabbi Solomon Goldstein. Stanley Marcus asked me to call you."

The voice became alert. "Yes? What can I do for you?"

"Have you seen this morning's paper, Miss Carpenter?"

"Not yet." The voice was worried now. "What is it?"

"There's an unfortunate ad there. The usual stuff. Kennedy being pro-Communist and whatnot. It's a full page."

"Oh, Christ!"

"Mr. Marcus thought you might know who placed it. It's signed by a Bernard Weissman."

"Weissman? Never heard of him."

"It's a Jewish name," Rabbi Goldstein said. "Jews don't often put their names on such things."

"How bad is the ad?"

"Well, bad for today. Otherwise, it wouldn't matter much."

"Christ. The White House press will pick it up. Especially if something happens."

"How are you expecting it to go, Miss Carpenter?"

"Who knows? I'm just keeping my fingers crossed. I've done everything I can think of. Is Weissman speaking for himself or a group?"

"The American Fact Finding Committee."

"That's a new one. Probably just the people who paid for the ad."

"Do you think the newspaper would tell us?" Rabbi Goldstein asked.

"I doubt it. They probably don't even know. Believe me, rabbi, nobody will be happier than I will when *Air Force One* takes off this afternoon."

"I can imagine. Well, thank you, Miss Carpenter. Sorry to disturb you so early."

"No problem. I'm just sorry it happened. I was hoping we had them buffaloed. For one lousy day, anyway."

When Rabbi Goldstein hung up, he swallowed his cold tea and picked up a yellow pencil and gathered the white sheets on which he had scrawled the beginning of his sermon. He tried to read his words, but couldn't focus his mind on them. He kept thinking of Bernard Weissman, trying to imagine the face of a man so ungrateful, the eyes of a Jew so stupid.

PRESLEY

Into the mirror, Presley Evans admitted he wasn't handsome enough to play Marcus Antonius before a snooty Dallas Theater Center audience. Too morose. Too jowly. Maybe too old, too.

> Into what dangers would you lead me, Cassius,
> That you would have me seek into myself
> For that which is not in me?

He spoke the words aloud and smiled. Not Cassius, either. The face and bare shoulders and chest in the mirror were too meaty for a lean and hungry look. The belly was beginning to run to paunch. But he wasn't hung over. He hadn't had a drink for a week, since Justice, playing the hard-nosed director, had told him to buckle down to the part or lose it. No booze, and good, hearty food. Early to bed and early to rise. Presley raised his fists above his head, drew in the belly, and flexed his biceps.

> Another general shout!
> I do believe that these applauses are
> For some new honours that are heap'd on Caesar.

Justice had been bluffing, of course. No one could have taken over the part a week before opening. Anyway, Presley had discovered that he liked getting up early when there was no hangover to dread. Already he had developed a routine. Plug in the coffee, brush the teeth, shower, shave, put on the robe, pour the coffee, and take it to the living room and set it on the coffee table. Put the big pillow at the end of the couch, take the first sip of coffee, light the cigarette, and pick up the script. He would have an hour, maybe two, of coziness and work before his wife woke up. Darlene didn't have to work hard. She was playing Calpurnia.

Presley turned on the warm water and ran the basin full, then opened the medicine cabinet and took out the can of shave cream and the razor. He shook the can and enjoyed the spewing-gurgling of the cream into his palm, then spread it over his jowls. No, Marcus Brutus was the part for him. The face in the mirror, the dark eyes, the jowls, the downturned mouth, revealed the brooding moodiness, the deep interior full of principle and patriotism that wouldn't bend, even for love.

Romans, countrymen, and lovers! hear me for my cause, and be silent. . . . Had you rather Caesar were living, and die all slaves, than that Caesar were dead, to live all freemen? As Caesar loved me, I weep for him; as he was fortunate, I rejoice at it; as he was valiant, I honour him; but as he was ambitious, I slew him. . . .

He didn't speak the words aloud. He didn't know all the lines, and Justice had given him an ultimatum. Or else what? Presley smiled. But Justice was right. It was an important speech. It had to be done right. It would be.

The razor against his cheek made a small, harsh sound severing the whiskers. Presley shook the razor in the warm water. Did barbers still offer shaves? He had had a real barber shave once, the summer he worked for the seismograph crew, back home in west Texas. He'd had a change of clothes in his car, but no razor. And when the girl he called agreed to a date, he changed and went to the barber shop. What was her name? Gloria. Yes. The barber laughed. A sixteen-year-old wanting a barber shave. But the hot, damp towels—God, they were delicious. They gave him a hard-on. Did barbers still wrap faces in hot, damp towels? Presley hadn't seen it in years. Maybe that's why the barber had laughed. He knew Presley was the last one.

Presley wiped the flecks of cream off his face with the towel and shook the razor in the water and opened the medicine chest and laid the razor back on the shelf. He poured a little Aqua Velva into his palm and spread it over his skin, smiling at its cool tingle, then pulled the plug in the basin and turned on the cold water to wash the soap and whiskers down. Lord, he felt good. He put on the robe and went to the kitchen for his coffee, then to the living room. He was irritated to find Darlene awake already, sitting on the couch, reading the paper, her dark hair standing out from her head as if she had received an electric shock.

"Hi, hon," she said. "Did you know Kennedy's going to be in Dallas today?"

"Christ," he said. "Are you the last to learn everything?"

RODNEY

"You shouldn't have done it," Rodney Dart said. "It's stupid."

"Done what?" Elsie asked.

"That fucking ad." He was standing in front of the dresser mirror, tying his necktie. Elsie, still in bed, laid the paper on her lap. Her eyes met his in the glass.

"What makes you think I did it?" she asked.

"Not you personally. One of your fucking groups. That American Committee for something-or-other."

"The American Fact Finding Committee isn't one of my groups," she said. "It must be new."

"Well, you'll be joining it, even if it's headed by a fucking kike." Rodney turned from the mirror, pulling the Windsor knot tight.

"Anyway, what's wrong with the ad? It's the truth. I'm glad *somebody's* saying something."

"I think you should have let the guy slip through town and be on his way," Rodney said.

"That's not what you told Betty Lou Carpenter last night."

"Fuck her. I was drunk. I think the guys who hired her knew what they were doing. Dallas can't stand another thing like that Stevenson thing. It's bad business, bad politics, bad everything."

"You thought that 'Stevenson thing,' as you call it, was great!" Elsie said.

"It was funny! But Kennedy isn't funny, dollface. He's got the Secret Service and the FBI and every fucking cop in Texas looking out for him. You try something like that on him and your sweet ass will wind up in jail."

"Oh, you believe in the *selective* right to free speech," Elsie said. "Speak up unless it offends a commie."

"Come on," Rodney said. "I just don't want to have to bail you out of jail. Your picture would be in every paper in the country."

"I don't have a thing planned for today—"

"Good."

"I may go downtown and watch."

"No, you're not."

"Sweetheart—"

"Forget it. I'm going to be as far away from downtown as I can get today, and so are you."

"Where are you going?"

"The Richardson site. To make sure the rain didn't scare off the fucking wetbacks. Half those houses are already sold, and I want them finished."

Elsie got up and put her arms around Rodney's neck. She pressed her heavy breasts against his chest. His hand moved over her soft back and hips. "Sweetheart . . ." she said.

"Forget it, honey. If I find out you were downtown today, I'll close every charge account you've got."

Elsie laid her head on his shoulder, her eyes toward the

mirror. "Look at us, Rod," she said. "We look like the cover of a paperback book."

Rodney didn't look. "I'm warning you," he said. "Tomorrow you can raise all the hell you want, but not today."

The Ninth Hour

R. QUENTIN

R. QUENTIN BABCOCK GLANCED at the "Impeach Earl Warren" sticker on the rear bumper of the lilac Cadillac and resisted an impulse to peel it off. He hated having to take Martha's car to the office. Lilac was a silly color for the president of a bank, especially J. L. Fisher's bank, and the bumper sticker offended his passion for discretion, a passion that Martha didn't share.

The semicircular concrete drive was wet, and Robert was wearing his raincoat. As Quentin approached, Robert put on his cap and opened the back door of the Cadillac. "Morning, Mr. Quentin," he said.

"Morning, Robert. Think it might clear?"

Robert glanced at the gray sky. "Yessir. I think we're going to get some sun."

Quentin slid onto the black leather seat and laid his own raincoat and his briefcase beside him. The odor of Martha's perfume was heavy and sweet, and he missed the stale cigar smell of his own car. The service manager had promised it would be ready by closing time yesterday, and hadn't delivered. "Robert, did you tell those bastards whose car you were leaving?" he asked.

"I sure did."

"Well."

Robert started the engine, and Quentin took off his hat and laid it on his raincoat. He selected a cigar from his leather case and bit the end and moistened it with his tongue. He crossed his long legs and lit the cigar and felt better. He considered opening the briefcase and selecting some proposal or application to study during the drive. But this was going to be a ceremonial day, anyway, and the rain had deepened the colors of the bare trees and brown lawns of the Highland Park mansions, had changed the landscape of his routine enough to attract his eye.

Thirty years ago, when he and Martha moved to Highland Park, he had remarked to her that if there was a heaven, it must be like their new town. "Didn't Jesus say, 'In my father's house are many mansions'? And aren't there many mansions in Highland Park?" Martha had repeated the remark many times, usually at cocktail parties honoring younger couples who had attained the ultimate symbol of success in Dallas, one of Highland Park's mansions. Quentin still admired the remark himself, but wished Martha would quit repeating it. It befitted a man who had just arrived, not one who had lived three decades in the place. In his mature opinion, Highland Park was simply evidence of the possibility of having cake and eating it, too.

He treasured the vision of the men years ago, men like himself, who had foreseen that Dallas might someday engulf their little enclave of wealth and beauty. They had incorporated their neighborhood to avoid annexation, hired their own policemen and firemen, established their own public school system, and still managed to continue their control of the city where they made their wealth but didn't live and vote. They invented a means for the tail to wag the dog.

The creator of the Dallas Citizens Council had wanted to call it the Yes and No Club. That's what it was, of course, but Quentin had been one of those who proposed the more discreet name. Even the chief officers of the city's largest cor-

porations need not be ashamed of the name "citizen," he told
them. Wasn't it the duty of a citizen to do whatever was right
for his city? Wasn't it the duty of the rich and the wise to be
the best citizens of all, as in Athens and early Rome and
Renaissance Italy? His colleagues agreed. They lived, after
all, in a democracy. They even went beyond Quentin's proposal and put "citizen" in the name of the council's political
arm, the even more exclusive group that selected the proper
candidates for the city council and provided the money for
their election.

Membership in the Citizens Charter Association was the
highest honor to which any man in Dallas might aspire. Quentin thought of the tiny group as the muscle that wagged the
tail that wagged the dog. Its meetings were as secret as the
College of Cardinals'. Its power over the political affairs of
the city was almost as complete as the pope's in the Vatican.
It convened only to select the appropriate candidates for the
Dallas City Council and provide them whatever money they
needed to win, then disbanded until the next municipal election year. Visiting journalists, who had no understanding of or
sympathy for Dallas ways, described the association as an
oligarchy. But any fair critic would have to look at the end as
well as the means. "We're assuming a civic responsibility,"
Quentin had told a reporter once. "You can quibble over the
meaning of 'civic' and 'political,' but I don't see the Citizens
Charter Association as a political organization. Our objective
is to keep Dallas government clean and good."

It was such statements that had made Quentin one of the
city's trusted leaders. Most other members of the association
were crusty, self-made men without a talent for discreet, well-
balanced public utterance. And wealth, after all, wasn't the
only criterion for leadership. J. L. Fisher, the board chairman
of Quentin's bank and certainly the wealthiest man in the city,
had never been invited to join the Citizens Council, much less
the Charter Association, for he was too outspoken and pos-

sessed no talent for secrecy. Quentin had slowly, carefully made himself the perfect liaison between the old bastard whose wealth couldn't be ignored and the wiser heads who knew that true authority is exercised with as little noise as possible. For many years now, Quentin had been trusted by both. He was as shrewd and tactful as any Charter Association man, but rough-hewn enough in his appearance and manner to get along with Fisher, who heartily despised the men he called "those dudes downtown."

Whatever Quentin might be called, it wasn't "dude." The most expensive, carefully fitted English suits hung on his large, bony frame like laundry on a fence. His long arms and big hands made all sleeves seem short. His angular, ruddy features and unruly gray hair seemed more appropriate to ranches and oil fields than mahogany desks and boardrooms. Quentin knew this, and enhanced the image by slowing and thickening his native west Texas twang whenever Fisher was in his company. He had overheard subordinates laugh and imitate his cowboy manner when they were drunk, but he didn't mind. That manner was the reason some of them were subordinates and he wasn't.

No matter what the weather, Quentin's favorite spot along his route to work was the point on Cedar Springs where the skyline first appeared through Robert's windshield. He had watched the magnificence of the vista grow from the early days, when the huge flying red horse atop the Magnolia Building was the city's only true landmark, visible from miles away. Today, Pegasus's wings flapped unnoticed among the shadowy canyons created by the towers of Quentin's bank and the other banks and insurance companies, who seemed determined to build their own version of Manhattan on the Texas prairie. Quentin's own tower, once the city's tallest, also had been overshadowed in recent years, and two more now under construction by rival banks would put it deeper into the shade. But Quentin and Fisher declined to participate in what they called the "pissing match" between their rivals to dominate the skyline. Quentin preferred to be in the shadows, where the real business of banks and cities was done.

"Dallas is a great city," Quentin said as the skyline appeared.

"Yessir," Robert said. "Sometimes I think it's getting too big for the likes of me."

Robert maneuvered the lilac Cadillac expertly into the flow of downtown rush-hour traffic, easing the car's long fenders into the lanes he wanted, daring drivers of smaller cars to challenge him.

"Do you know Mrs. Babcock's plans for today?" Quentin asked.

"Nosir. She ain't spoke to me yet."

"Well, I'm going to tell the agency to deliver my car by eleven o'clock or else. You be there to see that they did the work properly and give their driver a ride back. If Mrs. Babcock gives you trouble, just tell her to call me."

"Yessir."

"Let me off at the Main Street door," Quentin said. "And get this purple car out of here."

Robert pulled the car to the Main Street curb and jumped out and opened the door. "Have a good day, sir," he said.

"This day is going to be a pain in the ass," Quentin said.

BULL

"Is it still raining?" Bull asked when Mary Ellen raised the window shade.

"Not much. It's going to clear, I think."

"I can do without rain today."

Mary Ellen sat down on the bed and kissed Bull on the forehead. "Poor Bullard," she said.

"Yeah. Poor Bullard. You know, you're a great piece of ass, for an old lady."

Mary Ellen blushed. "Hush! The kids will hear you."

"Shut the door. Let's have another round."

"Bullard, hush! They'll think we're awful!"

Bull laughed. "Bad nights just make me horny, that's all."

"Last night must have *really* been bad."

"Yeah. Poor bastards."

"Drinking?"

"I don't know. Maybe just stupid. The kid puked."

Mary Ellen took a cigarette from the pack on the table and lit it and handed it to him. "What are you doing today?"

"Working the crowd. Then traffic afterward."

"Where?"

"I don't know."

"Maybe you'll see him," she said.

"I couldn't care less. I just want to get it over with."

"I'll watch it on TV. Maybe I'll see you."

"Yeah, watch for me. I'll be the handsome one in the blue uniform." He patted her on the ass. "Sure you don't have time for a quickie?"

"Bullard!"

"I don't see how you can blush, after all these years."

"It's the kids. If they weren't here, I'd turn you every which way but loose."

Kim came in, one hand holding her blonde hair gathered at the back of her head, the other offering a hairbrush and a rubber band. "Mom, fix my ponytail," she said.

"See?" Mary Ellen said. "Ask me again after they've grown up."

"Huh?" Kim said.

"Nothing. Say good morning to your father."

"Hi, daddy. Can I have some money?"

"How much?"

"A couple of dollars."

"What for?"

"A Coke after school. You know."

"Cokes don't cost a couple of dollars."

"A dollar then. Okay?"

"Okay," Bull said. "Your mother will give it to you."

"You're spoiling her," Mary Ellen said. She was brushing Kim's hair back, gathering the ponytail. They were pretty, Bull thought. They looked like one of those mother-daughter commercials on TV.

"I like pretty girls," he said.

"I don't think we should have to go to school today," Kim said. "They ought to give us a holiday."

"Sure," Bull said. "So you could run around downtown, getting in trouble."

"Oh, daddy!"

Joey appeared in the doorway, his face quizzical. "I wondered where everybody went," he said. "Hi, daddy." He sat down on the bed and hugged Bull's bare shoulders. He smelled of orange juice.

"Did you take Albert out of the high chair?" Mary Ellen asked.

"He's not through yet."

"What's Buster doing?"

"He's with Albert."

"Well, go stay with them till I finish here. If that dog jumps on Albert, he'll scream bloody murder."

Joey went back to the kitchen. "Sweet kid," Bull said.

"Wow, you're in a good mood today," Kim said. "What's up?"

"Nothing," Bull said. "A man's got a right to a good mood now and then, hasn't he?"

Mary Ellen fastened the ponytail in place with the rubber band. "Okay. Off with you."

"What about my money?"

"Get it for her, honey," Bull said.

Mary Ellen got Bull's wallet from the uniform trousers on

the chair and took a dollar bill out of it. "How about two?" Kim said.

"One's enough," Bull said. "Who do you think I am? J. L. Fisher?"

Kim accepted the bill and came to the bed and kissed her father. "You're J. Edgar Hoover," she said.

"J. Edgar's a tightwad," Bull said.

Kim raised her eyebrows. "So?"

Bull laughed. "Be good."

"I will. 'Bye, daddy. Say hello to Jackie for me."

"Nice kid," Bull said when she left the room.

"You *are* in a good mood," Mary Ellen said.

"I've been thinking of those kids last night. At least I think they were kids. I couldn't even tell. Things like that make you feel lucky to be alive. After you get over being blue."

"Speaking of blue . . ." Mary Ellen made a face and pointed at the blue uniform shirt on the hanger hooked over the top of the door.

"Yeah," Bull said.

"I'd better go take over Albert," Mary Ellen said. "It's time for Joey to go."

When she left the room, Bull threw back the covers and got up. Mary Ellen was fussing over Albert in her cooing way. Bull knew she was wiping his face and hands, that the high chair was a mess, that Buster was sitting on his haunches, watching, his long tongue lolling. Life felt good. He *was* lucky to be alive. Bull knew that.

THOMAS J.

Regis Watson was sitting behind his big desk, drinking coffee from a big white cup with his initials on it. There was nothing else on the desk except a green blotter that nearly covered the top and a telephone. Watson sat like the king of some Westernized African country, gently rocking in a brown leather chair with a thronelike back higher than his head. His black suit was expensive and perfectly pressed. The red handkerchief folded neatly into his breast pocket matched his necktie. When Thomas J. entered, Watson rose and extended his hand across the desk. "Ah. Reverend Durant," he said. "You're out early this morning."

"You have a member of my congregation," Thomas J. said. In his old brown tweed coat and scuffed black shoes, he felt humble in the presence of Watson's splendor.

"Ah." Watson smiled and waved Thomas J. to the smaller leather chair in front of the desk. "Coffee?"

"No, thanks."

"You're referring to Emma Rawlins, I believe. If you've come to view the remains, we haven't prepared her."

"No, I'm here to make the arrangements."

"Arrangements for what, Thomas J.?"

"Why, her funeral."

Watson leaned back in the huge chair and rocked. He smiled slightly and sighed. "I tried to sell her burial insurance for years, but she never purchased it."

"She was a poor woman, Regis."

"Ah, yes. But my terms were very reasonable. My terms are based more or less on the ability to pay, you know."

"She had no money. She was on welfare."

"Several of my older clients are on welfare. I make it easy to pay. Just a little a week. I'm a compassionate man, Thomas J."

Thomas J. smiled wearily. "Maybe I *will* have some coffee."

"Certainly." Watson swiveled his chair to a hot plate on a small table behind him and poured coffee into a paper cup with paper handles and handed it across the desk. "I suppose you'll miss Emma Rawlins. She nearly always got her picture in the papers, didn't she? On your picket lines? I've always envied your flair for showmanship. That sort of talent is valuable in my business, too."

"Our rights have nothing to do with putting on shows," Thomas J. said.

"Ah." Watson put his fingertips together in front of his mouth, as if praying, and gazed thoughtfully at the green blotter. "Sometimes I wonder if you've thought this thing through," he said. "This civil-rights business."

"What do you mean?"

"Well, what if you were to succeed? What if the lion suddenly lay down with the lamb, so to speak? What if it were suddenly 'black and white together,' as Dr. King wants. What would happen to Negro funeral homes—and Negro churches? What would happen to you and me, Thomas J.?"

"What does that have to do with the right to vote?"

"One thing tends to lead to another. . . ."

"Look, Regis, I didn't come here to recruit you to our cause, or even to ask for a donation. Your views are well known."

Watson spread his hands apologetically. "Forgive me. You came to make arrangements for Miss Rawlins. We're talking about a pauper burial, I assume."

Thomas J. half rose from his chair. "No! We're *not* talking about a pauper burial!"

"Well, Thomas J., if there's no money . . ." Watson shrugged. "Of course, if you wish to take Miss Rawlins elsewhere . . ."

Thomas J. leaned back into his chair and crossed his long legs. "How much have you done on her?"

"Nothing. She's back there on a slab, poor thing, just as she was brought in. She's at your disposal." Watson smiled. "No pun intended."

"The church owns a few burial plots," Thomas J. said. "How much would the rest of it cost?"

"It depends on what you want done."

"Something simple, but dignified."

"Not a pauper burial?"

"Sister Emma was poor, Regis, but she was respected. She lived a long time in this community. Everybody respected her. A pauper burial would be a disgrace."

"Well, burial insurance would have—"

"Just give me a price, Regis."

Watson opened a desk drawer and took out a yellow pad and a pencil. He wrote down a column of figures and pushed the pad to Thomas J.

"A thousand dollars, Regis? Come on!"

"Dignity is expensive," Watson said. "You're lucky you've got the plot."

"Give me a break," Thomas J. said. "You get nearly all the business from my congregation."

Watson gazed at Thomas J. a second, then took back the pad and studied it. "Seven-fifty. That's the best I can do."

"All right."

"Have you got seven-fifty?"

Thomas J. nodded. "I want the funeral to be tomorrow. How's three o'clock?"

"Fine."

"Can you have her laid out by tonight?"

"Yes, but I'll need the money. In cash."

"When?"

"Before she's laid out. By the way, that price doesn't include a stone, you know."

"I'll tend to that later. I can take up a collection for that."

"Will you have the seven-fifty?" Watson asked.

"Yes."

"When?"

"This evening."

Watson pushed himself away from the desk. He laid his hand on Thomas J.'s shoulder and walked him to the door. "Nice doing business with you," Watson said. "I'm giving you a good deal."

Thomas J. got into his Plymouth and drove to the church,

dodging the deep puddles that the rain had left in the pot-
holes. His small study behind the sanctuary was never reached
by the sun, and he shivered when he felt its damp darkness.
He switched on the light and scanned the clutter of Sunday
School materials and choir robes and hymnals, then stooped
and lit the gas heater. He stood before the flame a few minutes, toasting his hands, then reached for the phone on the
desk and dialed Sister Mamie Ezell, chairman of the Building
Committee.

"Sister Mamie? Reverend Durant. I guess you know about
Sister Emma?"

"Oh, reverend, I'm so distressed!" Sister Mamie said.

"Yes . . . Well, she lived a long life, sister, and a good one."

"Oh, I know! And now she's with the Lord. I know that,
but . . ." Sister Mamie began to cry.

"I was wondering . . ." Thomas J. said. "I was wondering
if you could see that the sanctuary is put in order. The funeral
is tomorrow afternoon. I would do it myself, but it's important
for me to take our message to the president."

"Oh, yes, reverend. Yes, the president ought to have your
witness. It's for all of us."

"Sister Emma would want it that way, don't you think?"

"Yes, I do, reverend. Don't you worry about a thing. I'll
call the Flower Committee, too."

"Good. Sister Emma will be at Watson's Funeral Home
tonight."

"All right, reverend. I'll call everybody. Don't you worry
about a thing except bearing our witness."

Thomas J. hung up and sat down in the oak chair behind the
desk and rubbed his eyes. His stomach felt a little weak. Where
was he going to get seven hundred and fifty dollars by evening? What would Regis do if he didn't?

JASON

Mrs. Claymore was standing at the door as she did every morning, greeting her pupils as they filed into the room. Jason thought she was the prettiest teacher in the school. Her short brown hair was always shiny, and she was smiling this morning, as she always did at the beginning of the day. "Good morning, Jason," she said.

"Good morning," Jason replied, returning her smile.

Jason loved his classroom. Its smell reminded him of apples, and he sometimes wondered why, since neither he nor his classmates often brought apples to school. But he liked the smell, and he liked the brightness of the sunshine that came through the room's wall of windows. He was glad his desk was near that wall, for at a certain time of the day the sun was strong on his back and it made him feel good. He liked the pictures of autumn and winter that Mrs. Claymore had thumbtacked to the big bulletin board between the examples of her pupils' best work. He was proud that one of his own essays was on the bulletin board, and he sometimes sneaked a peek at it as he passed the board on the way to his desk. His essay was about moving to Texas, and he remembered exactly what it said.

Texas is not like Connecticut at all. When my dad told my mom and me that we were moving to Texas, I looked up Texas and Connecticut on the map of the U.S. in our atlas, and Texas was very big and Connecticut was very small. I have not seen much of Texas yet, but my dad says we will go see the Alamo this summer. The main thing I like about Texas so far is Dallas, where I live. Everything in Dallas looks clean and new, and the weather is very nice. It is probably snowing in Connecticut by now, but in Dallas the sun still shines like summer.

The sun wasn't shining this morning, though, and Jason wondered if winter was coming, although it wasn't cold.

When all the children were seated, Mrs. Claymore called the roll, then everyone stood and sang "My Country, 'Tis of Thee" and "God Bless America" and said the Pledge of Allegiance, and Mrs. Claymore said a prayer, as she did every morning.

While Mrs. Claymore prayed, Jason wished that his mother weren't coming to get him this morning. He wanted to see President Kennedy, but he was afraid his mother was going to get into an argument with Mrs. Claymore. He wished his mother would try harder to be like everybody else.

The Tenth Hour

DENNIS

A FAINT VOICE WAS CALLING, "Where's Jackie?"

"Mrs. Kennedy is organizing herself. It takes her a little longer, but, of course, she looks better when she does it."

Kennedy's crisp accent stabbed Dennis with homesick longing, even over the radio. Maybe Judy was right. Maybe they should go home for Christmas. Judy hadn't been home in a year and a half, and he hadn't been home in two. He hadn't been much of anywhere, really. He had come to Texas to experience the South, but all he had seen of Dixie was the long, dull highway between Dallas and Broadway Junction. The only obviously southern thing about it was the big sign over the main street in Greenville.

GREENVILLE, TEXAS
THE BLACKEST LAND AND THE WHITEST PEOPLE

The sign amused him every weekend, for nearly all the people he saw on Greenville's streets were Negroes. Dennis had mentioned this over coffee at the Student Union once, and one of the Texans at the table had turned red and challenged him. The sign wasn't racist, he said. In Texas, "white" was a synonym for "nice" or "good," as in the saying "That's mighty white of you." Dennis laughed, and the Texan left the table.

And he had been to Fort Worth, where Kennedy was now
delivering a speech in praise of the aircraft workers for their
labor on the TFX fighter plane. Dennis liked Fort Worth,
with its cowboys and stockyards and blue-collar workers and
its slow, easygoing ways. Fort Worth had a sense of humor,
and Kennedy probably was having a good time there. Sometimes Dennis wished he had gone to Texas Christian University instead of Southern Methodist. A lot of Methodist
theologues went there, and Fort Worth was what Dennis had
expected Texas to be. Dallas looked down its nose at Texas.
Dallas wanted to be—what? Not Boston. New York? Well,
it hadn't succeeded. In its eagerness to be sophisticated, it
had wound up more provincial, isolated even from the rest of
Texas, more provincial than unpretentious Fort Worth.
Maybe more provincial than Greenville and Broadway Junction, whose farmers certainly would have turned out for the
president of the United States.

"That was President Kennedy, speaking about an hour ago
outside the Texas Hotel in downtown Fort Worth," the disc
jockey burbled.

Dennis opened his eyes and turned off the radio. Judy was
still asleep, her back to him, her hair a bird nest on the pillow.
Dennis touched her cheek. It was still hot, maybe with fever,
maybe just with the heat of sleep.

Dennis went to the kitchenette and prepared the coffee and
plugged in the pot. He was still logy with the coffee and
cigarettes of last night, and the thought of more didn't appeal
to him, but he was a slow waker and couldn't get along without them. What he hated most about his weekends at Broadway Junction was pretending he didn't smoke while the other
men lit up on the church porch or around the Sunday table.
He longed to be in his car then, heading south with the first
drag in his lungs. It had been a mistake, going back to sleep
after calling Judy's principal to keep the substitute another
day. He felt rotten.

He lit up now and poured a glass of orange juice and carried it to the bedroom. Judy opened her eyes. He shook the last two aspirin out of the bottle on the bookcase headboard and put his hand on her shoulder. "Medicine time," he said.

Judy rose to her elbow, blinked at him, and accepted the glass and the pills. "What time is it?" she asked.

"A little after nine. How do you feel?"

"I don't know." She swallowed the pills and made a face. "Did you call Wilkes?"

"Yes. He said the flu's going around. He had to get three subs today."

"Um. Poor Wilkes. He hates that."

"Do you want something to eat?"

"Maybe some toast."

"Dry or buttered?"

"Dry."

"Coffee?"

"No. Tea. Do you mind?"

"No."

"You're a dear."

Dennis ran water into a pot and put it on the stove, then got the bread from the bread box and inserted two slices into the toaster. He envied Judy's capacity for breakfast. He couldn't face a bite until his stomach started its rumbling during Greek class. That was his signal that his body was finally awake and that he would be hungry for the rest of the period.

The water came to a boil just as the toast popped up, and Dennis, pleased at his timing, put a tea bag in a cup and poured. He squeezed a large dose of lemon juice into the cup, too, then put the toast on a salad plate and carried it all to Judy.

"You're a dear," she said.

"Do you want something on the toast? Jelly?"

"No thanks. This is fine."

Dennis got his coffee and rejoined her, sitting on her side of the bed.

"How late did you work?" she asked.

"Not long after you went to sleep. Around three-thirty, I guess."

"Did you finish?"

"No, but I've got a good start. It'll be okay as soon as I figure out what I want to say. How are you feeling?"

"Better, I think."

"We're out of aspirin. I'll go down and get some. Do you want anything else?"

"Chocolate ice cream. And some Sucrets."

"Your throat's still sore?"

"A little. Oh, and a magazine."

"What magazine?"

"*Redbook* or *Mademoiselle*. I don't care."

Dennis finished the coffee and got his raincoat and umbrella out of the closet. Outside, he stood on the tiny porch, evaluating the rain. He decided not to open the umbrella. It was two blocks to the drugstore, and only a fine mist was falling. The carrier had delivered the newspaper in a waxed-paper wrapper. Dennis removed it and read the front-page headlines. STORM OF POLITICAL CONTROVERSY SWIRLS AROUND KENNEDY ON VISIT. YARBOROUGH SNUBS LBJ. He wasn't surprised. The rag wouldn't have said anything favorable about Kennedy if he had descended into Texas on a cloud.

Dennis folded the newspaper and dropped it by the door. He stepped onto the sidewalk and turned toward Lovers Lane. The sky was gray, but the sun was illuminating the clouds in the east, promising to break through, and it wasn't cold. In Boston he would have considered it a nice day for this time of year. The cool, moist air seemed a cleansing blessing to him, and he was glad to be walking. It was chickenshit of Weldon and Ben not to go to Love Field with him. Chickenshit. There was a Texas word he liked. Even a Bostonian knew exactly what it meant.

BYRON

In all the years that Byron had written editorials for the evening paper, he had never gotten used to the morning editorial conferences. The publisher, the editor, the other editorial writer, Frank Cavern, and himself filing into the cramped, ugly little room each day with coffee cups in hand, sitting in the same chairs around the table, scanning the day's first edition that the editor's secretary laid in front of each place, the aimless conversation, the publisher's newest nigger joke, the strained, obligatory laughter. It was like some handed-down religious ritual that continued to be performed long after its purpose had been forgotten. In theory, the meetings were supposed to be discussions of editorial policy. In practice, they were wasted hours of nondiscussions, nonopinions, nondecisions that made the page a pale, watery imitation of the morning paper's elegantly cruel conservatism.

"Your Kennedy editorial yesterday was damn good, Byron," the editor said.

"The hell it was," the publisher said. "What about that crap about Dallas being a city of hate?" His small, dark eyes squinted at Byron through the smoke of his cigar. "What the fuck did you mean by that?"

"I didn't say Dallas *is* a city of hate," Byron said. "I said we hoped Kennedy would discover that it *isn't* a city of hate.

"Well, damn it, Hayes, doesn't that imply that we *are* a city of hate?"

"You're right. I should have caught that," the editor said.

Byron gritted his teeth. It happened whenever he put a bite of meat, a real comment, a genuine opinion into an editorial on a local topic. The farther the issue was from Dallas, the bolder his opinion was permitted to be. But criticism of the city made the publisher uncomfortable among his friends in the Citizens Council. It required apologetic explanations for the appearance of discontent in print. The paper's unspoken rule was to say something nice or nothing at all about Dallas.

"Betty Lou's public relations don't come cheap," the publisher was saying. "That 'city of hate' nonsense pisses away a lot of money for nothing." He spoke to the editor as if they were alone in the room. "What have you got for the weekend?"

"I thought we might lead with a piece praising the friendly reception the city gave him," the editor said.

"Assuming that's the case," Byron said.

"It will be," the publisher said. "You're not going to get into political stuff, are you?"

"No," the editor said.

The publisher folded his newspaper and pushed his chair away from the table. "Well, I leave the rest of it to you gentlemen. I'm on the reception committee."

"Will you be at the luncheon?" the editor asked.

"With bells on." The publisher grinned around his cigar and departed in a cloud of smoke, closing the door behind him.

"Thanks a lot!" Byron said.

The editor shrugged. "It's best to let him speak his piece and leave. Who wants to write about the throngs cheering the president?"

"Not I," Byron said. "I'm not so sure they're going to."

"Frank?"

"Okay," Cavern said. "You want me to say anything about the trip healing the Connally-Yarborough split?" The Democratic party binding up its wounds? That sort of thing?"

"You heard him. No politics," the editor said.

"Shit," Byron said.

"You're cranky as hell this morning, Hayes. Is Jean on the rag?"

"I'm jumpy. You know the crazies are going to turn out today."

"Not if Betty Lou has done her job."

"You don't think the angels are going to roll over and play dead when the devil himself is in town, do you?" Byron said.

"That's exactly what I'm hoping. That's what this PR campaign is about. Even the opposition went along with it. And if they say be nice, the crazies will be nice."

"Well, they should have whispered something to their ad department," Byron said.

"Yeah," Cavern said. "I wonder why *we* didn't run that ad."

Byron laughed. "If they had brought it to us, we would have."

"Jesus, Hayes, are you hung over or something?" the editor asked.

"I'm sorry. Callison and I got a little shitfaced last night."

"How's he doing?"

"He misses his kid."

"Who's the American Fact Finding Committee?" Cavern asked.

"My guess is it's Bernard Weissman," the editor said.

"My guess is you're right," Byron said. "The question is, who's Bernard Weissman? My guess is he's Colonel Luther Byrd, U.S. Army, retired."

"Think so?"

"The ad has all his earmarks. The world view. The big picture. I imagine Colonel Byrd in boots and epaulets, perusing old war maps with Highland Park ladies in his Turtle Creek bunker."

"I wonder why he settled here," Cavern said.

"Where would *you* settle if you were Colonel Luther Byrd?" Byron asked. "Wouldn't you look for birds of a feather?"

"Come off it!" the editor said. His face was red.

"So I'm nasty this morning," Byron said. "I've got a headache."

"Well, take an aspirin. It's Friday. We've got the Sunday and Monday pages to put out. Unless you don't especially want the weekend off."

"How many pieces are on the bank?" Cavern asked.

"Three," the editor said. "That might fill one."

"God, I hate Fridays," Byron said.

"Think of it as the day before Saturday," the editor said.

"I'll be satisfied with Friday night," Byron said. "I don't think Kennedy should come here. I think we're in for trouble."

"Don't be paranoid," the editor said.

It came from hanging around Jake, Byron concluded. There was nothing as depressing as friends getting divorced. They were crybabies. They clung to you like leeches. They got you drunk and hung over, and always talked about leaving. Byron pushed himself away from the table. "I'll write anything you want," he said. "I'm going to get some aspirin."

As he walked through the newsroom, he glanced at Callison's desk. Jake wasn't there, of course. He was supposed to be at the courthouse, but he probably was still in bed. Byron wished to hell he was, too.

HENRY

Henry thought it was a cat vomiting. He had been dreaming about a cat, and he thought the sound was part of the dream. The cat was a tabby that had belonged to his sister when he was a kid, and Henry was trying to remember what he had been dreaming about it. It was the trying to remember that told him he was awake and that the sound wasn't a cat. It was Muffin. Muffin had the dry heaves.

"Hey, cut that out," Henry said.

Muffin heaved again. It was an awful sound. It reminded Henry of the times he had had the dry heaves, and he didn't like remembering them. "Cut it out, Muffin," he said.

"I can't, man," Muffin said. He sucked at the air like a man dying. He probably felt like he was dying. Henry raised himself onto an elbow and looked. Muffin was kneeling. His back was to Henry, and his head was bowed so low that Henry couldn't see it. Dead, wet grass was stuck to the back of Muffin's coat and the soles of his shoes. "Fuckin' scotch," Muffin said. Henry could barely hear him over the roar of engines and the whine of tires on the viaduct above.

"It's the scotch, all right," Henry said. "Niggers oughtn't drink no scotch. Their systems ain't made for it." He laughed.

"Son of a bitch," Muffin said. He heaved again, but not so loudly this time. He flopped back onto the grass and lay on his back with his eyes closed. Henry laughed again. He knew Muffin was hurting, but he felt like laughing. "Shit," he said.

"Fuckin' scotch," Muffin said.

"Yeh, scotch ain't for niggers," Henry said. "Gin's for niggers, and wine's for niggers, but scotch ain't." He picked up the green Cutty Sark bottle and held it before his eyes, but it was empty. He tried to throw it into the river, but the river was too far away.

"It ain't the scotch," Muffin said. "It's the rain."

"Rain never give nobody the dry heaves, Muffin. Anyways, it's about stopped."

"I'm cold. Build a fire," Muffin said.

Henry laughed. "Well, for one thing, Muffin, there ain't no wood. And if there was wood, it would be wet. And if it wasn't wet and I started a fire, this grass would start burning, and we would have cops and firemen down here, and you and me would go to jail. And anyways, I ain't got no matches. And that's a good thing, Muffin. If they was to put you in jail, they wouldn't never let you out."

"Fuckin' scotch," Muffin said.

"You said it, boy. If I hadn't give you that scotch, I'd have me some right now. You're just wasting it on the heaves."

"I'm cold," Muffin said.

Henry was chilly, too, and damp. He walked out from under the viaduct and a few steps down the brown grass that sloped toward the river bottom. He stopped and looked up at the sky. The sun would break through by and by, he thought, but he didn't like the shade of gray in the clouds. They had something of winter in them, and Henry hated winter. Some days in winter, the wind shot through him like arrows. On those days, people walked faster than usual along the sidewalks, and not many would stop and fumble under their coats for coins to drop into Henry's palm. In winter he would think sometimes of going home to Tyler and living with his sister. Then he would remember that his sister was dead and the house where they had grown up had been torn down to make a parking lot for a supermarket.

"Hey, Muffin, it ain't hardly raining at all," Henry said.

Muffin said nothing, but he stood up and leaned against one of the pylons of the viaduct, trying to steady himself. Henry returned to him. "Come on," he said. "Let's go get something to eat."

"I ain't hungry," Muffin said.

"Sure you are. You'll feel better after you get something in your belly."

"You got any money?"

"No, but we'll get some."

Muffin didn't reply, but when Henry laid his hand on his arm and urged him along, he allowed himself to be moved. They climbed the steep embankment and stood panting at the end of the viaduct, watching the cars and trucks whine back and forth between downtown and Oak Cliff. Muffin stepped off the curb. A truck's air horn blasted and he jumped back, his eyes big and scared.

Henry laughed. "You trying to get your coon ass killed, Muffin?"

They shuffled down Jefferson Street, then turned toward

the courthouse and the jail. There were several cheap eating joints in the area, and the lawyers and deputies and bail bondsmen were a soft touch.

"I need a cigarette," Muffin said. "You got a cigarette?"

"No, but we'll get one."

As they neared the ugly red stone courthouse, Henry noticed that more police cars than usual were parked around the place, and deputies and state highway patrolmen were standing around in groups, wearing slickers, talking to one another. "Maybe there's been a jailbreak," Henry said.

Muffin looked scared. "I ain't going up there," he said. "They'll put my ass in jail."

"Yeah, you hang back. I'll go look."

Henry tried to look casual, sauntering along the sidewalk. He hoped his back wasn't covered with grass, like Muffin's. Some of the officers gave him the eye, but said nothing, and he said nothing to them. Then he saw a deputy he knew, leaning against a patrol car alone, swinging his billy back and forth.

The deputy smirked when he saw Henry. "You getting out of the tank, Henry?" he asked.

"Nosir. I ain't been in the tank, Slim," Henry said.

"Clean as a whistle, are you?" Slim said.

"Yessir. Hungry, though. Could you spare a dollar for a bowl of chili? I'll pay you back."

Slim gave Henry a look. He was a young deputy, not tough enough yet to give Henry a really hard time. "Chili don't cost a dollar," he said. "You're just wanting some rotgut."

"Oh, nosir," Henry said. "I got a friend that's hungry, too."

Slim stuck his hand in his pocket and brought out a money clip with several bills folded in it. He peeled off a single and gave it to Henry. He pointed down the block with his billy. "I'm going to watch the door of that joint," he said. "I better see you go in."

"Oh, you will," Henry said. "What's going on, anyways? Somebody bust out?"

"Naw, President Kennedy's coming to town, Henry. Don't you read the papers?"

"How about a cigarette?" Henry asked.

Slim took a pack of Camels from the pocket of his slicker and shook one out for Henry.

"How about another one? For my buddy."

"Damn it, Henry. Why don't you take my billy and my car while you're at it?"

"I won't bother you no more."

Slim shook out another cigarette. "Okay," he said. "But stay away from the president, hear? You touch the president and I'll have to run you in." He laughed.

Henry touched his brow in a kind of salute. "Much obliged," he said. He sauntered back through the knots of officers, trying to look casual, toward the place in the next block where Muffin was sitting on the sidewalk with his head between his knees. The deputies were always kidding him, Henry thought. Somebody must have busted out.

SHERRY

"I wonder if we'll get to see her," Eileen said.

Sherry Murrell was counting out fifty dollars in small bills for the man at her window. She waited until she finished to ask, "Who?"

"Jackie. I just love her. She's so neat."

Eileen was the bubbly, brainless type that made it hard for men to take women seriously in business. She chatted incessantly over the glass partition that separated her cage from Sherry's, about movie and TV stars and players for the Dallas Cowboys whom she considered sexy. She claimed to have been an American Airlines stewardess before she came to the bank. She gave up flying, she said, because a stewardess was just a glorified waitress, and the pilots, from among whom she had hoped to pick a husband, turned out to be older men who were already married. Now she was looking for an up-and-coming banker or lawyer. Although they lived in the same apartment complex, Sherry had never accepted Eileen's invitations to come over and watch TV. She imagined an apartment cluttered with confession magazines and apple cores and nail polish bottles and dirty underwear.

"Today's payday," Sherry said. "We'll have the Friday lunch-hour rush. I'd just as soon watch it on the news, anyway."

"Why don't you come over and watch with me?" Eileen said.

"I can't. I have somebody coming for dinner."

"A fellow?"

"Yes."

"Oh, lucky you. Who is it?"

"You don't know him." Sherry resented the prying, confidential tone of the question. Eileen was a terrible gossip.

"Is he rich?"

"No."

"Is he handsome?"

"He has his points."

"Is he sexy?"

"Yes."

"Why don't you introduce me to him?"

"He's not your type, Eileen." Sherry pointedly turned her attention to her next customer, an old woman wanting to cash her social-security check. Sherry handed her a ballpoint pen and watched as she slowly, carefully scrawled her signature on the back.

Sherry was trying to fight her resentment of Jake. She didn't like his meeting Liz for lunch. Couples getting divorced had to get together and talk things over, but did it have to be for lunch? Lunch had an air of friendliness, almost of courtship, about it, and Jake hadn't been at all reluctant to accept Liz's invitation. Why couldn't he have met her at their house? There, in the privacy of their broken home, they could scream and yell at each other. At lunch, they would have to be polite, and the idea of Jake being polite to his wife made Sherry jealous.

There was no reason for jealousy, though. It made her feel lousy. Wasn't Jake having dinner with her tonight? At her place? She would set the mood. She would be in control. She would stroke his brown hair, kiss the lids over those sad blue eyes. She would make Jake glad he was with her, and not Liz. He wouldn't want to leave, and she wouldn't make him.

"Aren't you even going to tell me his name?" Eileen asked.

"No."

"Is he married?"

"No."

"Does he have a friend?"

"All his friends are married."

"He must be an older man, then."

"Cut it out, Eileen."

"I was just asking." Eileen was miffed, but Sherry didn't care.

Steak. She would serve steak. She would splurge and buy two nice T-bones. With baked potatoes and a nice green salad. The basics. Jake would like that. He hadn't been eating well lately. He hadn't been taking care of himself. And a good wine. A nice, dry Burgundy. Wine made Sherry feel warm and glowing. Sexy. Jake ought to drink more wine and less of the hard stuff. But she would buy a bottle of bourbon, too, in case he wanted it. She wanted Jake to be happy tonight. She wanted everything to be perfect. She wanted him to know she really loved him.

Jake wouldn't be happy at first. Liz would use the kid against him, would make him feel guilty about James. She would use James to try to get more money. It would work, too, if Jake had any more money to give. Jake was such a sap about James.

Sherry supposed she wanted to meet the kid. She had suggested an introduction a couple of times, a picnic at White Rock Lake, maybe, or a movie. The three of them. But Jake wouldn't agree to it. Not yet, he said. After the divorce. James had enough to handle right now. Sherry didn't really care. She would have been nervous, meeting the kid. She just wanted to show Jake that she could make James like her, that she could be good with him. She would feel more secure with Jake if he would let her meet James. It would mean the three of them were all right, that it was natural for them to be together sometimes.

Jake would be down when he arrived tonight, because James would be on his mind. Sherry would play him some music on the hi-fi. She liked the Beatles, and he liked hillbilly. It was one of the things that reminded her that he was quite a bit older. But she had bought some Mantovani and Percy Faith. Mood music.

The smile that Sherry kept on her face for her customers seemed tight and uncomfortable this morning. It made her nervous, thinking warm thoughts in the cold white marble of the bank.

"Oh, you know, we're heading into nut country today," the president said. He stopped his pacing and stood in front of her. "You know, last night would have been a hell of a night to assassinate a president."

She smiled, humoring him.

"I mean it," he said. "There was the rain, and the night, and we were all getting jostled. Suppose a man had a pistol in a briefcase."

He pointed a finger at the green wall and jerked his thumb back twice.

The Eleventh Hour

RAYMOND

RAYMOND CALLED THE TEXAS HOTEL in Fort Worth, and the White House guy put him on hold. Raymond's sharp jaw tensed in frustration. The White House people always put him on hold. It was part of the game the Washington flunkies played these days. They probably sat and watched the light on the phone blink for a couple of minutes whether they were busy or not. That was part of the game, too, pretending they were busy. This time, though, he didn't have to wait long.

"Yes?" the White House voice said.

"Agent Medley, sir. I'm at Love Field. Should we put on the bubble top?"

"Hold on." The White House voice faded, but didn't leave. It was talking to someone else in the room. "The Dallas paper is predicting rain," it said. "The weather bureau can't make up its mind." The voice returned to Raymond. "What do you think?"

"Sir?"

"What do you think? Is it going to rain or not?"

Raymond hesitated. *He* damn sure wasn't going to make the decision. The president would be pissed as hell if he decided wrong, and the White House guys would blame it on him. "Well, it's still drizzling," he said.

"But is it going to stop, or not?" the White House voice asked. "What's your hunch?'

Raymond hesitated again. Shit, he was going to have to gamble. "I think the clouds will blow off to the east," he said.

"Hold on." The voice faded again to consult the other person in the room, then returned. "O'Donnell says that if the weather is clear and it's not raining, have the bubble top off."

Wonderful. If he left the bubble top off, the president and Jackie would get rained on. If he put it on, they would swelter in a mobile hothouse all the way to the Trade Mart. They would be pissed, and the crowd would be disappointed, and Raymond would get the blame. Obviously the White House people had no idea how quickly and emphatically the weather could change in Texas.

Flying the thirty miles from Fort Worth to Dallas was stupid, anyway. It was a long drive from the Texas Hotel to Carswell Air Force Base, where the presidential plane was waiting. The plane would barely get into the air before it would descend into Love, and then the motorcade . . . The trip from the Texas Hotel to the Trade Mart would take almost two hours. Even with a parade at both ends, it could have been driven faster than that. But Kennedy couldn't resist an airport crowd. Raymond wished presidents hadn't stopped traveling by train.

He stepped out of the International Arrivals Building for another look at the clouds. They were thinning, all right. The western sky was almost clear, and there were a few frayed holes on the northern edge of the dome of gray. The sun would break through soon, then the overcast would burn away. He would gamble that it would happen before the president arrived. There would be no bubble top today.

Raymond's eyes scanned the roof of the terminal building's eastern concourse. The cops stood in groups of two and three there, talking, smoking, cradling their weapons in the sleeves of their yellow slickers. They had nothing to do yet. Maybe they had been put on the roof too early. Maybe they wouldn't be alert by the time the plane arrived. Maybe they were as bored as he was with the waiting. Raymond looked at his watch. There was still more than an hour to go. Well, the crowd would be here soon, if there was going to be one.

The chain-link fence would separate the crowd, if it came, from the presidential party. At intervals as he walked along it, Raymond grasped the heavy mesh with his hands and pulled, to test its strength. It seemed strong enough. He didn't expect much of a crush, anyway. The only people behind the fence so far were a bunch of kids who had come early to claim a spot against the mesh. Some of the boys were wearing letter jackets. Some of the girls were, too. They had their arms around the waists of boys not wearing letter jackets, which probably meant the jackets belonged to the boys and they were going steady. Raymond glanced at them as he passed.

"Hey, dad."

Raymond turned. "Are you talking to me?"

"Yeah." The kid stepped forward from the group. He had an Elvis Presley hairdo and stood hip-shot against the small blonde girl at his side. His arm was around her waist. She wore the letter jacket. He wore a black leather motorcycle jacket with lots of zippers. "When does the clan get here?" he asked.

"The Klan?" Raymond said, thinking of Kluxers.

"Yeah. The Kennedy clan." The teen-agers tittered.

Raymond looked the kid hard in the eye. "They'll be along. When you see them."

"You a cop?" the kid asked.

"Secret Service."

"Oh." The kid's smirk faded. He took a step back.

"Who are you?" Raymond asked.

"Thomas Jefferson High," the kid said. "We came to see Chairman John."

The kids tittered again. When Raymond turned to walk back to the International Arrivals Building, they hissed.

STACY

Stacy backed the station wagon out of the driveway, then looked at her watch. She should have time to stop by the Preston Shopping Center before she picked up Jason. She had noticed a small shop there that specialized in bathroom things, and she wanted a shower curtain for Jason. If the shop didn't have something childishly masculine, she would drive on to the school. She didn't have time to wander about the department stores today.

The parking lot was crowded, although the stores couldn't have been open long and the weather was hardly ideal for shopping. Stacy had never been to the center when the lot wasn't crowded. She wondered if north Dallas women ever did anything but shop. They shopped in pairs, sometimes even in groups, talking constantly, holding goods up to solicit the opinions of their friends. It was a strange custom, and Stacy wondered whether it was born of some desperate need for constant companionship or the women's lack of confidence in their own taste. Dallas was supposed to be a sophisticated, fashion-conscious town, but the women she had met and those she saw in the stores displayed no originality, no personal flair, in the clothes they chose or the way they wore them. They seemed to value safety and acceptability above everything, and that, she suspected, was why they shopped in packs. They needed the approval of their friends before they bought a dress or a pair of shoes. Maybe they were smart. The things they bought were nearly always expensive. It would be awful to spend a lot of money for something and then be embarrassed to wear it. Maybe Dallas women brought their friends along so someone would *know* the clothes they wore later to a party or a symphony concert were, indeed, expensive, and therefore okay.

Still, it seemed so silly. She would have gone mad, absolutely mad, if she had to listen to some languid, drawling woman at her elbow all day. Shopping alone was one of her true pleasures. She loved the freedom, the anonymity of browsing through beautiful things, hearing the hangers scrape against their rods as she worked her way through the dresses, undressing and trying things on in her own silence, sitting alone in the tearooms, watching the women at the other tables and eavesdropping on their conversations. She admitted to herself that she had done more shopping in the month she had lived in Dallas than during a whole year in Hartford. She told Mark it was because she was getting settled, and things had to be bought. But shopping was a way of getting out of the house, and she liked getting out in Dallas more than in Hartford, so long as she could go alone. She regretted there was no time today.

A gray Continental backed out of a space between two Cadillacs, and Stacy seized the spot. The driver of the Continental was an older woman, gray as her car and immaculately coiffed, already wearing a mink jacket. The car's windows were shut, and Stacy, suspecting the woman of running her air conditioner rather than take off the mink, smiled. The woman, mistaking the meaning of the smile, smiled too, and waved.

Stacy walked across the lot to the bathroom shop, and was greeted at the door by a woman in dark eyeshadow and red hair drawn back into a bun. A yellow pencil stuck out of the hair near the bun. The woman smiled and said, "Good morning. May I help you?"

Stacy hated having to deal with clerks before she had had time to look, but she and the woman were alone in the shop. There was no getting out of it. "Yes," she said. "I'm looking for a shower curtain. For a child."

"Boy or girl?"

"Boy."

"This way." The woman led Stacy toward the back of the store and flipped through the rack of shower curtains. She held out a brown one with cowboys on it. "This would be nice for a boy."

"I wanted blue," Stacy said.

"It comes in blue, too. Light blue."

"No, I need dark blue. And the cowboys are too young. They look four or five years old."

"How old is the boy?"

"Ten."

The woman smiled. It was a stiff, impersonal smile, and Stacy didn't like it. "I have a ten-year-old myself. It's a wonderful age. Would your boy be interested in airplanes? My boy loves airplanes."

Stacy was flipping through the curtains herself. She found a dark blue one with huge orange tigers on it. The tigers were leaping and growling. It was hideous. Jason would love it. "This. This is what I want," she said.

"Oh, any boy would love that," the woman said. "I have a matching window curtain to go with it. Would you like to see it?"

"No."

"All righty." The woman stretched to a stack of boxes on a shelf above the shower curtain display and took one down and opened it to make sure it was the tigers. "May I help you with something else?"

"No."

While the woman was writing the sales slip, Stacy asked, "Do you know where I might buy a flag?"

"A flag?"

"Yes. An American flag. A small one that you might hold in your hand and wave."

"A flag . . . Let me see now. . . . You might try the toy store, down this block and across the other little parking lot. That's the only place I know of in Preston that might have a flag."

"Thank you." Stacy paid the woman and left the store with her tiger shower curtain.

The man who greeted her at the door of the toy store smiled, too. He was an older, gentle-looking man, and his smile seemed genuine. He was a perfect guy to work in a toy store.

"Morning, ma'am," he said. "May I help you?"

"Yes. Do you sell flags? Small flags?"

"Yes, ma'am. Second aisle on your right."

Stacy found the aisle and the flags, arranged like flowers in plastic beach pails. There were Confederate flags and Texas flags and even pirate flags with the skull and bones on them, but no American flags. She went back to the man and said, "I can't find any American flags."

"Oh? I'm sure we have some." The man led her back down the aisle and looked at the flags. "By golly, you're right," he said. "We're clean out of American flags. How about a Confederate flag? They're pretty popular these days. Is it for party favors or something?"

"No. It's to wave at the president. A Confederate flag won't do."

"I guess not," the man said. "That is, if you *like* the president."

"I like him," Stacy said.

The man winked and leaned toward her. "I voted for him," he said. "I'm a yellow-dog Democrat."

"What in the world is that?" Stacy asked.

The man laughed. "A Democrat who would vote for a yellow dog before he would vote for a Republican. Even a Catholic. I don't think all Catholics are bad, do you?"

"No."

"I think Jack Kennedy has made a mighty fine president." He looked again at the flags. "You're going to see him, are you?"

"Yes."

"If I didn't have to work, I'd go, too." His blue eyes twinkled. "Young lady, would you do me a favor?"

"What's that?"

The man took a Texas flag out of its plastic pail and handed it to her. "Would you wave this for me?"

Stacy didn't know what to say, so she looked at the flag in her hands. It wasn't like a state flag. It seemed to belong on one of the slick color pages of her dictionary that portrayed the flags of all the nations. She had always been startled seeing it below the American flag on the pole at Jason's school, as if the pole marked the border between two countries. It was too vivid, too strong for a state flag.

"You're a newcomer, aren't you?" the man said.

"Yes."

"From the North?"

"Yes."

The man nodded. "I could tell from the accent. Anyway, I wish you'd wave the flag for me, just to show President Kennedy that Dallas isn't always what it seems. Not all of it, anyway. Will you do that?"

"Well . . . Yes, I'd be glad to."

"Good." The man turned to walk away.

"I need three of them," Stacy said.

The man took two more out of the pail and handed them to her. She followed him to the cash register at the front of the store. "How much are they?" she asked.

"Nothing. They're free. You're doing me a favor, aren't you?" He put the flags in a bag and handed them to her.

She was moved. She wanted to lean over the counter and kiss the man. "What's your name?" she asked.

"Norvell Jennings, ma'am. A yellow-dog Democrat." He winked again. "Us yellow-dog Democrats have to stick together, don't we?"

"Yes. Thank you, Mr. Jennings."

"My pleasure, ma'am. Just hold those flags way up high, so he can see them."

Stacy sat in her car for several minutes, staring at the dashboard. She didn't know why, but Norvell Jennings's gesture made her want to cry. Her eyes focused on the dashboard clock, which wasn't running, but reminded her to check her watch. She had to hurry. She started the engine and pulled into the traffic on Preston Road and turned south toward Jason's school.

The flags on the pole in front of the low, one-story building were hanging limp and damp when she walked up the sidewalk. Inside, the classroom doors were open and the corridor was filled with the rustle of paper and the crisp, efficient tones of teachers and a single child's voice calling, "I know! I know!" She noticed she had brought the bag with the flags with her. She found Jason's room and stood outside the door, out of sight of the children, smiling. Mrs. Claymore was writing on the blackboard. She saw Stacy and smiled back and lay down the chalk and came into the corridor.

"I'm Mrs. Leary—"

"Yes, I know," Mrs. Claymore said. "How do you do?"

"I came to pick up Jason."

Mrs. Claymore stopped smiling. "I told the children they couldn't be excused today," she said.

"Well, the superintendent said they could, if their parents picked them up." Stacy knew her voice had become brittle. She didn't care. "I am Jason's parent."

Mrs. Claymore was a fair, dark-haired woman. Quite young and pretty. "Mrs. Leary, I don't approve. The Kennedys are not the kind of people that children . . . Well, I don't approve. I told the children, and you're the only one . . ."

"Are you telling me that I don't have the right to take my son to see the president of the United States?"

"It isn't a matter of right, Mrs. Leary. It's what's best for the children."

Stacy opened the bag and took out one of the flags and waved it in Mrs. Claymore's face. "Bring me Jason immediately," she said.

Mrs. Claymore backed through the classroom door, her eyes wide. "Jason Leary," she said. "Come here, please."

Jason came, looking worried. "I'll have him back as soon as possible." Stacy said. "I'm sure he won't miss much."

Mrs. Claymore closed the door.

Stacy handed Jason the flag. "Come on," she said. "Today you're going to be a real Texan."

"Good," he said. "It's about time."

J. L.

"You'll catch your death of cold if you go out there, sir," Jonathan said, but J. L. Fisher put on his raincoat anyway.

"Jonathan," he said, "Buck Pool and I used to swim rivers on horseback with water up to our chins and lie on the bank shivering. Don't tell me a little old drizzle is going to kill me."

"Well, sir," Jonathan said, "you better wear a hat, anyway."

J.L. opened the closet door again and studied the hats on the shelf. He selected the old, sweat-stained five-gallon that he wore when taking the sun in the garden. That ought to fool them.

"If Miss Anna asks, where shall I say you are?" Jonathan asked.

"Walking around the grounds," J.L. said. "Checking security." He got through the door and closed it before Jonathan could answer. He leaned against one of the tall white columns of the portico and peered down the long, straight drive toward the street. The iron gate was closed, but he guessed it wasn't locked. Calvin wasn't as careful about security as he should be. Anyway, if it was locked, he had a key. He considered finding Calvin and ordering the car, but Anna probably had told Calvin to make himself scarce. He shouldn't stay too long on the portico, either. Jonathan might already be telling on him.

The lawn, flat and brown to the gate, offered no cover. The trunk of the huge live oak, to the right of the driveway half-way down, would hide him if he could get to it, but Anna or

Jonathan or Calvin might spot him first. He couldn't take the chance. He didn't move as fast as he used to. The creek path would be better. The creek flowed down to the street, almost parallel to the driveway, and the hedges along it were thick and evergreen. If he bent low enough, they would hide him until he got to the wall, then it would be only a short dash to the gate.

J.L. stepped off the portico and around to the side garden. He crossed the garden as quickly as he could. The three steps down to the creek path were slippery with the rain, and he slipped on the bottom one and fell. His hip hit the edge of the step and hurt like hell. He sat down on the step, breathing hard, enjoying the pain. It would have broken the hip of a lesser man. A lesser man would have to go to bed and die. All those years of horses and oil rigs weren't for nothing. You're a tough *hombre*, Fisher, he thought. He wished Buck Pool were here to help him up, though.

"Mr. J.L.? You out there, Mr. J.L.?" It was old Lanell, calling from the back door. Goddamn it.

J.L. got up and eased himself to the wet cobblestones of the creek path and hunkered behind the hedge. He would have to move fast now. If they came down to the path, they could see all the way to the wall, and the jig would be up. He made his way down the path in a sort of duck walk, trying to keep his head below the top of the hedge. He regretted that he was wearing boots. They slipped on the wet stones and made too much noise. It was a hell of a note, hiding out from a woman and a bunch of darkies. He would pretend they were Mexicans after the horses again, and that Buck Pool was sneaking around out by the live oak, trying to get behind them.

His unnatural crouch and his hurting hip made him pant. He felt himself sweating under the raincoat and the hat. He had to stop and blow every few steps, and he turned and looked behind him each time, expecting to see Jonathan or Calvin at the end of the walk, but they were never there. Since he hadn't demanded the car, maybe they really believed he was just out walking. He could hear the creek gurgling over the rocks, and after he checked his backtrail he would look at the rocks and listen to the water. The creek was very shallow and didn't even flow during the dry months, but last night's rain had made it a real stream. The water was dark and cold-looking, like streams that he and Buck had seen in Colorado.

By the time he reached the place where the creek flowed under the wall, J.L.'s lungs felt as if they were going to burst. He thought his legs might not lift him straight. But slowly he rose and risked a look over the hedge at the lawn and the house and the gate. No one was visible, so he left the path and limped as casually as he could to the gate. He was pleased to find it locked. Calvin was finally taking security seriously. J.L. pulled the big iron key from the pocket of his jeans. The lock was well oiled and moved smoothly. J.L. opened the gate barely wide enough to slide through, then closed it as quietly as he could and locked it again. Triumph swelled his chest, and he wanted to yell a Mexican *grito* as he and Buck used to do in their great moments, but Anna might hear.

The traffic swished on the boulevard, the tires sizzling on the wet pavement. A taxicab was stopped at the traffic light at the end of the block, and as soon as the light changed, J.L. stepped into the street and took off his hat and waved it. The cab changed lanes to avoid him, but he changed lanes, too. The driver hit the brakes, and the cab slid to a halt. J.L. hobbled to the door and opened it and got in beside the driver, who was a nigger.

"Hey, I almost killed you!" the nigger said. His eyes were big and white, like Amos on "Amos 'n' Andy." Amos drove a cab, too.

"Take me downtown," J.L. said.

"Mister, I can't." The nigger pulled over to the curb and stopped. "I'm on call. You have to get out."

"My name is J. L. Fisher. I want to go downtown."

"I can't help it, mister. I'm on call. I've got a fare waiting for me."

J.L. opened his wallet and took out a fifty-dollar bill and showed it to the nigger. "This is your tip, if you take me downtown."

The nigger's eyes got bigger. "Give me that right now and you've got yourself a ride. I'll just say I got lost."

J.L. gave the nigger the bill and he stuffed it into his jacket pocket. He put the cab in gear and moved back into the traffic. "J. L. Fisher," he said. "That name sure rings a bell, but I can't place you."

"I'm in the oil business," J.L. said.

"Oh."

"What's *your* name?"

"Lucius. Lucius Jackson."

"I didn't know they let coloreds drive cabs."

"Where you want to go downtown, Mr. Fisher?"

"I'll tell you when to stop," J.L. said. His hip hurt like hell.

TIM

"Why are you sweating?" the station manager asked.

"Because I'm fat," Tim Higgins said. "Fat people sweat a lot."

"Shit, it's not even hot. What are you going to do in July?"

"Is there going to be a press conference at the airport?"

The station manager checked his clipboard. "No, I don't think so. There's nothing on here about it. No, I don't think so." He was as nervous as Tim.

"I won't need the recorder, then."

"Better take it," the station manager said. "He might decide to say something. He might say how glad he is to be in Dallas or something. Better take it, just in case."

Tim lifted the recorder to his shoulder.

"The batteries working in that thing?" the station manager asked.

"Yes. I tested them." Tim hated it when the station manager tried to play news director. He did it every time there was an important story, and he just made everybody nervous and slowed them down.

"Okay. Call in as soon as the motorcade leaves Love Field. As soon as Kennedy leaves, hop on the phone and call in. Lonnie will finish his commercial or record or whatever he's doing, then he'll put you directly on the air. Got it? And for Christ's sake, be casual—you know, like this sort of thing happens all the time. Like you're a big-time broadcast honcho." The station manager scowled. "Jesus, I'm glad we're not on TV. You're sweating like a pig."

"I'm sorry. I'm a little nervous, that's all."

"Well, don't be nervous on the air. Just play it straight, okay? Just say what happened. If Lonnie has time, he might ask you a question or two. He'll probably hoke it up a little, but you play it straight, all right?"

"Right."

"And if somebody bops him with a sign or spits on him or something, try to interview whoever did it. Find out who he is, what organization he represents, why he did it, that sort of thing."

"The cops or the Secret Service will get to him first."

"Well, do the best you can. If there's a demonstration or chanting or anything, record it and bring it in."

"Right." Tim looked at his watch. "It's time to go. I want to look over the crowd before *Air Force One* gets here."

"Right. Good boy. And don't hang up after Lonnie takes you off the air. I want to talk to you."

When Tim opened the door, the station manager swatted him on the ass with his clipboard, like a football coach sending his team out of the locker room. Tim got into the red car with the station's call letters emblazoned on the side in shapes of lightning bolts. He was nervous, and hoped he wouldn't foul up the telephone report. He wished he hadn't told Callison and Hayes that he was in the press pool. If Jake was at the airport, he would never let Tim live it down.

MARTHA

Martha Babcock's hatred of the Kennedys had become the strongest emotion in her life. She hated them more than Earl Warren, who wanted niggers to go to white schools; more even than Martin Luther King, who wanted niggers to sit at the table with white people and eat with them. She didn't hate Caroline and John-John, since they were only children. But they would grow up to be like Jack and Jackie and Bobby, and if she still lived and America was still free when they grew up, she would hate them then. But America wouldn't be free by then. She dreamed sometimes of Communist firing squads lining American freedom fighters against a wall. She stood between Barry Goldwater and Bruce Alger, and when the Communists offered them blindfolds, they refused them.

Of the three Kennedys, she hated Jack the least. There was a boyish look about him that appealed to her. She didn't think he was the brains of the family, anyway. Bobby was the brains. He was so sneaky-looking. He had no charm to hide behind. His fancy Harvard accent sounded phony. But Jackie was the worst, redecorating the White House and showing it on TV, as if the White House had been nothing before she moved into it. Acting like a queen showing off her palace. She hated Jackie's breathy little voice. She hated old Rose and Joe, too, and their yacht, the *Honey Fitz*, and their fancy family compound on Cape Cod. Boston Irish masquerading as royalty. Maybe all the money she gave to her organizations and all the meetings she attended wouldn't bring them down, but if the Communists took over the country, Martha wouldn't be to blame. She hated them all.

This morning she hated Quentin, too. What right did he have to try to keep her in the house? What right did he have to tell Robert she couldn't use her own car?

"But, Miss Martha," Robert was saying, "I can't drive you. I have to see that Mr. Quentin's car gets here from the shop."

They were in the garage. Robert was standing between Martha and the lilac Cadillac, as if guarding it. Martha hated the odors of oil and rubber in the garage. It was demeaning, arguing with a servant. "I don't want you to drive me," she said. "I want the keys."

"Mr. Quentin said you should call him if you wanted to go somewhere," Robert said.

"Mr. Quentin can go to hell," Martha said.

Robert seemed shocked, and Martha regretted the words. Not that she minded shocking Robert, but she and Quentin took pains to keep their feelings private from the servants. "I want the keys," she said again, holding out her gloved hand.

Robert took the keys from his pocket and gave them to her. "Mr. Quentin's going to be mighty mad," he said.

Robert held the car door open for her, and she got in and started the engine. He opened the garage door, and she backed the car out and turned it quickly down the driveway. When she stopped at the exit to the street and looked in the mirror, Robert was standing by the open garage door, staring after her. Quentin would be angry, but she didn't care. She really hated him today.

Maybe it had begun when he stopped praising the way she dressed for parties. Or maybe it was when he stopped telling her stories at the dinner table about things that happened at the bank. But it was the hurt of his wanting a separate bedroom that made her admit what it was. There were many couples of their age in Highland Park who no longer slept together. She had been to enough bathrooms in enough houses to know that, and had discussed it with enough wives over enough luncheons. But the wives always claimed separate bedrooms were their idea, that they got tired of randy old men with liquor on their breath pawing them when they wanted to sleep. She believed them. She wouldn't want their husbands pawing her, either. But Quentin had insisted on keeping the room that had been theirs and moving her to another. Theirs was a masculine room, he said, and she could decorate the new one any way she wanted. She knew she hated him then. It was *her* money that had bought the house, after all. It was *her* family that had shone in Dallas society for three generations before she married an awkward country boy without a penny to his name and made him something. She had felt like a divorced woman until she met Bruce Alger at a party, and he recruited her as a volunteer for his congressional campaign.

The car ahead was a Volkswagen with a faded "JFK and LBJ" bumper sticker on the back. She pulled around it, leaning on her horn, then swerved back into its lane to make sure its driver could see her own sticker. In her mirror, the young man made an obscene gesture, and she honked again.

Quentin was a political coward. He liked to live in his smoke-filled rooms and be invisible. She remembered with pleasure how angry he had been after the incident with the Johnsons at the Adolphus. "You could have been arrested!" he said. And she just laughed and said, "You should have seen Lady Bird. I thought she was going to croak." And Quentin picked up his scotch and his newspaper and went to his bedroom and didn't come out all night. Well, he couldn't keep her muzzled. If something was going to happen today, she wanted to be part of it.

She hated the odor of Quentin's cigar in her Cadillac. She felt as if she had been invaded somehow, that Quentin had taken something of hers and made it his own, as he had the room. And trying to keep the keys from her. It was unforgivable.

When she pulled into the parking lot and the attendant opened her door for her, she noticed the lot was crowded. "Are there a lot of people downtown today?" she asked.

"Yes, ma'am," the attendant said. "Looks like there's going to be a big crowd."

She would browse at Neiman's, then grab a bite at the Zodiac and stroll toward the Adolphus. If her group was to gather, it would be there, or across Commerce Street at the Baker. She guessed it would be the Adolphus. One of its entrances was on Main Street. It bothered her that no one had called to inform her of the plans. Some of the younger women didn't take their responsibilities seriously enough.

She pushed through the doors with the golden "N-M" on the glass and walked briskly toward Cosmetics, ignoring the clerks who smiled and nodded as she passed. She loved the heady mixture of aromas in Cosmetics, and always began her tours there. A brown-haired woman stepped from behind a glass case and said, "Good morning, Mrs. Babcock. May I help you?" She wasn't one of the old familiar clerks, nor was she one of the young girls, either. Martha squinted, trying to place her. "I'm Liz Callison," the woman said. "I've waited on you before."

"Ah," Martha said. "Your memory is better than mine, young lady."

"What may I do for you? the woman asked.

"I need some perfume," Martha said. "I need some Joy."

R. QUENTIN

Quentin took the elevator to the lobby and almost bumped into J. L. Fisher when he got off. Jesus, why was the old fart downtown, today of all days? "J.L.!" he cried. "Were you coming to see me?"

"No, no, I came down to check the office." Fisher pointed upward. The offices of Fisher Oil occupied the top floors of the building, just above Quentin's own. Fisher was dressed in run-down boots, a sweaty rag of a hat, and faded jeans and denim jacket. A raincoat with a smear of mud on it was draped over his arm. They pumped each other's hand and laughed for no reason. The old man shifted his weight and winced.

"You all right, J.L.?" Quentin asked.

"Sure, sure. Just creaky in the joints, I guess. Where you headed, Quent?"

Quentin leaned close to the old man's face and lapsed into his west Texas twang. "Well, I'm moseying over to Republic," he said.

"What the hell's going on?" Fisher asked. "I just saw four hearses over there."

Quentin laughed. "They was limousines, J.L. We've got a little reception committee forming up over there."

Fisher looked alarmed. "Not for that Kennedy crowd, I hope!"

"Oh, nosiree!" Quentin said. "Governor Connally's flying in, and a bunch of the boys is driving out to meet him."

"John's coming to town, too, is he?"

"Yeah. I guess he wants to show them Kennedys whose range they'll be riding today."

The old man laughed. "Well, that's good. You be back later, Quent?"

"Yessir. Later this afternoon." Quentin wondered if J.L. was aware of the luncheon.

"I thought we'd get together for a little drink," Fisher said.

"You got Miss Anna's permission?" Quentin asked, and they laughed. "You just give me a holler and I'll come running. Whenever you get thirsty."

"Good, good."

Quentin shook Fisher's hand again and pulled away, pretending to be in a hurry. Rotten luck. What the hell was Fisher doing? He hadn't been downtown in months. If he found out Quentin was on Kennedy's reception committee, there would be hell to pay. Fisher didn't understand civic duty. Quentin would have to make up something, some story, before he went up for that drink. If the old man even remembered the invitation. There was a good chance he wouldn't.

Republic National Bank was one of the towers that overshadowed Quentin's on the Dallas skyline. The building had been written up and photographed by *Life* when it opened. The magazine had carried on about Texas money and Republic's gold-leaf decor. Quentin thought the whole thing was in bad taste. The building's steel-gray exterior, covered with some kind of impressionistic stars, was cold and ugly, and the neon star, or whatever it was, on top looked like an erect prick trying to fuck the sky. What had Bob Hope called it? A unicorn wrapped for mailing? Now Republic was building an office tower, a twin of the bank, next door. It would give the bank a mammoth presence downtown, but what the hell. Republic was the biggest bank in Texas. Let it put on the dog.

The black limousines were drawn up before the main entrance to the bank, and several men dressed in dark suits, some wearing white five-gallon hats, stood on the sidewalk talking. Quentin knew them all, of course, and they greeted him heartily. The U.S. attorney, Barefoot Sanders, was the first to shake his hand.

"How you doing, Barefoot?" Quentin asked.

"I'm looking for the Democrats," Barefoot said. "Are we going to meet Kennedy or Nixon?"

"Why, Kennedy," one of the other men said. "Nixon's probably leaving about now."

"Leaving?" Barefoot said. "You mean he was in town?"

"Yep. For the sody-pop convention. He's a lawyer for Coke or Pepsi or somebody now."

"Is that what Republicans do between election years?" Barefoot asked. "Sell cold drinks?"

The men laughed. "Well, don't put Nixon down," one of them said. "He'll get another run."

"Not if Goldwater has anything to say about it!" another replied.

Barefoot winked at Quentin. "I don't know how *I* got on this committee," he said. "I mean, I actually *voted* for Kennedy."

"That's why," Quentin said. "We drew straws between you, a nigger, a meskin, and a labor leader, and you won."

The Twelfth Hour

LIZ

LIZ AND JAKE ARRIVED at the Blue Front at the same time from opposite directions. "Well, at least you're on time," she said. Since nearly everyone in downtown Dallas lunched at noon, the place was almost empty. A waitress named Louise showed them to a table.

"You're early today, Jake," Louise said.

"Yeah," Jake said. He didn't look at the menu Louise set before him. "I'll have the usual."

"I'll have the same," Liz said. Louise picked up the menus and moved away. "What's the usual?" Liz asked.

"Polish and sauerkraut," Jake said. "And a Heineken's"

"I could do without the beer," Liz said. "So could you. You drink too much."

"Well, it's not your problem anymore, is it?"

Louise returned with two frosted glasses and the green bottles of Heineken's. Jake lit a cigarette and poured his beer. His face was drawn and grayish. He looked like he had lost weight. His suit was a mess. His shirt was dingy around the collar. "You look like hell," Liz said.

"That's not your problem, either." Jake raised his glass in a salute. "What *is* your problem, Liz?"

"I told you. I don't have enough money to pay the bills."

"Neither do I. You know what they pay me over at the snake pit. You're getting nearly all of it."

"*James* is getting it," Liz said.

"Okay, James is getting it. But you live there, too. I'm not keeping anything from you. What am I supposed to do?"

"I don't know. Could you borrow?"

"No. Banks and credit unions like to be paid back, and I couldn't do that. I don't even have any collateral. You're getting all there is, Liz."

Louise brought the Polish and sauerkraut. Its spicy aroma knotted Liz's stomach. She picked listlessly at the kraut, then set down her fork. Jake was eating like a starving man. "Your chippy isn't taking very good care of you," she said.

"Knock it off, Liz." Jake chewed a huge bite of Polish and made a gulping sound when he swallowed. "When are you going to file?"

"I don't know." Liz pushed her plate to the center of the table. "It's hard, ending something that you've been used to for eight years."

"Well, when you file, we'll have to make some kind of official financial arrangement. I can't live forever on seventy-five a week, and no judge will make me. The damn lawyers will have to be paid, too."

They had had the conversation before. Liz didn't know what she had expected. He was telling the truth, and she panicked every time she heard it.

"We'll have to sell the house, Liz. We have to face that."

Liz didn't want to face it. "Is she pretty?" she asked.

"Who?"

"Sherry."

"Yes."

Liz wished he hadn't answered so directly, so simply. She wished she didn't ask such things. It was like licking a sore in her mouth. It hurt, but it somehow felt good, too, and she couldn't stop. "Is she young?"

"Yes! Cut it out, damn it. She has nothing to do with us.

She wasn't in the picture before you kicked me out. You know that."

"There were plenty of others, though, weren't there?"

Jake wolfed the last bite of Polish and laid his fork on the plate. Louise saw him and came over. "Another beer, Jake?"

"Yes. How about you, Liz?"

"No, thanks."

When Louise went away, Liz said, "You drink too much, Jake. And you eat too fast. Something bad's going to happen to you. An ulcer or something."

Jake smiled. He looked like hell. "Not your problem, is it?"

"Well, James would like to keep his father, even if he's a rotten one."

"Imagine that. Dumb kid."

"There's no need to be sarcastic, Jake."

"Well, stop using James against me. Every time you pick at one of my faults or my *terrible* habits, you manage to throw James in, one way or another."

"He's the one person who might be able to influence you," Liz said. "He's the one person that you might think of sometimes."

"I *do* think of him. I think of him all the time." He pointed at Liz's plate and raised his eyebrows.

"Go ahead," she said.

Jake pulled the plate to him and attacked it as ferociously as he had the first. Liz watched in silence. She wanted to change the tone, the mood, of the conversation. "What are you going to do with him tomorrow?" she asked.

"Who?"

"James."

"I don't know. Maybe I'll take him to the zoo."

"You took him to the zoo last week. And two weeks before that."

"James likes the zoo."

"But don't you think he'd like to do something else sometimes?"

Jake stopped eating and glowered at her. "Like what, Liz? I can't take him to the dump where I'm living. It's depressing as hell, and he could catch something terminal just walking across the floor. You don't want me to take him to Sherry's place, and I agree—that wouldn't be good. You don't even want me to take him over to Byron and Jean's—"

"I can't stand the thought of all of you sitting around and talking about our mess," Liz said.

"Well, everything else costs money, which I haven't got. That leaves the fucking zoo."

"Okay, okay! I don't want to fight."

"What *do* you want, Liz? You know I can't give you any more money. Why did you call me?"

"I don't know. Maybe I just wanted to hear that— *woman's* voice. Maybe I wanted to find out how you're doing. Maybe I wanted to talk about something besides peanut butter and tennis shoes and lipstick and perfume and pancake makeup. I miss you sometimes, you know, even if you *are* a bastard."

"Withdrawal pains. You'll find somebody else before long." Jake glanced around the restaurant. The tables were full now, and a group was waiting at the door. "Either we order another beer, or Louise drives us out."

"I can't. I've got to get back to the store."

"Stick around. We'll watch the motorcade."

"I can't. I'm late already." She fumbled with her purse.

"Forget it," Jake said. "It's on me."

"But I said I'd pay."

"Forget it. I'll take it out of my recreation budget."

They stood up, and Louise noticed them and brought the check. "Are you going to see the president, Jake?" she asked.

"Maybe. If the crowd's not too big around the courthouse."

"I wish I could see him," Louise said. "I've never seen a president."

Liz and Jake squeezed through the crowd at the door and

paused on the sidewalk while Jake lit another cigarette. The last of the overcast had disappeared and the day suddenly was bright.

"Well, take it easy," Liz said.

"Tell James I'll pick him up around ten tomorrow," Jake said.

They waved and separated. Liz walked the block to Main Street and turned toward Neiman-Marcus. The crowd was heavy all along Main. A lot of people were skipping lunch.

THOMAS J.

Thomas J. leaned across the seat and opened the glove compartment and took out the pint of Early Times. His hand shook when he lifted the bottle to his lips, and that bothered him. He wasn't halfway through the day yet, and already he was full of stress and problems. He had hoped for peace of mind today, for the calm that he admired so much in Dr. King. Maybe Dr. King needed a belt of bourbon, too, before he stepped into the street, but Thomas J. didn't think so. Dr. King possessed the peace that passeth understanding. Thomas J. planned to use that thought when he buried Sister Emma. He always used it at funerals, for it was the simplest and truest definition of death that he knew. Death was a kind of peace, the absence of the weariness and stress that he felt now. Your hand didn't shake when you were dead. You didn't have to deal with Regis Watson when you were dead, or worry about where to get seven hundred and fifty dollars to put an old woman in the ground. Maybe Dr. King didn't have to worry about little things like that. Maybe he just worried about big things, and maybe big things were easier to worry about than little things like graves and caskets and Regis Watson.

The bourbon warmed Thomas J.'s throat and belly, and he took another belt before he returned the bottle to the glove compartment. He got out of the car and opened the trunk. The signs lay in a jumble, some of them dirty and dog-eared from use on the sidewalks and sliding against each other in the trunk. There were too many for Thomas J. to carry across the parking lot by himself, and maybe no one else would want to hold one, anyway. He chose one that said, DALLAS NEGROES WANT THEIR RIGHTS, and another that said, OUR RIGHTS, RIGHT NOW, and slammed the trunk lid. He lifted the signs to his shoulder and walked slowly toward the terminal building. The lot was crowded with cars, and, between the noises of planes landing and taking off, he heard the murmur of people and felt himself tensing again. A large crowd would mean the hostiles were out in force, and Thomas J.'s first glimpse of the throng along the chain-link fence confirmed his fear. Someone was waving a Confederate flag high above the heads of the people, beside a sign that said, YANKEE GO HOME AND TAKE YOUR EQUALS WITH YOU. A signboard atop a Volkswagen parked at the edge of the crowd read: MR. PRESIDENT, BECAUSE OF YOUR SOCIALIST TENDENCIES AND BECAUSE OF YOUR SURRENDER TO COMMUNISM, I HOLD YOU IN COMPLETE CONTEMPT.

"Hey, nigger!" The high-pitched voice came from behind Thomas J., and he didn't turn to acknowledge it. "Ain't you at the wrong airport? This is a white man that's coming in here!"

"No, it ain't," a lower voice replied. "It's a white nigger coming in!"

"Hey, nigger! Is that right?"

Thomas J. knew if he turned and looked at the taunters, he would be in trouble. He stood motionless, studying the signs, scanning the crowd for an ally.

HELP KENNEDY STAMP OUT DEMOCRACY
IN 1964 GOLDWATER AND FREEDOM

LET'S BARRY KING JOHN
YOUR A TRAITER
CAN THE CLAN
HOORAY FOR JFK

His eyes paused at this last crudely lettered square of cardboard, held aloft by two small black hands. He eased through the crowd toward the sign and laid his hand on the boy's shoulder. The boy turned. He was about eleven or twelve years old. "Morning, brother," Thomas J. said. "Mind if I join you?"

"Sure don't," the boy said.

"Do I know you?"

"Don't think so."

"I'm Reverend Durant."

"Hi."

"You come here by yourself?"

"My folks are here somewhere."

"I'll stay with you till they come back. Some of these folks aren't too friendly."

"Okay."

It was an odd crowd. Gangs of teen-agers wearing high-school letter jackets laughed and whooped and shouted jokes about niggers and commies. Here and there, gray-haired, tight-lipped men stood alone, gazing toward the runway. These, Thomas J. thought, were wishing they had the nerve to wear hoods and robes. A few couples, obviously married, stood silently, staring, too, trying to ignore the hubbub around them. They were Dallas liberals who had come to prove to the president, and perhaps to themselves, that they existed. A husband or wife would turn to whisper something, then look over a shoulder first, to see who might hear. Thomas J. knew how they felt. Like members of an underground. Like spies who would be interrogated and shot if they were discovered. Thomas J. saw a few that he knew, some who had contributed money to the Dallas County

United Poll Tax Committee. He fought the impulse to join them, or at least wave. That would make things worse for everybody. They might even pretend they didn't know him and find an excuse to walk away. It was better to let them pretend he wasn't there, or that they weren't.

But a young white man standing alone smiled when he saw Thomas J., and made his way through the crowd toward him. He was pudgy, soft-looking, wearing thick glasses that made his brown eyes seem larger than they were. He reached Thomas J. and the boy and held out his hand. "Hello, Brother Durant," he said.

Thomas J. didn't like white people who called him brother. There was something too easy about it, something too nice. White people who called him brother felt guilty. They hoped that calling him brother would take away the guilt. Or maybe calling him brother made white people feel righteous. Whatever their reason, Thomas J. didn't like them. "Hello," he said.

The way he said it made the young man uncomfortable. He blushed and squinted through the thick glasses. "You probably don't remember me," he said. "I've been to a few of your meetings. With a group from Perkins School of Theology. I'm Dennis Pointer."

"I remember," Thomas J. lied. "Is your group here?"

"No. I'm the only one who could make it." Pointer laughed, embarrassed. "Would you like me to take one of your signs?"

"If you want to." Thomas J. handed him the sign that said, OUR RIGHTS, RIGHT NOW, and lifted his own sign aloft.

A group of kids hissed. "Black and white niggers together," one of them said. Dennis Pointer ignored them. He knew something, at least. Pointer noticed the boy standing beside Thomas J. and said, "Is this your son, Brother Durant?"

"No. I don't know his name."

"Sammy," the boy said.

"Pleased to meet you," Pointer said.

"You talk funny," Sammy said.

Pointer laughed. "I'm a Yankee. From President Kennedy's hometown."

"So that's why you're out here," Thomas J. said.

Pointer gave him a hard look. "Not the only reason. I'm glad to hold your sign."

An awkward silence developed between them, and Thomas J. was sorry. The man was probably sincere. There was no reason to get smart with him. Pointer must have felt the awkwardness, too. "Did you ever see so many cops?" he said, scanning the roof of the terminal.

"Maybe they've finally learned something." Thomas J. said.

A murmur moved through the crowd, and Thomas J. felt himself being pushed toward the chain-link fence. He noticed a line of black limousines that had arrived noiselessly and stopped beyond the fence. The chauffeurs were opening the passenger doors, and dark-suited, white-hatted men were climbing out.

"Who are they?" Pointer asked.

Thomas J. stood on tiptoe, trying to make out the faces under the shade of the hatbrims. "Nine Republicans," he said. "Two Dixiecrats . . . and Barefoot Sanders." He lowered himself, laughing. "I wonder how old Barefoot got into that crowd. He's a liberal."

Pointer laughed, too. "Well, they *are* welcoming Kennedy."

"No, they aren't," Thomas J. said. "They're welcoming Connally."

"Who's that?" Sammy asked.

"The governor of Texas," Thomas J. said, "and no friend of yours."

The men in the dark suits huddled near their limousines, talking among themselves, ignoring the crowd beyond the fence, checking their watches, looking into the bright sky. Soon there was the roar of jet engines on the runway, then the whine of a huge plane taxiing toward the crowd.

"That's him!" Sammy cried.

"No, that's Lyndon Johnson," Thomas J. said.

An airport crew rolled a ramp to the plane. The door opened, and the vice president, tall and massive even from a distance, stepped onto the top step with his wife on his arm and waved. The crowd raised a polite cheer and a few boos, and the Johnsons stepped quickly down the stairs and shook hands with the men from the limousines. Then *Air Force One* whined into view and the volume of the cheers and boos increased. While another ramp was pushed into place, Lyndon and Lady Bird and the men from the limousines arranged themselves into a reception line. The door of *Air Force One* swung open then, and John and Nellie Connally loped down the stairs, smiling and waving. Dennis Pointer leaned to Thomas J. and shouted into his ear. "Shouldn't the president have come out first?"

"Not in Dallas," Thomas J. said.

MARY ELLEN

She was peeved at herself for running out of baby food. Albert didn't even have a teething cookie to gnaw on, and he was getting cranky. There was nothing left but to go to the store, and that meant loading the stroller and Albert into the station wagon. It was a lot of trouble for such a small chore, but at least the day had turned nice.

Mary Ellen returned to the house and picked up the child and slammed the door before Buster could dash through. "We beat him!" she said, and that pleased her, for whenever she didn't beat Buster through the door, he galloped down the street after the station wagon, and Mary Ellen had to stop and take him into the car before they reached the heavy traffic of Illinois Avenue. The dog would lick Albert then, and Albert would holler.

Mary Ellen strapped Albert into his kiddy seat and backed the wagon out of the carport and drove the two blocks to her mother's house and turned into the driveway. Her mother was sweeping dead grass and leaves off her sidewalk, so Mary Ellen didn't have to get out. She rolled down her window, and her mother waddled up, smiling. She stretched her fat arm through the window, and Albert grabbed her finger. "How's my baby?" she said.

"Cross as a bear," Mary Ellen said. "I don't have a thing in the house for him to eat. You want to go to the store with me?"

"No, I'm going to watch the Kennedys on TV. Didn't you want to see that?"

"Yes. I'll be back in time."

"Well, I don't want to miss it. I'll stay here."

"You want me to bring you something back?" Mary Ellen asked.

"I can't think of anything. Why don't you come on here when you're through? You and me can have a sandwich and watch together. I'll feed the youngun for you."

"All right. I'll get some lunch meat. And some Cokes."

"That'll be fine. Why don't you leave little Albert here with me? Maybe you can get done faster."

Mary Ellen unbuckled Albert from the kiddy seat and lifted him through the window. "Go to granny," she said.

"Upsy-daisy!" her mother said, pretending she was going to toss Albert into the air. He let out a yell.

"I told you he was cross," Mary Ellen said.

"That's all right. Everything's going to be all right, Albert." The old woman hugged the child to her large, soft bosom and patted his back. "Is Bullard working this shift?"

"Yeah. Everybody is, I reckon."

"He'll probably get to see them, then."

"Maybe. It depends on what they've got him doing."

"I sure hope there's no trouble."

"Surely there won't be," Mary Ellen said. "Not today."

"I just pray you're right."

"Well, I'll be right back."

When Mary Ellen turned into the street, she smiled and waved. Her mother lifted Albert's arm and waved it for him.

SHEILA

Sheila went in the back door, as usual, and stood for a moment, letting her eyes adjust to the darkness. She didn't need to see. Every detail of the place was stamped in her mind as indelibly as the house where she grew up. Even blind, she would have known it was Babe's joint. The air would have told her. No telling how long ago the last whiff of fresh air had come into the big, windowless room. The air in Babe's had been breathed and rebreathed so many times that Sheila imagined there was no oxygen left in it.

"Hi, hon," Babe said. He was sitting at the bar, as usual, with the newspaper spread out before him, peering at her over the dark rims of his reading glasses. The cigar in his hand was still long, which meant he hadn't been up long, either. "How about some coffee?" he said.

"Sure," Sheila said. Babe made no move to leave his stool and get it, so she walked behind the bar and poured her own from the glass pot on the hot plate. She carried the coffee around to Babe's side and settled onto the stool next to him. "How do you read in the dark?" she asked.

Babe licked a thumb and turned a page of the newspaper. "How'd it go?"

"You get right down to business, don't you?"

"Always. Business before pleasure. That's good advice. Where is it?"

Sheila stuck out her tongue at him. Babe ignored her, so she opened her purse and took out the fifty-dollar bill that Barnhill had given her for the extra fuck, then put it back. Exact change might make him ask questions. She took out the hundred and handed it to Babe. He looked at it, then pulled a big roll of bills from his pocket and gave her a fifty back.

"A fifty-percent commission is unfair," she said. "I do all the work."

"You do, huh? You know how long it took me to loosen up that son of a bitch? It ain't as easy as you think."

"Well, it isn't worth fifty. I could get my own guys without any trouble."

"Sure. And wind up with bruises all over, like Mavis. The guy noticed that bruise. That's why he picked you. You get any bruises from him?"

"No, he just put it in and passed out," Sheila said. "A real limp-dick."

"See there? A real easy fifty, right? If you'd picked him up on your own, you would have got a couple of bruises, like Mavis. You would have looked like shit on the stage."

"Mavis likes to fall in love. That's her problem."

"Yeah, and in a couple of years she's going to be putting out on street corners. You wait and see." Babe relit his cigar and waved out the match. "I'm thinking of firing her," he said.

"Fire Mavis? Oh, don't do that, Babe."

"She's getting to be a problem. She won't listen to me. This is a business, you know. I can't put up with them damn bruises."

"Let me talk to her," Sheila said. "Girl-to-girl."

"Go ahead," Babe said. "Put a scare in her, okay?"

"Yeah."

"I ain't going to take it much longer. I mean it."

"I'll tell her." Sheila wanted to mention her gold bracelet, but decided not to. He would tell her to kiss it bye-bye. She drank the last of her coffee and set the cup on the bar. "Well, she said, "I'm going. Nice doing business with you."

"Don't be late for the first show," Babe said. "We ought to have a good crowd today."

"Have I ever been late?"

"No. Just don't start today."

Sheila slid off the stool and picked up her purse. "You're like an old grouchy daddy," she said.

"That's exactly what I am," Babe said, "and don't you forget it."

Sheila kissed him on the cheek. "Can I get out the front?"

"Go ahead. I'll lock it behind you."

Sheila stepped into the sunlight and turned down the block toward the Plaza, then paused at the entrance of a liquor store, then went in. The phone book was hanging by a chain from the side of the phone. She lifted it and looked up the number and dropped a nickel into the slot and dialed.

"Adolphus Hotel."

"Mr. Barnhill's room, please."

"One moment."

Sheila was relieved to hear the buzz. Barnhill hadn't checked out.

"Mr. Barnhill doesn't answer."

"May I leave a message?"

"Certainly. What is the message?"

"My name is Thelma Ruth Green. Please tell Mr. Barnhill to leave my property at the front desk. I'll pick it up."

"Property?"

"Yes. He knows what it is."

"All right. I'll leave him the message."

"Thank you." Sheila hung up. She hoped Barnhill had found the bracelet before the maid stole it. She hoped he would want to return it.

On her way to the Plaza, she noticed there were more people on the street than usual, and remembered why Barnhill was in Dallas. At the corner, waiting for the light to change, she considered turning toward Main and finding a spot to watch the motorcade, then dropped the idea. Her first show was at two o'clock, and she didn't want to be tired.

T I M

"Our man Tim Higgins is standing by at Love Field to tell you about the arrival of *Numero Uno*, the president of the United States himself, and his lovely lady, Jacqueline! Yes, they're right here in Big D, friends and neighbors, and old Tim, as always, is on the spot! Tim, tell us what the heck's going on out there!"

"Well, Lonnie, the weatherman cooperated just beautifully! The rain has stopped, the sun has come out, the sky is a bright Texas blue, the crowd is large and in a truly festive mood! As the president and the first lady stepped out of *Air Force One*, a big cheer went up! They came down the steps smiling and waving! On the ground, they were greeted by Vice President and Mrs. Johnson, and the mayor's wife presented Mrs. Kennedy with a bouquet of red roses, which, I might add, looked just smashing with the pink suit she's wearing today! They were just beautiful, Lonnie! What can I say? Bert Parks should have been out here singing! It was that gorgeous!"

"Tell me about the crowd, Tim! It was friendly, I gather!"

"Oh, absolutely! Very, very enthusiastic! And the president seemed very pleased with his reception! He and the first lady walked along the cyclone fence here at Love Field for about fifty yards, smiling and waving and shaking hands with the people! I don't think they wanted to leave, Lonnie! I really don't! I think they would have stayed out here all day if an aide hadn't reminded Mr. Kennedy of that big blue convertible waiting! It was just great! What can I say?"

"Well, that's just great, Tim! Tell me! Some people were worried that the president wouldn't be well received in Dallas! Did you see any protestors or pickets out there, Tim?"

"Well, Lonnie, there *were* a few signs expressing disagreement with some of the president's policies! But I would say there were no more of them out here at Love Field than there would be in any other major city! This is America, after all, and every citizen has the right to express his views! But the president is the president of *all* the people, Lonnie, and I think this crowd out here was saying that's fine with them! The president is the president, and political differences are put aside when he comes to town, no matter who he is!"

"Well put, Tim! So what's happening out there now?"

"Well, the presidential motorcade has just left the airport to make its way downtown! Listeners who live or work in the vicinity of Lemmon Avenue or Turtle Creek Boulevard or Cedar Springs Road might want to run out and take a look! The president and Mrs. Kennedy are headed that way right now! And, of course, the *big* crowd will be along Main Street, I guess!"

"Right you are, Tim! Thank you very much! That was our man and yours, Tim Higgins, reporting from Love Field, where President John F. Kennedy and his lovely lady have just arrived on the latest stop of their whirlwind tour of Texas!"

Tim was off the air now. He listened while Lonnie set up a record, then returned to the phone. "Hold on, Tim," Lonnie said. "The boss wants to talk to you."

Tim waited so long he thought he had been forgotten. He was about to hang up when he heard the station manager's voice. "That was good, Tim. Just fine."

"Thanks, chief."

"How bad were those signs?"

"The usual stuff about niggers and commies."

"Nothing organized? No incidents?"

"No. It was about as I described it."

"Good."

The station manager said nothing else, and Tim thought he might have hung up, but he hadn't heard the click. Finally he said, "Is there anything else, chief?"

"No, you can come in now."

"You mind if I get some breakfast first? I haven't had a bite."

"Go ahead. No hurry."

The crowd was streaming through the terminal now, heading toward the parking lot. Tim wove his way among the people. He hoped the restaurant wouldn't be crowded. He was famished.

BETTY LOU

Even the ad manager at the paper claimed he didn't know who Bernard Weissman was. The ad had been cleared with the publisher himself, he said, and Mr. Weissman had paid for it in cash and left. He assumed that the man who paid for it was Mr. Weissman. He didn't handle the transaction himself, he said. He never saw Mr. Weissman at all. Why was everybody in such an uproar about the ad? he wanted to know. It said nothing that the paper's editorial page hadn't said many times before. Yes, he knew of the effort to make the president's day in Dallas a cordial one, but he didn't believe in suspending the First Amendment for Mr. Kennedy's sake. Had Miss Carpenter read the newspaper's editorial page this morning? The editorial welcoming Mr. Kennedy was, he thought, gracious. The paper, he said, had bent over backward to be cooperative, but it wouldn't censor a citizen who wanted to use its pages to petition for redress of grievances. That's what the publisher had said, and the ad manager agreed. Surely Miss Carpenter could understand their position.

Betty Lou had been chain-smoking all morning and had lost count of the cups of coffee. She felt saturated with nicotine and caffeine. She was jumpy. Maybe she was taking the damn ad too seriously. But she had wanted everything to be perfect today, and it wasn't. Even if everyone in Dallas was as nice as pie, those damn White House reporters would take that ad back to Washington and make something out of it. Some fucking columnist would be scrounging around for a topic one day and find that ad in his files and write another fucking "think piece" on fascism in Dallas, and the others would jump on the bandwagon, and all her work for two months would be for nothing. If Bernard Weissman or some other idiot spit on somebody or scuffled with somebody or shouted an obscenity within earshot of the press pool car, it would happen even sooner. Tomorrow the eastern papers would describe Kennedy moving through Texas as triumphantly as a Roman emperor. An outpouring of affection unmarred except by, of course, Dallas, which marches to its own strange drummer, they would say. The city would be picked apart like a frog in a zoology lab, and those who had hired Betty Lou would ask what the hell she had done to earn the money.

Her secretary opened the door and smiled the sweet smile that Betty Lou had begun to hate today. "More coffee?" she chirped.

"God, no!" Betty Lou said.

"Cheer up! Everything's going fine!"

"Says who?"

"The radio. The motorcade has left Love Field now, and the radio says they got a terrific welcome."

"Yeah?"

"Yeah. Come look out the window. You'll feel better."

In the worry of the morning, Betty Lou had forgotten the motorcade would pass her building. The secretary touched her arm as if to help her from her chair. Betty Lou pulled away. "I'm not crippled," she said.

"Well, come look."

Betty Lou went out to the reception area. The receptionist and several secretaries were standing at the windows, looking down into the street. When she appeared, they backed away, making tentative moves toward their desks. "It's okay," Betty Lou said. "You can watch." They moved back to the windows, but crowded closer, leaving one window clear for Betty Lou.

The windows were sealed, so she couldn't lean out and look at the sidewalk in front of her own building, but the sidewalk across Main Street was jammed with people, and not many were walking. They were jockeying for position on the sidewalk, crowding as close as possible toward the curb, seeking a clear view of the street. A cop stood with his arms and legs spread, apparently cajoling the crowd to stay on the sidewalk. Another cop stood in the center of the intersection down the block, whistling the Main Street traffic onto the side streets. The suits and dresses of the people told Betty Lou that most of them were office workers, although some of the women clutched shopping bags. She looked at her watch. It was exactly noon. The people in the street below were skipping lunch. "Would you girls like to go downstairs?" she asked.

"Oh, yes!" the receptionist said.

"Go ahead, then."

As they rushed to their desks to grab their purses, Betty Lou told her secretary, "Bring me a cheeseburger without onions and a Coke."

The girl looked disappointed.

"You've got time. If you hurry."

The girls rushed for the elevators in the hall, and Betty Lou was alone. She pulled the receptionist's chair to the window and settled down to study the crowd. All the faces visible from her window looked happy, and she saw no signs of any kind.

LUTHER

When the clock chimed twelve, Colonel Byrd was in the bedroom, studying himself in the full-length mirror. He had decided against full dress, after all. It was too formal, too ceremonial. Kennedy might interpret it as a gesture of respect. Colonel Byrd was wearing his greens. The ribands on his chest were ample testimony to his years of service and valor, more easily understood than the medals themselves would have been at the distance from which Kennedy would look at him. From Turtle Creek Boulevard, full dress uniform might have been mistaken for some sort of lodge costume, at least by the press. But there was no mistaking army green.

Colonel Byrd put on his hat and snapped to attention and saluted. He was a fine-looking soldier. Any right-thinking country would be proud to be served by such a man. Any right-thinking soldier would have followed him, even to death. Many had. His forced retirement said something about the kind of country the United States was becoming. It said something about the commander in chief who had forced that retirement, too. But Kennedy wouldn't be commander in chief forever. Already the country was wising up to him. It was happening in Dallas, in California, in many places. The people were beginning to see the menace, were beginning to realize what was happening to the United States. They were becoming worried and frightened. They were listening to

Goldwater and Edwin Walker and H. L. Hunt's radio program, "Lifeline." They were beginning to listen to Colonel Luther Byrd, too.

Colonel Byrd picked up the band of black cloth lying on the bed and pinned it around his left arm above the elbow. He examined the effect in the mirror. The black was more visible against the green than it would have been against the full dress. He picked up the empty martini glass from the table beside the bed and switched off the bedroom light and went to the kitchen. He poured another martini from the shaker and dropped an olive into it and carried it to his chair in the living room. He picked up the WANTED FOR TREASON leaflet from the ottoman and studied it again. Maybe it was good that it was so badly printed. It had the look of the people about it, the feel of the grass roots. By now, his people should be distributing it along Main Street. He hoped they hadn't wasted them all yesterday. They could be fools sometimes.

He looked at the clock on the table below the framed Nazi flag. He ought to be on the balcony now. The motorcade would pass at any moment. He gulped the martini and set the glass on the ottoman and walked to the door. He opened the drapes and removed the steel pipe that blocked the track of the sliding glass door, then turned the lock and stepped out.

The sun was bright and warm. The bare trees along the boulevard were so vivid and still that Colonel Byrd could distinguish their individual twigs. He was pleased that only a few people stood on the dead grass along the street, looking expectantly in the direction from which the motorcade would come. A man pointed toward his balcony and booed. Two women joined in, but Colonel Byrd ignored them. He stepped to the balcony wall to inspect the flag, which was suspended from a staff extending at an angle from the wall. There was no breeze. The people in the street could see that the field of stars was at the bottom.

Colonel Byrd decided to stand at the end of the balcony

nearest the street, in profile to the people below. No sooner had he moved into position than he heard the roar of motorcycles. He snapped to attention and focused on a spot of pavement that he could see through the tops of the trees. The motorcycles and cars moved, one by one, through the spot, but the limbs of the trees obstructed his view. He couldn't tell whether anyone was looking up at him. In one of the cars was a splash of pink, bright in the sun. That, he assumed, was Jackie.

Small children stood on the curb, holding a sign that asked him to stop and shake their hands. "Let's stop," he said. As he stepped into the street, the children charged forward, shrieking, almost sweeping him off his feet. He laughed and shook their hands. The children's parents stood on the curb, smiling, taking pictures.

She watched from the car. The wool suit had been a mistake. They weren't halfway there, and already she was wilting. The sun was so bright.

He returned to the car, still laughing, waving at the children. She put on her sunglasses. "Please don't wear those," he said. "The people have come out to see you." She laid the glasses in her lap, but raised them again whenever there were no crowds.

The car moved under an underpass. Its shadow was cool. The sun made all the difference.

The Thirteenth Hour

JASON

MARK HAD CONDUCTED A TOUR of the insurance offices for
Jason and Stacy. Whenever he brought them near a desk in
the big room where everyone was working, the person at the
desk would stop what he was doing and stand up and shake
hands with Stacy, and Jason, too, as if he were grown. Mark
called them all by their first names, but they called him Mr.
Leary. He didn't work in the big room where they did. He
had an office of his own, with pictures of horses on the walls
and heavy drapes over the big window that looked out over
the room where everyone else worked. His desk was bigger
than the others, and he had no typewriter. He also had a secretary, who smiled and asked Jason how he liked Texas.

"Love it," he said.

"That's fine."

Then Mark took them to lunch at a cafeteria in the same
building, and the woman who brought the coffeepot around
to refill Mark's cup called him Mr. Leary, too.

"You're famous, dad," Jason said. Mark looked pleased.

But this was the best part of all. The sidewalk was jammed
with people. They were laughing and trying to get as close
as they could to the street. Some were holding small Amer-

ican flags, and a few waved Texas flags like those that Jason and Stacy and Mark held. "We would have a better view from the office window," Mark said.

"I'd rather be down here," Stacy said.

"Me too," Jason said.

Stacy squeezed Jason's hand. "Isn't it exciting?"

Mark led the way, inching closer to the curb. The people were packed more tightly against each other nearer the street, though, and the Learys were still three-deep from the curb when they had to stop.

"What a happy crowd!" Stacy said.

"Dallas isn't always what you think it is," Mark replied.

"I can't see," Jason said. "Lift me up."

"You're too big for that."

"Oh, come on, Mark," Stacy said. "For just a little while."

Mark squatted, and Jason jumped on him piggyback. Stacy put her hand under Jason's rump and boosted him to Mark's shoulders. "You weigh a ton," Mark said. "Don't move or I'll lose my balance."

Jason felt like a giant, towering over the heads of the people. He could see all the way down the block. The policeman standing in the street winked at him. "Hi, big fella," he said. "Let me borrow your flag."

"I need it," Jason said.

"What's your name?"

"Jason. What's yours?"

"Bull." Down the block, two boys stepped off the curb, and the policeman blew his whistle and moved toward them, waving them back.

"Dad, that policeman's name is Bull," Jason said.

"He said Bill."

"No, he said—dad! Here they come!" Two policemen on motorcycles had turned the corner into Main Street. A cheer went up and got louder as the motorcycles moved down the block. Jason didn't recognize any of the men in the white car leading the procession, but after it came three motorcycles, then a big blue convertible with flags on the front fenders. "I see them!" he shouted. "I see them, dad!"

"Stop bouncing! Do you want us to fall?"

The president's hair was reddish in the sunlight, and Jackie's pink dress and hat were very bright. "Yea, Kennedy! Yea, Kennedy!" Jason yelled. He waved the Texas flag.

"Jason, stop bouncing!"

"Yea, Jackie! Look at me!"

The president looked straight at Jason and smiled and waved. Jason didn't look at the other cars at all. He watched the big convertible move slowly down the block until he couldn't see it anymore, then Mark squatted and Jason got off his back. Stacy was beaming. "Well, you've seen the president," she said. "Let's try to beat the traffic out of here."

"He waved at me, mom! Did you see it?"

Mark kissed them and walked back into the building, and Stacy took Jason by the hand. "This is the most important thing I've ever done," he said.

J. L.

He got the can opener and a can of Wolf Brand chili from the stock that he kept in the deep drawer of his desk. He opened the can and poured the chili into the pan on the two-burner electric hot plate on the file cabinet. He opened the top drawer of the cabinet and got the Jim Beam bourbon bottle and a tumbler and set them on the desk beside his bowl and the box of Sunshine Saltines.

It was the meal that he and Buck Pool had eaten just before Buck fell from the derrick, and J.L. thought of it as a sacrament, like the Last Supper of Jesus. He never varied the elements of the meal, not even the brand names, and whenever he ate it his mind dwelt on the details of that day. He remembered the heat of the sun and the sand and the small fire over which he and Buck had warmed the chili, and the flies that swarmed around them while they ate. "Funny thing about flies," Buck had said. "No matter how far out in the desert you get, they find you as soon as you open the chili can." That was about an hour before Buck fell off the derrick, and it was the last thing J.L. remembered him saying.

Anna had forbidden the sacred meal years ago, after a visit to the doctor, but J.L. had continued it at the office. He preferred eating it here, anyway, among the old photographs of him and Buck standing and grinning with some rig or another in the background, in the privacy of his own thoughts. It was easier to relive the details of Buck's last day without Anna whining about his health and Jonathan looking at him as if he were a little boy who had messed his pants.

The chili was still on the burner when J.L. heard the cheering and rolled his chair away from the desk. A sharp pain shot through his hip, but he hobbled to the window. The long cars of the enemy were passing below him, past buildings with faded red-white-and-blue bunting draped at the windows, and the cheers rose like a wind from the street. He could distinguish no words through the glass, but the faces along the sidewalk looked friendly. "They've come after our horses, Buck," he said aloud. He started to turn away, then saw the spot of pink and the roses. The Kennedys themselves. As if by accident, he focused on the couple seated in front of the Kennedys in the big car. Only slowly did J.L. realize who they were. John and Nellie Connally. "Son of a bitch!" he said. He stared at the car until it passed out of view, then hobbled back to the desk. He picked up the phone and dialed Quent Babcock's number. "Is Quent in?" he asked the secretary.

"No, sir. He's not."

"Where the hell is he? This is J. L. Fisher."

"Yes, sir. He's at the Trade Mart, sir. At the luncheon."

"When's he coming back?"

"I don't know, sir."

"Well, when you see him, tell him to get his skinny ass up here. He's got some tall explaining to do."

"Yes, Mr. Fisher. I'll give him your message."

J.L. slammed the phone down and checked the chili. It was almost ready to bubble. He opened the Jim Beam and filled his glass to the brim.

WARNER

The Trade Mart resembled a prison in which a riot had erupted. Dallas and Texas police, wearing mirrored sunglasses and grim faces, seemed to surround the huge building, standing at parade rest, holding riot sticks ready. They reminded Warner of the Birmingham and Alabama troopers he had seen on TV during the summer, when the dogs and fire hoses were loosed against the Negro demonstrators. As he got out of the cab, two plainclothesmen charged into a group of white pickets who held aloft signs reading HAIL CAESAR and YANKEE GO HOME. After a brief, silent struggle, the plainclothesmen emerged, shoving ahead of them two young men whose hands were handcuffed behind their backs. Their mouths, and the mouths of the other demonstrators, were swathed with adhesive tape. Warner approached a Dallas officer who looked younger and friendlier than the others. "Why the tape?" he asked.

The officer's expression hardened. "You belong here?"

Warner showed his ticket.

"They say it's because they're being muzzled," the officer said.

"They told you that?"

"They wrote it on a piece of paper for a reporter. Dumb nuts. They've been here since seven o'clock this morning, just so they can get tossed in the jug."

"Well, two of them made it," Warner said.

"I hope they all get sunstroke," the officer said. "This ain't good. Somebody could wind up getting shot."

Beyond the doors, Warner found that he had entered a different world. The heat and noise and confusion outside dropped from his mind in the huge hall where layers of balconies rose to a glass roof high above and live trees grew around a clear pond and a fountain spurted almost to the skylight. A blur of yellow fluttered past his face. Other blurs of blue and green were flitting among the trees, above the white-clothed tables set for luncheon. Parakeets, flying free, as if in the wild. Men and women were already seating themselves. Waiters were already serving. Warner ventured uncertainly in the direction of the head table, wondering if he was supposed to sit in a particular place. A man at a table near the front rose and waved at him. Warner waved back, then recognized him as a member of the Dallas County legislative delegation. The man pointed to a chair next to him and motioned for Warner to join him. Warner lurched forward, smiling, his arm extended for the handshake. "Tom! How the hell you doing?"

The legislator caught his hand and pumped it vigorously, simultaneously grasping Warner's elbow with his left hand in the manner of Lyndon Johnson. "Sit with me," he muttered into Warner's ear. "I've hung myself up in a nest of Republicans, including a goddamn Bircher." He led Warner to the table and introduced him around. Warner nodded and shook hands, not bothering to remember the names. "Warner's a colleague of mine in the House. From San Antonio," Tom said.

"Well, we'll let him sit down anyway," one of the Republicans said. The others laughed.

"Nice of you to run interference for me, Tom," Warner said as he sat down. They laughed again. "Quite a place," he said. He scanned the rows of balconies. "What do they sell here?"

"Clothes," one of the Republicans said. "Women's clothes, mostly. This place is going to make Dallas one of the fashion centers of the world."

"Well, I'll remember not to tell my wife about it," Warner said, and they laughed.

"Oh, they won't sell to her, anyway. This place is just for store buyers. They have to mark it all up a few hundred percent before they pass it on to *our* checkbooks."

"Do these parakeets fly around in here all the time?" Warner asked.

"Not these particular ones," replied a dour man across from Tom. "These are special birds, trained to shit in Kennedy's soup."

The man didn't smile. The Republicans chuckled and glanced nervously at Warner and Tom. The dour man, Warner guessed, was the Bircher.

During the awkward silence that fell, Warner studied the head table. It was adorned with dozens of yellow roses. The presidential seal hung from the rostrum. Near it, a high-backed leather chair awaited Kennedy. Where would Yarborough sit? If he could catch the senator's eye during the luncheon and give him some signal, maybe he could win a handshake with the president. A photograph, even. State Representative Warner Barnhill shaking hands with President Kennedy would look great on his campaign literature.

"Where's Ralph going to sit?" he asked Tom.

"I've been wondering myself. I'm hoping he might invite me up and introduce me."

Warner laughed and slapped Tom on the back.

"Well, you're welcome to him," the dour man said. "And all the rest of his kind."

Anger rose in Warner's cheeks. "If you feel that way, why are you here?" he asked.

The man looked straight at him, unblinking. "To meet the enemy face-to-face," he said.

MARTHA

When Martha Babcock stepped from the cool of Neiman-Marcus onto the sunny sidewalk, the crowd almost overwhelmed her. Businessmen were dashing across the street against the red light and disappearing into the restaurants and office buildings. Teen-agers were running to and fro in packs. A Mexican mother leaned against a wall, trying to shush her infant. An older child clutched her skirt and also cried. Martha thought the motorcade must be nearing the block. Then she noticed that the people were moving in all directions. Some were heading toward the parking lots. She looked at her watch, then held it to her ear. It was running. Cars were moving into Main from the side streets. A policeman stood in the intersection, whistling and waving them by. She went up to a man who was standing on the corner, waiting for the light to change. "Where are the Kennedys?" she asked.

The man looked surprised. "Why, right down the street there."

Martha tried to run, but her high heels and the crowd wouldn't let her. She moved along in a kind of hobbling jump toward the Adolphus, trying to remember whether Quentin had said he was riding in the motorcade or just greeting the Kennedys at the airport. The shopping bag containing her Joy perfume banged against her leg. But slow as her progress was, she was getting closer to the cheering. She scanned the crowd for protest signs, but saw none. At the Adolphus, she paused, panting, while the doorman opened the door for her. She dashed into the lobby. The place was empty. Even the desk clerk was gone. She turned. The doorman saw her coming and opened the door again. "Did any political groups meet here? In the lobby?" she asked.

"No, ma'am. Not that I know of," the doorman said.

"Where *is* everybody?"

"I guess they're out here, ma'am. Looking at Jackie." The doorman grinned. "I got a glimpse of her myself."

A block or two away, the cheering was getting louder. Martha dashed again, threading through the crowd, bumping people, not stopping to offer apologies or respond to theirs. A huge Negro woman turned from the street. Sidestepping to avoid her, Martha felt her ankle turn, and she went down. Two men in the crowd jumped to help. "Are you hurt, ma'am?" one of them asked.

"No. I don't think so," she said. "Just help me up, please."

The men grabbed her under the arms and lifted her. The heel of her right shoe was lying on the sidewalk. One of the men picked it up and handed it to her. "You sure you're all right?" he asked.

"Yes," she said. "Just embarrassed."

"Can we help you get somewhere?"

"No, thank you. I can manage."

The men released her and watched as she turned and moved slowly in the direction from which she had come. She was sure she looked silly, limping along, holding her heel in her hand. Tears were in her eyes. There were no protest signs anywhere. The Kennedys were getting away with it.

JAKE

"Good day for a picnic," said the guy from the county auditor's office. He and Jake leaned against the sandstone wall of the red Romanesque courthouse, squinting across Houston Street at a family sitting on a narrow strip of grass in Dealey Plaza. The man, the woman, the two little girls were eating fried chicken and dropping the bones into a white paper bag. One of the girls, holding a bottle of orange pop, ran to one of the reflecting pools and dipped her hand in the water.

"Don't get wet, honey," her father called.

"I'm washing my hands," she said.

She was about James's age. Watching her, Jake wondered if James would like to go on a picnic. If the weather held, they could drive to White Rock Lake tomorrow and roast hot dogs and go fishing on the pier. Or they could take some Kentucky Fried Chicken and eat it while they fished. Jake took off his suit coat and folded it over his arm. The man from the auditor's office said, "I'm glad I left mine inside." The man hadn't worked for the county long, and Jake didn't remember his name. He was in no mood for conversation, anyway.

He stepped off the curb and crossed the street before the man could offer to join him. It was a little cooler in the plaza, and the crowd was thinner than he had expected. Mostly office people from the courthouse and warehouse workers from the Dal-Tex Building and the Texas School Book Depository just north of the plaza. The motorcade would have to move slowly to make the right turn off Main onto Houston; then, only a block farther on, the sharp left onto Elm that would take the president under the Triple Underpass to Stemmons Freeway and the Trade Mart. The underpass marked the end of the motorcade route. Once through its shadows, the big cars would pick up speed and be gone. The plaza was the best spot in Dallas to watch. Jake wished Liz had come with him.

The cheers were swelling now, moving up Main. Jake slung his coat over his shoulder and looked around for the best vantage point. He chose the corner of Houston and Elm, where the motorcade would make the sharp left turn. He dashed across Main where it bisected Dealey Plaza and he hurried along the sidewalk in front of the reflecting pool. He found a place near the corner, beside a young man in work clothes and a boy. The boy, a little older than James, had hooked his thumb into the man's back belt loop. The man's arm was draped across the boy's shoulders. "Want to see a Secret Service agent?" the man asked.

"Yeah! Where?"

The man pointed. "Up there. The corner window on the sixth floor."

Jake looked, too. A man was standing in the shadows, a few feet behind the open window of the School Book Depository, but he was clearly visible. He was young and not wearing a necktie and was holding a rifle or a shotgun. The Secret Service knew its business. From his perch the man could see the whole crowd along Houston Street and in the plaza and at the corner where the motorcade would turn into Houston from Main. He could see all of Elm Street to the Triple Underpass. The man wasn't watching the crowd, though. His face was turned toward the right, almost in profile. He seemed to be gazing down Elm to the underpass. Jake glanced in that direction, too. Several men were standing on the railroad track on top of the underpass. They were Secret Service agents, too. Or maybe they weren't. Maybe they weren't supposed to be there. Maybe the man in the window was sizing them up. Jake expected him to speak into a walkie-talkie, to communicate with the men on the underpass if they were agents, to tell the cops to remove them if they weren't. But he stood motionless, gazing down Elm.

"Is that a machine gun he's got, dad?" the boy asked.

"Looks like a rifle," the man said. "With a scope."

Jake shaded his eyes with his hand. The man was right.

He could see the scope. His eyes moved to the roof, one story above the agent's head. A half-dozen pigeons were walking along the edge like portly tightrope walkers. Their pompous, awkward bearing reminded him of W. C. Fields. The clock on the Hertz Rent A Car sign behind the pigeons read 12:29.

A cheer rose from the plaza as the first pair of motorcycles turned from Main into Houston. The office workers alongside the red courthouse and the Criminal Courts Building clapped their hands. Somebody let out a rebel yell. Jake recognized the driver of the white lead car: Jesse Curry, chief of the Dallas Police. Beside him sat Bill Decker, the sheriff of Dallas County. Jake glanced back at the School Book Depository. The man in the window still stood like a stone, still gazed down Elm as if nothing had changed. Maybe that was his assignment. Maybe some other agent was watching Dealey Plaza.

Jake had known Curry and Decker for a long time. When the white car passed him and was about to make the left turn into Elm, Jake shouted, "Looking good, chief!" Curry recognized him and waved.

Behind the three motorcycles following Curry, the flags of the United States and the presidential office flapped lazily above the front fenders of the big blue convertible. The Secret Service agents riding the running boards stood high above the crowd. They watched the crowd while the crowd watched the president. John and Nellie Connally, in the jump seats behind the driver, smiled and waved to the crowd, and so did the Kennedys. The president seemed to be speaking to the crowd as the car moved along, but the motorcycles drowned out his words. Nellie Connally turned in her seat and said something to him, and he nodded. Jackie was dressed wrong for the day. Her pink suit must have been uncomfortable on such a warm afternoon.

"Hey, Jackie! Look at me!" cried the boy with his father.

"Wave at her, Kenny," the father said.

When the blue car made the tight left turn in front of the

School Book Depository and headed toward the Triple Underpass, Jake's eyes roved past the third car, full of anonymous faces, to the vice-presidential convertible. In the back seat, between her husband and Ralph Yarborough, Lady Bird smiled and waved. The vice president sat glumly, head bowed, not looking at the crowd. Yarborough grinned and raised his hands high above his head. From time to time he pointed a finger at someone on the sidewalk and shouted, "Hi there, y'all!" as if greeting a friend. Maybe he was. He was having a good time.

Jake was lying on the sidewalk before he realized that what he had heard was a gunshot. In that instant, the warm concrete against his face was the frozen earth of Korea, the last time he had heard rifle fire. He was looking at the white rubber sole of a tennis shoe. Maybe the kid had been hit. The father was saying, "Kenny! Kenny!" and the boy was crying. Jake saw his own arms wrapped around the boy's legs. Maybe he had pulled him down. A man, far off, was screaming, "No, no, no!" Another shot echoed off the buildings. Someone shrieked, "They killed him! They killed him! They killed him!" Jake looked up. Pigeons were flying above the roof of the School Book Depository. Hundreds of them, startled, trying to organize themselves into some kind of formation. The Hertz Rent A Car clock read 12:30. The rifle barrel was disappearing into the sixth-floor window.

When Jake stood up, the father picked up Kenny and ran up the sidewalk toward Main Street. Many were running on the grass of Dealey Plaza, screaming. A few were lying prostrate and still, as if dead. Near the underpass, a motorcycle lay crazily against the curb, its wheels spinning. A policeman wearing a helmet and brandishing a pistol was trying to climb the steep embankment. Someone in the car behind the president's limousine raised a rifle and waved it from side to side. A siren shrieked, drowning the screams. Jackie was crawling onto the trunk deck of the blue car. Someone grabbed her and pulled her back. The car spurted toward the shadow of the Triple Underpass. A little girl stood alone in the street in front of the School Book Depository, crying.

"Oh, my God!" Jake cried. "Oh, Jesus Christ! Oh, no!"

TIM

"More coffee?"

Tim waved the waitress away. "I'll take the check."

She licked the pencil and totaled his tab and laid it face-down on the table. "Hurry back," she said.

Tim took a swallow of ice water to wash away the black-coffee taste and slid out of the booth. He took a quarter from his pocket and dropped it on the table.

"Everything all right?" the cashier asked him.

"Fine."

The breakfast had refreshed him. There was nothing left but to check at the police station for any arrests connected with the visit and make his routine rounds of the rest of City Hall and the courthouse. He didn't expect much. There was only one real story in Dallas today, and he had already covered his part of it. Maybe he could go by City Hall now, tape a few quotes by the mayor about the visit, check with the cops, drop the stuff off at the station, and knock off early. He checked his watch. No, the mayor would be at the Trade Mart now, probably presenting cowboy hats to Jack and Jackie. He might as well go back to the station and give the boss another opportunity to praise him for the job he had done.

In the Love Field concourse, Tim passed the booth from which he had phoned in his report. On an impulse, he went back to it, dropped in a nickel, and dialed. Lonnie answered.

"Tim! Where the hell are you?"

"Love Field."

"Hold on. The boss want to talk to you."

"Jesus Christ, Higgins!" The station manager's voice was trembling. "Where the fuck have you been?"

"To breakfast, chief. You told me to." Tim's hand was sweating. The receiver was slippery. He switched hands and wiped his palm on his pants leg.

"Well, get your ass to Parkland," the station manager said. "There's been a shooting at Dealey Plaza."

"What kind of shooting?"

"UPI just moved a flash. They say three shots were fired at the motorcade."

"Holy shit!" Tim's heart was thumping so hard that he raised his hand to his breast.

"That's all we know. I hope to hell it's wrong, but Lonnie's putting the flash on the air now. Just get your ass to Parkland and find out if anybody's there. Call as soon as you find out. Got that?"

"Yeah."

"Well, *move!*"

Tim slung his tape recorder over his shoulder and dashed to the parking lot. He glanced frantically along the rows. In a burst of panic, he was sure his car had been stolen, then spotted the station's call letters on its door. His hand shook. He couldn't fit his key into the lock. "Be calm!" he whispered. "For God's sake, be calm!" He grabbed his right hand with his left and stabbed at the lock. The key slid in. He tried the stabbing motion on the ignition, and it succeeded again. At the exit, he thrust a five-dollar bill at the booth and screamed, "Keep the change! Let me out!" The startled attendant raised the barrier gate, and the car roared to Mockingbird Lane. Its tires squealed as it turned and sped toward Harry Hines Boulevard. Tim's eyes flickered between the windshield and the two rearview mirrors as he wove among the semis and pickups and delivery vans. "Shit!" he screamed. "Fuck!" *Actually*, he heard himself saying, *I hope there's a little action. Something like that Stevenson thing, you know?* Had he really said it? He had. To Callison and Hayes. Last night. The memory made him feel responsible for whatever he was about to see.

He expected guards at the entrance to Parkland Memorial Hospital, but there were none. A white ambulance stood in the parking bay designated AMBULANCE ONLY by the red neon sign. The big blue convertible was parked diagonally across the two bays marked EMERGENCY CASES ONLY, its trunk pointing toward the hospital door. Smaller convertibles and motorcycles were arrayed around it at crazy angles. The doors of all the cars were open. People milled and crowded and gestured.

Tim pulled onto the shoulder of Harry Hines and parked illegally. He walked casually up the driveway toward the buff brick hospital, expecting to be challenged and driven away, but no one seemed to notice him. He stopped a few feet from the edge of the crowd, afraid he would attract someone's attention. He could see nothing but the backs of men bending over the cars. "Oh, my God, Mr. President!" someone said. Tim caught a glimpse of Jackie's pink suit and heard her moan. Then the crowd seemed to start moving through the emergency doors.

As Tim was about to follow, more motorcycles roared up the drive, sirens wailing, and more convertibles. Henry Gonzalez alighted from one and joined the crowd. A policeman called Tim by name. "Where do you think you're going?" he asked.

Tim pointed at the hospital door.

"Try it and I'll kill you," the policeman said.

RODNEY

"Why do you chew gum while you're fucking?" Rodney asked.

"Fucking you makes me nervous," Wanda said. "The gum calms me down a little."

"Why do I make you nervous?"

"Lots of reasons." Wanda brushed her black hair from her eyes. "For one thing, you're married."

"So what?"

"Well, it means you can't get serious about me. I mean, where's it supposed to lead to? What's going to come of it?"

"I don't follow you," Rodney said. "You want to marry me or something?"

Wanda looked at him. "I wouldn't mind."

The bedsprings squeaked under his weight. He laughed. She nestled into his shoulder. "I hate this bed, too," she said. "I get to listening to it, and it makes me nervous."

"I think it's pretty sexy," Rodney said. "It takes me back to the good old days."

"This whole motel takes *me* back to the old days," Wanda said. "This crummy bed and that old stove and the filthy toilet and the cotton patch outside—"

"Corn patch," Rodney said.

"And that old man at the office. He looks out at me every time you register. And that picture of Jesus. It gives me the creeps."

"This ain't a motel, honey. It's a tourist court. The first people who stayed here drove up in Model A's. No telling how many folks have fucked in this bed. I think that's sexy."

"It's gross," Wanda said. "The only decent thing about it is the TV."

"What *is* that shit? What's that woman crying about?" They were watching the picture without the sound.

"It's 'As the World Turns.' All the women cry on 'As the World Turns.'"

"Turn it off."

"You're going to take me back to Dart Construction Company and my goddamn typewriter, aren't you?"

"No. We'll make love again."

"Let me get you a drink."

Rodney handed over his glass, and Wanda took it to the sink. He watched her drop in the ice cubes and pour the whiskey. "You're a helluva looker," he said.

"I know."

"How old are you, anyway?"

"You know."

"Nineteen."

"Twenty," she said. "I had a birthday. You forgot." She brought him his drink and crawled back into bed. "Make it up to me. Marry me."

"I'm old enough to be your daddy."

"So what?"

"I'm already married."

"So what?"

"No, Wanda. Think of something else."

"Okay, transfer me to the downtown office. We could use my apartment then."

"Elsie comes into the downtown office. I don't want her to know you even exist. Why don't you move out here to Richardson?"

"Are you kidding? Me? Live in the cotton patch? Even a kept woman needs *some* social life! I'm not going to live out here in Ozzie and Harriet Land."

"How about a raise, then?"

"How much?"

"It depends. How fast can you get rid of that gum and turn off the TV?"

"Wait, Rod. I have a surprise for you."

"What is it?"

"It wouldn't be a surprise if I told you. It'll be fun."

"Forget surprises. Tell me, or no raise."

"Well, they're going to broadcast Kennedy's speech after this. Wouldn't it be funny to fuck while he's talking?"

"What's funny about it?"

"Wouldn't you like to jiggle your ass in his face?"

Rodney laughed. "You have a truly weird sense of humor, Wanda."

"It *would* be funny, though. Wouldn't it?"

The face of the weeping woman disappeared. The screen went blank for a moment, then Walter Cronkite appeared, sitting behind a desk. Rodney unwound his arm from Wanda and crawled to the foot of the bed and turned up the sound.

"What's the matter?" Wanda asked.

"In Dallas, Texas," Cronkite said, "three shots were fired at President Kennedy's motorcade. The first reports say that the president was seriously wounded."

"Jesus H. Christ!" Rodney reached for his clothes and put on his shirt and pants and shoes, leaving the rest on the chair. He listened, but Cronkite was off the air. He reached for the doorknob.

"Rod—"

"Just sit tight," he said.

He crossed the sunny parking lot to the tourist court office. The old man sat in a lawn chair in the small area that served as a lobby. "What can I do for you, Mr. Dart?" he asked.

"Where's your phone?"

"Right behind the desk there. Help yourself."

Rodney dialed his house and got a busy signal. He pressed the cradle and dialed again and banged the receiver down. "Shit!"

"Something wrong, Mr. Dart?" the old man asked.

"Busy. Probably the goddamn maid." He walked to the screen door and looked out. "You been listening to the news?"

"No. Why?"

"Nothing. Thanks anyway."

He crossed the parking lot to his car and got in and drove slowly away. On U.S. 75 he kicked the accelerator hard and roared southward and turned on the radio. "If that bitch had anything to do with this . . ." he said.

The pool reporters ran to get close to Emergency Room No. 1. The first of the party they found was Senator Ralph Yarborough, standing in the Blood Bank. He was alone, hunched and pale. "Gentlemen," he said, "this has been a deed of horror." He turned his head away, whispering, "Excalibur has sunk beneath the waves. . . ."

The Fourteenth Hour

HENRY

THE PEOPLE IN THE GREYHOUND STATION were talking about Kennedy, so the deputy hadn't lied after all. The president really was in town. Henry couldn't figure out the people, though. Several were crying, and one woman kept repeating, "Horrible, horrible, horrible . . ." Henry had never seen the Greyhound station in such commotion. It made him nervous. It was time to think of another bottle of wine, and excited people never gave him money. He got up from the bench and went out to Lamar Street.

The sun felt more like the beginning of spring than the coming of winter. There were many sirens, and Henry turned south on Lamar, away from their sound, although the town got poorer farther south, and money was harder to ask for.

Two blocks from the station, a man stood alone on the corner. He looked young, and that pleased Henry. Young men were the easiest touches, especially when alone. "Excuse me, sir," Henry said to him. The young man didn't look at him, so Henry said it again. "Excuse me, sir."

The young man turned his head. He was very pale, and looked frightened. "I don't mean to bother you," Henry said. "It's just that I got a problem."

The young man looked at Henry, or in his direction. For

an awful instant, Henry thought he was blind. "I'm a truck driver," Henry said. "From Tyler. My rig's broke down on the Stemmons. I got no money to call my boss. I wondered if you—"

"Where's my car?" the young man said.

"Sir?"

"I left it around here somewhere. Where can it be?"

"I don't know," Henry said. The man was crazy. Henry began backing away.

"What did you say?" the young man asked. He was looking at Henry now. More sirens were screaming on Commerce and Main. Maybe they were looking for this guy.

"I said my truck's broke down on the Stemmons," Henry said.

"Oh," the young man said. "And I can't find my car."

Henry backed away. "Never mind," he said.

"The president," the young man said.

"What?"

"The president. Is he alive?"

"Oh, he's alive, I reckon," Henry said. "I reckon that's what that's all about." He jerked a thumb toward the sirens.

"God, how horrible," the young man said.

"Well, I gotta be going," Henry said. "Take care of yourself, hear?"

"He's still alive, isn't he?" the young man said.

Henry turned toward the Greyhound station. He would find Muffin. Maybe Muffin was having some luck. The sirens were so loud they hurt his head.

R. QUENTIN

R. Quentin Babcock looked at his watch. "They're late," he said.

"They're always late to these things," Barefoot Sanders said. "That's the trouble with motorcades. They always take longer than they're supposed to."

"Nixon would have been on time," Quentin said.

Sanders grinned. "Who would want to see Nixon?"

Quentin ignored him and addressed the rest of the table. "Look at this. We've nearly finished eating, and Kennedy isn't here. Have we got to sit here and watch Jackie eat before he speaks?"

"Democrats run on nigger time, Quent. You know that."

Quentin glanced at the man who said it and nodded. "I've got a mind to leave when I finish this steak," he said. "I've got a bank to run."

"You haven't foreclosed on an orphan all day, have you, Quent?" Sanders said.

Quentin ignored him. He hated banker jokes. He looked around the hall. It was a good turnout. More than two thousand, probably. The Kennedys couldn't say Dallas snubbed them. The hall was impressive, too. The balconies. The fountain. The trees. Even the damn birds. It was impressive. The Kennedys would know Dallas was no one-horse town. Quentin was proud that he and the bank had supported the Trade Mart from the beginning, that he'd known early what an asset it would be to the community.

He didn't hear what the woman screamed, but he heard her scream. The people near the entrance screamed, too. "What the hell?" he said.

"Oh, my God! It can't be true! It can't be true!" The cry became a chorus, moving from table to table.

"What the hell!" Quentin said.

"They've been shot! All of them! They've been shot! They're all dead!"

The men at Quentin's table stared at each other, scared. "It's crazy!" Quentin said. "It's a joke! That woman is crazy! It's just not true!"

People were getting up and moving from table to table. Some were heading for the exits. Two men walked quickly to the rostrum, behind the seal of the president of the United States. They were strangers. "Ladies and gentlemen . . ." one of them said into the microphone. "Ladies and gentlemen . . ."

The fountain stopped splashing. The man was going to say it was a joke, that the crazy woman had been arrested. He was going to say the president had arrived, and everyone would stand and applaud, and there would be embarrassed laughter that they had been fooled by the woman. Kennedy would make a joke about it when he came in.

"Ladies and gentlemen . . ." the stranger said again. The crowd got quiet. The silence was eerie without the fountain, with only the crazy parakeets fluttering. "There has been a mishap," the man said. "The president has been shot. . . ."

"It can't be true! It can't be true! It can't be true! It can't be true! It can't be true! It can't be true!" The cry rose and echoed like a chant at a football game. "It can't be true! It can't be true!"

A blond man rose near the front of the hall and threw his napkin on the table. "This fucking town!" he shouted.

Quentin stood, too, and the other men at his table. They suddenly looked worn and drawn. "Not in Dallas," one of them said. "The president wasn't shot in Dallas. Dallas didn't kill him."

"He's not dead," Quentin said. "They called it a mishap. They wouldn't call it a mishap if he were dead, would they? Some nut just . . ." He laid down his napkin. "Some nut just . . ." He turned and walked through the crowd, squeezing between the frantic people, pushing with them toward the door. He had to find a phone. He had to know where Martha was, and what she was doing.

MARY ELLEN

The first thought in Mary Ellen's mind was to go home at once. "Oh, don't," her mother said. "Don't leave me by myself at a time like this."

"Come with me," Mary Ellen said. She was crying, and her mother was crying, and Albert, alarmed, had started crying, too.

"But they'll have more news in a minute and we'll miss it."

"Well, do what you want. I'm going."

"Wait a minute," her mother said. "Here. Take him."

Mary Ellen lifted Albert. Her mother heaved herself out of the rocker. "Shh! Shh, honey!" Mary Ellen said. "It's all right!" Albert touched her cheek and felt the tears and cried harder.

"Maybe he's got the colic," her mother said.

"He's all right. Hurry, mother. I've got to go."

The old woman picked up the plates of sandwich remnants and potato chips from the coffee table in front of the TV. "Hurry, mother!" Mary Ellen said. "I'm going. They'll probably let school out. I don't want the kids coming home to an empty house."

Her mother set the plates back on the table and waddled out of the room. She returned, tying a plaid woolen scarf over her head, and opened the front door. Mary Ellen patted Albert's back. "There, there," she said. "It's all right."

In the car, she squeezed the steering wheel with both hands and leaned forward, squinting through the windshield as if driving through a storm. Her mother switched on the radio. A panicky voice confirmed the report that the president had been hit and had been rushed to Parkland. "Oh, Lordy," her mother sobbed. "Oh, Lord, please let him live."

Mary Ellen pulled into her own driveway and cut the engine and ran to the house, leaving her mother to bring Albert. When she opened the door, Buster jumped on her.

Mary Ellen burst into sobs. "Get down! Get down, you god-damn mutt!"

Buster got down and ran around her in tight circles. She kicked at him and missed. She switched on the TV in the living room and moved on to the kitchen. Beside the toaster sat the small black police monitor that Bullard and the kids had bought her for Mother's Day. She turned it on sometimes while she worked, hoping to hear Bullard's voice. She turned it on now. The policemen were close to panic, too. They weren't using the code that Mary Ellen had memorized to understand their conversations. They spoke as if in person, as if shouting at each other across a crowded room. Officers in Dealey Plaza and the School Book Depository, officers at Parkland and the Trade Mart, all shouting over the crowds and motorcycle engines and sirens. The dispatcher was broad-casting the description of a young man with dark hair, in-structing men to take witnesses to the sheriff's office. Mary Ellen strained to hear Bullard's voice.

"Mary Ellen?" Her mother stood in the kitchen door, hold-ing Albert.

"Shh!"

"I just thought I'd put Albert down for a nap."

"Yes. Fine."

A newscaster boomed from the TV in the living room, but Mary Ellen paid him no mind. She leaned close to the monitor, trying to picture the officers, trying to see their faces and what they were doing, trying to pick Bullard's voice out of the noise. Then the dispatcher broke in, his voice breaking with emotion. "Attention all units in the Oak Cliff area! A citizen has reported an officer shot at Tenth and Patton!"

"We'll take it," a unit replied. "We're near there."

"Roger," the dispatcher said. "I'll get you help."

There was a pause, then the unit asked, "How's the officer?"

Another pause.

"How's the officer?"

"The citizen says he's dead."

Mary Ellen's shriek reverberated through the house. Amidst it she was aware of Albert screaming and her mother trying to run. She shrieked again. She saw her mother standing over her and realized she was lying on the floor. "They've killed a policeman!" she screamed. "They've killed Bullard!"

"Oh, my Lord! Oh, my God! Oh, sweet Jesus!" Mary Ellen's mother was on her knees, bending over her, trying to shake her. "Did they say it was Bullard?"

"It was Oak Cliff! He was coming home!"

"Did they *say* it was Bullard! *Tell* me, sweetheart!"

Mary Ellen sat up. "It had to be! He was coming home!"

"He was working downtown, sweetheart. He wouldn't come home at a time like this."

"I'm on the Jefferson Viaduct," a unit was saying. "I'd like to take that Oak Cliff call. I know the area."

"Roger," the dispatcher replied. "The citizen says the suspect fled on foot. Check the alleys. And be careful."

"Roger," Bullard replied.

"Thank you, Jesus," Mary Ellen said.

DENNIS

Weldon closed his Hebrew Bible. "I don't think I'm cut out for Hebrew," he said.

"Neither am I," Dennis said.

"You've got to have it for graduate school," Weldon said. "I'm just going to be a pastor. I shouldn't have taken it."

"But think how impressed your flock will be when you spout a little genuine Hebrew at them."

Weldon smiled. "Got time for a cup of coffee?"

They shoved themselves away from the long seminar table where they and six others had suffered through an hour of Genesis, and went into the hallway. "How's Judy feeling?" Weldon asked.

"Better. She didn't teach today, though."

"How was it at Love Field?"

"Not bad. A pretty friendly crowd, actually. You should have gone."

"I wish I had."

"Hey," Dennis said. "You know a Negro preacher named Tom Durant?"

"Durant? No."

"Pretty interesting dude," Dennis said. "Kind of weird, though. Not very friendly."

Three secretaries were standing outside the dean's office, talking almost in whispers. Dennis and Weldon walked past them, then Weldon turned and said, "Did something happen?"

The secretaries looked at him, surprised. "Our president's been shot. Didn't you know?"

"Who would want to shoot the president of SMU?" Weldon said.

"No," the secretary said. "President Kennedy. Downtown."

"*What?*"

"The radio says Johnson and Connally were shot, too."

"I don't believe it!" Dennis said.

The secretary shrugged. "That's what the radio says."

Dennis and Weldon had moved on through the door before the impact of the secretary's words hit them. They stood at the top of the steps, gazing across the sunlit campus. Small knots of people stood on the grass and under the trees. Slowly Dennis realized what they were talking about. Weldon made a small choking sound in his throat.

"You still want some coffee?" Dennis asked.

"No, I think I'll go to the chapel. Want to come?"

"No, I think I'll go home."

Weldon started down the steps. At the bottom, he turned

back and spread his arms. "Look, I'm sorry," he said. "I mean, he's from your hometown and all...."

Dennis gave a little wave. Weldon walked slowly toward the chapel, not looking at the groups on the sidewalk. Dennis stayed for some time, looking at his shoes, not thinking of anything, then moved down the steps and toward the parking lot. He passed one of the groups on the sidewalk. "You think they'll cancel the Baylor game?" a girl was asking.

In the car, he turned on the radio. The newscaster was recounting the facts and rumors he had of the shots in Dealey Plaza. He sounded weary. He halted in midsentence, then said, "This just in from Parkland. President Kennedy's condition is reported as grave. He is said to be moribund, which means he is near death." The newscaster's voice cracked. He paused again. "To repeat ..." He paused. "President John F. Kennedy is said to be near death at Parkland Hospital from gunshot wounds he received from an unknown assailant as he was riding through downtown Dallas."

Dennis drove to the apartment. He parked at the curb and ran up the walk, afraid the president might die before he could get to another radio. Judy was asleep on the bed, hugging herself in her quilted robe. Dennis switched on the radio and shook her shoulder. "Judy! Darling! Wake up!"

Judy came awake, startled. "What is it?" She looked around wildly.

"Listen!"

". . . It was a huge and friendly crowd," the radio was saying, "possibly the largest of the president's Texas visit...."

"He's been shot," Dennis said. "The president has been shot. He's not expected to live."

"Oh, my God! Oh, no!"

"Listen!"

" . . . As the motorcade turned from Houston Street onto Elm Street, several shots rang out from a nearby building...."

"They say he can't recover," Dennis said. "They say he's going to die."

Judy buried her face in his shoulder and began to weep. They were standing beside the bed. Dennis didn't remember her getting up. Her neck was hot against his cheek.

" . . . moribund . . . "

Judy said something he didn't understand.

"What?"

She moved her face away from his shoulder. "I can't believe this is happening. Oh, Dennis, I'm so scared."

The radio's voice was gone. Only a faint hum came from it now. They stared at it, holding their breath. The hum seemed louder and louder, filling the room.

"Ladies and gentlemen—ladies and gentlemen—we've just received this report from Parkland Hospital—" The newscaster was struggling to talk. There was noise, someone else talking, in the background. "President John F. Kennedy is dead. The thirty-fifth president of the United States expired at Parkland Hospital at—at— Excuse me. I don't know what to say—I feel like I'm going to cry. . . ."

PRESLEY

O mighty Caesar! dost thou lie so low?
Are all thy conquests, glories, triumphs, spoils,
Shrunk to this little measure? Fare thee well. . . .

"Hold it, goddamn it! Hold it!" Justice screamed from the back row. "Damn it, Charlie, you sound like you've got a mouthful of oatmeal! You're Mark Antony, man! Project like the noble Roman you are!"

Presley Evans smiled privately. Justice had been rough all day. The assassination scene had been repeated over and over, with Justice screaming all the while that Caesar was falling like a drunken acrobat. Now this oatmeal thing. Where did he come up with that? An old movie?

"They've just murdered the most important fucking Roman of them all, Charlie, and Mark Antony's his friend, Charlie," Justice was saying. "He's also trying to save his own fucking hide. He's walking the fucking high wire, Charlie. He's not eating oatmeal at a time like this."

Where did he get those circus metaphors? Maybe he read a book last night. Read a book and saw a movie and stayed up too late and came to work cranky as hell. At least Charlie Thompson was his victim today.

"Okay, Charlie, take it from there again," Justice said.

O mighty Caesar! dost thou lie so low? . . .

Justice let them go on. Caesar lying on the stage. Cassius and Brutus standing over him bloody as hell, dickering with clean, innocent Antony. It was going well. Presley could feel the tension. Justice moved to the middle of the theater and watched and listened, strumming his moustache with his fingers.

O world, thou wast the forest for this hart;
And this, O world, the heart of thee.
How like a deer stricken by many princes
Dost thou here lie!

Charlie was into it. He actually sounded grief-stricken. Maybe there was something to that high-wire thing. Presley could feel the tension, the balance among the actors. They were cooking.

"That's okay for now," Justice said when they finished the scene. "Let's move on to Scene Two. We're in the Forum now. Jack, you read the lines of the crowd, okay?"

Jack Williams, who was playing Caesar, got up. A stagehand gave him a copy of the script. Presley's heart was beating faster than he liked.

"Presley, do you know the lines?" Justice asked.

"I think so."

"Well, do you or don't you?"

"Yes."

"Okay. Let's go."

The lines leading to Brutus's oration to the crowd went smoothly, and Presley took his stance and drew a deep breath.

> Romans, countrymen, and lovers! hear me for
> my cause, and be silent, that you may hear—

"They *can't* hear, Presley!" Justice cried. "You're explaining to Rome why you killed Caesar, for Christ's sake, not reciting 'Hiawatha' to the third grade! Start again."

Presley began again. The lines weren't set firmly in his brain. His mind raced ahead, trying to grasp the words and arrange them before his tongue reached them. Someone entered the theater and walked down the aisle to Justice and whispered in his ear.

> As Caesar loved me, I weep for him. . . .

From the corner of his eye, Presley saw Justice listening to the other man. What the man was saying apparently was important to Justice, his attention was so intent. The man left. Justice slumped in his seat for a moment, then got up and started down the aisle.

> Who is here so vile that will not love his country? If
> any, speak; for him have I offended. I pause for a reply.
> Jack Williams read: None, Brutus, none.

Justice stepped onto the stage. Tears were streaming down his cheeks.

RAYMOND

"I don't know where I'm going," the White House man said.

Raymond didn't know him. He was some kind of press-relations officer, but not the one who usually traveled with Kennedy. "Follow me," Raymond said.

He led the man down the long, crowded Parkland corridor toward the emergency entrance, into the maze of cubicles and nurses and crying children that was the Minor Medicine section, then around the final right turn, where Johnson's huge back came into view. Johnson was facing a window as if looking out, but the blinds were closed. Several agents stood with him. They looked at Raymond and the White House man, and so did Lady Bird, who was sitting on a chair, writing something in a small notebook. Johnson didn't turn around.

The White House man cleared his throat and said, "Mr. President."

Johnson turned. His face was gray and ghastly. Raymond remembered the massive heart attack he had suffered years before, when he was the Senate majority leader, and caught his breath.

"Mr. President," the White House man said, "don't you think I should make a statement to the press?"

Johnson shook his head. "Wait," he said. "We don't know whether it's a communist conspiracy or not. I'd better get out of here and back to the plane. Are they prepared to get me out of here?"

The agents, members of the vice-presidential detail, nodded. The announcement should be made after Johnson had escaped. Arrangements would have to be made.

The White House man left, but Raymond remained. One of the agents seemed to be taking over, doing the talking to Johnson, making the plans. Kellerman, the agent in charge for the Texas visit, wasn't there, and nobody sent for him. Raymond knew the man who was talking. Youngblood. Rufus Youngblood. "We don't know what type of conspiracy this is, or who else is marked," he was saying. "The only place we can be sure you're safe is Washington."

"What do we need?" Raymond asked.

"An exit that nobody knows about, two unmarked cars, a cop who knows Dallas like the back of his hand. Will you handle it?"

Raymond made his way back through the Minor Medicine maze, finally located Police Chief Jesse Curry, and whispered the demands to him. Curry beckoned Raymond to follow him.

There was no safe exit, but Curry arranged for the cars. Youngblood decided the Johnsons would leave the hospital behind a flying wedge of agents. Raymond felt as though he had been caught up by a tornado as they pressed through the corridor full of people and noise and movement, out the door and into the sunlight. The Parkland grounds were crowded with people, crying, screaming, wringing hands. From the center of the crowd, a sign popped up so suddenly that Raymond's hand moved instinctively to his gun. YANKEE GO HOME.

Youngblood shoved Johnson into the back seat of Curry's car and got in with him. Two of the congressmen jumped in, too. Johnson's head disappeared beneath the windows. Raymond arranged Lady Bird and her secretary, Liz Carpenter, and another woman in the back seat of the second car and climbed in beside the driver. He couldn't tell the women to get down. His car was intended to draw the fire of any snipers along the way. Lady Bird would have to remain visible.

The cars, behind an escort of several motorcycles, sped out Harry Hines Boulevard. They had traveled only a few blocks when a delivery van appeared out of nowhere, moved into Harry Hines, and seemed about to stop, about to block the street. Raymond leaned forward and drew his gun. A siren sounded from Curry's car. "Don't touch that siren!" Raymond ordered his own driver. "He's not supposed to do that!"

Curry's siren stopped, and the van moved on, but the motorcycles had already joined in. "God! We can be heard for miles!" Raymond cried. Then Curry's voice came over the radio: "Turn them off. No sirens, boys."

Without the sirens, the cars had to slow down at each red light, and every light seemed to be red. During the pauses, Raymond listened for rifle fire, then the cars would hurtle on. The women were quiet, scared. Parkland was only three miles from Love Field, but it seemed they had been riding for hours. Outside a building beside the street, a man was lowering the flag to half-mast.

The Fifteenth Hour

JASON

ALL THE ROOMS WERE EMPTY except Jason's. Mrs. Claymore was alone there, sitting at her desk, grading papers. She looked up and smiled at them.

"Where is everybody?" Stacy asked.

"They've gone home," Mrs. Claymore said. "School was dismissed after it was announced."

"After what was announced?" Stacy asked.

Mrs. Claymore smiled and frowned at the same time. "You don't know? I thought you were there."

"Where?"

"Why, downtown. Kennedy has been shot. He's dead. Didn't you know that?"

Stacy steadied herself on one of the pupils' desks. "You can't be serious," she said.

"Of course I'm serious," Mrs. Claymore said. "Surely everyone knows by now."

"Who did it?" Stacy asked.

"In my opinion," Mrs. Claymore said, "it was the hand of God."

Now they were sitting in the car in their own garage. The engine was running. Stacy was staring through the windshield at Mark's tools hanging on the wall. The radio was saying that President Johnson had been taken to a secluded place. They had been sitting there a long time.

"Mom?"

Stacy kept looking at the tools and didn't reply.

"Mom? Please say something."

She had a funny look on her face, as if she didn't know who he was. It scared him. "Why don't we get out of the car?" he asked.

"What?"

"Let's get out of the car. We've been sitting here a long time."

"You can get out. I just want to sit here."

"No. You get out, too. You can listen in the house."

"Do you know what's happened, Jason? Do you understand?"

"Yes. Somebody killed President Kennedy."

"Remember how they looked when they passed us, Jason? Remember how young he was, and how he waved at you?" Stacy covered her face with her hands. "And now he's dead. Dead, dead, dead. I can't stand it! We were among the last to see him smile." She switched off the engine and pulled out the key. The radio went off, but she made no move to get out of the car. Her eyes were red, and gray streaks of wet mascara lined her face. Jason reached over and touched her cheek. She grabbed him and pulled him to her. "Oh, Jason, don't ever forget how he was when he waved at you."

"I won't, mom. I think the phone is ringing."

He listened. It was ringing.

"I wonder how big a bomb it would take to blow the whole state of Texas off the map," Stacy said.

"Can I go answer it?" Jason asked.

"Yes. Go on. It's probably your dad."

LUIS

A wheel squeaked on the cart as Luis pushed it. It squeaked so loudly that it bothered him, but nobody else seemed to notice. Dishes were clattering into other carts like his. Some of the workers were pulling the white cloths off the tables and folding them. Others were folding the tables and carrying them away. The legs of the tables made a loud bang as they folded, and the bangs echoed in the huge hall. The parakeets still fluttered from tree to tree, fussing. Luis pushed the squeaking cart from table to table, scraping the garbage into the lower bin and piling the dishes into the upper bin, as he had been told.

Some of the guests were still there. Some stood in small groups, talking, as if nothing had happened, as if they were still waiting for something to begin. Some stood alone, saying nothing, lost in thought. Some would start to leave, then come back and pick up one of the little American flags or a yellow rose from one of the tables and gaze at it, then put it in a pocket or purse. Some would forget they had been about to leave. They would stand around some more, smoking cigarettes, not looking at anyone. *Gringos* were strange people. They never expected anything bad to happen.

The next table did look as if the party were just starting. Six plates in a row, the silverware still arranged beside them, the steaks never tasted. The chairs were back from the table, though, at funny angles. The people must have been served just as the news was announced. Luis left the cart and went to the kitchen and found a large paper bag. He picked up the steaks with his fingers and dropped them in and rolled the bag closed and laid it in the upper bin with the dishes. He wouldn't ask if he could take them home. They would tell him no. He would just take them. Warmed in a frying pan and covered with *salsa* and maybe fried eggs, they would make a feast tonight. Maybe one of the others would buy some beer.

One of the *Gringo* guests was walking toward Luis, straight to him. Maybe he had seen him take the steaks. Luis picked up the dishes and scraped the garbage into the lower bin and stacked the dishes in the upper bin, pretending he didn't notice.

"Hey," the man said. "Can you tell me where to find a phone?"

Luis shrugged, pretending he didn't understand, and the man went away.

Luis couldn't be too careful. Maybe there was going to be a revolution and these people who weren't going home were trying to decide which side to be on. Maybe the man looking for a phone would be on the wrong side, and somebody would remember Luis talking to him, and Luis would be in trouble. If a revolution came, Luis would go home. It was better to be poor than dead, and if he died in Texas, no one in Tamaulipas would ever know it.

Maybe the rat he had seen in the morning was an omen and he hadn't understood. If he were at home, maybe one of the witches in the village could have told him. Luis didn't know why he should be given an omen about Jack Kennedy, but it was possible.

BULL

Bull drove by Tenth and Patton. A crowd had gathered around the blood on the street, but two officers were there already, questioning them. The body had been removed. Bull didn't stop. He cruised the alleys, slowing the car to look into open garages and carports. No one was there. Oak Cliff seemed eerily normal compared to the chaos crackling over his radio. Who was the dead officer? Had he been killed by the same man who shot Kennedy? The descriptions of the two coming over the radio sounded much the same. The dispatcher was saying a man answering the description had been seen in an Oak Cliff branch of the public library. He assigned two units to go look.

Bull cruised the alleys. The guy had fled on foot. He might be here somewhere. He couldn't be far away. Unless he had a car waiting for him around a corner. That was a possibility. A lot of officers were being ordered to Love Field. Maybe the man, one of the men, was headed there in a car, trying to catch a plane. Bull took down the mike and radioed his location.

"The cashier at the Texas Theater says a man acting funny is holed up in the balcony," the dispatcher said. "Take a look."

"On my way," Bull said.

"Have report a suspect just went into the Texas Theater on West Jefferson," the dispatcher said.

Other units were responding to the call. Bull sped out of the alley and turned on his flashing lights. He heard sirens in the distance. When he pulled up in front of the theater, McDonald and an officer Bull didn't know were talking to the cashier through the box-office window. McDonald said, "Waggoner, take the balcony." As Bull passed the box office, the cashier said, "He didn't even buy a ticket."

Bull crossed the lobby and moved cautiously up the carpeted steps to the balcony. He kept his eyes away from the bright images on the screen. Slowly the ghostly forms of the patrons emerged, hunched in their seats, oblivious to him, eating popcorn. Three people. Sitting together. All women. He scanned the balcony rows. No one else was there.

A figure stepped from behind the curtain on the stage. Bull tensed. His hand touched the butt of his revolver. It was a war movie. Machine-gun fire rattled through the theater. The figure stood on the stage a second, in front of the screen. The movie made crazy lights and shapes on his face and body. It was McDonald. He jumped off the stage and moved up the aisle and squatted to talk to a man sitting in an end seat, then got up and moved up the aisle again. Another officer was walking slowly down the other aisle.

Bull ran down the stairs to the main floor. Twelve or fifteen people were there, but Bull could see only the backs of their heads. McDonald glanced at him, then turned into the third row from the rear in the theater's center section, toward a man sitting alone. The other officer moved in that direction, too. They had spotted their man. When McDonald got very close, the man jumped up and raised his hands. "It's all over now," he said.

As Bull started down the aisle, the man hit McDonald in the face, then reached inside his jacket and came up with a gun. McDonald grabbed him around the waist. They went down together, over the backs of the seats in front of them. Bull and the other officer rushed toward them. McDonald lashed at the man's face with his right fist, his left hand grabbing for the gun. The man pulled the trigger. The hammer fell, but nothing happened. "I protest this police brutality!" the man yelled. McDonald grabbed the revolver and yanked it from the man's hand. He looked around at Bull and handed him the gun, then grabbed the man in a bear hug. "Police brutality!" the man yelled. McDonald slapped the cuffs on him, and he and the other officer led him out the other aisle. Bull scanned the theater. Some of the patrons looked at him, but none got up.

In the lobby, McDonald was frisking the man. The man had calmed down and had a little smile on his face. He was an ordinary-looking punk. "You okay?" Bull asked McDonald.

"Yeah," he said. "The son of a bitch tried to shoot me, but it misfired."

"I saw it," Bull said.

McDonald shoved the man toward the theater door. "Police brutality!" the man said.

"Brutality, my ass," McDonald said.

On the sidewalk Bull said, "Maybe I'd better come in with you."

"I guess so," McDonald said. "Follow us. We can handle him."

"Who did he kill?"

"I don't know."

McDonald and the other officer shoved the man into the back seat of their cruiser. The other officer got in beside him. McDonald got behind the wheel and they took off. Bull dropped the prisoner's revolver on the seat beside him and heard McDonald inform the dispatcher that the suspect had been apprehended. Bull took down his mike and said he was following them in.

At headquarters, a sergeant said the dead officer was J. D. Tippit. He had been shot four times. Bull knew him. The man from the theater was still being processed when Captain Will Fritz came in. "One of the School Book Depository employees is missing," he said. "His name is Lee Harvey Oswald. I want him arrested."

The sergeant pointed a pencil at the man from the theater. "There he sits," he said.

S H E R R Y

The line at Sherry Murrell's window looked like any other Friday. People were waiting to deposit their paychecks and withdraw their weekend money. Usually on Friday people talked in the line. About work and how glad they were that it was Friday. About their weekend plans. Today nobody was talking. They stood in silence and stared straight ahead, not even exchanging the usual pleasantries with Sherry at her window. The two Negro men, who were standing together, said nothing to each other. When they got to the window, the taller Negro pushed a check across the counter without a word. It was made out to cash, on the account of the Dallas County United Poll Tax Committee, signed by Thomas J. Durant, chairman, for seven hundred fifty dollars.

"You want to cash this?" Sherry asked.

The tall Negro nodded.

"Just a moment." Sherry stepped away from the window and picked up the phone and dialed Bookkeeping. Negroes often had no idea how much money they had in their accounts. Bookkeeping said the Dallas County United Poll Tax Committee had it, though. Barely. She returned to the window and slid the check and a ballpoint pen toward the tall Negro. "Are you Mr. Durant?" she asked.

"Yes."

"Endorse it, please."

"But I'm the one who wrote the check," the Negro said.

"It's made out to cash," Sherry said. "You have to endorse it, to show that you got the money."

Reluctantly, the Negro took the pen and signed his name. The other Negro watched him carefully.

"Will seven hundreds and a fifty do, or would you like something smaller?" Sherry asked.

"That'll do," the Negro said.

Sherry counted out the money, and the Negro counted it again before he put it in his wallet.

One of the vice-presidents poked his head into Sherry's cage. "When you've finished with these customers, go ahead and balance," he said. "We're locking the doors."

"We're closing?"

"Yes." He moved on down the line of cages, passing the word.

Eileen smiled at Sherry over the partition. "Well, every cloud has a silver lining," she said.

The two Negroes glared at her, then walked slowly to-

ward the entrance. A guard held the door open for them,
and locked it behind them.

"It's a terrible thing," said the next man in the line.

"Yes, it is," Sherry said.

"Dallas will never live it down," he said.

Sherry balanced on the first try and was in a good mood
when she drove out of the parking garage. Her shopping
could be leisurely. She would even have time to straighten
the apartment before Jake arrived. He would be tired tonight.
And tense. Depressed from having to listen to Liz's com-
plaints. He would lay his head on her shoulder while he had
his drink, and she would massage the back of his neck.
Slowly he would relax. If Liz had thought to do things like
that, she would probably have Jake still. It was little things
like that that kept marriages from becoming stale and boring.
Sherry's mother had told her that. It was so easy to avoid
mistakes if you kept your head. Mrs. Callison. Mrs. Jake
Callison. Sherry Callison. Callison was such a pretty name.
She would enjoy using it. C-a-double l-i-s-o-n. Callison. Yes,
as a matter of fact I *am* kin to Jake Callison, the writer. He's
my husband. Yes, he *is* good. He's working on a novel, you
know.

The traffic was so heavy it seemed like rush hour. Everyone must have closed early. Men are only grown-up boys,
her mother had told her. Treat them like boys and you'll
never lose them. They want mothers and lovers. They need
somebody to tell them they're good, no matter what they do.
Their lives aren't as easy as they look. They're all scared
inside.

The liquor store was crowded. Sherry had to stand in line
to pay for the bourbon and the Burgundy. It was like the
line at the bank. Nobody was talking except the cashier.
"Everybody's stocking up for the weekend," he said. "Everybody's going to sit in front of the TV."

At Safeway, Sherry chose the steaks carefully. Jake claimed
to know about steaks. He talked of marbling and aging. He

learned it in high school, he said, when he was on the meat-judging team of the Future Farmers of America. Housewives were dumb to choose the reddest meat, he said. You looked for the marbling and the slight gray tinge of age. There were no gray steaks, but Sherry found two T-bones that looked marbled. They had fat on them, anyway.

"I think Johnson will make a good president," the cashier was saying. "He has so much experience." He was a slight, studious-looking boy with pimples. A college student, probably. The customer he was checking out didn't reply. "What do you think?" the boy asked. "You think the Birchers did it? What do you think history's going to say about Dallas? I mean, it's like the Ford Theater. Some crazy asshole . . ."

The customer didn't reply. When Sherry laid her groceries on the counter, she realized the boy wasn't talking to the customers. His fingers trembled on the keys of the cash register. "You know what Robert E. Lee said, don't you? Next to losing the war, Lincoln's assassination was the worst thing that could happen to the South." He didn't look at her. He didn't know she was there. "Well, that's what this is. The very worst thing . . ."

At the apartment, Sherry set the grocery bags on the breakfast bar and sat down on the bed and dialed the phone.

"City Desk."

Newspaper people all answered the phone the same way. The voice was always abrupt and metallic and hard, almost daring you to talk. So different from the bank.

"Jake Callison, please."

"Just a minute." The man laid down the phone. "Callison!" he shouted. "Where's Callison?" Other people were shouting in the background, over ringing phones and typewriters. How did they get anything done in that noise? She wished Jake would show her the newsroom sometime. The man picked up the phone again. "Jake isn't in right now," he said.

"Will you take a message?" Sherry asked.

"Is this Liz?"

"No."

"Well, listen. We're awfully busy right now."

"Just tell him to call Sherry, okay?"

"Yeah, fine, If I see him." The man hung up.

RAYMOND

The rear of the hearse was full of men. Secret Service agents, air force officers, members of the Kennedy staff, pushing and tugging on the casket. It wasn't budging. Raymond pushed. The men looked across the casket at each other, baffled, sweating. The hearse was an oven. Jackie stood outside, watching them, waiting, the skirt of her pink suit a smear of blood, her white gloves bloody. The men pushed and pulled again, together. Something ripped, broke. One of the air force men said something under his breath. The casket moved. Its molding had broken. Part of the handle had come off. "It was latched to the floor," the air force man said. Even unlatched, the casket slid slowly.

In the sunlight, Raymond saw that the casket was bronze. It gleamed. When it cleared the door, the men almost lost their balance. "Dear God, it weighs a ton," Raymond said. They carried it across the concrete toward *Air Force One*. The concrete was littered with signs and debris from the arrival. WELCOME JFK. HELLO JACKIE. YANKEE GO HOME. The casket was solid bronze, probably. The men carried it to the foot of the stairs at the tail door of *Air Force One*. Jackie stood aside, waiting for them to lift the casket up the stairs. The steps were steep and narrow. The men tilted the casket, rearranged themselves at the handles, lifted, pushed. Dear God, it was heavy. Raymond's shirt was sticking to his back.

Sweat was rolling into his eyes. He pushed harder, afraid they would drop the casket, that it would bounce down the stairs and crash on the concrete.

At the top of the stairs, they turned. Seats had been removed. Someone had made a place for the casket. They set it down and pushed it flush against the bulkhead. The men looked at each other, panting, sweating. The braid and the ribands on the air force uniforms were disheveled, as if the officers had been in a fight. An agent of the vice-presidential detail came to them from the front of the plane. "Medley," he said. He clutched Raymond's arm and led him to the door and onto the top of the stairs. "You know Sarah Hughes," he said.

"Yes."

"Go meet her at the gate. She's coming to administer the oath."

Raymond found Jesse Curry and led him to the car that had brought Lyndon Johnson to Love. As they drove away, one of the engines of *Air Force One* began its warm-up whine.

"Are they taking off?" Curry asked.

"I don't know."

Curry slowed the car, uncertain what to do. The engine stopped whining. "Everybody's confused," Curry said.

"Can you believe this is really happening, Jesse? Can you believe it really turned out like this?"

"No," Curry said. "It's like Pearl Harbor. Hell, it's worse."

They were at the winged statue of the Spirit of Flight at the airport entrance when the little sports car turned in. "There she is," Curry said. He waved her down and got out of the car and spoke to her. She nodded absently. Curry returned to his car and led the little car up the avenue, through the police barricades, to the plane. Raymond opened the sports car door and pointed at the steps. "Up there, Sarah," he said.

Curry followed the judge along the crowded aisle toward

the stateroom. Raymond stopped inside the door and leaned against the partition that separated him from the bronze casket.

"How do you want us? Can you get us all in?" Johnson was saying.

"I'll put the judge so I'm looking over her shoulder, Mr. President," someone replied.

"We'll wait for Mrs. Kennedy. I want her here," Johnson said.

There was a brief commotion, then Judge Hughes cleared her throat and said, "Hold up your right hand and repeat after me. I do solemnly swear—"

"Just a minute, judge," someone said.

There was a pause. The judge began again. "I do solemnly swear . . ."

Outside, a jet touched the runway and roared into a landing. As its noise diminished, Johnson was saying, "Now let's get airborne."

Raymond went down the steps and posted himself on the concrete and watched the door. Several men came down the steps and went into the terminal, talking. Judge Hughes came down and got into the little car. She waved at Raymond and drove away. The plane door closed. The jet engines began their whine again, one after another. Men in overalls wheeled the stairs away, and the plane lumbered toward the runway. Raymond squinted at the blue words on its side: THE PRESIDENT OF THE UNITED STATES. "Two presidents," he said. The plane poised at the end of the runway, then hurtled down the long, barren stretch. As the wheels lifted, Raymond glanced at his watch. Only 2:47. The goddamn sun was still shining.

The Sixteenth Hour

SHEILA

BILLY HAMILTON, THE BANDLEADER, stuck his head into Babe's office. "We gonna have a show or not?" he said.

"I'm ready," Sheila said. She was sitting beside Babe's desk in her long red dress, her G-string, her red garter belt and net stockings, her pasties with the tassels. Her red high-heeled shoes were on the desk. She never put them on until she had to.

"Me and the boys is ready, too," Billy said. "But there ain't nobody out there."

"Still nobody?" Babe said.

"Not a soul," Billy said. "The boys say nearly everybody downtown is closing up. There ain't gonna be nobody down here in a little while. We wondered if you want us to go on waiting around."

"You got any suggestions?" Babe asked.

Billy shrugged. "It don't matter to us. Our meter's running every minute we're here, whether we're playing or not."

"Well, shit." Babe removed the cigar from his mouth and inspected the chewed end. "I guess we might as well forget the afternoon shows. Where can I get you if I decide to go ahead with the evening?"

"At my place," Billy said. "We're all going over there and watch TV. You want to come?"

"No," Babe said. "I'll call you."

"Don't wait too late," Billy said. "We're liable to get a little drunk."

"I'll call you in two or three hours."

Billy nodded and ducked out, closing the door behind him. Through the thin wall, Sheila heard the musicians laughing and packing their instruments.

"At least I won't have to pay that bitch Mavis," Babe said. "Where the hell is she?"

"How should I know?" Sheila said.

"I thought you were going to talk to her."

"I was going to do that tonight. I don't know where she is."

"Probably giving some john a quickie in the back seat of a car. For free. If you see her, tell her don't bother to come back. Tell her I don't even know her."

"Oh, Babe."

Babe picked up a book and slammed it back on the desk. "What kind of show would we have with one stripper, huh? You feel like dancing all day?"

"I don't feel like dancing at all," Sheila said. "I don't think you should open tonight, either."

"Yeah? Tell me about it. How are the fucking bills going to get paid around here?"

"Nobody's going to come in here tonight, Babe. And you'll still have to pay the boys and me. And Mavis, if she shows up."

"Not Mavis."

"Well, nobody's going to come. You'll just go deeper in the hole."

Babe struck a kitchen match on the top of the desk and relit the cigar. "Where will you be?"

"At home, I guess."

"If you decide to go out, give me a call, okay? Otherwise, I'll call you."

"I'm getting out of this rig," Sheila said. She went to the small dressing room next door to the office and changed into her street clothes. As she was about to leave, Babe opened her door.

"Where am I going to find another dancer?" he asked.

"Don't worry. Things will work out. Okay if I go out the front?"

"Sure. I'll lock up." He put his arm around her waist and they walked together through the dark club. Sheila turned the knob and pushed, but the door didn't move.

"It's locked!" she said. "Babe, you didn't even unlock the door!"

"Don't that beat all? Well, it don't matter. Nobody was trying to bust it down." He unlocked the door and held it open. "I'll call you in a couple of hours," he said.

Traffic was backed up along Commerce Street, bumper-to-bumper, as far as she could see. The people on the sidewalks were hurrying, as if it were raining. A man ran up behind her, bumped her, and ran on without looking at her. A few steps ahead, he slipped and fell hard against the concrete. His briefcase slid across the sidewalk and hit a wall and opened. A sheaf of papers flew out and scattered along the sidewalk. People stepped on them, not noticing. The man got up and grabbed the briefcase and ran on, not bothering to gather the papers.

An old man wearing an army raincoat and a red corduroy cap stood on the street corner beside a high pile of newspapers. "Extra! Extra!" he called. It was the first time Sheila had heard the cry, except in the movies. "The president is dead!" he called. "Get your paper here!"

Sheila bought one and glanced at the thick black headline. PRESIDENT DEAD. The picture under it was of the cheering crowd at Love Field and Kennedy smiling and shaking hands with someone and Jackie in a pillbox hat, holding roses. Sheila folded the paper and tucked it under her arm.

In the Adolphus lobby, crowds stood around the two TV sets. Walter Cronkite boomed from one, David Brinkley from the other. The watchers weren't talking, and the TV voices sounded crazy, talking about the same thing in different words, jarring against each other. Nobody was behind the desk. Sheila waited a few minutes, then ran the bell. She waited, but nobody came, so she rang again. A man in front of the Cronkite TV looked around, then loped across the lobby. "I'm sorry," he said. "May I help you?"

"Are you the clerk?"

"Yes. What may I do for you?"

"My name is Thelma Ruth Green," Sheila said. "A Mr. Barnhill was supposed to leave something for me at the desk."

The man went behind the desk and checked the mail cubbyholes. "Yes, here it is," he said. He drew a folded slip of paper from one of the holes. "Miss Green, you said."

"Yes."

"Here you are."

Sheila unfolded the paper. "Come on up," it said.

"Is Mr. Barnhill still registered?" she asked.

"Yes, ma'am."

"And where is the house phone?"

The man pointed to a row of phones, then came from behind the desk. Sheila started toward the phones, but the man returned to the TV, so she went to the elevators instead.

"What floor, ma'am?" the old man asked.

"Eleven, please."

"It sure is terrible, ain't it?" he said, closing the door.

"Yes. It's terrible."

"I hope you won't think unkindly of Dallas, ma'am. Dallas ain't that bad a town."

"No," she said. "Dallas is a good town."

The old man braked the elevator at the eleventh floor and moved it up and down several times, trying to align it perfectly. Finally, he opened the door and said, "Thank you, ma'am."

Room Service dishes lay on trays outside some of the rooms. The voices of Cronkite and Brinkley drifted through some of the doors. Eleven-oh-nine was one of the Cronkite rooms. Sheila knocked and heard a stirring. "Who is it?" Barnhill said through the door.

"Sheila."

Barnhill opened the door. His white shirt was wrinkled and wet-looking. His collar was unbuttoned and his blue tie hung like a limp noose. His eyes were red. He held a glass of whiskey with no ice. "Come on in," he said. "I'm glad you could make it."

JONATHAN

"He just ain't in the house, Miss Anna," Lanell said. "I've searched this place from top to bottom, and he ain't here. I swear it." Lanell looked guilty. It was Miss Anna that made her feel that way. Jonathan felt guilty, too. Miss Anna's hands were shaking so. If anyone was guilty, he, Jonathan, was. He was the one who let Mr. J.L. go out alone. He shifted uneasily on the sofa. Lanell laid her hand on his leg, and he laid his hand on hers.

Calvin coughed and mumbled, "Pardon me, ma'am." The three of them were sitting on the sofa properly, as if on a church pew, facing Miss Anna in the rocking chair. The sunlight from the window behind Miss Anna was shining through her hair, making a silver halo. She wove a twisted white handkerchief in and out among her fingers. Her diamonds flashed.

"I ain't seen him all day. I swear," Lanell said.

"I put his hat and raincoat on him," Jonathan said. "It was raining then. He said he was going for a walk."

"He didn't say where he was going?" Miss Anna had asked the question maybe fifty times this afternoon.

"Just around the grounds," Jonathan said. "Checking security, he said."

"And the gate's locked?"

"Yes, ma'am. But maybe he had a key."

"And you didn't drive him to town, Calvin?"

"Oh, no, ma'am. I ain't seen him neither. I swear on a stack of Bibles."

"Well, there's no need for all this swearing. Jonathan, ring the office again."

He went to the phone in the hall and dialed Mr. J.L.'s private line. He let it ring eight times, then dialed the Fisher Oil Company switchboard. He let it ring eight times, then dialed Quentin Babcock's number. No one answered there, either. "I guess everything's closed up," he said. "You want me to call the police?"

"Heavens, no," Miss Anna said. "If they found him and he started talking about his conspiracy . . . The police don't have time to look for him now, anyway."

They sat, thinking. Lanell laid her hand on Jonathan's leg again, then moved it away. Miss Anna rocked, twisting the handkerchief. "I hope he's all right," she said.

"Why don't Calvin and I drive down to the office?" Jonathan said. "If he isn't there, maybe we can find out where he went."

"Yes, Jonathan," Miss Anna said. "Yes, I think that would be wise. . . ."

When Jonathan saw that she wasn't going to continue, he rose and made a little bow. "We'll call you from the office, Miss Anna. Don't you worry," he said. Calvin got up, too, and followed him out the back door to the garage.

As Calvin turned the big car down the drive, he said, "Where you reckon that old buzzard is at?"

"Lord only knows," Jonathan said.

Calvin stopped at the iron gate and got the key from his coat pocket and gave it to Jonathan. Jonathan got out and unlocked the gate, and locked it again after Calvin drove through. "Maybe he lost his key," he said when he got back into the car. "Maybe he locked himself out."

"I believe it," Calvin said. "It would be just like the old buzzard to do that."

"The bad part is, we were supposed to keep him in," Jonathan said. "That's the bad part. We were supposed to keep him in."

"Well, keep your eyes on the sidewalks," Calvin said. "Maybe he's wandering around here somewhere."

The sidewalks of Highland Park were empty, though, and only a few cars were in the streets. In Oak Lawn, the traffic was heavier, and downtown it became a crush. "Look at this," Calvin said. "Just like rush hour."

"I guess those that were downtown are going home, and those that were home are coming downtown," Jonathan said. "To see where it happened."

"It sure is a crazy day," Calvin said. He crept his way to the bank's parking garage and pulled into the reserved space with J. L. Fisher's name on it.

The lobby was almost deserted. Two women stood staring through the glass doors, waiting for their rides. The security guard, a wrinkled old white man, stood at parade rest by the elevators. "Hello, Calvin," he said.

"What's happening?" Calvin asked.

"Most everybody's closing early," the guard said.

"You know if Mr. Fisher's up there?"

"No, I don't. I ain't seen him."

"Okay if we go up?"

"Sure. We ain't closing the building. People don't have to go home if they don't want to."

Jonathan and Calvin rode the elevator to the Fisher Oil floor. No one was at the receptionist's desk. There were no sounds of voices or typewriters. "Kind of spooky," Calvin said.

Another security guard, a younger white man, stepped around the corner. "I thought I heard the elevator," he said. "How are you, Calvin?" He shook Calvin's hand.

"Hello, Sam. This here's Jonathan."

Sam nodded, but didn't offer his hand. "I'm glad you came," he said to Calvin.

"Is he here?" Calvin asked.

"Boy, is he!"

"Why didn't you call us?"

"He gave orders not to," Sam said. "And he's still the boss, you know."

"Where is he?"

"In his office."

Jonathan and Calvin walked around the corner and down the hall to the outer office where Mr. J.L.'s secretary used to sit before he fired her and never hired another. The covered typewriter was still there, though, and fresh flowers were in the vase on the desk. Jonathan knocked on the door beside the desk.

"What the hell is it?"

"It's Jonathan, Mr. J.L."

"I don't want any Ovaltine tonight, Jonathan."

"Oh, Lord, he's gone batty," Calvin whispered.

Jonathan said, "I don't have any Ovaltine, sir. I just need to see you."

"Come in! Come in!"

Mr. J.L. was wearing the raincoat and the old hat. He sat in the big leather chair, smiling. Chili stains and cracker crumbs dotted the desk blotter. An empty bowl was sitting beside the telephone. Mr. J.L. was pouring a drink. "Jonathan, get a couple of glasses out of that file drawer," he said. "A man shouldn't have to drink alone."

"You know we don't drink, Mr. J.L.," Jonathan said.

Mr. J.L. squinted from under the sweaty old hatbrim.

"When a white man tells a nigger to drink, he drinks," he said.

Jonathan got two tumblers from the drawer and set them on the desk. Mr. J.L. poured them half full, his hand shaking. Jonathan thought he was going to drop the bottle. "Miss Anna isn't going to like this," Jonathan said.

"You saying I'm henpecked?"

"Nosir."

"Well, sit."

Jonathan and Calvin sat down in the two deep, soft chairs in front of the desk, holding the glasses but not drinking. Mr. J.L. leaned back in the big leather chair and cupped his own glass between his hands. "Well, well," he said. "They came after our horses, didn't they? Just like I said."

"Yessir," Jonathan said. Calvin gave him a look, but Jonathan ignored him. "Yessir, they came after the horses, all right."

"But they didn't get them, did they?"

"Nosir, they didn't get them. That's for sure."

Mr. J.L. sipped the bourbon. He pushed back the old hat and smiled at Jonathan. "Old Buck sure fooled us, didn't he?"

"How's that, sir?"

"Well, all this time we've been thinking he was dead, and he was sitting up there with that old Winchester, just waiting for them. All this time, Jonathan."

Calvin's eyes widened. He set his glass on the desk. "Miss Anna sent us to bring you home," he said.

"She did, did she? Well, when a man's got something to celebrate, he can't let his woman boss him around, can he? You just sit there and enjoy your drink."

"Maybe we ought to call her," Jonathan said. "We ought to tell her where we are."

"No, you sit tight, Jonathan. Everything's all right."

"She sure would like to hear about Mr. Pool, I bet," Jonathan said.

"I'll tell her when I get home," Mr. J.L. said. "He just cut down on them with that Winchester, Jonathan. Just like the old days. A Winchester's a fine rifle. I told you that."

"Yessir, I remember that. I sure do."

"We can't go yet," Mr. J.L. said. "Quent's got to explain about John Connally, you know."

"Mr. Connally? What about him, sir?"

"Well, he was right there, Jonathan. Right there with those bandits. Thick as thieves."

SOLOMON

Beyond the parking lot, the North Central Expressway was full of cars moving stop-and-go toward north Dallas and Richardson. Rabbi Goldstein imagined the radios in all the cars blaring the same awful news. It looked like any Friday afternoon, but the rush was early and it was warmer than it ought to be so late in November. Rabbi Goldstein locked his car door and folded the newspaper under his arm and crossed the lot. He climbed the three steps to the door of the office. He inserted his key into the lock and glanced again toward the expressway. Another car pulled in and parked at the other end of the lot. A man got out and walked toward him. The man was wearing an old-fashioned fedora pulled low over his eyes, and a dark suit. Rabbi Goldstein waited for him.

"I'm glad you're here," the man said when he reached the steps.

"You wanted to see me?" Rabbi Goldstein asked.

"Yes."

The man's head was bowed. From the top of the steps Rabbi Goldstein couldn't see his face. He was sure he didn't know him. "What can I do for you?" he asked.

"I want to pray," the man said. "I need to pray about this terrible thing."

"Come in. I'll pray with you, if you like."

The man started up the steps and raised his head. He was a red-faced man with a red moustache. About fifty. He looked startled. "Are you the pastor here?" he asked.

"I'm the rabbi here."

"This is a synagogue?"

"Yes."

"Oh. I thought it was a church. I guess I didn't see the sign."

"The sign is in front of the building. This is the back."

"It looked like a church to me," the man said. "I'm sorry."

"We pray to the same God," Rabbi Goldstein said. "It doesn't matter where we do it. You're welcome here." He swung open the office door.

The man backed down the steps. "It's easy to get confused at times like this," he said. "It was silly of me not to notice. I just got confused."

"I understand," Rabbi Goldstein said. "You may come in if you wish. You're welcome."

The man raised his arms, then slapped them hard against his legs. "I'm so confused. . . ." He turned and walked back to his car. He drove out of the lot and up the expressway ramp and stopped to wait for a break in the traffic.

Rabbi Goldstein went into his office and spread the newspaper on his desk.

Welcome, Mr. Kennedy,
to Dallas . . .

He must say something about it in the service this evening. His sermon would be recorded for broadcast on Sunday night, and the city must hear that Bernard Weissman wasn't of Solomon Goldstein's congregation.

JAKE

"Chief Curry told me you were at Dealey Plaza. I figured you would come right in. Why didn't you?" Captain Will Fritz, chief of Homicide, set a cup of coffee in front of Jake on the scarred wooden desk. He leaned back in his chair and clasped his hands over his belt buckle, waiting for Jake's reply. His gray five-gallon hat was tilted back from his forehead, his eyes placid behind the tortoiseshell glasses.

"I had a job to do, Will. You know that."

Fritz grunted. "Did you get it done?"

Jake drew the newspaper from his coat pocket and handed it across the desk. Fritz unrolled it and laid it on top of the pile of papers in front of him. His eyes scanned the bold, black type, the picture of the smiling faces at Love Field, the huge, simple headline: PRESIDENT DEAD. Fritz said, "I guess somebody hollered, 'Stop the presses,' huh?"

"I guess. They were stopped by the time I got back."

"I've always wanted to be in a newsroom when they hollered that," Fritz said. "It must be pretty exciting." His placid eyes flickered over the page, as if looking for something worth reading. "You've got a lot of stuff here."

"It's pretty rough," Jake said. "We were in a hurry."

"Still, you've got a lot of stuff. You guys reacted fast." Fritz sipped his coffee casually, as if at breakfast. "This town's going to catch hell. You know that."

"Yeah, I know."

"Reporters from all over the world are probably on their way here right now."

"No 'probably' about it," Jake said. "They'll be coming."

"We've got to do everything right. Know what I mean? We're going to catch hell, no matter what we do. But we've got to do everything just right."

"That's right."

"You should've come to us first," Fritz said. "That would've been the right thing to do, Jake. Your duty as a citizen."

"I don't know a hell of a lot," Jake said. "I didn't think you would mind."

"That's presuming on friendship, isn't it, Jake? There's no room for friendship in a situation like this. You understand my position, don't you?"

"Am I in some kind of trouble?"

Fritz folded the newspaper. "You mind if I keep this?"

"Go ahead."

Fritz opened a desk drawer and laid the paper inside. "Nope, you're not in trouble. It would've been better the other way, that's all." He closed the drawer and leaned back and clasped his hands again. "Okay, tell me what you saw."

"I didn't see a hell of a lot."

"Where were you standing?"

"At the corner of Houston and Elm."

"Is that where Chief Curry saw you?"

"Yes."

"Which corner of Houston and Elm?"

"Southwest."

"Across Elm from the School Book Depository?"

"That's right."

"Okay, tell me what you saw."

"A man standing in a window."

"Which window?"

"The right-hand corner of the Depository. Sixth floor. There were other men standing in other windows. Hanging out of them, you know."

"Uh-huh. So why did you notice this particular guy?"

"Because he wasn't leaning out like the others. He was standing back from the window, in the shadows, and he wasn't watching the motorcade. And he was holding something."

"What was he holding?"

"It looked like a rifle."

"Didn't you think that was kind of funny, Jake? A man

standing in the shadows, holding a rifle? Didn't you get curious at all?"

"I thought he was a Secret Service agent. The guy standing next to me said he was a Secret Service agent, and I figured he was right. Jesus Christ, Will! Wouldn't you have thought the same thing? With all the cops and Secret Service around, would you expect some ordinary asshole to be standing in a window holding a rifle?"

"Okay. Then what?"

"I heard the shots."

"How many?"

"Two. Three. I don't know. There were echoes, and all hell broke loose then."

"Did you see the guy fire the shots?"

"No."

"Why not? You were looking right at him, weren't you?"

"No. I was looking at Kennedy then. I think I was looking at Kennedy. I didn't see him get hit, though."

"Why not, if you were looking at him?"

"I hit the dirt. The sidewalk. I was holding some kid around the ankles. I guess I pulled him down with me. Everybody was screaming and crying."

"You didn't see anything else?"

"I saw the rifle barrel go back into the window."

"Did you see the guy?"

"No. Just the rifle barrel."

"What did you do then?"

"Well, I was pretty shook up. After I *knew* what I was doing, I ran back to the paper to tell them Kennedy had been shot."

"How did you know he'd been shot if you didn't see it?"

"People were screaming that he'd been shot. And the way the cars took off, I knew *something* had happened."

"Didn't you ask anybody any questions? Didn't you interview anybody?"

"They weren't in a mood to be interviewed, Will. They were running and screaming. So was I."

"Did you notice anything about the guy in the window that might help us identify him? Did you get a look at his face?"

"No. He was in the shadows. He looked young, though."

"Could you see what he was wearing?"

"No. Except that he wasn't wearing a coat. Or a tie."

"He didn't really look like a Secret Service agent, did he?"

"I don't know, Will. I don't know beans about the Secret Service."

"Okay." Fritz stood up and shook Jake's hand. "That's all, I guess. For now. You going to stick around?"

"It looks like it," Jake said.

"You think you could pick this guy out of a lineup?"

"I don't know. I doubt it. You've got the guy, haven't you?"

"Well, we've got *a* guy. He looks good."

"I could try, if you want me to."

"We'll see. We've got other witnesses. We're pretty sure he's the guy who hit Tippit, anyway. That's not for publication, Jake. Not yet."

"You've got our last edition. No more from us today."

"Yeah, thanks for bringing that," Fritz said. "I'll keep it for a souvenir."

"Do you really want to remember this day, Will?"

"There's not much chance of forgetting it, is there? I feel like running and screaming, like all those others. This town's in for a hard time, Jake. We've got to do everything just right."

"Yeah, I know," Jake said. "Thanks for the coffee."

"My pleasure," Fritz said.

Eight miles up, night rushed toward the plane, met it, and enveloped it. Storms below shattered the TV faces to dizzying patterns, reduced their voices to gibberish. The president paced back and forth across the stateroom, pausing at the TV whenever the faces and voices would clear. "We still don't know it isn't a conspiracy," he said. "We still don't know how big it is." The Texans nodded, spoke to him, did his will.

The Irishmen shuttled back and forth from the forward area to the tail, squeezing past the Texans, glaring at them, hating their drawling voices. Irishmen knelt in the aisle beside the long casket and stood bracing themselves against the bulkheads, talking, remembering, drinking, trying to comfort her. The gentlest Texan, Bill Moyers, followed them there. "The bedroom is free," he said, "if you'd like to clean up."

She shook her head, and Moyers went away. "Why not change?" the Irishmen said. "Another dress?" The blood had caked like rust on her skirt, under the bracelet on her wrist.

"No," she said. "Let them see what they've done."

The Seventeenth Hour

BETTY LOU

SHE HAD DONE EVERYTHING she could. They couldn't say she hadn't done her work. Two months of smiling at newspaper editors, pushing her news releases into their hands, begging them to use them any way they wanted. Two months of chirping to disc jockeys and civic club program chairmen and ministers. No one had ever done what she did. Nobody else had ever had to run a public-relations campaign to persuade people not to spit on the president of the United States or hit him with a picket sign. It had worked, too. Her crowds were bigger and louder and friendlier than San Antonio or Houston or Fort Worth. Not a single ugly incident. Hardly even a nutty sign. She had worked her butt off and had done the job. Except for that fucking Bernard Weissman and one lousy fucker with a gun.

In the mirror, the skin around her eyes was so dark she looked as if she had been in a fight. Fatigue. Plain old bone weariness. Her eyes were red, too. Not so much for Kennedy as for herself. She had been hired to make sure the Dallas faces on the television sets and in the newspapers were happy ones. To make the country forget the picture of Bruce Alger snarling at Adlai Stevenson. And the picture of Lyndon Johnson hugging a frightened Lady Bird in the Adolphus lobby.

The ugly, turned-down mouths of the Birchers. The IMPEACH
EARL WARREN billboards. The world thought there was something small, black, and hard in the soul of Dallas, and she had
been hired to prove there wasn't. She had almost done it, too.

Rubbing cold cream on the weary face in the mirror, Betty
Lou began crying. She daubed at her eyes with the greasy
Kleenex, determined not to give way again. The world would
crucify Dallas this time. There must be a thousand reporters
on their way now, already knowing what they were going to
look for, already phrasing their stories in their heads. Dallas,
the city of hate. Dallas, the only city where it could happen.
Dallas, the city where it *did* happen. They would crucify
Dallas, and maybe Dallas would crucify her. She had been
hired to do a job, and didn't do it. She had been paid a lot of
money, and produced negative results. She was supposed to
persuade Dallas not to spit on Kennedy, and it had shot him.
They would look for someone to blame. It could be her.

When the phone rang, she froze, asking the eyes in the
mirror if she should answer. The eyes said no. She couldn't
manage a cheerful voice. She didn't want to talk and try to
make sense. She waited. The phone rang ten times. Eleven.
Twelve. It seemed to be getting louder, more urgent. It wasn't
going to stop. She sat down on the bed and picked it up.

"I knew you were there," the voice said. "I knew you
would answer."

"Who *is* this?"

"A friend. Just a dear, dear friend, deary." The voice
laughed. It was a woman's voice. "Why did you take so long
to answer? Did you have to compose yourself? Were you
crying over your dear, dear president, deary?"

"Who *are* you? What do you want?"

"Such a nasty thing they did to your cute little president,
blowing his head off like that. So impolite. After all you did
for him, too."

Betty Lou started to hang up, but something in the voice
stopped her. It was familiar. Not a friend, but someone she

knew. Someone who knew about the job she had done. Her mind scanned the faces of the women she had met at the clubs, the churches. "Yes, it *was* nasty," she said.

"Well, deary, you should have expected it. Dallas doesn't like Communists, you know. It was dumb to expect Dallas to be sweet to a Communist, even for a day."

"Why don't you tell me who you are?" Betty Lou asked. "Are you a coward?"

"Oh, no, no, no, deary! I'm not a coward. The cowards spent the day kissing Kennedy's ass. I wasn't there. You didn't see me there, did you?"

"I don't know. Who are you?"

The voice laughed. It was a throaty, happy laugh. Almost drunken, but not really. Giddy. "That's for me to know and you to find out," it said.

"Give me a hint," Betty Lou said. "Do I know you?"

"Of course you know me. Wasn't Jackie a mess, though? She'll *never* get that suit clean."

"Why did you call me?" Betty Lou asked.

"I thought you would need cheering up, deary! I know how depressing it can be when a job just blows up in your face, so to speak. Sometimes Rod comes home—"

There were sounds of a struggle at the other end of the line. A man's voice, whispering. "Hey, cut it *out!*" the woman's voice said. The receiver clattered, dropped on the floor, maybe. Then someone hung up.

Elsie Dart was such an idiot that she couldn't even make an anonymous phone call right. Betty Lou rummaged in her purse for the slip of paper with Rabbi Goldstein's number on it, found it, and dialed.

Mrs. Goldstein answered. "Sol's already gone to the temple," she said. She gave Betty Lou the number.

The rabbi answered on the first ring. "Ah, yes, Miss Carpenter," he said. "How are you?"

"Not so hot at the moment, rabbi."

"No. I'm sorry. It's just a habit, you know."

"I wondered if you located Bernard Weissman," Betty Lou said.

"I didn't. Nobody seems to know him."

"Well, I had a thought. Have you considered the possibility that he's a woman?"

"A woman? Well, I hadn't—"

"There are some nasty women in this town, you know. I just got a call from one of them. I have a hunch that your man may be a woman. What do you think of that, rabbi?"

"I don't know. . . ."

"Not a Jewish woman, either," Betty Lou said. "How about that? Think about it."

"All right, Miss Carpenter, but—"

"Call me next week, if you're interested. Not that it matters now, I guess. Goodnight, rabbi. I'm going to take a pill and go to bed."

"Goodnight, Miss Carpenter."

Betty Lou hung up and dug in her purse for the bottle of Miltown. She shook a pill into her hand and walked to the kitchen and poured a glass of white wine, then went back to the bed and fluffed her pillows and propped herself against them. She took the pill and a sip of wine. She wished there would be something silly on TV until she went to sleep, some situation comedy. Of course, there wouldn't be. Elsie Dart probably wasn't Bernard Weissman, either. But maybe the old rabbi wouldn't think she was crazy.

LUCIUS

Outside the window of Thomas J.'s study, the wind whipped the bare branches of the elms. Scraps of newspaper and hamburger wrappers blew past, bouncing like tumbleweeds. A black-and-white dog trotted, head down, tail between his legs. "Looks like we're in for a cold spell," Lucius said. Thomas J. made no reply. Lucius turned from the window. Thomas J. was sitting at his desk, staring at nothing, rubbing his chin. "Looks like we might have a norther coming," Lucius said. "It's funny, ain't it? How the weather got good just long enough for him to ride down the street and get shot, and then got bad again. It's enough to make you wonder."

Thomas J. looked at Lucius. "What did you say?"

"I said it's funny how the weather got bad again after Kennedy was killed. It's kind of like what happened in the Bible after Jesus was crucified. The darkness and the earthquake and all. It ain't going to get as bad as that, I guess, but Kennedy ain't Jesus, either."

"No," Thomas J. said, "but he was the best we had."

Lucius unfolded one of the wooden Sunday School chairs stacked against the wall and sat down. "I'm worried, Thomas J.," he said. "How are we going to get seven hundred and fifty dollars back in that bank before somebody finds out?"

"That's not your problem," Thomas J. said. "I'm the chairman of the Poll Tax Commitee, and I signed the check."

"But what if the cops find out about it? What if the newspapers get a hold of it and make a big thing out of it? It would be bad for the movement. They would say, 'What do you expect from them uppity niggers? They're crooks.' They would be tickled to find a way to make us look bad, you know."

"Well," Thomas J. said, "don't you think it would look bad if we let Regis put Sister Emma in a pauper's grave? She was a fine old woman, Lucius. She was a slave and a Christian and was at all our meetings and on TV and in the papers."

"The way things are today," Lucius said, "I don't think anybody's going to notice what we do with Sister Emma."

"*We* will," Thomas J. said. "Our *people* will, Lucius. You know how hard it is to get them to even *ask* for their rights, much less fight for them. They'll say, 'Yeah, Emma Rawlins fought for her rights, and look what it got her. Buried like a dog.'"

"You don't need to preach to me about Sister Emma," Lucius said. "I loved her as much as you did, and you know it. I'm just worried about that money."

"Well, don't be. I'll get it. I'll go to some of the white folks she used to work for. They get sentimental about their mammies. Especially after they're dead. They like to do nice things for dead niggers." Thomas J. stood up. "Come on, Lucius. Let's get it over with."

Blowing dust stung Lucius's eyes when they left the church. The temperature was dropping fast. Thomas J. turned on the heater in the car. "First time I've used it this year," he said.

Watson greeted them at the door, bowing, rubbing his hands together. "Good evening, Thomas J. Good evening, Lucius," he said. "You have the money, I presume?"

Thomas J. nodded.

Watson made a sweeping gesture with his hands. "Come into my office."

Watson seated himself in the big, thronelike chair. "I think you'll be pleased," he said. "The old lady made a surprisingly good-looking corpse. You have the money, you say?"

Thomas J. took out his wallet and counted the bills onto Watson's desk. Watson watched him, and then smiled. "Thank you. I knew I could depend on you, Thomas J. I swear, I don't know where you civil-rights fellows keep coming up with the cash."

"You do pretty well yourself, Regis," Thomas J. said.

"This?" Watson pointed at the bills. "This, Thomas J., is a pittance. And hard-earned, at that. I'll tell you who made a killing today. The undertaker who furnished that Kennedy casket. Did you see them unload it on TV?"

"No," Thomas J. said.

"Magnificent. A huge bronze model. It must have cost a mint. I tell you, Thomas J., if we ever become equal, every

Negro in Dallas is going to want a casket like that. And a white undertaker, and a white preacher to say the words. You ought to think about that."

"We'd like to see Sister Emma," Thomas J. said. "To see what we're getting for our pittance."

Watson smiled. "Of course." He got up and led them to a dark room with green velvet curtains on the walls. The casket was in the center of the room. Tall, wrought-iron candelabra with electric candles in the sockets stood at the head and foot of the casket. The lid was open. "Pink felt exterior," Watson said. "White satin lining. The best I could provide for the money."

"Is it metal?" Thomas J. asked.

"Wood. But good stuff. It'll hold up a lot longer than she'll need it."

Sister Emma's thin hair was neatly combed. She was wearing a simple black dress with a white lace collar and a small cameo brooch. Her hands were folded on her belly. She looked healthier than Lucius had remembered her in years.

Thomas J. nodded. "Nice, Regis. She looks lovely. I didn't know she owned such a pretty dress."

"Oh, I provided that," Watson said. "Miss Rawlins's wardrobe was very skimpy. The dress is a token of my esteem for you, Thomas J., and my appreciation for your business."

Lucius looked at him, but couldn't tell whether he meant it. "What do you think, Lucius?" Watson asked.

"Good," Lucius said. "She looks good."

"Mamie Ezell provided the little cameo," Watson said. "It's just costume jewelry, but it adds a nice touch, don't you think?"

"Yeah," Lucius said. "Real nice."

"Are the services still to be at three o'clock tomorrow?" Watson asked.

"That's right," Thomas J. said.

"Good. Miss Rawlins and I will be there."

"I'd like a receipt, Regis," Thomas J. said.

Outside the funeral home, he said, "That's the thing about Regis. He gives you a hard time, but he does a good job."

"There ain't any flowers in there," Lucius said.

"Well, not many people bring flowers to the funeral home. There'll be plenty at the church."

"What if they forget?" Lucius said. "They might, you know, with this murder and everything on their minds."

"Don't worry, Lucius. She'll have a fine funeral. You'll be proud of it."

At the church, Lucius said goodbye to Thomas J. and climbed into his cab and headed downtown. The streets were so full of cars that they reminded him of rivers loaded bank-to-bank with fish, squirming, fighting for water, for oxygen, for room to swim. He fought his way toward a small florist's shop he knew of and found an empty parking lot behind an abandoned store building. When he reached the shop, a woman was hanging a CLOSED sign on the glass door. The door was locked. Lucius knocked, and the woman opened it a crack. "Can you help me?" he asked. "I need a small wreath for a friend of mine that's died. I need it right now."

"I'm out of flowers," the woman said. "They just came down on me like a swarm of grasshoppers and bought every flower I had."

"Who did?"

"Everybody. They bought everything they could get their hands on. If I had any flowers left, I wouldn't be closing. I've never had as good a day as this."

"What are they doing with them?" Lucius asked.

"Taking them down to Dealey Plaza, where the killing happened. Somebody said they're just laying them on the grass down there. It seems kind of silly to me."

"Do you know some other shop that would have some flowers? All I need is a wreath."

"I sure don't," the woman said. "There's probably not a flower left in Dallas. Not downtown."

"Well, thanks, anyway."

The woman nodded and locked the door. Lucius returned to the cab and drove toward Dealey Plaza. Houston, Elm, Commerce, every street near the plaza was jammed. As Lucius neared the courthouse, he saw why. Drivers were stopping to stare at the School Book Depository. Some got out of their cars and stood on the sidewalk, pointing upward. Lucius nudged the cab to the plaza side of the street. There, too, people stood, staring up at the Depository as if checking the time on the Hertz Rent A Car clock. Traffic was at a standstill. Bouquets and wreaths, some of them huge, littered the brown lawn. At the edge of the grass, almost on the sidewalk, lay a bunch of white carnations. Lucius jumped out of the cab, ran across the sidewalk, grabbed the bouquet, leaped back behind the wheel, and closed the door. The driver behind him honked, but Lucius didn't look around.

PRESLEY

"*O piteous spectacle!*" Justice said.

"*O noble Caesar!*" Presley said.

"*O woeful day!*" Justice said.

"*O traitors, villains!*" Presley said.

"*O most bloody sight!*" Justice said.

"*We will be revenged!*" Presley said.

Justice laid his arm around Presley's shoulders and they shouted together: "*Revenge! About! Seek! Burn! Fire! Kill! Slay! Let not a traitor live!*"

The men at the bar turned and glanced at them. "Could you keep it down?" one of them said. "We can't hear the TV."

Presley clicked his heels together under the table and shot

his hand up in a Nazi salute. The man gave him the finger and turned back to the TV. The pinched face of David Brinkley was talking about Kennedy's service in the navy. Brinkley's face was replaced by a smiling, boyish JFK in an officer's uniform, posing on the deck of PT-109.

"Did you ever see a picture of a World War Two guy where he wasn't smiling?" Presley said. "It must have been a very funny war."

"Presley, I've never loved you more than now," Justice said. "You may be the only man in Dallas who isn't an asshole. Besides me. Have another drink." He tilted the scotch bottle into Presley's glass. They had stopped calling for setups and ice an hour ago. Donnie didn't seem to mind. He opened a beer or made a setup whenever somebody asked him, but left the customers alone. He was absorbed in the TV, which was almost directly over his head behind the bar. He must have been getting a stiff neck.

"I was in World War Two," Justice said. "In the navy, too. But I never got closer to the enemy than San Diego. It *was* kind of a funny war. In San Diego."

"What you said about assholes is right," Presley said. "If this town had any balls, there would be a mob down at the jail now, hollering for Oswald's head. The commie bastard would be dangling from some light pole."

"Well, Oswald shot the wrong guy," Justice said. "If Barry Goldwater had been hit, they'd be down there tearing *down* the fucking jail."

"I'd like to burn something right now," Presley said. "Or kill somebody. Shit, it would be pure pleasure to kill somebody right now. Just for the hell of it. I knew a guy out in west Texas who did that. He just got pissed off at somebody in a bar one night and killed his ass. He never got paroled, either, because he would never say he was sorry."

Justice didn't reply, so Presley tried to focus on the backs of the men at the bar. There were five of them. The only

people in the place besides him and Justice and Donnie. Presley could see their faces vaguely in the mirror behind the bar,
glowing in the blue light of the TV. They were talking to
each other, smiling. "Look at those fuckers," he said. "Look
at them smile."

Justice glanced, then turned back to his drink.

"I tell you," Presley said, "I felt creepy as hell when you
walked down that aisle and said he was dead. I mean, I'd been
standing there with the fucking *dagger* in my hand. I felt like
I'd fucking killed him myself."

"I know," Justice said. "*Julius Caesar*, for Christ's sake.
What a thing to be doing."

Presley took a long pull at the scotch and coughed. He
hadn't eaten all day. The scotch was raw in his gut, making
noises.

"Did you vote for Kennedy?" Justice asked.

"Yeah, I did."

"Did you really? You're not just saying that?"

"No. I voted for Truman and twice for Eisenhower and
then for Kennedy."

"Why did you vote for him?"

"Oh, I thought he was pretty exciting after Ike, and he
chose LBJ for his running mate. I liked that. I thought old
Lyndon deserved some recognition."

"I voted for Nixon," Justice said. "I didn't like the son of a
bitch, but I thought he would make a better president. I
figured Kennedy for just a rich prick from Boston. I didn't
think he knew much."

"Hell, I still don't think he knew much," Presley said. "Not
compared to Johnson. But he was fun. He didn't take the
assholes too seriously."

"Assholes," Justice said. "You know, Presley, the main
thing that's wrong with the world today is assholery. If we
could get rid of the assholes, we'd be okay."

"There's five assholes up there," Presley said. The men at

the bar were talking loudly now, laughing at whatever appeared on the TV screen. "That's where I would start, if we were getting rid of assholes."

Donnie called, "Hey, you guys okay?"

"How about some ice, Donnie?" Justice said.

Donnie brought two glasses of ice and set them on the table. "Hey, you guys are making a dent in that bottle," he said. "Ain't there no play tonight?"

"The house is dark tonight," Justice said. "A little holiday in honor of the—occasion."

"Yeah, everybody's closing up, I guess," Donnie said. "I ought to close, too. I ain't doing shit. But I figured some of the newspaper guys would come around. Later, I guess."

"Who are those assholes up there?" Presley asked.

"I don't know," Donnie said. "They just came in looking for a beer. Everybody's closing up, they said."

"I'd like to close *them* up," Presley said.

"Hey, Presley, don't pay any attention to them," Donnie said. "They're just a bunch of jerks."

"Assholes," Justice said.

"You got any food?" Presley asked. "Sandwiches or anything?"

"Hey, you know I don't. I got potato chips. That's it. I'm even out of beer nuts."

"Potato chips don't go with scotch," Presley said. "You expect us to eat potato chips with scotch? Shit."

"Take it or leave it," Donnie said. He went away.

"*O woeful day!*" Justice said.

"You said it," Presley said.

"*Burn! Fire! Kill! Slay!*" Justice said.

"Damn right."

On the TV screen, a big forklift was lowering the casket from *Air Force One*. Then the tail door opened and Jackie walked down the steps, surrounded by men.

"If Oswald had been any kind of shot at all, he would have

gotten her, too," said one of the men at the bar. The others laughed.

"Excuse me," Presley said. He pushed away from the table and picked up his chair. He lurched to the bar and slammed it into the back of the man who had spoken. The man's face bounced on the bar, then he fell to the floor.

"Hey!" Donnie said.

The man on the floor writhed, holding his face. His companions stared at Presley, wide-eyed, not moving.

"If any of you other assholes want it, come ahead," Presley said. He raised the chair above his head.

"Hey! Cut it out!" Donnie said. "You want me to call the cops?"

Presley lowered the chair and carried it with him to the door, walking backward. Justice raised his glass. "*Burn! Fire! Kill! Slay!*" he said. "*Slaying is the word. It is a deed in fashion.*"

The Eighteenth Hour

WARNER

"WHAT TIME IS IT?" Sheila asked.

"A little after five."

"I've got to make a call." She picked up the phone and told the operator the number she wanted. She waited, then put her finger on the cradle to break the connection. "Babe's still closed, I guess. I'll have to call him at home. Will you turn off the TV a minute? Just the sound?"

Warner moved to the foot of the bed and reached for the knob. He turned off the picture, too, and moved back to his pillow and watched the pinpoint of light slowly fade from the screen. The networks had canceled all scheduled programming and commercials until after the funeral, and already they were getting repetitive, digging into the files for anything they could find about John Kennedy and Lyndon Johnson.

"Hi, Babe. Sheila. What's the story?"

Again, the face of the sour-faced Bircher at his table flashed into his mind. Warner would never forget the look on his face when the news was announced. What was it? Pleasure? Fear? Both? Not just surprise. Not surprise at all, really. What was the man thinking, now that the FBI was saying a Marxist did it? A defector to Russia and then back again. An admirer of Castro. An American with a Russian wife. In the John Birch scheme of things, Oswald and Kennedy should have been on the same side. Unless Oswald had become a Bircher. Or a Friend of General Walker. Or a Texan for America. It was possible. Not many Marxists would choose to live in Dallas. Unless they were crazy. Which was possible. A lot of crazy people chose to live in Dallas.

"I know, Babe. I was out. I'm still out. I'm calling from the drugstore."

President Lyndon Baines Johnson. Unbelievable. Fucking incredible. So much for the Yarborough Democrats and the Connally Democrats. There would be only Johnson Democrats in Texas now. Lyndon would holler, "Jump!" and everybody would ask, "How high?" Yarborough, too. Warner Barnhill, too, if Lyndon ever flattered him with an invitation to jump. Lyndon owned it all. Hell, he owned the whole fucking country now.

"There won't be any action tonight, Babe. I'm going to stay home and watch TV. . . . Right. . . . No. I haven't seen Mavis. Didn't she call? . . . Did you try her place? . . . Well, I don't know. I haven't seen her."

It was decent of Connally to get hit, too. He had saved the ass of Texas. Hell, the liberals would have concocted their own conspiracy theory: Lyndon is going to be dropped from the ticket in '64; Lyndon invites Kennedy to Texas; Kennedy gets bumped off in Texas; Lyndon is responsible for everything that happens in Texas; *ergo*, Lyndon is responsible for Kennedy's death. They would have believed it in the East. Jesus, maybe Warner Barnhill would have believed it if Connally hadn't been hit. It was a real hit. Not just a flesh wound. He might die. But that wouldn't save the ass of Dallas. The ass of Dallas was in a crack for sure. Dallas had inserted its ass into the crack, and now it had closed the crack. All by itself. It couldn't happen to a nicer town. If Kennedy had to die, this was the right place.

Sheila hung up. "Well," she said. "No show tonight. I'm at your service."

"Good. How much?"

Sheila screwed up her mouth and squinted at him appraisingly. "Oh ... How about three hundred?"

"You're kidding!"

"For it all, I mean. Including this afternoon."

"No."

"You're not the easiest date I've had, you know."

"Forget it," Warner said.

"Okay. How about two-fifty?"

"How about two hundred?" Warner said.

"Can't do it. I have to pay Babe, you know."

"No, you don't. You're home watching TV tonight."

Sheila shrugged. "Okay. Two hundred. In advance. You don't have to treat me like a Juarez whore."

"Then don't treat me like a *turista*," Warner said. He gave her the bills from his wallet on the table and watched her stash them in her purse.

"Turn on the TV," she said.

"Wait. Hand me the phone." He picked up the receiver and waited for the hotel operator. "I want to make a long-distance call," he said. "San Antonio." He gave her his home number.

"One moment."

Warner lit a cigarette while he waited. The smoke, attracted to the heat of the bedside lamp, rose up the shade like a chimney.

"I'm sorry, sir. I can't get a long-distance circuit right now," the operator said. "We're having a horrible time this evening."

"Well, keep trying, will you? It's important."

"Yes, sir. I'll ring you when I can complete your call."

Warner thanked her and handed the phone back to Sheila. "Were you calling your wife?" she asked.

"Yeah. She's expecting me home tonight."

"Why aren't you going?" Sheila was cuddling close now, stroking his chest with her fingertips.

"I really don't know," he said.

"Do you love your wife?"

"Yes. I love her very much."

"But she doesn't understand you, right?"

"She understands me very well."

"Is she good in bed?"

"Yes. She's great."

"Then why are you here?"

"I don't know."

"You're really upset, aren't you."

"Yes."

"Tell me what you want me to do."

"Nothing. Let's just watch TV for a while."

R. QUENTIN

R. Quentin Babcock studied the note on his desk as if his secretary's clear, round handwriting were difficult to decipher. *JLF wants to see you right away. Sounds angry.* Perhaps he could pretend he hadn't returned to the office and hadn't gotten the message. But he would have to pretend until Monday. Or Tuesday, if the funeral was going to be Monday. The bank would have to close for that. And when he called Fisher he would have to apologize, have to explain where he had been and why he didn't get the message. He would have to answer uncomfortable questions. It would be more discreet to call Fisher's office and hope nobody answered. If nobody answered, he wouldn't call Fisher's house. He would say he didn't want to disturb Fisher's dinner, or that he and

Martha went out and he didn't get a chance. . . . No, that wouldn't work. It wouldn't be discreet to go out tonight, or pretend to. Fisher would want to know where he went and who was there, and that could get sticky. He picked up the phone.

"J. L. Fisher residence."

"What?"

"Oh, I'm sorry. This is Mr. Fisher's office."

"Who *is* this?"

"Jonathan Waters, sir. May I ask who's calling?"

"Oh. Quentin Babcock, Jonathan. Is Mr. Fisher there?"

"Yessir."

"I have a message that he wants to see me. May I speak to him?"

"Sir, it would be better if you came on up."

"You sound funny, Jonathan. Is something wrong?"

"Well . . . yessir. That's right, sir. We'll be expecting you right away."

Rotten luck. What the hell was that nigger up to? What was he doing at the office? What was Fisher up to?

Puzzled and a little scared, Quentin took the elevator to the top floor and turned the corner to Fisher's office. Jonathan opened the door immediately. He looked tired and relieved. "Evening, Mr. Babcock," he said.

"Evening, Jonathan."

Calvin rose from a chair by the desk. "Evening, Mr. Babcock," he said.

"Evening, Calvin."

Fisher was wearing his raincoat and the old, sweat-stained hat. His small face gazed slack-jawed from between the turned-up collar and the turned-down hatbrim. He looked like an ancient desert rat, a cowboy gnome, grotesque behind the big mahogany desk.

"Evening, J.L.," Quentin said.

"Sit down," Fisher said.

Calvin moved away from the chair he had occupied and

leaned against the wall. Quentin sat down and tried to laugh in a jolly way, but the sound came out wrong. He cleared his throat.

"Jonathan, see if we have another glass," Fisher said. "You know, Quent, niggers can't drink worth a damn. I've been trying to get these boys drunk all afternoon, and it's just been a waste of good whiskey. They've hardly touched the stuff."

"Well, J.L., good whiskey's never wasted on me."

Quentin watched Jonathan get a glass from the file cabinet and pour two fingers of Jim Beam. Quentin hated bourbon. Thank God, the bottle was nearly empty. He accepted the glass and raised it. "*Salud!*" he said.

"*Sal—sal—salud!*" The old coot was stewed to the gills. "Where the hell have you been, Quent?"

"Oh, here and there. I didn't know you were still here, or I would have come sooner."

"Yes . . ." Fisher's eyes seemed focused on some invisible point in space, as if he were trying to remember something. "What I want to know, Quent, is why John Connally was with those horse thieves."

"He's been traveling around the state with them," Quentin said. "It was his duty, you know. As governor."

"Duty be damned!" Fisher said. He slammed the glass down so hard that whiskey splashed onto the desk. "Where *is* that two-faced son of a bitch? I want to talk to him."

"Why, he's in Parkland, J.L. He's having surgery."

"Surgery? Did he get a bellyache cavorting with those thieves?"

"He was shot, J.L. Didn't you know that?"

"*Shot?* Are you telling me Buck shot Connally, too?"

Jonathan, standing behind Fisher, raised his eyes to the ceiling and twirled his finger at his temple.

"Why the hell would Buck shoot John Connally?" Fisher asked.

"Uh—maybe it was an accident," Quentin said.

"Accident, my ass! Buck never shot anybody by accident. He always hit what he was aiming at. He nailed Kennedy good and proper, didn't he?"

"J.L., are you talking about Buck *Pool?*"

"Damn right." Fisher waved his arm at the pictures on the wall. "*That* Buck Pool."

"J.L., ain't he *dead?*"

Fisher leaned over the desk and gave Quentin a conspiratorial leer. "Dead, my ass," he said. "That sneaky son of a bitch has made me *think* he was dead all these years. And all the while he was just biding his time, just waiting for today. That son of a bitch knew about the conspiracy before any of us, Quent. He saw those horse thieves coming, and he's been laying for them. And he got them, by God. He nailed their ass good."

Quentin didn't know what to say. He gazed into his glass.

Fisher leaned back. "But why would Buck want to shoot John Connally, Quent? Answer me that."

"I have no idea," Quentin said.

"You think John might have been in on the conspiracy?"

"It doesn't seem possible."

"No, it doesn't," Fisher said. "But things are seldom what they seem, Quent. Seldom what they seem. I don't think Buck would do it if he didn't know something. He must know something, Quent."

Quentin didn't reply.

"So John Connally's dead, too. . . ."

"Well, he ain't dead," Quentin said. "He's having surgery. He might die, though."

"You reckon the sun got in his eyes, Quent? Buck's eyes, I mean. It's not like him to leave something to do surgery on. Think of it. John in on the conspiracy. After all the money I've spent to get that bastard elected."

"They're saying a fellow named Oswald did it," Quentin said.

Fisher laughed. "They can say anything they want to. That doesn't change the facts."

"Does Miss Anna know where you are?" Quentin asked. Fisher laughed again.

"Miss Anna sent us down here to find him," Calvin said. "We're supposed to take him home. Miss Anna doesn't even know where we are."

"Yeah, I think we'd better go," Quentin said. "It's time to go home, J.L. They'll be closing up the building soon."

"Home, my ass," Fisher said. "I'm going to stay here and get drunk."

"We're out of whiskey, J.L. Don't you want to go home and crack open a new one?"

Fisher looked at the empty Jim Beam bottle. "By God, you're right, Quent. You're a helluva man. Yeah, let's go. Anna will want to hear about Buck, anyway."

"Jonathan, you and Calvin take him downstairs," Quentin said. "I'll meet you in the lobby. I have to make a couple of calls."

"You coming with us, Mr. Quentin?" Jonathan asked.

"Yes. I think you're going to need me."

Jonathan and Calvin went behind the desk and helped the old man out of the chair. He couldn't stand alone. Jonathan and Calvin each grabbed an arm and moved him slowly toward the door. "Oh, my God, I think I'm drunk," Fisher muttered.

When they were gone, Quentin closed the door and dialed the Fisher house. "Hello, Lanell," he said. "This is Quentin Babcock. Let me speak to Miss Anna."

"Quent! Have you seen J.L.?" Miss Anna asked. "I'm about to go out of my mind."

"Yes, ma'am, I'm with him," Quentin said. "I'm bringing him home. With Jonathan and Calvin."

"Is he all right?"

"I think so. He's just very drunk, Miss Anna."

"Oh, my stars!"

"So drunk he thinks Buck Pool shot Kennedy," Quentin said. "I think we'd better humor him, Miss Anna. Until he's sober."

"Oh, dear!" Miss Anna said.

"Don't worry. We'll be there shortly. Everything's all right."

"Thank you, Quent. I'll have Lanell turn down his bed."

He hung up and dialed his own number. "Where are you?" Martha asked. "Where have you been all day?"

"I don't have time to explain now," he said. "Listen, old Fisher's drunk out of his mind. I've got to take him home."

"Well, hurry. I want to talk to you about the party."

"What party?"

"The funeral party. I'm going to give a party on the day of the funeral."

"Jesus Christ, Martha!"

"I don't have time to talk now. 'Bye."

Jonathan was standing with Fisher, holding him up, in the lobby. "Calvin's gone to get the car," he said.

When the car appeared, Quentin grabbed Fisher's arm and helped Jonathan steer him to the sidewalk and ease him into the back seat. Jonathan climbed in after him, and Quentin sat in the front with Calvin. By the time they left the curb, Fisher had passed out.

He wouldn't go into the White House tonight. He gathered the Texans around him in his old office, in the Executive Office Building. "There must be no gap," he said. "The government must go forward. We've had a tremendous shock, and we have to keep going."

He reached for the phone, called Truman, called Eisenhower, called his old neighbor, J. Edgar Hoover. He wanted a complete FBI report on the assassination, he said, no stone unturned. Hoover said he would get it. He reached for a sheet of White House stationery and wrote. His words were small and cramped, unlike his usual strong, angular scrawl:

Dear John—

It will be many years before you understand fully what a great man your father was. . . .

"The senators and congressmen are waiting in the anteroom," one of the Texans said.

"They'll have to wait a little longer," he replied. On another sheet he wrote:

Dearest Caroline—

Your father's death has been a great tragedy for the Nation, as well as for you, and I wanted you to know how much my thoughts are of you at this time. . . .

He handed the letters to one of the Texans and went into the anteroom.

The Nineteenth Hour

RODNEY

CHET HUNTLEY AND DAVID BRINKLEY were rerunning Kennedy's speech of October 22, 1962. The Cuban Missile Crisis. "Remember that?" Rodney said. "Remember how we loaded our car trunks with canned food, and everybody started building bomb shelters? That was a good business for a while, building bomb shelters. I must have built a dozen of them. I wonder what people use them for."

"Why are they running this bullshit?" Elsie said. "It's boring."

"Jesus, it seems like a hundred years ago," Rodney said. "It was only last year. We were supposed to be one of the top ten targets. Remember? I wonder how they figured that out."

"They made it up," Elsie said. "There wasn't any crisis. Castro and Kennedy made it up."

"You didn't think that at the time. You're the one who bought the damn canned goods. You thought the Russians were going to land at Galveston."

"Change the channel, will you? This is awful."

Rodney got up and switched to Cronkite. "How's the eye?" he asked.

Elsie removed the ice pack, and Rodney bent to look. "You're going to have a shiner," he said.

"Great. Why did you hit me, Rod? You didn't have to do that."

"Listen, dollface, you know I love you. You know I respect your views. Hell, I agree with most of them—"

"You didn't have to hit me, Rod. You hit me hard."

"Look, if you want to call that Carpenter bitch, that's your business," Rodney said. "If you want to play games with her, that's your business. But you brought *my* name into it, and that made it *my* business. I had to stop you, that's all. I'm sorry."

"Well, you said plenty last night. You didn't care what Betty Lou thought of you then. I was proud of you, Rod. I thought you were wonderful."

"I was drunk. Besides, I didn't know this was going to happen. If I'd known what was going to happen, I wouldn't have said a fucking word."

"*Why*, Rod? That's why the country's going to hell, darling. The niggers and the commies riot in the streets and yell about what they want, and they get it. They run the country because people like you keep quiet. Don't you understand that? If people like you would speak up like they do, *you* would be running the country. *We* would be running the country. Don't you see that?"

"I don't think you understand what's about to happen to this town," Rodney said.

"What do you mean?"

"Do you know what it feels like to be hated? I mean, really hated? By everybody in the fucking world? That's what you're about to find out."

"It doesn't matter, Rod. When you know you're right, it doesn't matter. Knowing that you're right is what matters. It's the only thing that matters."

"Yeah? Well, tell me that next week, and maybe I'll believe you."

Elsie moved away from him and huddled in the corner of the couch. She laid the ice pack on her eye and turned her attention to the TV, ignoring him. Cronkite was talking about Lyndon Johnson. His hill-country background. His worship of Franklin Roosevelt and Sam Rayburn. His power and genius as the Senate majority leader, elected by his Democratic colleagues during his first term, the first to ever lead the Senate so soon. Lyndon Johnson was strong. Lyndon Johnson was smart. Lyndon Johnson was great. The country was lucky to have Lyndon Johnson at its helm in this dire hour.

"God," Elsie said. "Last week they were saying Kennedy was going to dump him. Now they're saying he's the greatest thing since sliced bread. Barry Goldwater will whip his ass next year."

"I don't think he'll get the chance," Rodney said.

"You don't think Goldwater will get the nomination?"

"Oh, sure. But I don't think *Johnson* will get the nomination. I don't think the Yankees will let him run. I bet those Catholic sons of bitches have got their heads together right now, deciding who's going to take the place of dear old Jack."

Cronkite was rerunning the film of the arrival of *Air Force One* at Andrews Air Force Base. The big plane was easing to a stop in the dark, the TV lights glaring off its fuselage. "We've seen this," Rodney said. "Let's switch."

"No. Wait. I love it."

The casket was lowered. The stairs were rolled to the tail door. Jackie walked down in her bloody skirt. "Look at her," Elsie said. "Acting like a fucking madonna. Didn't even change her dress. You *know* she had another dress, Rod. Oh, I love it, Rod. It's so silly. Oh, look, Rod. There's Bobby. What a dope. See how sad he is? Oh, it's so lovely I can't stand it."

Johnson was standing at the microphones. The TV lights were reflecting off his glasses. "This is a sad time for all people," he said. Planes and helicopters were roaring in the darkness. Johnson was hollering. He sounded like a south Texas county judge. "We have suffered a loss that cannot be weighed. For me it is a deep personal tragedy. I know the world shares the sorrow that Mrs. Kennedy and her family bear. I will do my best. That is all I can do. I ask for your help—and God's."

"See what I mean?" Rodney said. "The Yankees aren't going to put up with him. Hell, he'll be playing hillbilly music in Jackie's White House."

"I think I'll call those Learys," Elsie said. "I'll ask them how they like their new president."

"Don't do it. Unless you want another shiner."

"I was kidding, darling."

The phone rang. They looked at each other and laughed. "Maybe Mrs. Leary's calling *you*," Rodney said. He made no move to answer.

Elsie set her ice pack on the coffee table. "I'll get it in the kitchen," she said.

When she returned, she was smiling. "We're invited to a party," she said. "At the Babcocks'."

"What Babcocks?"

"Why, *the* Babcocks, sweetie. The *R. Quentin* Babcocks."

"No shit? When?"

"The day of the funeral," she said. "Whenever that is."

"I'll be damned." Rodney slapped his thighs. "Well. Looks like the Darts are moving up."

"What did I tell you?" Elsie said. "It pays to be right. All the right people are right."

Rodney kissed her bruised eye. "I love you," he said.

LUIS

Luis didn't have enough frying pans to warm all the steaks at once, so he was warming them two at a time in one pan and frying eggs in the other. He had already fried the potatoes and was keeping them warm on a cookie sheet in the oven. The other men—Ignacio, Antonio, Rogelio, Juan, and the new man from Oaxaca, whose name was Pablo—sat around the table, drinking beer and watching him. Ignacio and Rogelio had bought a whole case of Pearl, and the men were drinking it from the cans, picking up the saltshaker now and then to shake salt into the holes in the tops of the cans. Luis was drinking a Pearl, too, while he cooked. It was the first time the men had watched him cook, and he felt important and a little nervous.

"These steaks came from the table where Kennedy would have sat," he said. "One of them came from the very place. It's the one he would have eaten. But I don't know which one it is. We all can pretend it's the one we're eating, if we want. Another of the steaks came from the place where Jackie would have sat."

Antonio shook his head. "Maybe we shouldn't eat them," he said. "Maybe they have poison in them. Maybe they're cursed."

Ignacio laughed. The wrinkles in his face when he laughed made his knife scar look more horrible than ever. "Antonio is about to eat the best meat of his life," he said, "and he's afraid."

"If they were going to poison Kennedy, they wouldn't have shot him," Rogelio said. "It would make no sense."

"Maybe it's Luis who's going to poison *us*," Ignacio said.

Rogelio and Juan laughed, but Antonio looked worried. Pablo didn't laugh, either. He hadn't said a word since he came to the table. Maybe it was because he was new.

Luis forked the first two steaks out of the pan and put them on plates. He laid a fried egg on each of them without breaking the yolks and spooned some *salsa picante* over them. He put a generous helping of potatoes and a bright green jalapeño on each plate and carried them to the table. "One is for Ignacio, who knows a feast when he sees one," Luis said. "Who wants the other?"

"I'll take it," Antonio said. "I think Ignacio got the poison one."

"Are you putting the curse on me?" Ignacio asked.

"No," Antonio said. "Your belly is so strong that poison wouldn't hurt it, anyway."

Ignacio raised his shirt and pounded his belly with his fist. "You're right," he said. "I'm a rock."

All the men said good things about the meal. Even Pablo caught Luis's eye across the table and nodded appreciation. Juan said, "This meat is so tender, are you sure it came from a steer, Luis?"

"I know only that it came from the president's table," Luis said. "I don't know where it was before that."

"Kennedy missed a great meal," Antonio said. "It's a pity."

"Have the Americans ever killed a president before?" Rogelio asked.

"Yes," Antonio said, "they killed Abraham Lincoln."

"Is he the only one?"

"I think so. I know of no others."

"Was he killed in Texas, too?" Luis asked.

"I don't think so," Antonio said. "It was a long time ago. Maybe Texas was still in Mexico then."

Ignacio went to the refrigerator and brought back six more beers. Rogelio picked up the opener and opened them. "The *Tejanos* are violent people," Ignacio said. "Isn't that so, Pablo?"

Pablo shrugged. "I don't know," he said. "I don't think *Tejanos* come to Oaxaca. If they do, I don't know of them."

"If there's oil in Oaxaca, the *Tejanos* go there," Antonio said. "They go wherever there's oil. They can smell it, I think, like dogs. Is there oil in Oaxaca?"

"I don't know," Pablo said. "Not in my village."

"So who will be president now?" Ignacio asked.

"Lyndon Johnson," Antonio said. "He's a *Tejano* himself."

Ignacio whistled softly. "Kennedy should never have come here. He should have known they would shoot him."

"I didn't know *Gringos* did such things," Juan said. "In their own country, I mean."

"*Tejanos* aren't like other *Gringos*," Ignacio said. "The devil lives in them, I think."

The Twentieth Hour

BULL

THERE WERE MAYBE A hundred reporters in the corridor, and the closeness of their bodies and the television lights made the place as hot and stuffy as a tomb. The reporters tugged at the sleeves of detectives, poked microphones into the faces of uniformed officers. Whenever the television lights flashed on, the officers in their glare would draw in their bellies and stand straighter, trying to look solemn and official. "I don't know what they're doing," the officers would say. "We just brought the prisoner down and put him in Captain Fritz's office. You'll have to ask Captain Fritz about what they're doing in there."

"Who's Captain Fritz?" one of the Yankee reporters would ask.

The word had come down: For God's sake, be nice to the press. Bull didn't know the source of the word. Captain Fritz, maybe. Or Chief Curry. Maybe even the mayor. Every officer at headquarters had gotten the word, one way or another. Bull didn't mind. It was good for the public to know the police were doing their job. Mary Ellen kept a scrapbook of clippings with Bull's name in them. For the children. He had his picture in the paper once, helping with the stretcher of a liquor store clerk who had been shot.

Bull was off duty. He could go home if he wanted, but this was no time to leave. That was his prisoner in Fritz's office, the most important prisoner in the history of America. He would stick around a while, just in case. In case Captain Fritz or somebody wanted to ask him something about Oswald. He had barely seen the man. He had helped McDonald arrest him, and that was all. He didn't even ride downtown with him. But still, there might be something they would want to ask Bull, and Bull ought to be here. He didn't want to leave, anyway. This was history going on here, and he was part of it. There would never be another night like this, never this many reporters in the dingy corridors, never this many television lights and cables, never so many questions shouted so urgently. He should call Mary Ellen and tell her he was okay, but the reporters were using every phone booth in the station, and as many office phones as they were allowed. Mary Ellen would assume he was safe. Anyway, he would have plenty to tell her when he got home.

The fat man coming toward Bull wasn't a TV reporter. TV reporters were never fat, and they weren't sweating and rumpled, either, as this man was. No entourage of lights and cameras followed him, although he carried a microphone, which he poked ahead of him tentatively, like a blindman's cane. He seemed shy, confused, unaccustomed to the noise and the press of bodies around him. His microphone was attached to a tape recorder, slung over his shoulder. He wiped his forehead with his coat sleeve. "Hot in here, isn't it?" he said to Bull.

"Sure is," Bull said.

"Mind if I ask you a few questions?"

"Go ahead. I'll help any way I can."

"Could we go someplace a little quieter?" The man pointed at his tape recorder.

"Maybe around the corner there," Bull said.

They maneuvered through the crush and turned down a quieter corridor. "I'm Tim Higgins," the man said. He mumbled the letters of a radio station.

Bull shook his sweaty hand. "My kids listen to your station all the time."

"Do *you* listen to it?" Higgins asked.

"I don't get much chance to listen to the radio. Except police radio." Bull smiled apologetically.

"What's your name?" Higgins asked.

"Officer Bullard Waggoner."

Higgins fumbled with the buttons on the tape recorder and cleared his throat. "Ready?"

Bull nodded.

"This is Tim Higgins at Dallas Police Headquarters. The place is a madhouse. The corridors are jammed with reporters from all over the country, and at this moment Lee Harvey Oswald, the suspected assassin, is in the office of the chief of Homicide, Captain Will Fritz. With them behind closed doors are District Attorney Henry Wade, agents of the FBI and the Secret Service, Texas Rangers, and Justice of the Peace David L. Johnston. Here with me in the corridor is Dallas police officer Bullard Waggoner. Officer Waggoner, will you tell our listeners what's going on behind that door?"

"Well, Tim, all I know is that the prisoner was brought down from his cell a few minutes ago and is in there with the men you mentioned. Captain Fritz and others have been questioning him off and on all afternoon, and maybe that's what they're doing now. Since Judge Johnston is here, they may be arraigning him. I just don't know."

"Arraigning him for the murder of President Kennedy," Higgins said.

"Yes. Or maybe for the murder of Officer Tippit. Or both. I just don't know, Tim."

"Officer Waggoner, as an ordinary cop on the beat, so to

speak, what's your most vivid memory of this day? What personal detail of this day will stay in your mind forever?"

Bull opened his mouth to describe his part in the arrest at the Texas Theater, but a hubbub broke out around the corner. Higgins looked at him, startled. "Excuse me," he said. He ran around the corner into the crowd of reporters at Captain Fritz's office. Bull followed him.

They had brought Oswald out of the office, and he was just standing there, flanked by detectives. Reporters were screaming questions at him, and he was smiling slightly. His left eye was bruised, probably by McDonald's fist in the theater. He was answering the questions, but Bull, standing behind the shouting reporters, didn't hear all his words.

". . . I was not allowed legal representation during that very short and sweet hearing," Oswald was saying. His voice was soft, mocking. He looked smaller in the glare of the television lights than Bull remembered him, and very young. "I really don't know what the situation is all about," Oswald said.

The detectives nudged him forward, waving for the crowd to stand back. The reporters moved, reluctantly, making a path to the elevators. They followed, shouting more questions, but Oswald didn't answer.

"What happened?" Bull asked a television cameraman.

"They charged him with killing the cop," the cameraman said.

Bull looked around for Tim Higgins. He wanted to tell him that J. D. Tippit was only thirty-nine years old, that he had a wife and three children, and that his youngest son was born only five months ago. He wanted to say that Tippit was an ordinary cop on the beat, too, and that he wouldn't remember a single thing about this day. But Higgins was gone.

LIZ

"Let me get it," James said. He pushed aside the TV tray that still held his bowl and the remains of his spaghetti and his empty Coke bottle and ran into Liz's bedroom. Liz lowered the volume and listened, trying to guess who was calling. James came back to the bedroom door, looking disappointed.

"Who is it?" Liz asked.

"Dad," James said. "He wants to talk to you."

"So what's so bad about that? Why are you looking so glum?"

"He's going to say we can't do anything tomorrow," James said. "He's going to say he has to work. He just didn't want to tell me."

"Oh, come on. It's probably not that at all," Liz said.

James slumped past her and turned up the volume and flopped onto the couch. He probably would cry now. Liz closed the bedroom door and picked up the phone. "What is it, Jake?"

"Liz, I'm at the Police Department. I'm in a phone booth, and about fifty reporters are waiting to use the phone, so I can't talk long. But I wanted to say some things to you."

"Okay, so say them."

There was silence a moment, then he said, "You should have stayed with me today, Liz. You would have seen it happen. I actually saw the son of a bitch holding the rifle."

"Jesus, Jake," Liz said. "You think I'd want to see that?"

"No, of course not. I don't know what I'm saying. I'm so fucking tired I think I'm going to die."

There was another pause, so long that Liz asked, "What did you want to talk to me about? I assume you're awfully busy and can't pick up James tomorrow. Is that it?"

"No, it isn't, Liz. What I wanted to say—what I wanted to ask—I wanted to ask if I could come over after I get through here. If I *ever* get through here."

"What's happening down there?"

"Jesus, it's a fucking circus. You wouldn't believe it."

"I believe it," Liz said. "That was a cute little press conference Oswald had. Have the cops gone out of their minds?"

"I think they have. They may try the little bastard right here, tonight, and take him out and hang him. Just to get it over with. Wade, Curry, all of them. They're popping out and making statements to the press every ten minutes. I never saw anything like it."

"Well, you can come over if you want to. It's still your house. Sort of."

"Okay. Look, it'll probably be late. And I *will* have to go in to the office tomorrow and write my story. You understand that."

"Yeah, I understand it," Liz said. "I don't think James will, though."

"Well, don't say anything to James. I'll explain it after I get there."

"He'll probably be asleep, if it's going to be really late."

"Let him stay up," Jake said. "As a favor. To me."

"Why should I do *you* any favors?"

"Okay, Liz, forget it. I'm sorry I bothered you."

"No, wait," Liz said. "I didn't mean to get snotty. But won't your—girl friend get mad? Isn't she keeping a light in the window for you?"

"I don't know. I guess she is. . . . Look, Liz, I know this must seem strange to you, but the way I feel right now— well, I want to be with James tonight. And I want to be with you. With *you*, Liz."

A sadness rose within her. A kind of sweet pain. "Well, come over then, Jake. James will be up. And so will I."

"Thanks."

Another silence. It was so long that Liz wasn't sure he hadn't hung up. "Jake?" she said.

"Yeah," he said. "Listen. If I come, I'll want to stay. For the night, I mean. . . . With you, Liz."

The pain sharpened. "Well, I can't promise anything," she said. "But I'll think about it."

THOMAS J.

Thomas J. had thought he would walk to the funeral home until Mamie Ezell called and asked for a ride. She was a huge, arthritic woman and walking was painful for her. On any other night he would have called and invited her to ride with him, for she went nowhere unless he or Lucius Jackson or some other member of the congregation drove her. But he wasn't thinking right today, and he forgot.

When he left his house, he saw it was just as well that he was driving. The wind was blustery and had the chill of winter in it. Had he walked, he would have regretted his decision along the way to Regis Watson's place and would have arrived in no mood for pastoral duties. He was less comfortable with his duty concerning death and burial than any other. There was something unfair about death, unjust, whether its victim was a child or had lived a century like Sister Emma. Death never waited for any life to complete itself. There was always something still undone when death came like an expected visitor who always shows up early, before the house has been put in order. Sister Emma had vowed to live until her people were free, but she didn't. John Kennedy had vowed to make them free, but he hadn't. They were dead, and the work was still to be done. It didn't matter whether you died old and in bed or young with a bullet in your brain, the work remained for others. And others after them.

Preachers were expected to explain that. It doesn't matter, they were supposed to say. Sister Emma and John Kennedy will look down from heaven and see our victory when it comes. They've gotten their reward early, that's all. That's what death is, brothers and sisters, a reward for doing a job here. Sister Emma and John Kennedy were put here for a purpose, and they fulfilled that purpose and were taken. Why now? We can't know. Death is God's decision, and God always decides right, and heaven is our reward. Praise God and be happy for those who die. The Lord is my shepherd, I shall not want. In my Father's house are many mansions. If it weren't so, I would have told you. Believe it, brothers and sisters. It's all we've got and all we need. It's plenty.

Thomas J. had said these things many times, and the members of his congregation believed him, or thought they did, or pretended to. Thomas J. believed these things, too, sometimes. Sometimes, standing in his pulpit and saying them, he felt the Holy Spirit move through his body like a wind and he believed them and was able to make the others believe. After such a sermon, he would feel peaceful all day and know he had said the right things. Other times, though, he felt deader inside than Sister Emma would ever be, and the words of comfort came out like lies. Tonight of all nights, Thomas J. didn't feel the Holy Spirit blowing within him.

On an impulse, he turned off the pavement onto the dirt road that led to Sister Emma's house. He stopped in front and cupped his hands to the car window to look out. The house was dark, of course. The bare branches of the chinaberry tree in the front yard, silhouetted against the reflection of the city lights off the clouds, moved in the wind. He had thought he would sit in the car and get himself together, compose his thoughts, then drive on. But just sitting did him no good, so he got out.

The odors of Sister Emma's privy and the other privies on the street were on the wind. A dog barked, and someone yelled for him to shut up, the voices of both dog and master blown thin and ghostly. The porch boards creaked under his weight. The door wasn't locked. Thomas J. doubted that it had ever been, in all the years it had hung there. The window shades had been pulled and the room was dark and still full of the musk of sickness. Thomas J. crept his way to what he thought was the center of the room and groped for the chain of the light bulb that dangled from the ceiling. He found it and pulled it and bathed the room in yellow light.

Someone had made up the bed and spread the army blanket over it like a counterpane. The TV was still on the chair where Lucius had left it last night. Today, actually, but it seemed a long time ago. Thomas J. walked through to the kitchen and turned on the light. The bucket of water he had brought still sat on the bench, and he took down the dipper and drank and looked around and turned off the light. He went back to the front room and sat on the edge of the bed. Nothing had changed. It was as he had seen it a hundred times. More times than that. Sister Emma was all that was missing. "Ain't gonna be no hate in heaven," he said aloud. "Heaven's gonna be Juneteenth every day." He got up and turned off the light and closed the door and drove to Mamie Ezell's house.

She was waiting behind the glass panes of her front door and came out as soon as he pulled up. Thomas J. met her at the curb and opened the car door for her and helped her in. "Oh, reverend, I'm so distressed," she said. "I've been grieving all day."

In the foyer of the funeral home, Regis Watson bowed. He smiled at Thomas J. "You know the way, reverend," he said.

Thomas J. nodded and led Mamie Ezell into the room where Sister Emma's casket stood. Seventeen people, all members of his congregation, sat on folding metal chairs in front of the casket. Some of the women were daubing their eyes with handkerchiefs. The men looked nervous and uncomfortable. They stood up when they saw Thomas J. and came forward to shake his hand. "I'm so glad you're here, reverend," one of the women said. "Would you lead us in a word of prayer?"

"Later," he said. "First I want us to do something that Sister Emma would want us to do." He clasped hands with the woman and Mamie Ezell and nodded for the others to do the same. They made a circle, hand in hand, around the casket, and Thomas J. began the song.

> We shall o-ver-come!
> We shall o-ver-come!
> We shall o-ver-come some-day!

The others joined in, timidly at first, then with more noise and feeling as the Holy Spirit came into them.

The Twenty-first Hour

DENNIS

JUDY HELD OUT THE RECEIVER. "Talk to papa," she said. "I can't get through to him."

Dennis took the phone. "Hi, Ed," he said. "How are you?"

"Where the hell have you taken my daughter? What kind of place is that down there, anyway, your goddamn Texas? We finally elect a good president, and the goddamn Texans don't even let him finish a term. They blow his goddamn head off. What kind of people are those, huh? What are you and Judy doing in a place like that?"

"Ed ... Ed ... "

"I tried to get you to go to Boston University. Remember? I said, 'BU's a fine school, Denny, a fine Methodist school, better than SMU, probably. Especially if you want to go to graduate school up here. Most people up here never heard of SMU. You're better off at BU.' Remember that, Denny? Remember my saying that?"

"I remember it, Ed. Listen—"

"But, no, you had to go south. Who did you think you were? Some kind of missionary? Did you think those people were going to be better because you were there? They're crazy, Denny. They're violent people. My daughter's in danger, Denny, and I don't like it. I don't like it one bit."

"Listen, Ed, calm down a minute. Let me say something, okay?"

"All right. Say something. I'm listening. Say something."

Now that Ed was listening, Dennis couldn't think of anything to say.

"Go ahead. Say something. I'm listening."

"Well, it's just not the way you think it is," Dennis said. "Judy isn't in danger. I'm not either. We're as safe here as we would be in Boston."

"Yeah? You're telling me Jack Kennedy would have been shot in Boston? Come on, Denny!"

"I mean he could have been killed anywhere. Chicago. Los Angeles—"

"Those cities don't have all those nuts."

"Los Angeles has nuts. Maybe more nuts than Dallas."

"Okay, Denny! Los Angeles has nuts! But Dallas killed him, son! L.A. didn't kill him, Chicago didn't. Dallas did, and I want you and my daughter out of there."

"Look, Ed. You're overwrought. All of us are overwrought. Judy and I can't just pack up tonight and move out. I'm in the middle of a semester. So is Judy. She couldn't get a job now, and I couldn't get into BU, and I'd lose credit for the whole semester. Would that make sense? If you were in my place, would you do that?"

Ed was sobbing softly. Dennis waited, listening to him trying to regain control. Ed blew his nose, then said, "Okay, son. But I don't understand it. I don't see how it happened. Tell me."

"I don't know, Ed. I don't know how it happened."

"Those cops are blowing their case, you know." Ed was calm now, the cool, tough lawyer. "They're trampling all over that bastard's rights. They've been questioning him, charging him, parading him in front of those reporters, and he doesn't even have an attorney. Is everybody down there stupid? If they get a conviction, the appeals court will throw it right out the window. The Supreme Court will, anyway. What the hell do they think they're doing?"

"I don't know, Ed. Maybe they know what they're doing."

"The hell they do! It's a goddamn carnival on TV. The little bastard's going to get away with it. Don't you have the ACLU down there?"

"Sure we do."

"Well, where the hell are they? I tell you, Denny, they're blowing it right out the window."

"Why don't you come down and defend him, Ed?" Dennis grinned at Judy.

Ed laughed. "Sure. Then Boston would kill *me*. Are you after Judy's inheritance or something? When are you coming home, son? It's been so long."

"I don't know, Ed. We've been thinking Christmas, maybe."

"Yeah? It's a deal. I want your promise on that."

"I can't promise, Ed. I'll promise for Judy, though. Judy will come."

"Not good enough," Ed said. "I want you, too, Denny. I want us to have a good old family Christmas, like we used to. No empty chairs around the table."

"Look, Ed—"

"Promise, goddamn it! Promise, and I'll mail you the plane tickets tomorrow. We'll go up to New Hampshire and do some skiing. What do you say? Huh? Would you like that?"

The loneliness in Ed's voice, the memories of Christmas tables and sun glinting on the ski slope, broke Dennis's resistance. "Okay," he said. "Christmas. We'll come." Judy gave a silent cheer.

"Swell," Ed said. "I'll mail the tickets tomorrow. I love you kids. You know that."

"We love you, too, Ed."

"Hey, listen, Denny. Christmas is near the end of the semester, right? Maybe we could drop by BU, look around, ask a few questions, huh? Just for the hell of it."

"Maybe."

"Good enough." Ed paused. Dennis thought he might be crying again. "I love you kids. You know that."

"We know, Ed."

"Jesus, I can't believe this day. I just can't believe this thing happened."

BYRON

The first and final editions of the evening paper were spread side by side on Byron's desk. Both featured the big picture of a smiling JFK shaking hands with the smiling crowd at Love Field. Both carried a blurb beside the masthead promoting the Christmas book section, coming Sunday.

The first edition, which had rolled from the presses as the motorcade moved through Dallas toward Dealey Plaza, was so full of cheer.

DALLAS GREETS PRESIDENT

Security Boys Play It Cool	Jackie Sparkles, Lady Bird Too	Crowds Cheer Wildly for JFK

A celebration, turned to ashes so quickly.

PRESIDENT DEAD

Byron flipped through the final edition again, not reading the body type this time, just scanning the headlines and the pictures. The pictures, grotesque now, of Kennedy greeting two cowboys on horseback in Fort Worth; of the Kennedys and the Connallys smiling and waving from the convertible in San Antonio; of Kennedy and Johnson chatting at the Fort Worth breakfast table; of Kennedy at the microphone in the Texas Hotel parking lot, with Yarborough and Connally and Johnson arranged behind him like solemn soldiers; of the Kennedys and the Johnsons smiling at each other at Love Field, Jackie holding the roses. They all were so cheerful, so political, so normal, so turned to ashes.

A stranger in a raincoat appeared at the door. "Mind if I use one of your phones?" he asked. "They're all busy in the newsroom."

"Sure," Byron said. "Come in."

The stranger sat down at one of the empty desks. "What are you doing in here all by yourself?" he asked. "What room is this?"

"The Editorial Department," Byron said. "I'm an editorial writer."

"Trying to think of something to say, huh?" The stranger was short and dark. He spoke with some kind of eastern accent. Philadelphia, maybe. "I don't envy you," he said, "trying to explain this thing." He got his connection with his paper surprisingly quickly. "Look, Jerry, I haven't written anything," he was saying. "I got some good notes, though. Would you believe the high schools are playing football tonight?"

Byron folded the paper and went to the newsroom. It didn't look like his newsroom. More than half the men at the typewriters and telephones were strangers, some still wearing overcoats, many with suitcases and portable typewriter cases sitting beside their chairs. Copyboys trotted hither and yon, delivering coffee and sandwiches, delivering reporters' carbons to the Associated Press Bureau in the next room. The kids were flushed with excitement. This was what they had expected the newspaper business to be like all the time. The way

it was in the movies. Byron moved through the clatter of the
typewriters and the Teletypes and the jangle of phones to the
city desk. "McGrath," he said, "have you seen Callison?"

"He's at the cop shop. Why?"

"I just wanted to talk to him."

"Well, he may be there all night. They may charge Oswald
with the assassination tonight, and Callison's bird-dogging it.
You want to talk to him if he calls in?"

"No. I'll catch him later."

The publisher, across the room, talking to one of the
visitors, caught Byron's eye and waved. He said something to
the visitor, then picked his way among the desks, greeting the
out-of-towners, spreading hospitality. His white shirt sleeves
were rolled above the elbows, his necktie loose, his collar open.
He grabbed Byron's elbow and steered him toward the Editorial Department. "I want you to write something, Hayes,"
he said. "For tomorrow."

"I've been thinking about that," Byron said. "But tomorrow's Saturday. We've got no editorial page tomorrow."

"We'll run it on page one, if it's good enough. It's got to
be just right, Hayes. Those fuckers out there are going to
burn Dallas."

"What do you want me to say?"

"Hell, I don't know. You're the writer. It's got to be short
and to the point. It's got to say how Dallas really feels about
this thing."

"How *does* Dallas feel about it?"

The publisher glared at him. "Well, goddamn it, do you
know how *you* feel about it?"

"Yes. I think so."

"Write that, then. But don't make it some first-person
thumb-sucker. And show it to me before you give it to the
desk."

"Where will you be?"

"In the newsroom somewhere. Or in my office. You can

find me." The publisher slapped Byron on the back. "This will be the most important goddamn editorial you've ever written, Hayes. And it's going on page one."

Byron returned to his desk and rolled a sheet of paper into his typewriter. The stranger in the raincoat was still there, still talking. Byron tried to block out his voice, tried to focus his attention on the sheet in front of him. Before he had thought of a word to write, the man finished his call and stood up. "You figured out how to explain it?" he asked.

"I can't explain it," Byron said. "Can you?"

"Yeah, I can," the stranger said. "But your paper would never run it. Thanks for the phone." He picked up his note-book and left the room.

In the quiet, Byron began to write.

Terrible history has been made in Dallas, and the magnitude of our city's sorrow can only be measured against the enormity of the deed.

John F. Kennedy, President of the United States of America, is dead. Killed in Dallas. No matter what the explanation of the act, the awul reality of it overwhelms us. He died here.

We do not know now, we may never know why it happened in Dallas. And it is no comfort to our grief that an insane chance, operating with blind destiny, brought our President's death to us.

But this we know, that as a city we must show the world the deep unity of our grief, the depths of the stunned void that is in each of us.

Let us go into the open churches, the cathedrals, the synagogues, and there let us pray to God to teach us love and forgiveness. In the quiet of our homes, let us search our hearts and, through the terrible cleansing power of our grief, remove any vestiges of bitterness and hate.

What happened here could have happened in any city. But first there had to be the seeds of hate—and we must pray that Dallas can never supply the atmosphere for tragedy to grow again.

The bullet that felled our President was molded in an unstable world. But to our great sorrow, it found its mark here.

Byron took a long time to write it, and when he finished, he worried that maybe the grief it expressed was more for Dallas than for Kennedy, that maybe the visitors in the newsroom would take it and twist it into another expression of the city's sickness. But they would be gone in a few days, a few weeks, a few months, and Dallas would remain. The event of this day would have to change the city. Dallas would have to become better or worse than it was.

At the top of the page, he wrote, LET US SEARCH OUR HEARTS. He rolled it out of the typewriter and went to the newsroom. The publisher wasn't there, so he took the elevator to the first floor.

The lobby was dark, and light shone from only one of the executive offices. It was the lamp on the publisher's desk. A bottle of scotch and an empty glass sat on the desk, and when Byron entered, the publisher poured from the bottle and handed the glass to him. "Sit down, Hayes," he said. He refilled his own glass and accepted Byron's page and leaned to read it in the light of the lamp. He finished it and relaxed into the shadows and sipped his scotch, then leaned forward and read it again. He handed the page back to Byron. "It's just right, Hayes," he said. "Take it upstairs and tell them to run it. Then come back and finish your drink."

J. L.

He heard the wind before he opened his eyes. There was never a wind that he didn't hear, and he could tell by listening whether it was a cold wind or a hot wind, without feeling it. This was a cold wind, not like the hot, gritty wind that was blowing when Buck climbed to the top of the derrick. But he didn't feel the wind, and he opened his eyes to see why. He was between his white sheets, under the white wool blanket. His head was on his white feather pillow, but something wasn't right. He shifted in the bed. He was dressed, wearing all his clothes except his boots and coat and hat. He had come to bed without undressing, which was very odd. The lamp beside the wing chair by the fireplace was burning. Had he had his Ovaltine? He didn't think so. He didn't remember it. Where was Jonathan?

He shifted in the bed, turning toward the bedside table and the little black button on it that he could press to call Jonathan. But the movement made his head hurt, and his arm didn't want to stretch out and touch the button. He closed his eyes. The wind was outside. He couldn't feel it at all, but he heard it and knew it was cold, not like the wind that had blown the day Buck climbed the derrick.

He could see Buck climbing. The chili pot was on the hard-packed sand beside the fire. The fire was still burning. The bourbon bottle was beside the pot, near his foot where he hunkered by the fire. It was nearly empty, and the wind was shaking the tops of the mesquite and blowing grit into his eyes and between his teeth as he laughed at Buck climbing. The wind smelled of oil, and Buck was laughing as he climbed, and when he got to the top of the derrick he stood erect without holding on to anything, then he waved, flapping both arms like a huge bird, and hollered something that couldn't be heard over the wind. He came down, still hollering, his arms spread like the wings of a bird soaring, drifting, drifting until he lay still on the sand.

That was the way he had always remembered it. He would have sworn he wasn't mistaken, that it happened that way and Buck Pool was dead. But it was a trick. Buck had known something. Buck found out the bandits were coming and circled around and ambushed them clean as a whistle. Kennedy. Connally. All of them. Surprised as hell, never expecting Buck up there with the Winchester, cutting down on them like lightning out of nowhere, bursting their skulls like gourds. They lay so still in the canyon, the sun glinting yellow off the cartridges in their belts, the flies buzzing about their ruined faces, the horses nickering, their flesh quivering at the odor of blood, their hooves stamping on the rocks, anxious to leave, the buzzards circling, waiting.

Buck knew. He knew them better than they knew themselves, and the wind whipping through the canyon like a hail of knife blades. Sandals they wore, tied on with pieces of rope; and straw sombreros, no good with winter coming; and thin, greasy sarapes tied behind their saddles. Praise God, from whom all blessings flow. The Lord helps those who help themselves. Buck dancing like an Indian, holding the Winchester over his head, hair blowing in the wind, stripping Kennedy and Connally of cartridge belts, guns, knives, leading the horses back to camp, turning to watch the buzzards' circles get smaller and tighter and lower and lower.

SHEILA

"The trouble is, I'm not getting drunk," he said. "I keep drinking, but nothing happens."

"Maybe they watered it down," Sheila said. "Some places do that, you know."

"Come on! This was a new bottle. The seal hadn't been

broken. The Adolphus isn't just any joint." Barnhill was on the phone. "This is room eleven-oh-nine," he said when Room Service finally answered. "Barnhill. B-a-r-n-h-i-l-l. I want another bottle of Cutty Sark. Yes. Scotch. *Sabe?* And ice. Scotch. A whole bottle. And ice." He turned to her. "You want something?"

"Yes. Something to eat."

"What to eat?"

"I don't know. A sandwich. Some kind of sandwich."

"Christ! What *kind* of sandwich?"

"A cheeseburger. And French fries."

"A cheeseburger and fries," Barnhill said into the phone. "What to drink?" he asked her.

"Wine," she said. "Some white wine."

"And a bottle of white wine," he said into the phone. "And make it snappy, yes? Pronto? Big tip. Okay?" He hung up. "Stupid fuckers. They'll get something wrong."

"I didn't want a whole bottle," Sheila said. "Just a glass."

"Well, count your blessings. It isn't every lady who gets more to drink than she wants."

"You should have ordered something to eat. When was the last time you ate?"

Barnhill looked at the ceiling. "Breakfast. A fine, greasy, hangover breakfast. They never brought me my steak at the Trade Mart."

"I think you're getting drunk," Sheila said. "You sound drunk to me."

"No, I'm not. I'm tired as shit, but not drunk. I've got to get drunk, lady. This whole thing is going to be a big fucking bust if I don't get drunk."

"I think you're going to make it. I really do."

"God, I hope so." Barnhill leaned against the pillow and rubbed his chest. He stuck a cigarette into his mouth and struck a match. The hand holding the match trembled.

On the TV, a man in an overcoat was standing in front of a building, talking into a microphone. The sound was off. The man looked very somber. "What building is that?" Sheila asked.

"The Executive Office Building. The vice president's office is in there." Barnhill took a long drag on the cigarette and coughed.

"Those things are going to kill you someday," Sheila said.

"You sound like my mother," Barnhill said. "Fuck health. When you can get your head blown off anytime, fuck health. Hey, have you ever noticed that those TV mikes look like pricks? Those TV guys always look like they're about to go down on somebody. Have you noticed that?"

Sheila laughed. "I have! I *have* noticed that! Jesus, I knew I had something in common with you."

Warner took her hand and shook it. "Great minds," he said. "Great minds run in the same gutter." He removed his hand from hers and laid it on her breast. He moved closer. "Hey," he said, "want to knock off another chunk before Room Service gets here? I bet we could. Those fuckers are so damn slow."

"Not now," she said. "I want to eat and clean up. I want to take a shower. We stink, you know. We smell like old sex and cigarettes. *Your* cigarettes."

"*Our* sex," Barnhill said. "Did I ever tell you you're one hell of a dancer? You're the best dancer I ever saw. Epecially lying down. Mattress dancing. That's what you're really good at."

"Hmm. Should I take that as a compliment?"

"Damn right. That's what the world needs, more good mattress dancers. Give us more women like you and there'll be no more wars. That's what causes wars, you know. Deprived men."

When Room Service knocked, Barnhill went to the door naked. Sheila pulled the sheet over her, and the Mexican with the tray tried not to notice either of them. "Just set it on the bed," Barnhill said. "The lady's an invalid. She can't get up." The Mexican opened the wine and presented the check. Barnhill signed it and handed it back. "Big tip," he said. "Big, big tip." The Mexican mumbled something and backed out of the room.

"I'm starved," Sheila said. She picked up the cheeseburger and bit into it. "It's good. It's even warm. Want a bite?"

"No." Barnhill was opening the scotch, clinking ice into the glass, pouring. "Fuck health."

"Have a bite. Have a French fry. Have something."

"No."

Sheila wolfed down the cheeseburger. "God, I really needed that," she said. "I was starved."

"Now," Barnhill said. "Now let's knock off a chunk."

"Not now. Let me shower first. I won't be a minute." She escaped Barnhill's hands and went into the bathroom and turned on the shower. The hot water came quickly. She adjusted it and climbed into the tub and pulled the curtain. She was lathering herself when Barnhill swept the curtain aside.

"Oh, nice," he said. "Move over. I need a shower, too."

He almost fell, trying to climb into the tub, but Sheila grabbed and held him until he found his balance. She moved the soap bar over his body. Their bodies were slippery against each other. She let him kiss her on the mouth. "Now," he said. "Here."

"Not here," she said. "We'll fall." She stepped out of the tub and grabbed a towel.

"Forget the towel," he said. He grabbed her arm and led her to the bed and eased her down. Their bodies were so slippery. The sheet was getting wet.

"Have you gone crazy?" she said.

"I'm trying to believe I'm still alive," he said.

Elsewhere in Bethesda Hospital physicians worked, discovering why he died.

He should be buried in Boston, the Irishmen argued, in Brookline, where he was born. He should be taken home to rest.

The Secretary of Defense disagreed. "A president," he said, "particularly this president, who has done so much for the nation's spiritual growth and enlarged our horizons, and who has been martyred this way, belongs in a national environment. I feel this is imperative. Boston is just too parochial." He went to the room where she sat, still in her bloody skirt and stockings.

"Where am I going to live?" she asked.

The Twenty-second Hour

SHERRY

THE BAKED POTATOES LOOKED TOO DRY and puckered, so Sherry turned off the oven. The greens were a little wilted, too. She had washed them and left them on the drainboard, not guessing they would be there so long. The steaks were laid out, seasoned, waiting. The Burgundy was open and on the table with the candles. The bed was turned down, inviting with clean sheets. Percy Faith was on the hi-fi. The son of a bitch hadn't even called. Okay, he was a reporter. Okay, he had to work tonight. Okay, he was caught up in the thrill of it all and didn't have time to eat, to be with her. She could understand that. But he could have called. Honey, I'll be late. Honey, I have to work all night. Honey, don't wait up. I'm sorry. I love you. He could have done that. Two minutes. Three minutes. That's all it would have taken.

She took the candles off the table and put them in the drawer. She forced the cork back into the wine bottle. She went to the bathroom and stood in front of the full-length mirror on the door. The black nylon negligee hugged every curve. Her nipples were visible through the thin cloth. The contrast of her white cleavage against the black nylon was stark and stunning. It was obvious she was wearing nothing else. Her short blonde curls glistened. She was beautiful. Any

man would be proud to have her. It could have been one hell
of a night. She bent over the sink and scrubbed off the
mascara and the pancake makeup and the lipstick and took
off the negligee and changed into the jeans and the Dallas
Cowboys sweatshirt that hung over the shower curtain rod.

She returned to the kitchenette and took the roll of alu-
minum foil out of the cabinet and was about to tear off a piece
to wrap the steaks. But what the hell. She was hungry. Why
should it all go to waste? Why should she eat alone? She lit
the broiler and set the temperature and went to her purse on
the breakfast bar and got her keys. She left the apartment and
locked the door and stood for a moment against the iron rail-
ing of the veranda, looking down into the courtyard. The
spindly, leafless trees were swaying in the wind. It was
getting cold. It would have been a hell of a night to spend
in bed. She walked down the steps and around the building
into the next courtyard, identical to her own, and looked at
the names on the mailboxes until she found Eileen's, and rang
the bell.

Eileen peeked at her with the chain latch on, then closed
the door to loose the latch and opened it. She was wrapped
in a blue chenille robe. Her hair was rolled in pink curlers.
"Well, hi," she said. "What a surprise. Come in."

Sherry stepped inside, and Eileen closed the door and fixed
the chain again. The place reeked of cosmetics. Fashion
magazines were strewn on the couch and on the floor around
it. The bed was unmade. A bra hung on the lampshade beside
the bed. "The place is a mess," Eileen said. "So am I. I wasn't
expecting company." She laughed nervously.

"Don't worry about it," Sherry said. "I just wondered if
you had eaten."

"Well, I've nibbled. I didn't feel up to fixing anything.
Just sort of holing up, you know. A good night for it, huh?"
She motioned toward the couch and they sat down.

"Yeah, well . . ." Sherry said. "I've got these two good

steaks, and I wondered if you might come over and cook them with me."

"Would you like something to drink?" Eileen asked. "I've just got beer."

"No, thanks."

"I thought your boy friend was coming over."

"Well, he was, but he called. He has to work late. He doesn't know when he'll be through. He's working on the assassination."

"Really? Is he a cop or something?"

"He's a reporter. A writer."

"Wow. How neat."

"Yeah. Sometimes. But right now I could kill him. I had this big evening planned, and then this happens and everything goes blooey." Sherry tried to laugh.

"Well, don't be too hard on him," Eileen said. "I mean, it's not his fault."

"No."

"These things happen. Women just have to put up with them."

"I know. But they always happen at the wrong time."

Eileen shrugged. "When's the right time, sweetie? Things just happen, that's all."

"Well, what do you say? Would you like a big T-bone steak and a salad and a baked potato and a bottle of wine?"

"Mmm. My mouth's watering. Let me put on some clothes."

"Maybe we can watch TV or something later," Sherry said.

"Not TV. I watched some of it and it's just too depressing. Kennedy's dead, and they caught the guy, and now they're just repeating the same things over and over. Can you believe Lyndon Johnson is president? I mean, after Jack Kennedy? And Lady Bird taking Jackie's place? My God, that's depressing!"

"I've got some new records," Sherry said. "Or we could just talk."

"Fine. Let me throw something on." Eileen got up and went into the bathroom. "Why are you so mysterious about this boy friend of yours?" she called. "I'm just *dying* with curiosity, and you haven't told me a thing."

Sherry drew a deep breath. What the hell. "He's married," she said.

"*Ahhh!*"

"Well, he's separated. But he's still married. Sort of. Don't comb out your hair. My salad greens are wilting."

"I won't. Are you going to marry him? After he's divorced?"

"I don't know. I haven't thought about it. We just take it one day at a time, you know?"

"Yeah. That's what you have to do with married men, I guess. Not that I've had that experience." Eileen came out of the bathroom, tucking her shirttail into a pair of black corduroy slacks. "Are you going to tell me his name?"

"No. I don't think that would be fair."

"Would I recognize his name? Is he famous?"

"I don't know. If you read the papers, I guess he is."

"Does he write about sports or movies?"

"No."

"I probably wouldn't know him then. But that's exciting, going with a reporter. They're pretty interesting, I bet. Okay, I'm ready."

They walked around to Sherry's apartment, and Eileen stood in the doorway, taking the place in. "Oh, it's so neat!" she said. "You're going to make some man a great wife someday."

Sherry burst into tears. "Oh, Eileen!" she said. "I'm so unhappy!"

Eileen hugged her. "Don't worry," she said. "It'll turn out all right."

MARTHA

"You would think Jackie would have the decency to change clothes," Martha said. "Why must she be so tacky?"

Quentin, hunched in his chair, watching the TV, said nothing.

"Why do you keep watching that?" Martha said. "It's just the same thing over and over. I think they're trying to drive us insane."

Quentin said nothing, and Martha slid her reading glasses down her nose and looked at him. Quentin was ignoring her. She knew she was getting under his skin. "So the people at the Trade Mart were upset?" she said.

"Yes. Very."

He was trying to shut her up. He was always trying to shut her up, but she didn't care. He knew he couldn't shut her up anymore, and she didn't mind showing him that he couldn't. Spread before her on the little cherrywood secretary were her party books, which she consulted while she needled him. He didn't even know what she was doing. He hadn't looked at her since he came home from old man Fisher's.

"Why should they be upset?" she said. "Most of them didn't like him much."

"It's bad for the city."

"But so good for the country, darling. So very, very deliciously good for the country."

Quentin reached for the Waterford decanter on the coffee table and poured another brandy.

"They say the man who did it is a Marxist," Martha said. "Is that true?"

"How should I know?"

"But that doesn't make sense, does it? Why should a Marxist do anything for the United States? To help it, I mean. Does that make sense to you?"

Quentin didn't say anything. He leaned farther forward, as if her voice were interfering with the TV.

"Well, does it?"

"No," he said. "It doesn't."

"Do you realize how easily Barry Goldwater's going to be elected, Quentin? Can you imagine sullen old Lyndon Johnson going up against him?"

Quentin grunted something she didn't understand. "What?" she asked.

"I said, I wouldn't make any bets on it. That Goldwater can beat Johnson."

"Oh, Quentin, you're such a grouch tonight. Are you upset because Robert didn't pick up your car?"

"You know damn well that's not it."

Martha stayed quiet, and after a while Quentin settled back into his chair. When he did, she said, "I wonder if Neiman's has any of that smoked Scotch salmon. It was so good last Christmas."

Quentin looked at her. "What are you doing?"

"Why, I'm planning the party."

"You're actually going through with it?"

"Of course. Did you think I was kidding?"

"Don't." he said. "Please don't. I'm begging you."

"Oh, Quentin, it's just a small get-together. Only about twenty people from some of my groups." Martha thumbed through her books.

"I want no part of it," he said.

"Well, that's up to you. You can stay in your room if you want. Or go out. I can say you had to go out of town. But you'll have to tell me where you're supposed to have gone. Some of your big accounts will be here, and they'll ask."

"Who are you inviting?"

"I haven't finished the list yet."

"You don't even know when the funeral is going to be."

"Oh, I figure Monday or Tuesday," Martha said. "If Marie does the shopping tomorrow, it won't matter much. It's just a small, informal get-together. Just to watch TV. You should come, Quentin. You seem to be enjoying TV so much tonight."

"I'm ordering you not to do it," Quentin said.

"I wonder if it will be a long funeral," Martha said. "I guess it will. Jackie will want to play it to the hilt." She slapped the open page of one of the books. "Here it is!" she cried. "An inspiration! Steak tartare, Quentin! What could be more perfect? Raw red meat!"

Quentin rose from the chair and picked up the decanter and stood glowering at her. "And champagne," she said. "Lots of champagne. But if it's going to be a long funeral, maybe we should have some beer and sherry on hand. We don't want people passing out before he's buried."

Quentin went to his room and closed the door. Martha heard the lock turn. Why in the world did he think she would want to go in there? Maybe spareribs, too. Glazed spareribs. That would be yummy. And what? Something vegetable. And breads and crackers. Nothing fancy. Something just right for a simple celebration.

MARY ELLEN

Buster, lying beside Mary Ellen's rocking chair, raised his head and pricked his ears. Mary Ellen stopped rocking and listened. "What is it?" Kim asked. She was on the couch, her legs tucked under her. Joey, wide-eyed and worried-looking, sat beside her.

"I think your father's home," Mary Ellen said. The children turned back to the TV. Buster got up and followed Mary Ellen to the patio. In the carport, Bullard slammed the pickup door.

"Hi, hon." His voice was delicious in the darkness. So alive. So normal. He stepped onto the patio and took her in his arms. He kissed her gently on the mouth.

"Oh, Bullard, I was so worried," she said.

"Is everything okay?" he asked. "Are the kids okay?"

"Yes, everything's fine. You're okay, aren't you? You're so late."

"Yeah, I'm okay." Bullard held her close and moved his hand slowly up and down her back.

"I nearly went crazy," she said. "For a while, I thought it was you."

"It was Tippit."

"You knew him, didn't you?"

"Yeah. We worked the same shift a lot."

"It's awful. To be happy when you hear it's somebody else. But I *was* happy, Bullard. I didn't care who it was, just so it wasn't you."

"That's natural, I guess." He kissed the top of her head. "Hey, do you mind if we stay out here a few minutes? Are you cold?"

"No, it's okay."

He walked her over to the redwood picnic table and they sat down on the bench. Bullard felt in his pocket and got a cigarette and lit it. His face looked worn in the light of the match, but he was alive. Just tired. He took a long drag on the cigarette and let the smoke out in a kind of sigh. "I was in on the arrest," he said.

"Of Oswald?"

"Yeah. I was at the theater. McDonald got to him first, but I was there. I helped. You want to know the crazy thing, Mary Ellen? He's a punk. Just another punk kid. I've arrested hundreds just like him. Hell, he didn't even put up much of a fight. I wish he had, so McDonald could have killed him. Or I could have."

Mary Ellen took his hand. "I'm so proud of you," she said.

"Let me tell you another thing," Bullard said. "You know

those reporters down at the department? There must be a hundred of them."

"I know. I've been watching on TV."

"Well, they're not asking a damn thing about Tippit. A hundred reporters down there, and nobody gives a shit about the poor, dumb, dead cop. Just Kennedy. But that's natural, I guess. Who cares about a poor, dumb, dead cop when the president of the United States has been murdered? You would think *somebody* would ask, though, wouldn't you?"

Buster trotted up, his tongue lolling, and laid a paw on Bullard's knee. Bullard rubbed him behind the ears. "Hello, boy," he said. "How's it going?"

"Tell me about him," Mary Ellen said.

"Tippit? Oh, there ain't really much to tell, I guess. He was about my age, had a wife, three kids. One of them a baby. He'd been on the force ten years or so, I guess." Bullard laughed. "Sounds a lot like me, doesn't it? He even lives over here in Oak Cliff somewhere. Lived here, I mean. That's about all there is to old J. D. Tippit. It could have been me, and it wouldn't have made a damn bit of difference to anybody but you and the kids and Tippit's wife and their kids. And Tippit. Just another cop that stops one punk too many."

The back door opened. "Mom?" Joey said.

"Yes?"

"Is dad here?"

"Yes, he's here."

"What are y'all doing out there?"

"Just talking."

"Can I come out?"

"Sure."

Joey sat down beside Bullard and hugged him. "Hi, dad," he said.

"Hi, son. How's it going?"

"Fine." Joey took Bullard's other hand and held it. "Why don't you guys come inside? It's cold out here."

"Okay," Bullard said. "All right with you, honey?"

"Sure."

Buster's nails clicked on the linoleum tile of the kitchen, following Mary Ellen. "Would you like a beer?" she asked.

"I sure would," Bullard said. He went into the living room. "Hi, Kim."

"Hi, dad."

Mary Ellen opened the beer can and went to the living room, but Bullard wasn't there. "Where did your father go?" she asked.

"I don't know," Kim said.

She found him in the boys' room, standing beside the crib, watching Albert sleep. Joey was with him, still holding his hand. She handed Bullard the beer. "Thanks, hon," he said.

"Are the Tippits listed in the phone book?" she asked.

"I guess so. Why?"

"I thought I might go over there. To see if there's anything I can do."

"Why don't you wait till morning?" Bullard said. "Why don't we stay home together tonight?"

HENRY

The wind gathered the tattered scraps of newspapers, dots of confetti, cigarette packs, and candy wrappers into the center of the intersection, then lifted them. Around and around they swirled, upward and upward, as high as five or six stories of the buildings on the corners. "Dust devils," Muffin said. "We got dust devils in Dallas."

"You don't know shit," Henry said. "Dust devils is caused by heat. It's colder than a well digger's ass out here."

"What do you call that, then?" Muffin pointed at the rising cloud of debris.

"Tornado," Henry said. "That there's a tornado if I ever seen one."

"You ever seen a tornado?" Muffin asked.

"No."

"Well, you don't know shit, then," Muffin said. "I seen a tornado once. Right here in Dallas. It weren't nothing like that."

"I never knowed a nigger dumber than you," Henry said. They were standing on the corner. Their coat collars were turned up. Henry was shivering. "Colder than a well digger's ass," he said. "Why ain't you shivering, Muffin? Ain't you cold?"

"Yeah, I'm cold. That don't mean I got to shiver, does it?"

Down the block on Main, a man was walking alone. His shoulders were hunched against the wind. "Come on," Henry said. They moved after the man, caught him before he reached the corner, he was moving so slowly. "Hey, buddy," Henry said. "Let me ask you something."

The man stopped. He was carrying a newspaper under his arm. He looked at Henry without much interest.

"Me and my partner here, our truck's broke down on the Stemmons—"

"You're standing only a few blocks from history," the man said.

"What?"

"Go to hell." The man turned and walked on, as slowly as before.

"Don't that beat all?" Henry said. "What kind of nut is that?"

"A nut that ain't gonna give us no money," Muffin said. "Let me ask you something. You notice anything strange about this town?"

"Yeah. Nobody's here. You and me and that nut are the only ones down here, I think."

"Yeah. And the fucking sirens," Muffin said. "We been

hearing sirens all night. Now, why would there be sirens when there ain't nobody out? Tell me that."

"Oh, come on," Henry said. He grabbed Muffin's arm and urged him along the sidewalk.

"And them dust devils. I think they mean something. I think something's going on here."

"Nigger voodoo," Henry said. "Come on. Let's go to Babe's. I bet we can get a drink at Babe's, and then you'll feel better."

They moved on to Commerce and turned left. "And the lightning," Muffin said. "That's another thing. It's been lightning all night, and nothing close to rain. Just cold and wind and dust devils."

The liquor stores were closed. Nobody was getting in or out of taxicabs or cars at the Baker or the Adolphus. "What's going on?" Henry asked the Baker doorman.

"Get out of here," the man replied.

Babe's sign was off. Henry tried the door. It wouldn't open. Then he saw the paper taped to the door.

CLOSED—COME BACK SATURDAY
NOT YOU MAVIS

"Well, Muffin," Henry said, "maybe you're right. There's something sure different about this town tonight."

The Twenty-third Hour

LUTHER

COLONEL LUTHER BYRD PUT ON his pajamas and his fleece-lined slippers and his brown silk robe and brushed his hair, but knew he couldn't go to bed right away. Things needed figuring out. Strategy had to be planned for the new situation, and things had to be figured out if the possible pitfalls were to be avoided. If things were thought through correctly, the situation could be used to great advantage. The right strategy at this moment might prove, in the end, to be decisive to the outcome of the struggle. Everything couldn't be figured out tonight, of course, but a beginning must be made. It was no time for soldiers to sleep.

He went to the bar and poured a snifter of Courvoisier and wished his apartment had a fireplace. The wind was howling around his corner of the building, and nothing would have been finer than to sit in his big chair with his Courvoisier and feel the heat of the flames while he thought. He had done some of his finest thinking in front of fires, but a soldier had to make do. He sat in the big chair and rested his feet on the ottoman and listened to the wind and the ticking of the brass clock on the carved table under the Nazi flag. His eye fell on the WANTED FOR TREASON leaflet on the ottoman, and he picked it up and studied it. How quickly the situation had changed.

Yesterday, wanted for treason; today, dead. It was the kind of justice that traitors should get, of course, but so unexpected. Patriots no longer expected justice in the United States, certainly not the quick, final justice without appeal that had been meted out to Kennedy. The way the sentence of an outraged people had been executed was beautiful. Despite the pomp and power of his office, despite the vigilance of his Secret Service, the traitor had been brought low.

What puzzled Colonel Byrd was the executioner. Who was Lee Harvey Oswald? The commies' media lackeys were calling him a Marxist, but were being oh so careful not to call him a Communist. Why? What the hell was the difference? Maybe he was a Trotskyite or some other off-brand, but so what? Their ends were the same, no matter how much they bickered over means. Or pretended to bicker. And hadn't Oswald lived in the Soviet Union? Wasn't he married to a Russian wife? Didn't he agitate for Castro's Cuba? According to Walter Cronkite, anyway.

All right. Assuming Oswald was a Communist, why would he kill Kennedy? Not of his own volition, certainly. He must have known he would be caught, and Communists never did anything without orders from above. Oswald would have to be a Communist agent. Of whom? The Russians? The Cubans? Why would they want to kill Kennedy? Revenge for the missile crisis? Bullshit. The missiles were still there, despite Kennedy's brave speeches and saber rattling. Even the idiots knew that. Why would the Communists no longer want Kennedy in the White House? Wasn't he giving the country to them as quickly as he could? Could Lyndon Johnson do it faster? Possibly, but probably not. Not enough faster to justify such radical action, anyway. Communists killing Kennedy didn't make sense. A professional Communist assassin would never be taken alive. He would kill himself rather than submit to interrogation. A Communist agent would never be paraded around the Dallas Police Department like a pet monkey.

Perhaps the media were lying. God knows, they lied often enough. But if they were lying, why would they blame the deed on a Communist? Wouldn't they more likely accuse some American patriotic organization, especially since the assassin chose Dallas for his work? Wouldn't they seize the opportunity to foment public reaction against Americanism, as they had so many times before?

Maybe the media were lying for a different reason. What if Oswald's motives were as pure and patriotic as Colonel Byrd's own? Perhaps he was an agent of the Birchers or the Minutemen, or simply a lone American citizen who saw what had to be done and did it. Maybe he was waiting in the jail now for his countrymen to rise and demand his release. Maybe he was waiting for the people to seize control of their own destinies and the destiny of their country again. Maybe he didn't know the media would lie, never dreamed that he would be painted as a traitor himself so that patriots wouldn't rally to his support.

The thought both warmed Colonel Byrd and embarrassed him. The motorcade had passed his balcony, and he had done nothing. Oh, he had made his gesture of protest, but what was that compared to what Oswald had done? On the other hand, it wasn't the duty of colonels to fire guns. Colonels, hell! He would have been a general long ago if the leftists in the Pentagon and the White House hadn't hated him. It wasn't the duty of generals to fire guns, to expose themselves to the detriment of their troops and their country. The sacrifices had to be made by those who had the least to lose and the least to offer for the good of all. Oswald, bless his soul, had the wisdom to see that and had declined to involve Colonel Luther Byrd. Oswald—at least according to the lying media—had been a marine. And whatever else one might say about the marines, they weren't cowardly draftees.

Colonel Byrd studied his leaflet carefully. Perhaps he had been involved, after all. He could see that such a work could inspire a simple patriot. Tom Paine's pamphlets hadn't been printed from glossy pictures on slick magazine paper, either, and look what they had inspired. He could see that a certain kind of man, upon reading such an honest and strongly phrased indictment of such a powerful and dangerous traitor, could be moved to take arms against him. The media were calling the assassination a tragedy, which it wasn't. The tragedy would be the failure of other patriots to take advantage of the opportunity that Oswald had given them.

Colonel Byrd got up and poured himself another Courvoisier and raised his glass in a silent toast to Oswald. Tomorrow he would call his agent and make himself available for another speaking tour.

The Dallas casket was too battered to use, so four of the Irishmen went out to find another.

"You know," one of them said, "the Irish always measure the importance of people by the number of friends who come to their wakes. All my life I've thought of my wake being held in a Boston three-decker tenement. I just assumed he'd live longer than me, and I'd be so proud to have the president of the United States at my wake. And now here I am, going to get a casket for him."

They asked the undertaker to show them something plain in the middle price range. But the one they bought was built of hand-rubbed, five-hundred-year-old solid African mahogany. It cost $2,460.

The Last Hour

DENNIS

ONLY FOUR DIM LIGHTS BURNED behind the communion rail, and no minister or choir was in the chancel. The door of the sanctuary simply had been unlocked and the four lights turned on. "As the mayor of a grief-stricken city," Mayor Earle Cabell had said on TV, "I hereby declare a day of prayer following the tragic and untimely death of our president, John F. Kennedy. In order that every person may claim for himself resources which God alone can provide, I further request that every house of worship, regardless of denomination, remain open continuously until midnight Saturday." A few had already come here. A few heads were visible in the gloom—some erect, eerily still, staring toward the chancel; some leaning on the pews in front of them, as if exhausted or wounded.

Dennis and Judy walked halfway down the carpeted aisle and slid into an empty pew. He helped her out of her coat and laid it and his own on the pew beside him. Judy shivered and rubbed her hands together. "Are you all right?" he whispered.

"Yes. It's just a little cool in here."

"We don't have to stay."

"No, I'm all right."

It was cold in the sanctuary. The feel of the place irritated him. He wasn't comfortable with private prayer. Sometimes he had tried. He would close his eyes and try to empty his mind of all but God, but his thoughts always rushed back in a dizzy, circular procession of fears and desires and problems and plans that were much more real and more insistent than God. He couldn't summon an image of God into his head and commune with him there. God always appeared as Michelangelo's white-bearded Creator, stretching his arm along the Sistine Chapel ceiling to zap Adam with the spark of life, and Dennis hated the picture. How many people in this sanctuary were really praying? Not many. They were recuperating from their shock, maybe, waiting for some divine salve to sooth their souls. Or they had come to be pious, to win points in heaven.

Judy's eyes were closed. Her hand covered her lower face. What was she doing? Dennis closed his eyes, tried to form a phrase to address to God. His mind went instead to the farmers of Broadway Junction who would come to hear him Sunday. What would he say to them? How would he explain this terrible thing? The will of God? The work of the same Satan who brought the boll weevils to the cotton fields? Simply the act of a sinful man? Where was justice? Where was mercy? Where was love? None of it worked. There ought to be a minister here, reading scripture, leading prayers, directing the thoughts of these people, making some kind of sense of what they were feeling. It didn't have to be true. There ought to be a choir here, singing, making the people sing, making them hear their own voices and the voices of the others, making them know they weren't alone, that somewhere was a reason for this confusion and grief, that somehow it all made sense, even though anyone who claimed it made sense was probably a liar.

Dennis pulled a hymnal from the rack on the back of the pew ahead and opened it at random.

Our God, our help in ages past,
    Our hope for years to come,
Our shelter from the stormy blast,
    And our eternal home.

The preposterous lie of faith was what these people needed, what he needed. The will, the guts, the stupidity to call death good and the dead fortunate, to shout the goodness of an eternal scheme of things that can't be seen, that the evidence declares doesn't exist, the absurdity of saints singing as they burn, looking skyward for a sign that never comes, turning to ashes from which they never return.

Time, like an ever-rolling stream,
    Bears all its sons away;
They fly, forgotten as a dream
    Dies at the opening day.

A woman sitting near the front of the sanctuary broke into coughing. She coughed and coughed, wet and racking, holding a handkerchief to her mouth. She couldn't stop. People raised their heads, opened their eyes, cleared their throats. Judy looked at Dennis. "Are you all right?" he whispered.

She laid her hand on his arm. "Yes, I'm all right."

The coughing woman left the pew. She stood in the aisle and faced the communion table and genuflected and crossed herself, although there was no crucifix. Maybe she had been a Catholic or an Episcopalian when she was young and was reverting to old habit. Maybe she had just wandered into the church because it was close and the wind was cold. She walked up the aisle, coughing into the handkerchief, her face contorted.

Our God, our help in ages past,
    Our hope for years to come,
Be Thou our guard while troubles last,
    And our eternal home.

"Let's get out of here," Dennis said.

Judy nodded, and he gathered their coats and left the pew. They followed the coughing woman out of the sanctuary. In the vestibule, he helped Judy into her coat and put on his own and held open the heavy door to the street. The coughing woman was standing under the streetlight, waiting for someone. On the steps, Judy asked, "Are we really going home for Christmas?"

RAYMOND

Theodore Roosevelt, William Howard Taft, Woodrow Wilson, Warren G. Harding, Calvin Coolidge, Herbert Hoover, Franklin D. Roosevelt, Harry S. Truman, Dwight D. Eisenhower, blustering Teddy, fat William, naïve Woodrow, randy Warren, silent Cal, bland Herbert, grinning Franklin, peppery Harry, likable Ike, dead in their beds or alive and as well as can be expected of men of their years. Abe and Garfield and McKinley, three presidents shot in less than forty years, and the country caught on. Maybe somebody doesn't like presidents, any president, all presidents; maybe all Americans aren't sane and happy and loyal, maybe a few are sick and crazy and angry and have guns. Maybe the White House isn't a parsonage, maybe presidents make enemies who want to see them dead. They didn't get Teddy or William or Woodrow or Warren or Calvin or Herbert or Franklin. Puerto Ricans stormed Blair House, but didn't get Harry. Ike's still playing golf, Harry's still taking walks, Herbert's still dozing on park benches. The rest died in their time, no poison in their veins, no bullets in their brains, no blood on their wives. Millions of miles on trains, on planes, in cars, on boats, even submarines; thousands of towns, villages, cities; dozens of foreign countries, planning routes, checking buildings, scouting roof-tops, riding guard, watching crowds, making lists—criminals, agitators, crazies, letter writers, commies, Nazis, Birchers; learning where they might be, guessing what they might do, looking, expecting them, guns within reach, watching en-trances, checking guest rolls. No, you may not prepare a special dish for the president. The president shall eat what everyone eats. The president's steak shall be chosen at random. You won't know which one until it's cooked and the agent points and says, "That one, give him that one," and goes with the waiter to the table. Five thousand yellow roses poked, probed, studied. No bombs there, no poison gas, just roses. No bombs in the red bouquet. No more presidents shot.

But today, Friday, the twenty-second day of November, the year of our Lord one thousand nine hundred and sixty-three, in the city of Dallas, county of Dallas, state of Texas, United States of America, John Fitzgerald Kennedy, youngest man ever to be elected president of the United States, while riding with his wife along a street chosen by Raymond Alvin Medley, an agent of the United States Secret Service, and his fellow experts, riding toward a luncheon hall chosen by Ray-mond Alvin Medley and his fellow experts, a luncheon hall situated in the city, county, and state where Raymond Alvin Medley has protected the United States and its chief executive for more than a decade, John Fitzgerald Kennedy is shot in the head by one Lee Harvey Oswald, twenty-four, whose his-tory, pictures, and fingerprints are in the files of the Federal Bureau of Investigation because he was a United States Marine and he went to the Soviet Union, renounced his citizenship, married a Russian wife, and made threatening noises against the United States. But Raymond Alvin Medley and his fellow experts don't know that Lee Harvey Oswald is standing in a window of the Texas School Book Depository holding a rifle, and so he fires one, two, three—how many bullets into the head of John Fitzgerald Kennedy?—making him the youngest president ever to die, the first ever to be loaded onto a plane in a bronze casket that weighs a ton and has a broken handle, and Raymond Alvin Medley is a member of the first Secret Service detail ever to fail to protect its president, and this occurs in Raymond Alvin Medley's own town, on the way to the safest luncheon hall he could find, along the safest motorcade route he could map, and Lee Harvey Oswald is in violation of no federal law, because it isn't a crime against the United States of America to shoot its president.

Raymond picked up the phone and dialed Will Fritz's office and identified himself.

"Hello, Ray," Fritz said.

"Are you going to charge him?"

"Yeah."

"When?"

"As soon as the judge gets here."

"I thought the judge was there."

"He went home. He's coming back, though."

"Is he guilty?"

"Sure. Guilty as sin. You coming over?"

"No," Raymond said. "I'll talk to you tomorrow. He hasn't confessed, has he?"

"We're not having that kind of luck," Fritz said. "But he's guilty."

STACY

"Do I have to go to bed?"

"Yes. It's almost midnight."

"There's no school tomorrow."

"I know, but you need your rest. It's been a long day."

Jason climbed into bed, and Stacy pulled the covers up and tucked him in. He squirmed, making a nest for himself.

"Is the bed cold?"

"A little. It feels good, though."

She bent and kissed him. He squeezed her around the neck. "Goodnight, darling," she said.

"Mom?"

"What is it?"

"I've never known anyone who died before."

"No, you haven't."

"He was pretty young, wasn't he? To die, I mean."

"Yes, he was young."

"Was he younger than you?"

"No. Not younger than me."

"Younger than dad?"

"No, Jason, not younger than dad. Now go to sleep." She turned off the lamp and started to the door.

"Mom?"

"What *is* it Jason?"

"Am I going to die?"

Stacy went back and sat on the side of the bed. "President Kennedy was killed by an evil man," she said. "That's not going to happen to you. You'll live to be an old, old man. A granddaddy."

"Where is he, mom? In heaven?"

"Yes. Don't worry about it. Go to sleep." She tucked the covers under his chin. "Goodnight."

"Goodnight, mom."

She left the door open a crack and returned to the den. Mark had turned off the TV. He was standing by the bar. "How about a nightcap?" he said.

"Yes. Thank you."

He took the glasses to the kitchen for ice and came back and poured the whiskey. "What took so long?" he asked. "Is he okay?"

"Yes. Just a little scared."

"Who can blame him? It'll stay with him always. It'll stay with all of us, I guess."

JAKE

The corridor was full of cigarette smoke and voices. Tim Higgins was leaning against the wall at the far end, away from the crowd. His shirt was soaked with sweat. "What are you doing here, Higgins?" Jake asked.

Higgins gave him a thin smile. "Same as you. Trying to stay out of the way of the majestic national media."

"Quite an honor, isn't it?" Jake said. "Getting your toes stepped on by so many stars. Got a cigarette?"

Higgins took a pack from the sweaty shirt and shook one out for Jake and one for himself. He struck a match and held it for Jake. "Everybody in town is a reporter tonight," he said. "Even Jack Ruby."

"Ruby? Who's he?"

"You know. Nightclub operator. Runs the Colony and the Carousel. Except tonight he's a translator for the Israeli press."

"Shit."

"That's what he told me."

"What the hell's he translating?"

Higgins laughed. "Not a goddamn thing. He wanted to see the show, so they let him in."

"Tight security they've got tonight, isn't it?"

"Well, better this than Parkland," Higgins said. "A cop out there threatened to shoot me."

"Did you flash your pool pass at him?"

"I didn't have a pool pass. I said that to you and Hayes just to keep you in your place. You newspaper guys are such arrogant assholes sometimes."

"We think of it as our natural superiority shining through," Jake said. "Can you spare one more cigarette? God knows when I'll see the outside of this fucking place."

"Bumming cigarettes," Higgins said. "That much class, Callison. The stars don't do that." He gave Jake another. Jake stashed it in his shirt pocket. "You reckon they're going to charge Oswald tonight, or are we just wasting our youth here?"

"Who knows?" Jake said. "They're playing it for all it's worth. Did you ever see so many cops having so much fun?"

"It's the TV," Higgins said. "They would drop their pants to get on TV. You're looking at big-time stuff."

The voices down the corridor got louder. The TV cameras were moving again toward the elevators. The reporters were following, pushing, shouting. "Here we go," Jake said. He and Higgins joined the mob.

The elevator door slid open. Jake found himself staring into the glassy eyes of Lee Harvey Oswald. He looked frail. His hands were cuffed in front of him. Two Secret Service agents held him tightly by the arms.

"Are you going to charge him now?" a reporter shouted.

"Move aside, boys," one of the agents said. "We've got to get through here."

Oswald smiled. He faced the TV lights without blinking.

"Did you kill the president?" a reporter shouted.

"I didn't shoot anybody," Oswald said. "That's ridiculous."

The body is that of a muscular, well-developed and well-nourished Caucasian male measuring 72½ inches and weighing approximately 170 pounds.